Praise for Paul Kane...

"Paul Kane is a first-rate storyteller, never failing to marry his insights into the world and its anguish with the pleasures of phrases eloquently turned."

–Clive Barker, Bestselling author of *The Hellbound Heart*, *Abarat*, *Mister B. Gone*, and *The Scarlet Gospels*

"Paul Kane's lean, stripped-back prose is a tool that's very much fit for purpose. He knows how to make you want to avoid the shadows and the cracks in the pavement."

–Mike Carey, Bestselling author of the Felix Castor series of novels and *The Girl With All the Gifts*, *Fellside*, *The Boy on the Bridge*, and *The Book of Koli* as M.R. Carey

"Kane finds the everyday horrors buried within us, rips them out and serves them up in these deliciously dark tales."

–Kelley Armstrong, Bestselling author of *Bitten*, *Haunted*, *Broken*, *Waking the Witch*, *Spell Bound*, and *A Turn of the Tide*

"Paul Kane is a name to watch. His work is disturbing and very creepy."

–Tim Lebbon, *New York Times* bestselling author of *The Cabin in the Woods*, *The Silence*, and *The Last Storm*

Zombies!

Paul Kane

Introduction by
Brian Keene

A
Grinning Skull Press
Publication

P.O. Box 67
Bridgewater, MA

DEDICATION

For George, a lovely guy who showed us all the way.

CONTENTS

ACKNOWLEDGMENTS

My thanks to Michael and Harrison at Grinning Skull Press for being willing to take this one on, to Brian Keene for the amazing and extremely flattering introduction, and also Dominic Harman for the gorgeous cover. As always, hugs and massive thank yous to all my friends in the writing and film/TV world, for their continual help and their support in the past. A very special thank you, though, to people like Mike Carey, Joe Hill, Jason Arnopp, Neil Gaiman, AK Benedict, Cavan Scott, George Mann, Michael Marshall Smith, Kelley Armstrong, Rio Youers, Stephen Volk, Peter James, Simon Clark and *loads* more. Finally, a massive thank you to my family, in particular my amazing wife Marie, who makes me glad to be alive.

Introduction
by Brian Keene

There's a line in Paul Kane's "Dig (This)"—one of the stories included in this collection—that reads: *"The small chapel to which it belonged had long since been abandoned, its structure unsound, its congregation now either dead themselves or worshiping in much more modern, centrally heated temples."*

Paul is talking about a building there, specifically a church. But he could also be talking about the state of horror fiction, circa the late-1990s. Before that, Horror (as a marketing category to be stamped on the spines of books) had just experienced nearly a decade of mainstream success, particularly here in the United States, with new novels and anthologies being mass-produced on a monthly basis by a multitude of publishers. But that ultimately led to oversaturation, bad books, and a contraction in the marketplace. Suddenly, the horror shelves at the local bookstore disappeared, replaced by expanding romance and self-help sections. Sure, the big names—folks like Stephen King, Clive Barker, Dean Koontz, and Anne Rice—were still selling, but horror fiction itself went underground for a while, surviving mostly in the small press and fanzines. (For more on that, I'll refer you to Grady Hendrix's *Paperbacks from Hell* or my own *End of the Road*). The zombie subgenre experienced this crash as well, with Phil Nutman's *Wet Work* and Skipp & Spector's *Books of the Dead 1* and *2* serving as denouements of sorts to the living dead.

A number of us writers came of age during the good years, and we began getting published during that dry spell. Paul and I were among that number, as were many of our peers who you read today—Tim Lebbon, Bryan Smith, Joe Hill, Mark Morris, Paul Tremblay, Sarah Pinborough, Christopher Golden, Mary SanGiovanni, Simon Clark, Sarah Langan, J.F. Gonzalez, Tom Piccirilli, Gemma Files, Wrath James White, Rio Youers... To provide a complete list would be exhausting and would double the page count of this collection, but you get the idea. Indeed, many of the stories included in this collection first saw publication during that fertile time—the early 2000s. And it was our efforts during that time that pretty much brought the horror genre back into vogue again. By the time we were ready for "prime time" publishing, there were a legion of readers hungry for horror fiction, and a host of publishers eager to provide it to them.

Like zombies, horror fiction rose from the grave, and like zombies, the audience was ravenous for it. Not for the first time, either. If you study the history of the genre, this sort of thing happens over and over again. It runs in cycles. The same can be said of the zombie subgenre itself. Critics and pop-culture historians point to late-2003 and early-2004, when almost back-to-back, my novel *The Rising*, Danny Boyle's film *28 Days Later*, and Robert Kirkman's comic book *The Walking Dead* all came out. It has been said repeatedly that this trio reignited pop culture's preoccupation with zombies, but I would argue that the desire had been there all along—it just wasn't being served to the masses. And it wasn't just the three of us. Plenty of the writers I mentioned above, as well as others among our peers, put their own stamp on the zombie subgenre during that time.

But none of them did it quite like Paul Kane. And we, as readers, should be very grateful for that. Paul's prose voice has always been distinct, but so are his *ideas* and his *delivery*, as you will soon see.

Here then, are some of the best of his contributions—full of scares, grim situations, beautiful imagery, and occasional bursts of humor. The first story I ever read by Paul— "The Face of Death" —is here, as is a favorite of mine, "Nine Tenths" (previously published on *Horror Drive-In*). There are also stories that are original to this collection.

All of them will leave you hungry for more. I know I am. Here's hoping Paul serves up a second volume soon...

Brian Keene
Somewhere along the
Susquehanna River
December 2022

We Have Become Mechanical

He'd made up his mind,
They had to become—
Wrestled with it, day and night.
The moral and religious implications.
Not that he believed in all that.
Not anymore.
Indeed, what Edward Telford
was planning flew in the face of
The Powers That Be.
Or Didn't Be.
Depending on your
Point of view.

A genius, he'd leaned toward
The sciences, but also his father
had been a man of industry.
Made his name in trains and
moving, mechanical toys.
Some of which had wowed the crowds,
at Crystal Palace.

Edward could be found from

an early age, tinkering
in his father's barn.
Experimenting. Building.
Things of pipe and steam.
Then later, at university, a student.
Of physics, of chemistry, of biology.
Of Nature and Human nature.
Human machinery.

That was where he'd met her.
Madeline. His one, true love.
A meeting of minds, her
curiosity, her intellect, the only match
he'd ever found for his own.
They were in sync, mirrored each other.
They'd laughed together, stepped out
together.
They'd married. Become one.
His other half, his wife.
And then he had lost her.
When she had died.

A body no longer able to
sustain life. Just a vessel for
the sickness.
Coughing. Blood. And finally...
Death. Sorrow. Dangerous thoughts,
on dark, lonely nights.
Of a book they'd both loved.
Shelley's creation from earlier
that century.
What if—

It would take more than mere
science, though.
Edward understood that.

Zombies!

They would also have to be—
To recreate movement. Replicate...
His first experiments were crude.
As crude as the means by which he
acquired the raw material.
Men who would give Burke & Hare
pause for thought.
Unscrupulous, uncouth.
Whose deity was
the coin.

Experiments out in his own barn now.
Limbs to begin with, extremities.
A combination of chemicals and
pistons. Twitching, movement.
Working and working.
Whole bodies then, encouraging them
to walk, like the first steps of
a baby. Lumbering, awkward.
Unthinking. Unfeeling.
Toys. Just toys again.

Because the real trick would be
the heart, the mind.
The soul.
Unquantifiable things.
But still he tried, got so far.
Clockwork and muscles.
The illusion of life if nothing
else.

Dozens of them. Re-animated from
the grave, strengthening them as he went.
No weakness; vessels fit for purpose.
That would never break down.
Until he could wait no longer.

Madeline had rotted enough.
Edward worked all the hours...
Not that God sent, but simply were.
The cruel work of time.
The cruel work that he did, looking back.

Until finally, at last, she was finished.
The best yet. Better even than his last.
Her gait, her walk more steady.
Recognition in her eyes?
Those bloodshot eyes?
The noise of the metal, the hiss of the
steam that powered her.
But Madeline. He recognized her.
Inside, it was her. It had to be.
Otherwise...

The right thing to do, he still thought that.
He'd just missed her so, so much.
Didn't question himself, the madness.
Not until the end.
Until she snapped his neck.
Ended his life.
So it could start again.

She had observed him, without him
knowing. In sync again.
Mirroring, a meeting of minds.
Had known Edward must become—
She'd set to work.
With chemicals, with metal.
So they could be one again.
Her other half, her groom.
The Groom of...

It was only then, when she had him back,

the hiss of steam, the click of
clockwork. Only then
that they had both known,
looking around at the others.
The start of a new world.
No need to wrestle with
moral and religious ramifications.
No powers that be.
Or didn't be.
No death.

Just them. The start of it all.
A meeting of minds.
Making up their minds.
Realizing, understanding.
That they needed to change
everyone.
That all the people would be better.
Stronger vessels, they'd never break down.
Cough up blood. Lose someone.
Die.
That they needed to be—
That they should become.
Finally, absolutely, unequivocally:
Mechanical.

He Is Legend

So this is the end…

June 2

Today is the first chance I've had to bring my journal up to date since what happened, happened. It's the first time I've felt like talking…*writing* about what me and my family went through, either. That's still so—

No, I can't. Not yet. I need another drink—then maybe. But I will say this. It went down just like I kept saying it would, more or less. They tried their best to cover things up, but I know the truth. I predicted it. I was always saying to Nat, one day they'll really go and fuck things up and—

Gotta stop now. I can't get the image of little Rosie's face out of my mind.

Christ, where's that other bottle of whisky I brought back with me?

✕✕✕✕✕

Right, I'm set. Just this side of off my face and still able to write.

If you're reading this at some point down the line—if there's anyone human still *left* to read it, that is—chances are you probably know all about the last several weeks. About the shit that went down at The New Festival of Britain, that cloud of red we saw on the TV, heard about on the radio—until everything got shut down and they started to suppress what was really going on.

That the dead were coming back to life. No, not life—not like Nat and my girl Rosie used to have. They were *so* alive. On weekends, when I had time off, or if I could rearrange my shifts—I was a workman for the council—we'd go to parks, go to the cinema, go out to eat. Rosie would order the most gigantic fudge sundaes you've ever seen in your life, then—

No, I need to stop thinking about all that. The life before. There's only this. I felt numb for such a long time afterward, but now I'm just angry.

Now I just want revenge.

But I do need to get it all down, to explain our story and what happened to us. There needs to be some kind of record...

It was on one of those weekends that everything changed for us. We were at the local shopping precinct, Meadow Hall—yeah, I know... the irony wasn't lost on me either... once I'd stopped crying my eyes out—when it all kicked off. We'd had a nice day out, even though I hate...hated being dragged around clothes shops by Nat and Rosie, my daughter having developed her mother's obsession for Next as she got older. It was still a nice break and made a change from digging up roads. That's right, I was one of those guys—annoying, but the job had to be done, and we always *got* it done.

So, we knew stuff was going on down south, and as I said, I'd been talk-ing about *something* kicking off for years, though nobody in our household really took me seriously: "Ssh, you're scaring Rosie," Nat used to say to me. That seems so ridiculous to me now. Scaring her? She *should* have been bloody scared; we all should. But I never thought it would hit us so quickly. I was worried, sure, and in retrospect I should have bundled my family up and made for the nearest harbor as soon as possible, got off this island and gone...

Where?

Was there any place that was safe anymore? Doesn't matter now; I didn't do it. All that bloody talk, and when it came right down to it... Maybe there was some part of me that couldn't believe the moment was actually here. That we'd gone and done it, caused the End of Days to come about.

They've been developing stuff like this for years, you know. Working on try-ing to reanimate dead tissue. But something went seriously wrong, and their experiments at the church with those dead folk were just the beginning.

But that's beside the point. There we were, sitting in the Oasis—that's the place where they sell food and drink—after our day out. Looking back, perhaps I was trying to give them that one final family day before the shit hit the fan. Because my radar was definitely up. Something was coming our way.

I just didn't expect it to be a shopping mall full of fucking zombies.

Our first sense that something was wrong came when groups of people started running toward us. Nat put down her latte and looked over at me, frowning—that look she always got when she knew we were in trouble (usually financially, I have to say). Worried and confused and silently asking what we should do. That's the thing about having a ten-year-old around; you can't ask these things openly, can't show your concern. You have to try and shield them, protect...

I rose, kicking back the chair I'd been sitting on. Trying to get a better look at exactly why those people were so panicked. Then I saw what was chasing them and realized that we should be running, too. At first, it didn't really register as anything other than more people, another group following them. Attacking them, to be precise, dragging them down to the ground—and, yes, I could see now they were biting into the ones they'd got hold of.

"Nat," I said slowly, but seriously. "Grab Rosie. We need to get out of here. Right now!"

My wife did as I asked, Rosie frightened enough now to follow our lead, and we backed off, turning, hoping to find some kind of emergency exit or something. Casting a look back over my shoulder, I saw more and more of the dead, all gray and rotting, scars covering their faces, mouths open wide and making those loud moaning noises. In fact, they were starting to outnumber the living—overwhelming them like hooligans at a football match. Even the security staff were being brought down.

Those bastards were spilling out of everywhere, filling the upper and lower floors.

And ahead of us, surrounding us. They came on us so quickly that we never really stood much of a chance. I looked around for anything I could use as a weapon, snatching up a baby chair and slamming that into the nearest one as it bore down on me. It was when I turned that I saw Nat and Rosie being dragged off, being dragged under the hordes.

I reached out but was yanked back myself. Jesus, they were strong those things, especially in large numbers. I managed to wrestle myself free a little, ducking out from under a pair of arms that were threatening to crush me in a bear hug. I dodged left, but someone had me by the arm. I punched backward, not even looking, managing to escape and get up to look for my wife and kid. I couldn't see them, only zombies bending and—

There was blood, so much it looked like a tin of red paint had been splashed around. Or a ketchup bottle had exploded. Then there was the pain, teeth biting into my shoulder. It was what had happened to my family, torn apart by the mob. So I really didn't care anymore, let them do their worst.

I really can't remember much more because I started to black out. When I woke up again, I was out in the car park. It was nighttime, and I was alone. All I can think is that someone got me out of there, rescued me and pulled me free of the mall, then had to leave me for whatever reason. Rescued me when I couldn't even do that for my own wife and child.

Sometimes I wonder if I really did die that day and this is Hell. Feels like Hell.

I went back inside, of course, but like the car park, it was deserted. Just smears of red everywhere, a few body parts. No sign of Nat or Rosie. At least I was spared the aftermath of what was done to them, though I think sometimes—and not without this amount of drink inside me, or more—that makes it worse. You *imagine* worse, if that's possible.

I need to break now, need another drink before I can go on.

June 3

Okay, that drink turned into several. Yesterday turned into today. And I woke up realizing that I hadn't finished my account properly. Hadn't told you about what happened next. After the bite, which hurt like fuck, by the way… Now, I know what's supposed to happen, what I've actually seen happen after one of them gets you—seen it up close and personal. Doesn't take that long, either, before you turn.

Except I never did. Don't get me wrong, I was as sick as a dog—made my hangover this morning look like mild food poisoning. Lucky I had a place to hole up while I went through it (slunk off back there, if the truth be told, probably thinking this was the end). Oh, I didn't tell you about my place, did I? My basement, or perhaps I should say bunker, as that's what Nat always used to call it: "Where you do your Mel Gibson thing, Bob." Not *Lethal Weapon*, though I can see the parallels now—in how I go about things out there, not giving a shit, and how that guy felt about ending it all when he lost his wife. Not *Mad Max* either, though again, things have worked out a bit like that.

No, she was on about the film where he keeps all those clippings, where he's obsessed with all the dodgy stuff the higher powers get up to. All the conspiracies, all the hidden agendas. It was a sort of hobby of mine, kept me off the streets. Or I should say, it's what I did when I wasn't on the streets and roads laboring; I know them like the back of my hand, you see. Except now they're kind of my stomping ground. Hunting ground, I probably should say. Night or day, makes no difference; it's not like they're vampires or whatever.

The stuff I've compiled over the years is one of the reasons why I knew something like this—but not *exactly* this—was going to occur at some point. All those experiments scientists were doing, all those genetically engineered viruses injected into insects and animals. You think Bird Flu or AIDS came out of fucking nowhere? Mother Nature? She had a massive helping hand.

They were playing with fire, though. Something was bound to go wrong at some point; it was only a matter of time. Man shall destroy himself, doesn't it say that somewhere in the Bible?

But I've gotten off track again. Where was I? Oh yeah, the sickness. I locked myself away down here, knowing it was well stocked—there's a concealed section with a fridge, tins, medicine (I treated the wound itself, but their shit was in me by then). Even a loo and backup generator. I also had one eye on some kind of nuclear disaster. You remember *Threads*, right?

I do. It was even bloody based here in Sheffield.

I wanted...wanted to keep my family safe, in case—

Stupid.

The bite, the sickness, stick to that. So, I was boiling hot one minute, freezing cold the next—then throwing up for England. It seemed to go on forever, but I came out the other side. Obviously, or I wouldn't be writing this. And sitting there sipping from a bottle of water after my shakes had worn off, I realized that all this had been my body's way of fighting the infection. That I must be immune in some way. Maybe that's why they left me alone. Because I didn't taste right.

Which gave me an advantage, meant that although I couldn't be silly about things, it gave me the upper hand in a scrap.

Once I'd fed myself up again, got stronger, I went out armed with what I could find around my house. A place I've since trashed, I should add; made it look deserted to avoid trouble. I thought it would be hard, all those memories, but in the end, it was easy. I needed to wipe them out, become hardened. I grabbed knives from the kitchen, tucked them into my belt, a hammer from the "man drawer" shoved in my pocket, plus a solid, pretty lethal-looking handsaw and an ax from my shed outside. Rough and ready, that's what I was. More than ready—and it wasn't as if there was a shortage of them out there. I could take my pick.

So that's exactly what I did. I suppose I did go a bit Mad Max, really; I went *something* at any rate. Wasn't the first time, sure as fuck won't be the last. Especially now that I have better weapons, abandoned by some of those military types in their failed bid to clean up the city.

They're long gone, by the way, the authorities. They've given up on this place, just like they must have done with so many across the country. Maybe they're concentrating on the capital still; who knows? Maybe everyone else has turned. I can't find out anything, can't even get a signal on the radio.

All I know is, all I can *rely* on is what I see out there. This city now belongs to them.

But I'm going to take it back.

June 15

Busy time again recently. I finally sat down and came up with some better ways to tackle those creatures. I mean, a stand-up fight is one thing, but it's still only me out there against them.

Fire's pretty good, for a start. It's one of the reasons why I've rigged the street outside, the house above, in case they ever find out where my base of operations is. Home-made explosives; they're not that difficult to make if you know what you're doing and have a grasp of basic chemistry. I might have messed around a lot in class at school and wound up doing what I was doing before all this, but I've made up for it since, and anyway, I'm a fast learner.

I've cooked up some nasty batches of acid as well, for instance. That works a treat—and from a distance if you spray it, like you're killing weeds in the garden. Which, y'know, isn't that far from the truth.

Then there was the head thing. You place a line of sharpened wire across a street, say between two lampposts, at a certain height. Then you walk around, trying to attract their attention, which, in all fairness, isn't that difficult. When they follow, lead them to the street and then duck as they reach the wire. Hey presto, instant Louis XVI, but without all that fuss with the guillotine. You don't even need an ax.

There are other methods I've used. For example, in my search of the city for anything useful, I came across one of those industrial strimmers they clear overgrown wasteland with. The really tough jobs that run on petrol and make domestic ones look like kids' toys; they make a real mess of those things, and pretty instantly. Splatters them into tiny pieces. Can't tell you how satisfying it is for me to see that.

Then there's the ramming: if you hit them hard enough, and with a fast-enough car (the thing about the end of the world is there's no shortage of those, you can even drive them out of showrooms), then they tend not to get up again any time soon. I'd imagine I've become a bit of a local attraction doing that.

It all gets the job done.

Last night I took on a crowd of them near what used to be old Heston's place back in the day. I remember us being scared of him as kids, running past the house in case he came out and tried to catch one of us. Looking back, he was just some lonely old guy. I see that now. And there are much worse things to be afraid of.

But, just like I'm not afraid of old man Heston anymore, I'm not afraid of them either. I'm too angry to be scared.

Like when I waded into that group. There's nothing like getting in there every now and again, getting back to that first hunt, that first fight. Getting down and dirty, only now I jam pistols under chins, wedge serrated bowie knives into skulls, hack off limbs with machetes.

They try to bite me, try to infect me, of course—not realizing that they actually can't. I do wear padding, protective clothing scrounged from the police station on Atlas Way; body armor, that kind of thing (the batons were handy, too, for any close combat). I know I'm immune, but I'm not stupid—I don't actually *want* to get bitten again because I can't risk being incapacitated, especially in the middle of an attack. I need to be able to get out of there before more of their kind arrive to help. Which they eventually always do, like they know when one of them is in trouble.

I like to make sure I'm long gone before then, if I can help it. I scope places out so I know what my exit strategy is. I was caught on the hop once, and it cost me dearly.

It...

I can't stop thinking about the life that might have been, if... Yeah, I used to be into the conspiracy stuff and was always talking about how things would go to pot, but I guess I never thought... No, I *hoped* it was all a load of crap. I was only looking into it so I'd be prepared. So we wouldn't—

I keep seeing Nat and me growing old together, me worrying about Rosie when she heads off to uni on her own. The amount of gray hair I'd get just from that! Nat telling me that kids have to find their own path, but me having trouble letting go. She was my little girl, you know? And I loved—*still* love her so, so much. I miss her.

I miss them both.

Drink now. I need another drink.

June 18

I think… I think I've finally… That I'm going insane. I know what's going through your mind: not much of a stretch in my current state. But, well, this was different. I think.

Never had a hallucination before, unless you count when I was very little and I had a fever that made me see horses coming through the walls. Not bad training for when I was bitten, come to think of it, but what I saw has got nothing to do with that. Least I don't… No, it doesn't. There were no other after-effects.

Maybe it was lack of sleep, then? My sleep's been shit since the apocalypse began, just don't seem to be able to relax—ha, ha! The booze puts me under most nights, and when I raided that *Boots* for essential medical supplies, I came away with some sleeping pills that do the same. But I never really stay asleep for long. I fight it, you see. I've always been a fighter, just like Dad was, right up to the very end of his life. I wonder if he—

No, don't even go there. Can't think about that. Mum was cremated, so there's no chance of bumping into her out there. But Dad?

Off on a tangent, I know, but it does relate to what I'm trying to talk/write about. Which is Rosie. I was out on the streets doing a recon for my next ambush and keeping out of the way of any lurkers, when I could have sworn I saw— It was a little girl, at any rate. Same kind of hair as my Rosie, dressed very similarly to how she'd been at Meadow Hall (Meadow Hell, as I tend to think of it now). Jeans, jumper, those white pumps she'd pestered us to buy and I'd grumbled were too expensive. God, I'd buy her a million pairs of the things without complaint if she was here today. Not that you need to buy anything anymore, but you know what I mean.

Anyway, there she was, turning the corner on Deansgate. I stopped, the breath catching in my mouth—throat dry, I could hardly swallow. Rosie. My Rosie. No, I shook my head. It couldn't be! And yet I found myself following, chasing after her. Or what I thought I'd seen anyway, conscious now that I was out in the open, but I didn't give a shit. That's where my mind was at.

Of course, there was nothing there when I got to the corner. No sign of Ros— Of the little girl. Wasn't inconceivable that someone like that might have survived the last couple of months or more, but at the same time...

She was so like my little girl.

Yes, I am drinking again. I have to. It's the only way I can make myself numb.

June 25

Last night I set another trap.

Only this time it wasn't designed to bring down the creature, but to capture it. I was thinking at first that I could study what I caught, figure out new ways to hurt or destroy them. Funny thing is, once I got it back here— Oh, the trap was a success, by the way, a variation on the old bear pit, but this time involving some weakened pub cellar doors, the creature falling into a metal trap beneath, which could then be wheeled home... Yeah, the funny thing is, when I'd got it back—it, not he, I refuse to call it that yet— and secured it down in the basement (which wasn't an easy task, but it's amazing the shit you can find in old museums!), I got the sense that it was watching me, trying to work me out. It even opened and closed its mouth a few times like it was going to say something. But it didn't.

Did get me thinking, though. What if there was something left inside there, some semblance of humanity? Crazy, I know, but I couldn't help wondering...

I shook the thoughts away because they were dangerous. Then I set about doing what I was going to do originally, studying the monster. My foe. Con-ducting some experiments of my own, testing its limits.

At one point, I swear it was looking at me with sadness in its eyes.

June 30

Can't shake the feeling that something might still be inside them. It was one of the reasons why I stopped doing what I was doing, torturing that thing. Probably wasn't even his fault he turned; he only looks young—bitten maybe, just like I was, or had he died at an early age? 'Course, the rotting, the peeling skin, and pallor like the side of a battleship will age a person (or should that be former person, or un-person? I never was one for all that PC shit), but I'd say what? Twenty-something at most? Made me wonder about his life, who he'd been, what his aspirations were.

Maybe to have a family of his own, a wife and kid. More than one, even? Nat and I had tried but were only blessed the once. God, I bloody loved that child. Perhaps this dead guy would have felt the same way, would have done anything for his daughter, or son. Given his life for them. It would have been better than giving his life over to this.

It preyed on my mind, the way he watched me, the way he looked so sad, even with those eyes rolling back into their sockets the way they did. I began thinking that perhaps I was going about this all the wrong way. What if he could be brought back? What if I could restore his humanity, give him back that life? Christ knows mine was fucked, but it might even help with the pain of that. Especially if I could use my blood to do it.

I'm no scientist; I don't profess to be. But I know a little about what makes things tick. If you're immune, that means a cure can be developed from your tissue, doesn't it? What I don't know, I can find out from the library. Now there's no Net, we're back to old school ways.

Back to school. Back to doing things over, getting it right this time. Putting all this frigging mess right.

July 10

Well, that didn't fucking work, did it?

I did what I said I was going to do, raided the City Library on Surrey Street—an impressive building that looks like it belongs back in ancient Greece or something—but only after making sure there were no nasty surprises inside. Do zombies hang out in libraries? What kind of things would they read? Cookbooks? Naw, they like their meat raw, which is handy for setting some of those traps actually; they're drawn to the smell. One of the reasons I mask my own.

It was empty, thankfully. So, after locating the science and medical stuff, I loaded anything I thought might be useful into a backpack—not a holdall, I needed to keep my hands free in case I had to spring into action. That makes me sound more like Chuck Norris or Bruce Lee than Mel.

I'm no ninja, but I do get the job done.

Made it back without incident, though, and began my studies. I pored over those books, taking it all in. Learning how if someone has had a virus and appears to be immune, has developed antibodies, you can try and create your own cure from that. Like I said, fast learner. Would mean another run for equipment I'd need, probably to the Hallamshire or Northern General Hospitals—maybe even both—but I could sort that, I figured. I *did* sort it, in fact. Took a van this time and filled up the back of that. Not as good for a fast getaway, but sturdy if I got into trouble.

By the time I was finished in my basement, it looked like a lab. Then came the hard part: not the science or any of that. Drawing my own blood. I've never been great with needles; it's why I wouldn't have made a very good junkie. Drink, yeah. The occasional puff on something when I was younger, even. But nothing that involved puncturing my skin. Just couldn't face it. Not until I really had a reason to.

Took a while to build up to that, but I did it—fighting the waves of nausea, the urge to just pass out in the chair.

But I got my samples, then I got to work.

Once you know what you're doing, it's actually pretty easy. Or at least I thought so. The problem is the quantities you're dealing with, because you never know whether it's going to be too much or too little. It's like baking a cake, I guess. Trial and error. Too much of one ingredient and your cake deflates, or rises too much and—

It's quite an apt analogy. You'll see that when I tell you what happened to the boy I tried to cure. I went over to him, chained as he was to the wall. Saw the fear and panic in his eyes. "I'm not going to hurt you," I promised him, realizing that all he had to go on were my previous actions in this department. "I'm trying to help you. Don't you understand?" What was I talking about? Of course, he didn't. Some level of recognition there, but nothing major. Nothing you could call human.

Not yet.

I pulled out another needle and stuck it in him, pumping him full of my cobbled-together antidote. He roared, straining against the shackles holding him. His eyes went wider than I'd ever seen them; he snarled and shook and brought up a kind of black, tar-like bile. Going through a similar thing to me when I was first bitten, I noted.

Then something incredible started to happen. His gray skin began to gradually have more color to it, turning a shade of pink again. I'm not saying he looked the best; if he'd been admitted to the hospital before all this, then they'd have probably given him about a 5% chance. But any change was a good one as far as I was concerned.

"Come on, come on," I said, cheering him on from the sidelines. All I could think about was that future I'd been denied, the one he might yet have. The one I might be able to give all the victims of this fucking disease. And they *were* victims; I could see that now I wasn't so blinded by hatred and bent on revenge.

The boy was shaking so much I thought he might pull the chains out of the wall where I'd drilled them in. But he wasn't trying to escape, his body was attempting to reject what I'd stuck in it, and with good reason. I opened my mouth, standing back just a moment or so too late, as his body shook itself to pieces and exploded. You see why that cake comparison was so apt now?

Bits of flesh, bits of what had once been blood and bone covered the walls of my basement. Covered *me!* I sank back into my chair, stunned. There was a time when I would have congratulated myself on developing what must surely be one of the greatest weapons against their kind, but all I could see now was failure.

The fear and terror in that lad's eyes.

In spite of my intentions, I'd actually made things worse. It took me a long time to move again after witnessing that. Even longer to begin the clean-up.

Cursing myself all the time, with one eye on a new bottle of Jack Daniels I'd brought back with me on my last run. I had hoped I might be able to celebrate with it, but now I just wanted to get plastered again.

So that's what I did...and spent the next day suffering for it. As I'm writing, I'm thinking I might do it again tonight.

Maybe I am becoming an addict after all? Or maybe I'm just so sick and tired of this life that oblivion looks like the better option?

Sick and tired...

Of life.

July 25

Test Subject Number Ten showed the greatest improvement yet.

Subjects Two through Nine all displayed different reactions to the serum, which I've varied with each subsequent injection. Some got almost to the point of eruption, then it settled down. Some did actually deflate, their bodies collapsing in on themselves (once again, the baking thing). All went into a state of shock I can only call some sort of coma. More failures, but I'm not going to keep beating myself up about it anymore. I need these subjects, need to do these tests so that I can get it right. I never thought I'd be the one saying this, but the end sometimes really does justify the means.

As in the case of Ten, a woman who'd been in her late forties by the looks of things when this hit her. I almost, *almost* got her back all the way. She even spoke a little, mouthing words I couldn't quite catch—and fairly quickly after I'd injected her at that. It sounded like, "H-H-Help me."

"Yes, that's what I'm doing," I told her, nodding. "You just hold on!"

That same fear was in her eyes, the color now returning to the pupils same as it was in her arms, hands, face. There was the shaking, of course, but that was only to be expected.

"P-Please..." she begged, clenching and unclenching one of her hands. I stepped over and grabbed it, holding it as if that might actually help with the process. But I'd done everything I could do; what was happening inside was up to her now. Her own private battle.

It was one that she ultimately lost.

Just when I thought the tide was turning, she gritted her teeth and that was that. She slumped forward, hanging there on the wall. In a similar inanimate state to the rest of the test subjects. But she didn't revert back to her gray, rotting form. She just looked peaceful, like that woman in the old painting, the one under the water.

Unlike the rest of them, I felt compelled to bury this one rather than take her to the pit. I even mumbled something resembling a prayer over the grave, though I'm not sure why. I was never much of a church-going person before all this, and nothing I've seen since has made me want to embrace religion. It just seemed like the *proper* thing to do, if that makes sense?

It just made me want to succeed even more, bring all of them back.

I was going to try harder; I vowed to do it.

August 1

Doing my usual trawl of the city, I spotted something odd today. Groupings of them, all heading in one direction, joining together. I watched from a good vantage point on top of one of the buildings, through my binoculars.

They were heading toward the Town Hall; I hesitate to say flocking but, yeah, that's really the only way to describe it. Congregating, as if following some silent call—silent to human ears anyway. Like they had their own religion. From what I could see, and for whatever reason, they were moving toward the City Council building.

I decided that, although it was risky, I would try to get closer. So I raced down the stairs, keeping an eye on the street as I went. By the time I got to the ground floor, the herds had thinned out a little—which at least allowed me to move a bit more freely and catch them up.

Hefting my automatic rifle, moving between the buildings, I managed to get a little closer. *Very* close, in fact.

I peered around the corner of a building a street or two away from all the commotion. And guess what I saw? You never will in a million years! So, I'll tell you.

There was this man standing outside the building, which has, in all honesty, seen better days—its Stoke stone more worn and tired-looking than I've ever seen it, clock stuck on twelve like some kind of doomsday device. He was standing on this thrown-together platform of junk. The zombie crowds had gathered around him, in the plaza, where the fountain used to be when it still worked—the grass sections now overgrown and wild (in need of those strimmers I once used). They seemed to be listening to him. I wasn't close enough to hear those murmurs, those mumblings. But through the binoculars, I got a good look at the zombie doing all the pontificating, like he was giving his very own Sermon on the Mount.

It was the Mayor, or at least the man who was standing again for Mayor at the time of the apocalypse. Was tipped to actually take the position, mainly because of his cut-throat dealings—none of which could be proven, of course. Typical politician then, I hear you say. You can imagine how much respect I have for them! My old fucking bosses.

Councilor Brandon Fleming his name was, back when he was alive. We were well used to seeing his face on local TV, on flyers, and posters. I was used to seeing him give speeches like this, too, though not usually in such circumstances. Was he... Were these people all recreating some base memory of before the fall?

Going through the motions, doing something they could only half remember? It made me all the more determined to bring them back again. To carry on with my attempts at a cure. There was something still inside from the old days, had to be.

I just needed to hit on the right formula.

Get the job done.

August 15

Subjects Twenty through Twenty-five, a total bust.

Need to rest, need to get some sleep before I carry on with this.

Need another drink.

August 20

Something's changed out there in the city. I can't put my finger on it, but definitely something. Ever since the meeting, since the speech.

It's been harder and harder to find test subjects, like they've spread the word or something. Like they know—as a whole—that I'm out here, that I've been setting traps.

I'm going to have to get smarter, that's all. Just going to have to think outside of the box.

Come on, Bob, get with the program.

August 27

Stupid, stupid, stupid.

I can't believe what an idiot I was today. Out trying to catch more test subjects—I'm getting a bit desperate now, running out of readily available ones—and I saw her. *Thought* I saw her. Nat, near the Winter Gardens. Going in.

As was the case when I thought I saw Rosie, I let my guard down, didn't I. Followed her in a kind of daze, half wanting, *needing* it to be her—even a zombie version of her I could fix—half hoping it was some sort of dream come true. But I wasn't going mad, I couldn't be. She was real, damn it!

I *think* she was real.

Shit. My fucking side hurts so much, and as for my ankle...

I'll write more later; I can feel the painkillers kicking in now, the ones I washed down with Jim Beam. Probably shouldn't have started writing in the journal at all, just wanted to get...some of it down before I forgot.

Before... I can hardly keep my eyes—

August 29

Still not in great shape, but I'm slowly recovering.

Just read back through what I wrote before. I nearly ripped the page out, started again. But it's all part of the journal, the record of what I've gone through here. The highs and the lows and the complete fuck-ups, complemented by drugs and alcohol. Necessary, I promise you. I'm still not an addict. Not really.

Okay, Nat.

I followed her inside, the place like a jungle now that there's nobody around to keep it tidy. So much so, I didn't see any of it coming. I wasn't expecting it, for starters. I mean: *I'm the thinking one, right?* Apart from those I've *almost cured*—and I still haven't given up on that, thank you very much— I'm the only person in this city still capable of it. The only one I've come across in all this time, anyway.

I just didn't think—ha!—they'd be capable of… Maybe they were still going through the motions again, and some of them knew how to do this kind of thing before. But it would still require—

I stumbled into the tripwire before I even realized it was there. A miniature version of the ones I used to leave for beheading *them*, only they didn't want me dead. No sir, not if the spring-loaded piece of wood that hit me in the ribs was anything to go by. It knocked all the air out of my body, sending me sprawling across into some overgrown plants. My rifle went flying in the opposite direction, out of reach.

Shaking my head, I started to clamber to my feet, then winced at the pain in my side. As if that wasn't enough, I'd barely taken a step or two when I trod on the mantrap, covered over with foliage. They must have been scattered about the place in the hopes that I'd stumble onto one, which is exactly what I did.

I wear combat trousers, which are quite thick, but they did nothing to protect me from those metal jaws as they snapped shut on my calf. I yelled out in pain, couldn't help myself. But I didn't have the luxury of taking my time. Already I could see shapes, movement all around me. I had to get out of there, and quickly. Shouldn't have even gone inside without an exit strategy.

Took two or three attempts, and I thought I was going to pass out again while I was doing it, but I managed to open up the clamp and get my leg out. Using a nearby tree to drag myself up, I scanned the floor, trying to make out which direction might be safe. One that wouldn't have any more nasty surprises in store.

Again, I didn't have time to stand around—had to make a decision and stick with it, hoping I could get free. In the end, I just thought, *Fuck it,* and launched myself sideways at the glass wall not far away.

I fell, tumbling over and over on the concrete outside—which actually probably put some distance between me and my pursuers. Maybe even saved my life.

Not that it felt like it at the time, as I limped away down the road, looking over my shoulder, clutching my side. I rounded a corner, risking a glance back to see a grouping of a dozen or more zombies outside the Winter Gardens, searching left and right. And was it my imagination, or did one of them point, grunt some kind of instruction like a captain giving orders to his troops?

No time to think on this back then, just had to get away. So, limping through the streets, I hobbled onwards—pausing only once to rip some material from my sleeve and tie it around the wound on my leg. I needed to stem the blood-flow, not only to save my life, but also so they wouldn't have a scent to track. I've seen what their heightened senses can do.

On and on I went, conscious of the fact I was out in the open. That I needed to get inside somewhere. I chose a shop that looked deserted, gaining access through the smashed window display at the front, shoes and sporting equipment having gone everywhere in some of the fighting from a few months ago.

In a back room, I collapsed, waiting until it was "safe" to move again. Until I'd recovered enough to get moving, and under cover of darkness (yeah, I know, heightened senses, but it was something—made me feel better at least). Then I went out through the back door, smashing it open with my shoulder, which wasn't a good idea and caused me to see stars.

From there: home. Or what had become of it. I'd stopped thinking about it like that once Nat and Rosie had been snatched from me. Once I'd trashed it.

I began to think about that as I slipped under from the pills and whisky. First Rosie, then Nat. I'd seen them…seen something, hadn't I?

Something that had led me right into a trap, just like the ones I had been setting for test subjects.

Using bait.

September 3

Healing, slowly. And drinking. A lot.

Not able to get out, not able to find test subjects. Not able to do *anything*. Useless, absolutely fucking useless.

September 11

I ventured out too soon, and they spotted me. Not surprising, really; I was like a bull in a china shop out there. My injuries have slowed me down; I've lost my edge.

Not only did they see me, they *followed* me. Tracked me back here. They're good, so much better than I realized. Organized and—

They gathered outside the house, just like they'd done outside the Town Hall, to listen to that speech. They hung back while I watched through one of the windows I'd cracked to make this place look like every other one in town: decayed, just like them. I've come to think of it like that, this city. I said once it belonged to them, but it's also come to resemble them. Like a pet with an owner, I guess.

Probably only right that I should bow out then. I was always fighting against a rising tide.

Within the hour, there were hundreds of the buggers outside. And him, the Mayor. He wanted to talk to me personally. Yes, they can talk—and not just to each other. I realized that when he began calling to me. It was definitely a shock at first, but then I thought: *what's one more shock to me now?*

"You cannot possibly win, you know," he said. Pretty good opening. I was starting to understand that truth myself. "You have inflicted untold horrors on our people," he continued. That rankled. *Untold horrors? On them? Fuck off!* I thought at first he was talking about my rampage, how I took my revenge, but there were reasons for that. Then he said, "We found the results of your 'work.' What you've been doing to our...my people." I thought for a moment he was going to say constituents like he used to do in those campaigns of his. "Trying to go against the natural order, trying to alter people when it wasn't necessary."

Natural order? There was nothing natural about the state of them. And it was necessary. Things needed to be put right, put back how they were.

Nat. Rosie.

And it was then that I saw them; they were close by him, maybe not intentionally, but it was like he was using them somehow to get at me. Not Nat and Rosie, but they looked so much like them it hurt. Perhaps I was imagining them again, I dunno, or I just wanted those...those *people* to look like Nat and Rosie. The woman was definitely real, wasn't she? The one they'd used to lure me into the Winter Gardens. Couldn't have been Nat—she'd *know* where I was hiding out, surely?

"It's our time now," the Mayor was ranting on. Still liked the sound of his own voice. Death hadn't changed that. "A superior race. We are cleansing the world. There's nothing you can do to stop us, and you will pay, mark my words, for the fear you have instilled in us. For the members of our family that you corrupted."

Family?

"The family is one. Outside of the family, there is nothing at all!"

It was then that he gave the order for them to attack my old home. And, as a knee-jerk reaction more than anything, I set off the explosives by remote control. The explosions weren't huge, but they did a lot of damage to those advancing, probably because of the nails and bits of torn metal I packed into each one. They shredded zombie flesh as easily as they would have done humans in some sort of terrorist act.

Was that what I'd become to them, a terrorist? A thing of nightmares? A legend that would be talked about many years from now? The boogie man, the thing that these—what, "intelligent zombies"—might fear?

While they were regrouping, recovering, getting ready to strike again, I retreated to the basement and locked the door from the inside. It's where I am now, writing this, though I can hear them outside, trying to gain entrance. I can—

Sorry about that... The door gave in under the weight of them. I've had to lock myself inside the other room in the bunker, though it won't be long before they're in here as well.

So, this is the end.

I just wanted to finish this journal, get the job done. To leave something of myself behind—Christ knows what they have planned for me after what I've done to them. The greatest sin as far as they're concerned, those tortures from earlier on nothing compared to the experiments I conducted trying to bring them back.

I was thinking that I might end up a legend amongst them: me, Bob Nevill, imagine that! But then history is written by the victors, and I've lost. Lost everything. My family, my...myself. *I* am lost. I was mad—heh—to think I could ever take this city back from them. It *belongs* in their hands, and so does this world now. It's guys like the Mayor who will paint themselves as the legends.

But that's for another time; all I can do now is

Dig (This)

Like all stupid ideas, it had seemed like a good one "at the time."

Although now, as they walked past these plots in the darkness, the gravestones like ragged, gray teeth sticking up out of the ground, Davy was wondering if they should go ahead with their half-baked scheme at all. It was one thing to say you were going to do something, but to actually do it was another matter entirely.

The more he mulled it over, the more stupid the idea became. Just whose suggestion had it been anyway? His? No, at least Davy didn't think so. Had to be Travis's, then. Yeah, Travis's stupid idea.

Travis suddenly stopped dead, and Davy ran into his back.

"Hey, watch it!" shouted Travis, then realized his voice was about ten times louder than it needed to be. Bringing up the rear, Stevo collided with Davy and muttered a pitiful sorry. It certainly hadn't been Stevo's idea. Travis, definitely Travis. He was the "brains" behind this operation.

Mind you, they were all to blame to some extent. Hadn't they chosen this place to hang out week after week? Why exactly was that? Because it was as quiet as the *grave*? It was true that nobody ever came up here. The small chapel it belonged to had long since been abandoned, its structure unsound, its congregation now either dead themselves or worshiping in much more modern, centrally heated temples. Which meant that the 'yard—as they called it—had also become neglected, the grass only cut once in a blue moon. Those buried here had been all but forgotten by their surviving relatives. If, indeed, they had any. In this age, the pace of life was just too great, problems too numerous. It left little time to visit people you couldn't even remember, let alone missed.

Which made the 'yard such a brilliant place for them to congregate. No one to disturb them, no one interfering. No one telling them what to do; the poor buggers in those plots were past telling anyone anything. Stevo came here to escape from the madhouse he lived in. It was more like an old folks' home since his sick grandparents had come to stay. You couldn't move for Zimmer frames and commodes at his place. Travis came to get away from his exboxer dad, who couldn't be arsed to go down the gym anymore, preferring instead to use his own son as a punching bag. And Davyboy? Well, he just came here to escape from the disappointment of his own existence. The fact that he'd never amount to anything, unlike his older brother, who'd been to university and snagged a job with a large banking firm in the city immediately after leaving.

"David, you're a complete waste of space," his mother would tell him every other minute. "Just like your father was." A father he'd never known and would have to take his mum's word about. So, he figured he might as well come here to waste that space rather than anywhere else. It was his space to waste, after all.

The three of them had been making the trek up to this small but deceptively capacious graveyard for about two or three months now. Ever since they found it on one of their famous walks—trying to alleviate the boredom of being a teenager in one of the most dreary localities known (or unknown?) to mankind. If Travis hadn't taken that shortcut through the hedge behind Old Parson's field, they might have missed it altogether.

None of them had ever had a death in the family—worst luck—so they'd never actually had cause to visit a graveyard before. It was one of those things they knew existed but hadn't really thought too much about. Until that day in late July, at the start of the summer holidays.

Travis had stopped and stared at the 'yard, the headstones

lined up in rows on the overgrown pasture.

"Now this I *can* dig," he said, smiling broadly.

Stevo didn't like it at first, sitting on the stones and smoking, or discussing which girls in their year—or even in the year above—were hot. (Sara Miles usually came top of the list for all three of them: she looked a bit like Angelina Jolie without the lips, and the boys called her "Angel" for short.)

But Stevo was soon talked around by Travis.

"Don't you see... This is perfect!"

It was. Davy thought the same. A really great "get-away-from-it-all" sort of place. Plus, if the company of Travis and Stevo got too much for him, he could always read the 'stones. There were plenty to choose from: some your standard crosses atop plinths or rocks; some more ornamental crosses with edges that looked like three-leafed clovers. Some were arch-shaped, and some were pointed—the idea being to suggest the way to Heaven, presumably—some had more rounded tops like big, flat shoes. But the vast majority were simple rectangular slabs; no frills or fuss. Davy spent hours and hours going up and down the rows, peeling away moss, parting the grass, taking in the dates, the names. Stevo laughed at him sometimes, but Davy found it all fascinating. Found the whole graveyard fascinating, if he was honest.

Maybe he *had* suggested this!

No, Davy could remember the conversation quite clearly in his mind now. He'd been reading the names on the 'stones again, coming back to a particular favorite of his—the plainest one of all, with the shortest inscription chiseled into the rough textured granite. *Here Rests Frederick Fullerton 1899–1965.* Travis and Stevo joined him, sitting opposite, and they drank the tins of beer Travis had stolen from his old man's fridge. Someone would be in for a thrashing when he found out; Davy was just glad it wouldn't be him.

Somewhere along the line, they'd started to talk about dying and death and ending up in a cemetery just like this one someday. Davy was amazed the subject hadn't cropped up before.

"So what do you think?" asked Stevo. "Is there a God and Heaven and all that?"

"What do I look like," Travis had retorted, "the Archbishop of bastard Canterbury?"

"Not exactly."

"What d'*you* think, Stevo?" Davy said, sipping the now-luke-warm beer. "What's after this? D'you go on to live forever?"

"I fucking well hope not," said Travis. "What's so great about life?"

"I wasn't asking you."

Stevo looked out thoughtfully over the horizon. This was heavy stuff to be discussing at such a tender age. But they were all old enough to have sex, no matter what the law said. It wouldn't be long before they could vote and work or sign on—if the statistics in this area were anything to go by. Why shouldn't they talk about the other "biggie?" "I think..."

"Yeah?"

"I think we'll all find out when the time comes."

Travis snorted. "'Course we will, *moron*. But by then we won't be able to tell anyone about it, will we?"

"Not unless we come back from the dead," said Davy, quick as a flash.

Stevo raised an eyebrow. "What, you mean like a ghost or a zombie or some bollocks like that?"

Davy nodded.

"You've been watching too many horror flicks, Davy-boy," said Stevo.

Travis felt sufficiently motivated to say, "All horror films are shit."

Davy wasn't impressed by his blitzkrieg method of critique but was willing to hear him out. "Explain."

"It's obvious, isn't it? The monsters and stuff. You know at the back of your mind it's all make-up. Special effects, computer animation. What's so frightening about that?"

"Better ask Stevo. He's the one who almost shit himself when we watched *Hellraiser* at Marty Finn's party that time."

"I was only a kid back then."

"*Hello*, it was last year."

Stevo showed Davy his middle finger. Davy raised his beer in salute.

"Well, they don't do jack for me," said Travis. "It's like watching soft porn or something. It's not real."

Davy smiled. "And when was the last time *you* watched porn—soft or otherwise?"

Travis smirked. "You'd be surprised at what's hidden under my old man's bed."

"No, I wouldn't."

"So what's the alternative?" Stevo innocently enquired. "Snuff movies? Those things are all faked as well."

"He's talking about those documentaries on Channel 5, those autopsy programs, aren't you? Or the ones about serial killers?"

Frowning, Travis said, "They're okay. But they still don't show you much of anything." His next question was off on a tangent but sort of made sense within the context of the meandering debate they were having. "I bet neither of you have ever seen a dead body up close, have you?"

Davy and Stevo looked at each other.

"Well, *have* you?"

They shook their heads.

"But then," said Davy, "neither have you."

Travis conceded the point. "You're right. I haven't."

That's when it started to get interesting. Travis pointed to the grave Davy was sitting next to. "Aren't you just a little bit curious?"

"About what?"

"You spend most of your time here looking at the head-stones, reading the names... Hasn't it ever crossed your mind?'

The funny thing was, it had. And Davy knew without speaking to Stevo that it'd crossed his mind, too, as spineless as he was. Travis had simply brought it out into the open. They were all wondering, at that precise moment, what the corpses in the 'yard looked like after being buried in the earth all this time.

So exactly when had they decided to find out?

Davy still couldn't recall. It hadn't been straight away, he knew that. But when, and whose idea had it been?

Travis's giant flashlight in his face brought Davy back to the here-and-now. Should he voice his concerns? Tell Travis he wanted to turn back? Stevo would go with him, there was no doubt about that. He was only here to start with out of a misplaced sense of pride, to stop them both from ragging him. If Davy wanted to high-tail it out of there, then that gave Stevo the perfect excuse to bail.

"Listen, Travis—"

"You're not chickening out, are you? Nah, I know you too well, Davy-boy. You want to see old Fullerton just as much as I do."

"Why'd we have to come at night, though, Travis?" whined Stevo. "There's never anybody here in the day, only us. Everyone's forgotten about this place."

Travis moved the light over to shine in Stevo's face. "Do you want to risk it? Just because we've never seen anybody the entire summer doesn't mean nobody *ever* comes. It'd be just our luck for someone to catch us in the middle of... You know... The middle of doing what we're going to do."

"But—" started Stevo.

"What's the matter, anyway? Are you scared of the dark?" He said this in a mocking tone of voice.

"No!"

Travis laughed. "Don't worry; I won't let anybody hurt you." He pulled something out of his pocket. There was a clicking sound, and the switchblade in his hand sprang open.

"Shit!" said Stevo. "Where the hell d'you get that from?"

"Ask me no questions..."

"Just...just put it away before someone gets hurt!"

Travis folded the blade on his thigh and hid it away again.

"Why d'you stop anyway?" Davy asked.

Travis flashed his light on the gravestone to their left. "We're here," he said.

Davy followed the beam and saw the name: Frederick Fullerton. They had indeed arrived.

"Right, time to go to work," said Travis. He waved his beam over the high grass next to the grave, looking for the spot where they'd hidden the shovels and pick earlier on. He found them easily enough, then handed out the implements: keeping the pick for himself. Stevo and Davy just stood there looking at the shovels as if they didn't know quite what they were for.

"Come on, then. Get started!" Travis snapped at them, but they still waited for him to begin digging before they joined in. The ground was hard, and shockwaves vibrated up along the shovels and pick as they worked. Time seemed to pass quickly, though, and it wasn't long before they were quite a ways down—the piles of earth by the side of the grave a testament to their labors.

"If we go much further, we're going to have a job getting out of the hole again," warned Stevo. The torch resting on the side of the fissure illuminated his worried face.

"Just keep digging," said Travis.

Davy had to admit that he felt the same. A sense of determination was surging through him now; he felt a need to get to the bottom of this hole they were digging, to finish what they'd started, to reach the—

There was a clumping sound. Travis stopped, his pick buried in the earth.

"Was that...?" Stevo half-asked.

"Pass me the torch," demanded Travis. With a shaking hand, Stevo reached up and did as he was told. Travis got down on his haunches, held the flashlight in one hand, and brushed away the soil with the other. "Pay dirt," he whispered.

"I don't think that's very funny," said Stevo. "Do you think that's funny, Davy? I said—"

"Shhh," Davy urged, leaning over Travis's shoulder. He was clearing away all the dirt, revealing the outline of the coffin they were standing on. Travis whistled, again a little too loudly.

"I don't like this," muttered Stevo. "Don't like it one bit."

When Travis suggested getting the lid off, Davy didn't know whether he liked it, either.

"What's the problem? I thought you wanted to see it."

"Me? I never said—"

"Look," said Travis. "Are either of you two wet nurses going to help me or not?"

His companions just stood there looking at him.

"Right, well, get out of the fucking way, then. Make some room." Travis motioned for them to get out of the hole, and they did. But they still squatted down on the side next to the mounds of earth they'd shifted—just in case they missed anything.

Travis used the pick to get underneath one corner of the coffin. It was tough to dislodge, but eventually it gave, old nails submitting to his pressure. There was a loud crack as the wooden lid opened up a fraction. In fact, it splintered halfway down, and Davy thought the whole thing was going to break in two.

It didn't, though. Quite the opposite: it came away in one piece, and Travis reared it up alongside the coffin itself.

"Christ, the smell," said Stevo. It reached them even up there, a foul odor that defied description.

Travis was pulling back, standing up on the edges of the coffin. He'd dropped the pick and now only had the flashlight in his grasp, trained on the casket below. But Stevo and Davy couldn't see a thing because of him.

"Travis," said Davy. "What is it? What's he look like?"

Travis didn't answer; he simply tip-toed around the edge of the coffin, allowing them a view of the corpse. It was old, as they'd expected. Mere bones covered with dried skin that looked like it would blow away in a mild breeze. There were hollows where the eyes should have been, cheeks sunken so much you could fit your entire fist inside them. Lower down, the ribs were completely bared, and Davy thought he saw something scurry very quickly through the cage. All three of them wanted to look away but couldn't; the fascination was too great. They felt compelled to drink in every sight of this, record every possible moment.

"Should... Shouldn't he be just a skeleton by now?" whispered Stevo eventually. "I mean, there shouldn't be—"

"Don't ask me," Davy answered. "I'm no expert. Travis? Travis...?"

The youth didn't answer. He just stood there as if he couldn't believe he'd actually had the guts to do this. To disturb the final resting place of Frederick Fullerton.

"Travis?" Davy called out in one of those cautious semi-shouts.

"I-I'm just coming," he said, putting down the torch.

Then he pulled out his switchblade.

Stevo clutched Davy's arm. "What's he doing? Tell him to put that away."

But Davy could only stare at his friend down in the pit, wondering what he was going to do with that knife. And hoping it wasn't what he was thinking; maybe collect a souvenir for their efforts. Jewelry? Was he after a watch or a ring or something? God, not a finger or—

Travis held the knife out at his side, giving the impression that he didn't really know himself what he was going to do. It *snicked* open, the sound much louder than before, the blade glinting in the light from the downed torch.

Then he held out his other hand in front of him, exposing his wrist.

In one swift movement, he ran the sharpened metal across his vein, like a musician playing a violin. Travis let out a shriek of pain and surprise at his own actions, but didn't stop. Instead, he cut deeper, causing a fountain of blood to spurt from the wound.

Now Davy did shout, properly this time: "Travis! What the hell are you—"

Travis turned his head and looked up at Davy. His expression was one of puzzlement mixed with pleading as he worked away on his wrist, knife-edge jagging open the flesh, sawing right through. Davy rose to jump in, to prevent him from hurting himself any more than he already had. To pull Travis out and get him some help.

But Stevo squeezed his arm tighter. "Look!"

Davy followed his gaze, past Travis and into the open coffin. Where the blood had landed on old Frederick Fullerton, and was still landing as they watched, it seemed to be drying up like the corpse itself—as if simply touching the dead man was having some sort of effect on it.

The body twitched.

"Fuck!" said Stevo. "Did you see that? Did you fucking see that?"

Davy saw, but he didn't know whether to believe it. The torch's beam was far from reliable and even—

It moved again. Now there could be no denying what was happening.

Travis divided his attention between his wrist and the bizarre scene before him. This wasn't right. This wasn't how it was supposed to go. They only wanted to see, to look at him. They weren't really doing any harm.

Well, now they could all see Fullerton, and more besides.

Could see how his worthless and ragged body was sucking up the blood greedily. How it was energizing and reanimating the thing that shouldn't be lifting itself up, two worm-infested hands clutching the sides of the coffin. He looked for all the world like a man in a bath, ready to reach out for a rubber duck, or maybe a loofah. Except what Frederick Fullerton really wanted to bathe in wasn't water. His nonsense of a face twisted around, jellied eyes appearing and seeing again after so long. It was Travis he desired. And Travis knew it.

"Jesus-God-Jesus-God-Jesus-God-Jesus..." ranted Stevo, wishing now he'd paid more attention during Religious Education; wishing he'd been more religious, full stop. At least that might've protected him from...from whatever this was.

What happens when you die? Do you go on living forever? Maybe somewhere, but not here. Not in this world! You don't go on living down here. In your grave...

Here RESTS Frederick Fullerton.

More blood splattered onto him, and Davy was wondering just *how* much there could be left inside Travis; not that much, surely. And wasn't there something he should be doing? Something he'd started to do before he saw this Lazarus return from the dead? Help Travis. That's what he was about to do.

Only now there seemed little point.

Fullerton drew himself up, knees cracking like dead wood, *things* falling from his ragged clothing, withered features contorting with the effort of it all. But the blood, oh so much *life*-blood, all gratefully received. Unwilling donor Travis looked like he wanted to get away and still couldn't. Davy doubted whether he'd be able to climb out of that pit now anyway; he wouldn't have the strength. His eyelids were fluttering, although the pupils beneath those lids were still alive with fear.

Fullerton stepped forward and grabbed Travis, snatching the knife out of his hand at the same time. He held up the blade, examining it for a moment. Then Fullerton smiled; it was a repugnant sight. Teeth with no gums—or what gums were left receding so badly you could hardly see them at all. Yet there was saliva. Where before Frederick had been so dry, almost like dust, he was now revitalized, had quenched at least some of his thirst for new existence.

But he needed more.

With one stroke, he opened Travis's throat, and Davy saw that there was *plenty* of blood still inside. It jetted across Fullerton's face and upper body, and he had to catch Travis as he slumped—almost certainly dead himself by this time. The corpse ground against his young hostage, obscene noises coming from the pair.

That was it. Stevo could no longer hold back his vomit. Turning away, he brought up his last meal (his last supper?), heaving until he thought he'd go blind.

Davy wasn't as fortunate. He kept his eyes locked on the drama unfolding. On Fullerton's inflating cadaver, the muscles filling out, sinews straining, a body given new form. At the same time, Travis seemed to be shriveling up before his eyes as his juice was transferred to Fullerton. And not just blood, either—everything, his whole being.

What's wrong? You wanted to meet him, always wondered about him lying down there with six feet of earth between you? Well, now's your chance! In a moment, he'll get out of that hole, and he'll come after you next. Then you'll meet him; you'll finally meet him!

Davy wasn't so sure he wanted to anymore. Wasn't sure he'd wanted it in the first place. Travis's fault. All Travis's—

Fullerton let Travis go. The teenager didn't make much of a

sound as he fell into the open coffin; there wasn't much of him left *to* make a sound. Davy watched as Travis rolled back into the wooden box.

The exchange was complete. One corpse for another, one *life* for another. Fullerton turned his attention to Davy.

"Quick, get up," he shouted at Stevo, who was still bringing his guts up next to the grave. *If he doesn't shift himself, they'll be spilling all over the ground for real*, Davy thought.

Davy stood and moved away from the edge of the opening, a shovel in his hand. He backed up, placing a hand on Stevo's shoulder. "Come *on!*"

Stevo got up, staggered about, then fell back down.

A hand came over the side of the grave. Not quite normal, but nothing like the hand that had clutched the side of that coffin just minutes ago. Another joined it, this one with a switch-blade in its grip.

"Fucking well, get your arse up!" shouted Davy, grabbing *his* arm this time and pulling him onto his knees. "We've got to—"

Davy froze. Fullerton was up and out of the grave in one lithe movement. The moon, in its infinite wisdom, chose that moment to sneak out from behind a cloud and illuminate the scene. Ful-lerton smiled that smile again.

Stevo looked over and just about saw the dead man through watery eyes.

Fullerton started to walk towards them.

Neither Davy nor Stevo could move. They wanted to but were stuck to the spot. Was it fear? Was it the inevitability of what was happening? Davy had no idea; all he knew was that his feet seemed to have taken root in the unkempt grass.

Doing the only thing he could, Davy raised his shovel and swung it—a warning for Fullerton to stay back. It didn't work. He kept on coming, narrowing the gap between the three of them. Fullerton shook his head.

"D-D-D-D-Davvvy..." Stevo spluttered.

Davy looked at Stevo, then back at Fullerton. Without another second's thought, he dropped the shovel.

"Davy, what're you—"

Davy suddenly found he could move, and he backed off.

Fullerton grinned once more, quickening his pace. He lunged at the kneeling figure of Stevo, slashing and stabbing him with the knife.

Davy turned his back on the sight but couldn't shut out the sounds. The gurgling noises, the terrible cries. He began to run, away from that place, away from what they'd just done.

Got to help him, got to—

But instead, Davy just kept on running. Suddenly, his existence seemed so very important; his space—even if it was a waste—was precious. His legs were going up and down of their own accord, and he was leaving the nightmare behind. Leaving Travis and Stevo, leaving Fullerton and his grave. He was running, desperate to get home and re-adjust his reality.

Had to pretend it hadn't happened at all, slip under the covers of his bed, and go to sleep.

✕✖✕✖✕✖

By the time Fullerton looked up again, Davy was a black speck in the distance. It didn't matter. He still had Stevo.

He stood, his own body now strong, remade. How easy it had been to reach out to these weak-willed youngsters, to influence them, to plant the seed in their minds. Just as they'd given him the idea in the first place with all their talk of horror and life after death, the images, the descriptions. He'd been waiting so long for just such an opportunity. Using their own preconceptions against them was a stroke of genius, even if he did say so himself.

So they were bored, were they? They ought to try being him.

It had been so easy to get Travis to offer up his spirit, such as it was. To persuade Davy to drop his "weapon" and abandon his friend. Actually, that last one puzzled him. Fullerton hardly had to break a sweat; it was almost as though Davy knew that he *had to* sacrifice Stevo in order to get away. That alone would haunt him for the rest of his short life.

For Frederick Fullerton had friends of his own here. Names on gravestones, whispered promises of revolution, of the dead stealing life from the ungrateful living. Those who no longer cared, nor remembered, who were determined to simply fritter away their precious gift in mindless monotony. It was...it was...*wasted* upon them.

Christ! Who would *choose* to spend their time in a place like this?

He smiled one last smile and stooped to pick up Davy's discarded shovel. Fullerton looked around him at the burial site, then at Stevo's remains. There was much to be done, many to free, many to feed. But he felt strong—and soon they would, too. Walking over to one of the nearby plots, he stuck the shovel in the earth.

Then, slowly but surely...

He began to dig.

Dalton Quayle and the Teatime of the Evil Resident Living Dead
(aka the Voodoo Hullabaloo)

Taken from the memoirs of Dr. Humphrey Pemberton, as always.

It was on a gorgeously bright, if nippy, mid-September morning that I again took the familiar trip to see my associate, colleague, and dearest personal chum, Dalton Quayle. For many years now, myself and this living legend of a man—master sleuth, adventurer, swashbuckler, and all-round good egg—have been battling the forces of darkness in all its various shapes and forms. And let me tell you, it comes in some very singular and uncanny forms indeed; from giant worms to dinosaurs in the Wild West, from weresheep to Egyptian demons, we've seen our fair share of peculiarities. Things that would turn your hair white, unless, of course, you happened to be of a certain age where nature has already taken care of that (although I'm told it's quite distinguished on some gentlemen), in which instance, it would simply cause it all to fall out (not quite as distinguished, but very smooth). Now, I'm not saying I haven't dined out on these stories from time to time. Indeed, as I've said before, you'll find certain pages of my memoirs published in installments in *The Strump* magazine, a monthly periodical of some note (they did want me to pen a spin-off called *Dalton's Weekly*, but that would have been going just a shade too far). However, if there was ever a tale I wish I didn't have to relate or set to paper, it is this one, for it challenges the very notion of all that is accepted in the world of modern science and religion. Not only that, it also gives me a case of the raging heebie-jeebies.

Quayle and I had arranged to play a round or two of golf that Wednesday, so I had canceled all my appointments at the surgery for that day and the next—instructing my receptionist to tell the patients I was off sick. Well, most of them are hypochondriacs anyway. Therefore, I was dressed in my finest yellow Rupert Bear trousers tucked into my socks, a jumper my old mother knitted me for Christmas, a bow tie, and a huge, flat cap with a bobble on the top. The very attire for a jaunt out on the fairway. Naturally, I anticipated us ending up on the 20th hole by the end of the day—the one after the 19th. And when I say on the hole, I should really say *in* it, as we don't tend to watch where we're going after a few dozen rounds of port. (Now you know why I canceled my appointments for the day after as well.)

But, as per usual in stories of this ilk, things didn't exactly pan out the way I thought they would. For one thing, when I knocked on the door of Quayle's residence in Butcher Street, it wasn't his housekeeper who let me in—the vision of loveliness that is Mrs. Hudsucker, apron just about covering her stoutly proportions, rolling pin in hand, ready to whack me on the head for some *faux pas* I would undoubtedly commit by accident around her personage—but rather the great man himself, his firm chin jutting out, lustrous hair tied back in that distinctive ponytail, which had been often imitated, but never rivaled.

He looked me up and down, then shook his head. "Halloween comes around so quickly these days," Quayle said after a moment or two.

"Halloween...? Oh, I see. It's just my golfing gear, old bean. Fashionable, don't you think?"

He raised one eyebrow. "It certainly makes a statement. And

that statement is 'I'm color-blind.'"

I laughed at his little joke, but peculiarly Quayle didn't join in. It was at this point I noticed that he was dressed much more somberly than I, completely in black as it happened. "So, is that what you're planning to wear as 'par for the course,' my good fellow? A tad depressing, if you don't mind me saying so."

"You'd better come in," was all Quayle said in response.

With a worried look on my face, I hauled in my set of clubs, catching them on the doorstep and almost sending them flying everywhere. As it was, a couple of Titlists broke free and bounced onto the floor. I slipped on one, falling backward into the vase of flowers in the hallway and knocking it crashing to the floor. Shaking his head again, Quayle held out his hand to help me up.

"Balls," I offered by way of an explanation—picking up one of the spherical white objects to show him. Then I cocked my head, waiting expectantly for the scream of anger that would usually follow, the rolling pin blow I'd have to duck to avoid. But there was nothing, no sign at all of Mrs. H. I stooped to pick up the fallen flowers from the floor.

"Come on, follow me," Quayle instructed.

"What on Earth's the matter? Has something happened? You're so *deadly* serious."

"Ssh," Quayle said, pressing his finger to his lips.

"But why so *grave*?"

"Pemberton!" Quayle fixed me with a stare that shut me up instantly. "Show a little tact, man." As we passed into Quayle's living room, which he barely used, preferring instead to loiter upstairs in his study, I saw Mrs. Hudsucker, also dressed in subdued attire (I didn't know they sold black aprons), sitting on the settee in tears. I swiftly hid the evidence of my little accident—the battered flowers—behind my back.

My first instinct was to go to her, place her head on my shoulder, and tell her everything was all right. But, for one thing, that would have resulted in a swift kick in a certain vulnerable area, and for another, I had absolutely no idea whether it would be "all right" or not, as I didn't have the faintest clue what was going on.

Not an unusual occurrence, I have to state.

Mrs. Hudsucker let out an almighty wail when she saw me, a pretty standard reaction, it has to be said, but I felt sure on this occasion there was more to it than just my presence.

"Quayle, what the devil's the matter with her?" I asked. "She looks like *death* warmed up."

Mrs. Hudsucker wailed even louder at this remark.

"What did I say?" I was genuinely dumbfounded.

Quayle took me to one side and explained that today was the tenth anniversary of Mrs. Hudsucker's husband's passing.

"Passing what?"

"Just passing, Pemberton."

"Oh. *Just* passing what?"

Another sigh. "Passing *on*—as in expired and gone to meet his maker, run up the curtain and joined the choir invisible. As in the *late* Mr. Hudsucker."

A look of enlightenment dawned on my face. "Ah, I see. What exactly was he late for, then?"

"Late for dinner, late for tea, late for pretty much everything," Quayle snapped, "because he was dead, Pemberton. D. E. A. D. *DEAD!*" My colleague said the last word a little too loudly, and Mrs. Hudsucker broke down again in a flood of tears, dabbing at them with her handkerchief. "I'm so sorry, my good woman," he apologized.

"For goodness sake, Quayle, show a little tact," I chastised, the boot on the other foot.

Quayle's eyes narrowed, and I was under no illusions as to where the boot would be in a moment, the opposite end to where Mrs. Hudsucker's would have been had I attempted to console her.

In all the time I had known this lady and, yes, held a torch for her, I must disclose, she had only spoken on the very rarest of occasions about her deceased spouse. But Quayle had told me enough (and when I say "told," I, of course, mean when I read his private journal, if I could decipher his spidery scrawl, but that is strictly between you and I). The man had been a gambler and a womanizer who hadn't deserved a devoted wife like her. He'd left her with scarcely a penny to her name, forcing her to take a job as Quayle's housekeeper all those years ago. With a severe advance on her wages, she'd secured a plot at Eveningstar Cemetery and Funeral Home and paid for the best embalming she could find. According to Quayle, the whole package had cost a tidy sum, which she was probably still paying back. It would certainly explain why she remained his dogsbody and all-round nursemaid.

Yet anyone would think, to hear her talk about her husband, that he was a saint. She simply wouldn't hear a word against the fellow.

"I completely forgot the date," Quayle admitted to me, "so I'm afraid our teeing off will have to wait until another time. I shall be accompanying Mrs. Hudsucker to visit Mr. Hudsucker's final resting place—God have mercy... I mean, God *rest* his soul—for moral support, you understand."

I nodded sagely. "Then I feel my place is also there, by her...I mean *your* side."

Quayle chewed his bottom lip. "I'm not so sure that would be a good idea, Pemberton. For one thing, the way you're dressed—"

"Nonsense." I turned to Mrs. Hudsucker. "You'd have no objections to me tagging along, would you, my good woman?" She let out the loudest wail I'd ever heard. In fact, it didn't even really sound human.

"Oh, come, come," I urged, tentatively walking a few steps toward her.

"What..." she wailed, "what are those?"

Mrs. Hudsucker was pointing at the flowers behind my back, the drooping heads of which were jutting out.

"Er, oh, nothing..."

"There, in your hand?" she sobbed, blowing her nose on her hanky. The noise sounded like a ship coming into dock.

"Oh, er, these, well, they're—"

"You brought flowers," she said, sniffing. "Why, Dr. Pemberton, that is ever so thoughtful of you."

I smiled an uneasy smile. "Ah, yes, that's right. As a mark of respect, my dear lady." I brought them out into the open, such as they were.

"Oh, they're, er, different," Mrs. Hudsucker commented between sobs. "We have a bunch much like them, only less…trampled. Well, that settles the matter; you simply must come along with us. Mustn't he, Mr. Quayle?"

"He must?" Quayle said, shocked, then, "Oh, yes, all right, I suppose." He turned to me, "But make yourself ready, Pemberton. The cab will be here anytime to take us to Eveningstar."

And indeed it was, the bell ringing mere minutes later. I opened the door, kicking the bits of glass from the vase under the hall table, then stood in front of it to let Quayle and Mrs. Hudsucker out. I needn't have worried about her spotting the mess, though, as her mind was definitely on other things.

"I still can't quite believe he's gone, you know," she said to Quayle as he armed her to the waiting cab.

Once they were through, I hoisted up my clubs and, head bowed, more to watch out for rogue golf balls than any kind of mark of respect, I slammed the door shut behind me and followed them to our transportation.

We called on the way for Mrs. Hudsucker's own flowers, a massive bunch of lilies that must have added yet more to the staggering amount she owed Quayle. They certainly put my offering in the shade—quite literally—when she brought them back into the cab. We sat in silence for the duration of the hour-long journey, apart from Mrs. Hudsucker's various displays of grief, that was. Then we were at the gates of the cemetery, huge iron things that were cast wide open, "inviting" us to come inside. Above the entranceway read the legend: "Eveningstar Funeral Home: Proprietor Mr. T. Man."

I should perhaps point out that I've never been comfortable in graveyards, or even around death; somewhat unusual talk for a doctor, I know. But when the most you have to deal with on a day-to-day basis is a stubbed toe or a slight case of halitosis, being confronted with one's own mortality doesn't exactly rate on my list of fun things to do. (Perhaps some of it harks back to my time in the army abroad, battling—well, all right, mainly *running away from*—natives in the name of The Empire. Many was the time over there I'd listened out for the whistle of the spear with my name on it; I was lucky to have made it out alive...)

So, all things considered, I'd definitely rather have been playing a round with my wood that morning.

We alighted from the cab, informing the driver to wait for us, and made our way along the path on foot. The place was deserted, and I couldn't say I was that surprised. It was a beautiful day, the sun beaming, though there was a slight chill to the breeze in here. And yes, there was greenery on either side of us, but it was hardly what I'd had in mind for today: tombstones and crosses littering the view, with the funeral home itself in the far distance. Angels stared back at us—I swear one of them was pointing, as if to say, "It won't be long now, Humphrey, so you'd better start brushing up on that harp playing!"

Still bawling her eyes out, Mrs. Hudsucker stopped when we reached the appropriate plot. No expense had been spared for her very late hubby's memorial: a huge stone monolith with cherubs playing trumpets and intricate carvings that spiraled upward, dwarfing the burial mounds of those close by. The inscription read: "Here Lies Reginald Hudsucker. Husband of Barbara. 'The Grim Reaper came for me without any warning. Fit and well that night, I'd popped my clogs by the morning.'"

I looked at Quayle, who shrugged.

"He always was a joker," said Mrs. Hudsucker, smiling faintly. Kneeling, the tearful woman placed her gigantic bunch of flowers on the grave, completely covering it, leaving no room for my offering, and closed her eyes. "Oh, I'd give anything to see him just one more time."

Quayle and I stood back and allowed her a moment with her thoughts. I fought the urge to whistle, though, when we'd been there more than half an hour or so. "How much longer do we have to dwell here?" I whispered to him.

"As long as it takes," Quayle replied sternly. "This is for Mrs. Hudsucker, remember?"

After a second or two, I nodded and said, "Fancy practicing our putting while we're waiting?" I tapped the clubs I was still carrying around. "It's a bit hilly, but I could make a little hole and—"

The look he shot me told me all I needed to know.

Bored, I gazed up at the sky, then from side to side. I saw that there were now a few more people in the previously unpopulated grounds, some to the left, some to the right. At first, there were just one or two, then a few more, and they didn't appear to be pausing at any particular graves. As a matter of fact, they appeared to be heading in our very direction.

"Erm, old boy..."

"What is it now?" said Quayle, exasperated.

"Look at that. Doesn't it strike you as dashed odd?" I commented, pointing to the increasing number of people on the horizon(s).

"Hhmm... Those other mourners, you mean? What about them?"

"Well, just the way they're moving, really. In that slow, loping way."

Quayle frowned. "What do you expect them to be doing, jumping for joy? This *is* a cemetery when all's said and done."

As the figures approached, I was granted more details of their appearance. One was staggering in an awkward way, as though his leg was giving out on him with each step. One was hobbling sideways like a crab, head twisted so he could see ahead of him, and another was virtually on his hands and knees. At first numbering only a handful, and spread out, their ranks were rapidly growing in size, the gaps between them decreasing.

"Ah, Quayle," I said, pulling his jacket sleeve. "I really do think this warrants a closer inspection."

"My dear Pemberton, will you be told. There is nothing strange going on h—" His gist was interrupted by a man appearing from behind a tombstone to his right and pouncing on him. Quayle fell backward, gripping his attacker by the wrists. "What in blazes! Have you taken leave of your senses, sir?" he shouted at the person on top of him.

"My God, look at his eyes, Quayle!" I urged. These were as

white as the golf balls in my bag. "He's...he's blind. That's probably why he tripped."

The man let out a moan in Quayle's face, and I saw my friend's
features crinkle up in disgust. "I think he should make an ap-
pointment at your surgery," he said, looking over. "This is the
worst case of halitosis I've ever come across!"

There was a sudden scream from behind us. I turned to see
Mrs. Hudsucker pointing at a grave not too far away. The soil was
relatively fresh over the top, and two hands had clawed their way
through it. They were reaching up toward the sky.

Glancing from Quayle to the burial place, I quickly put two
and two together. "Good Lord, Quayle. I think these...these poor
beggars have...have been...buried prematurely! Poe will be turning in his grave, if you'll pardon the expression."

Luckily, Quayle had more wits about him—as per usual—and
reached the correct conclusion. He shoved off his snapping as-
sailant, careful not to let him bite. "Pemberton, they haven't been
buried alive at all. You were right before."

"I was?" I said smiling, quite chuffed that I'd got something
correct for a change. "How so?"

"There *is* something rum going on here. These people are dead
on their feet!" Quayle scrambled to his own feet, toeing his felled
attacker.

"They do look a bit tired."

"No," said Quayle, exasperated. "That's not what I mean: they
really *are* dead."

Mrs. Hudsucker raised her hand to her mouth. "By all that's
holy. H-How can that be?"

"I hesitate to use it, but I think we're dealing with the 'Z' word
here."

"What? Surely you don't mean... No, it can't be... Not Zulus!
However have they tracked me down?" I ducked, listening out for
that spear.

"Not Zulus, Pemberton—zombies!"

I suppose I should really have twigged before; the shuffling
walk, the bad dress sense, the lack of conversation. But, you see,

the only zombies we have ever encountered were of the nautical kind, during our adventure in the Sarcasso Sea. Those were fast-moving and deadly with a sword. They had been in various states of decay, while these blighters seemed hardly to have decomposed at all! But they were to prove just as dangerous in great numbers.

Which were massing *en masse*, encircling us as we stood there wondering what to do.

"Er, Pemberton. I don't suppose you—"

"Do I have any firearms with me? You know me far too well, old peanut." Quayle was relying on the fact that I won't set out from my house without sufficient protection of the lethal variety—in fact I have been known to tuck away a flamethrower or two about my person. Stuffing the by-now wilting flowers in my enormous trouser pocket, I slipped my golf bag off my shoulder and rooted around inside. I tossed a shotgun over to Quayle, and I myself took out two huge revolvers. "You never know when you're going to need a shooter or three on the golf course," I said, tapping my nose with one of the barrels.

"Erm, quite." Not being the kind of bod who approves of using such implements himself, Quayle appeared uncomfortable even holding the shotgun.

I, on the other hand, relish any opportunity to shoot my load, and it wasn't long before I was doing just that, firing in all directions at the sallow-faced hordes zeroing in on us. "Take that, eat hot lead, say hello to my little friends…and so forth," I cried as I squeezed the trigger, pumping out one bullet after the next until I was spent. I stood there getting my breath back, a wild grin on my face.

When the smoke cleared, I couldn't believe my eyes. There they all were, still untouched. Somehow I'd missed every last one of them! No, that wasn't true. I had managed a hole-in-one, again not of the variety I'd imagined that day. I could see right through the wound in that fellow's chest to the other side, which he ignored as if it were a mere scratch.

"I-I don't understand," I gasped, mouth hanging open.

"Pemberton," Quayle said, tutting. "Have you learned nothing in your time with me? You have to aim for the head if you're going to aim at all."

"I thought that was vampires?"

Quayle shook his head. "Cross."

"Not really, although I would have liked to have picked off a couple."

"Stakes."

"I'm not sure this is the time to be thinking about food, although all that shooting has made me hungry and—"

"Oh, do shut up, Pemberton!"

"Well, you're the one with the shotgun, my good fellow," I reminded him. "Time to get 'a head.'"

Quayle looked like he'd totally forgotten he even had the weapon. I don't think he would have brandished it at all had another one of the zombies not broken free of the ranks and lumbered toward him. Quayle was forced to raise the gun, prodding the creature's nose with the twin barrels. "Stay back," he warned. "I'm not afraid to use this." But he so obviously was. The zombie, whose eyes were slightly less milky than the last one who'd attacked Quayle, gazed down at the metal rods and went cross-eyed.

My friend was hesitant, and I thought he wasn't going to pull the trigger at all. But finally, he closed his own eyes and did just that. There was a loud click but no blast.

"Quayle, you have to cock it!" I reminded him, throwing down my empty and useless pistols.

"I believe I just have," admitted my companion. Then a look of recognition dawned on his face. "Oh, I see." Quayle pulled back the gun and attempted to prime it for use. But before he could aim again, the zombie had reached out and grabbed the barrel, forcing it up in the air. There was a loud bang, and the zombie let go, causing Quayle to stagger backward.

"It's no good," he said as he joined me. "We're going to have to take our leave."

"Where are we taking it to?" I asked, but instead of answering, he grabbed my arm, and then Mrs. Hudsucker's.

"Come on." Quayle shouldered aside a couple of the corpses, careful to avoid their grasp, and created enough of an exit for us to escape the tightening circle. When I saw one of them reaching out for Mrs. H, I swung my bag of clubs—on purpose this time—and sent the devil flying. We ran away from the mob, who were turning and following. A couple slipped from sight, keeling over onto the floor. I frowned, puzzled, then Quayle pointed to the ground. Not only had we escaped—for the time being—but so had more of those golf balls from my bag.

Looking across to where our cab was, we saw that it had been overturned by another group of zombies. Of the driver, there was no sign; he'd either left us to our fate or been taken by surprise, becoming the first course of a menu of human flesh. I don't think any of us fancied being mains.

"Where to now?" I asked Quayle.

He nodded toward the funeral home. "We need somewhere to hole up."

"Bet you wish we'd gone to the golf course now, then, eh?"

We'd barely made it a few yards when there was an awful bellow. "Baaaarbaaaarraaaa...." it came. There was a throaty, guttural timbre to it, but there was no mistaking the name it had called out. Mrs. Hudsucker turned, then inhaled sharply.

The grave by which she had previously been kneeling was now also disturbed. The hands were having difficulty moving the gigantic bunch of flowers out of the way, but already a head had appeared. Reginald Hudsucker was attempting to crawl from his "final" resting place, calling out to his fleeing widow. She'd asked to see him again and had been granted her wish, it would seem.

"Baaaarbaaaarraaaa!" he shouted once again. "Baaaarbaaaarraaaa!"

"Reggie?" Mrs. Hudsucker replied, taking a step back in his direction.

Quayle and I caught her by the arm, both shaking our heads at the same time. "You can't go back there, Mrs. Hudsucker," Quayle warned her. "It's not safe."

"Let me go," she demanded, shrugging off my hand and reaching into her mourning apron. She lashed out with her rolling pin, bashing Quayle on the arm. Luckily, I have had more experience avoiding its blows and ducked when she turned on me.

I grabbed her by the wrist, aware that the zombies behind were gaining on us. "Stop struggling, my good lady. This is for your own good! That man is no longer the husband you once knew. Think of the pong if you went out on a date."

Mrs. H was having none of it. So Quayle reached up and grabbed the crook of her neck with his fingers. She froze, as still as the angel statues all around us.

"I-I can't move," murmured Mrs. Hudsucker through gritted teeth.

"A little something I picked up in the massage parlors of Taiwan," he revealed. "The ladies there are masters of reflexology."

I raised an eyebrow. "I'll bet!"

"It's used when the customers won't pay their bills. Induces a state of catalepsy; ironically, which looks like death. She'll be fine when I tweak the appropriate place."

We each took an arm and pulled Mrs. Hudsucker along the ground, her heels raking up the grass. Ordinarily, we would have been able to outrun the slow-swarming brutes behind us, but to say that Mrs. H is on the plump side would be like saying that King Kong needs a bit of a shave. By the time we reached the funeral home, puffing and panting, the zombies were not only right behind us, they had increased in number.

The white building was a mix of classical—with its large pillars at the entrance—and country, almost like a townhouse. As with the gates to the cemetery, the heavy front doors were wide open here, and we dragged Mrs. Hudsucker inside. Pushing the doors to, we found that there was no way of locking them—so Quayle grabbed a chair with his free hand and jammed it up against the handle.

"Should hold them for a little while."

That was when we heard the smashing of the first window. It came from a room to our left, so, leaving Mrs. H in the hallway, we ran inside. It was an office of some sort, and the window was indeed in a ruined state. A zombie woman had entered through the gap. She was the thinnest thing I'd ever seen, with auburn hair, white skin, and a bright red mouth. She was wearing a torn dress with leggings underneath, and as she got up and shuffled toward me, she moaned out loud.

"Quayle," I said, trying to control my voice, "do something!"

He still had one shot left in the shotgun, so he raised it. "Wait a second," he said, then eased back the hammer on the second barrel. "Don't want to go off half-cocked."

"Mmmmnnnn," she groaned as she grew nearer.

"Now, Quayle," I said, trying to hide the fact I was quaking in my golf shoes.

He aimed at her head, finger on the trigger.

"Mmmnnmnnnnnnnnnnnoooooo!" she cried. "No, wait, please. I'm not one of them."

Quayle lowered his weapon.

"I'm... I was out riding, and then one of those things staggered in front of my horse, which threw me." She touched her head and showed us the blood there. "I-I managed to find this place and smash the window with a tree branch."

"What's your name?" asked Quayle.

"Alicia, I think... Alicia Yoyobitch. I'm sorry, everything's a bit fuzzy."

"Pemberton, see to this woman immediately," instructed Quayle.

"Now, steady on. We've only just met."

"Her head wound, Pemberton."

"Oh, right."

But at that precise moment, two zombies burst through the broken window, lumbering toward her. Almost instinctively, Alicia jumped up in the air, pivoting around and kicking one zombie across the face, snapping his neck, then landing and bringing her other foot up under the second zombie's chin, which produced another cracking noise.

Quayle and I stood there with our mouths gaping open.

Alicia let out a little titter. "Erm, I have no idea how I just did that."

Snapping out of his daze, Quayle realized we should do something about the window—as apart from the draught, it was an open invitation for our zombie friends. On his instruction, we hefted a table up against the orifice, then pulled across a filing cabinet to brace against it. "That should hold them off for a little while," Quayle said once again. "Now maybe we can figure out why the dead are coming back to life...aside from boredom, obviously."

But he was to be sidetracked. "Help, help!" came a tiny voice from back in the corridor.

"Oh no," Quayle said, "Mrs. Hudsucker!"

We dashed back out into the hallway to see what was the matter.

"Zulu!" I shrieked when I saw the man out there, for his skin was dark as night. But then I spotted he was wearing a shirt, tie, and trousers; more importantly, he wasn't brandishing a spear... that I could see. The question of whether he was alive or not, however, was another thing entirely.

"Zulu?" said the man. "Is he havin' a chuffin' laugh or somethin'?"

"I apologize sincerely for my colleague's behavior," Quayle said. "He has a few unresolved issues from his time spent abroad. Who are you?"

"Name's Ken," said the man in the shirt. "I let myself in through the back door."

"Let me guess... You were attacked by the living dead and sought refuge here?"

Ken nodded. "It wos the first place I came across, cocker."

I thought about making a joke connected with the shotgun but decided against it.

Quayle introduced everyone, then fielded the inevitable questions about what was going on. "I have absolutely no clue," he was forced to say. "Perhaps a look around this place might shed some light on the situation, wot?"

"What?" asked Ken.

"Exactly, wot. But first, let's secure that back door, shall we? If you could wander in, so could they!"

Another chair up against the handle and a "That should hold them for a little while" later, and we were exploring the rest of the funeral home, dragging Mrs. H around with us. It was filled with long, white corridors, and I had the distinct feeling we were being watched as we traversed them. There was a music room down one of these—at least I assumed it was, because there resided a giant tuning fork in the middle. Other than that, we found nothing untoward.

Opening the roof of the building, we looked over the side and saw the size of our predicament. An army of zombies had gathered at the funeral home, no doubt because they could sense the food inside. Just as they'd done earlier with us, they'd encircled the place, leaving no way out—even if we could break free. By this time, it was late afternoon. Very soon it would be teatime, and I do so hate to miss my tea, especially when I've missed out on lunch as well.

All that remained was the basement to investigate now.

This was reachable via a small wooden trapdoor with a looped handle right in the center of the long hallway corridor. Quayle tugged on it, dropping it quickly and aiming the gun at the stairs. Nothing happened. One by one, we descended into a cellar that was part laboratory and part slaughterhouse.

Dead bodies hung from meat hooks, twitching involuntarily. Two metal "tuning forks" like the ones I'd seen upstairs were generating the electricity to power this hidden chamber, energy sparking between them. Metal trays with body parts on them covered the table tops, including a human head. Quayle strayed too close to this, and its eyes opened, mouth moaning, almost pleading. My good friend pulled a face in disgust.

"What manner of place is this?" Alicia said, horrified. No-one answered.

Then we saw them: the vials of glowing turquoise liquid in a rack. Turning, I accidentally knocked one over with my golf bag, and it spilled the concoction down my legs. "Look at that, my favorite Rupert Bear trousers," I complained.

"But look at *that*!" Quayle said, pointing at the flowers I'd for-gotten about in my pocket. The dead flora were suddenly blooming into life, growing bigger and stronger with each second. I took the unnatural things out and cast them down on the floor. "It's 're-invigorated' them," exclaimed my old friend.

"Exactly," came a voice from behind. We all spun around to see a bespectacled man in a white coat standing there. "I call it the T-Rage Fluid. Finally, a way to bring the dead back to life and none of that tedious messing about with books made from skin and written in blood... Just imagine it." There was an insane glint in his eye as he talked.

"I don't need to; I've seen it," Quayle replied, his jutting chin firmly set.

"I've been attempting to perfect it for so long, and now," con-tinued the chap with glasses, barely hearing Quayle, "at long last... You can be the first to witness my glory. For I, ladies and gentle-men, have today become a God."

"You've become a loony," I corrected him.

He simply laughed at this.

"Does Mr. Man know what you've been doing down here?" asked Quayle.

"I am he, and he is me," he sniggered. "I made him up years ago so I could take over this place without anyone asking too many questions. Even did a little embalming on the side for the sake of appearances. But no, I'm afraid he doesn't really exist. There's just little old me, Dr. Harold Vest."

"Never heard of you."

Vest pulled a face. "And nor should you have, Mister..."

"Why, he's the *famous* Dalton Quayle!" I spluttered.

"Really?" Vest looked him up and down. "Then your reputa-tion precedes you."

"Well, don't hold that against him," I said, and Quayle gave me a filthy look.

"Mine, however, is yet to be made," Vest carried on. "You see, I was thrown out of Mad Scientists school at fourteen, spurned by the medical community because of my experiments in the N'kabonaklulu jungle involving serpents and rainbows, upstaged by the likes of Doctor Frankenstein and his cobbled-together creature. Why should he be the only one getting a piece of the action, I ask? The fame and glory? I want my own franchise as well!" He stamped his foot like a spoiled child.

Quayle stepped forward. "You do know that I can't let you continue your work down here, don't you, Vest?"

My friend raised his gun, but Vest was way ahead of him. He held up a hand. "Now, I don't believe you want to do that. In fact, I believe you're going to drop that gun right this instant." Vest gestured towards the base of the stairs, where a second man with short yellow hair, dressed no less geekily, was holding the still-paralyzed Mrs. Hudsucker captive, a needle filled with T-Rage at her throat. "Permit me to introduce my assistant, Shane Pugg."

"What if I don't," said Quayle.

"Eh?" asked Vest.

"What if I don't permit you?"

Vest frowned and thought about it for a second. "Look, it doesn't matter; he's just over there, all right?"

Ken was edging nearer to Pugg, but he saw the fellow and told him to stay away.

"Now, about dropping that shotgun," Vest reminded my friend.

Quayle had little choice. He held his arms out at his sides, then let the weapon go. Already cocked, it hit the floor and went off. Everyone jumped, including Shane Pugg, who pressed the needle against Mrs. H's neck. Luckily, it didn't go in far enough to inject the T-Rage Fluid, but the little prick—the needle, not Pugg, although if the cap fits—had the odd effect of reversing the woman's paralysis. Before he could defend himself, Pugg was on the receiving end of a rather nasty rolling pin blow that completely felled him.

Before anything else could happen, there came a crashing noise from the upper floors.

"They've broken in," Quayle said, looking up. "The evil living dead are resident!"

Vest gazed at him, puzzled. "The what?"

"Reggie," said Mrs. Hudsucker, clapping her hands together, then making her way swiftly up the stairs.

"She's got the right idea," said Alicia, getting entirely the wrong one about why Mrs. H was ascending, "we have to defend ourselves." The thin woman snatched one of the golf clubs from my bag and sprinted up the stairs after her.

"Come on," said Quayle, grabbing my arm. I won't say I was keen to go up there—indeed, I did a bit of stamping myself as I was dragged up the stairs—but up I went nonetheless. "We'll be back for you later," my colleague warned Vest, who wasn't going anywhere in that basement laboratory.

Sticking our heads up through the trapdoor again, we surveyed the situation. The front door had been flattened, a consequence of the many hordes of zombies battering it. They were also entering from the office room and the back of the house, filtering in through the entrances Quayle had tried to fortify.

"I did say it would only hold them *for a while,*" he explained.

We saw Mrs. Hudsucker being carried out by several zombies, disappearing in the throng.

"Nooooo!" I called out.

Quayle placed a hand on my arm. "Don't worry; we'll get her back." Then he locked the trapdoor to make sure Vest didn't escape.

Alicia was kicking some serious bottom, as the Americans are fond of saying. First, she'd whack one zombie with the club, then head-butt another, and punch a third so hard its head almost came away from its shoulders. She certainly lived up to her name; it was like watching a Yo-Yo at times.

"Wow!" Quayle and I both said in unison.

Ken, who must have been the first one up even ahead of Mrs. H, was making his way toward the door, ready to defend the funeral home. Quayle had a better idea.

He hauled me up out of the gap, then took out another couple of golf clubs. "You wanted to get in some practice, I believe?"

Frowning, I watched as he took a golf ball from my bag, placed it on the floor. Then he took a swing and shouted, "Fore!" as the ball hurtled toward the pack of zombies in front. Ken stepped to one side as it hit the first zombie in the head, who then took down three more as he fell.

Smiling, I took his lead but aimed my balls at the zombies breaching the rear—and after a couple of divots in the carpet, I finally got into my swing. "I say, Quayle—look at that, straight down the middle!"

"Well done, Pemberton," replied Quayle, looking over his shoulder at the zombies I'd knocked down. "Keep them coming."

It soon became clear, though, that the zombies far outweighed the golf balls I'd brought with me (not to mention the ones I'd accidentally lost along the way). But we had created a parting in the wall—enough to run through and try to rescue Mrs. Hudsucker.

"Ready?" Quayle asked, to which my answer was always a shake of the head. We went anyway, using my bag as a temporary shield. If it could knock things over without my even trying, I reasoned I might as well try on purpose this time. And it worked, battering zombies away from us and making sure we could get out to the other side.

Where we saw Mrs. H patiently waiting, for her knight on horseback... Well, it was the zombie Reginald Hudsucker on horseback, actually. Somehow he'd found and mounted Alicia's lost steed and was heading for the ecstatic Mrs. H. "Aiiiimmmeee coooomingg toooo geeeeet yooooo, Baaaarbaaaara," he drawled.

"Oh no," I gulped, "we have to do something."

But before we even had a chance, Alicia had joined us outside the house and was shouting her horse's name. "Savinero! Savinero! I thought he was dead. What's that man doing on my Savinero?"

"Slumping over, mostly," Quayle observed.

She ran toward the approaching horse. Now, I don't know if it was the animal that recognized Alicia or whether Reginald Hudsucker changed its direction himself—for he did have a very lustful look on his face—but the consequence was the same. Mrs. Hudsucker was bypassed altogether in favor of the younger, thinner model. Reginald reached down and grabbed Alicia, pulling her up onto the horse with him—and at the same time, signaling the other zombies to take care of his wife.

Mrs. Hudsucker folded her arms, which is not an easy thing to do when you have her chest, and snorted. "Horses and women. Nothing ever changes, does it? Even after ten years in the ground!" She then whacked a couple of zombies with her rolling pin, and chased after the steed—this time, I had no doubt, to do her former husband some serious damage rather than pick up their relationship. I couldn't help but smile.

My reverie didn't last long, however. We had other, more pressing matters, to contend with—I say pressing because that's what the zombies were doing up against us. More and more of them, coming from nowhere.

"Right," said Quayle. "Time to end this."

He pushed through them, searching. I followed in his wake, still using my bag to protect myself...er...us. Then he suddenly paused, and I ran into him.

Steadying himself and sighing, Quayle said, "This has gone far enough now, don't you think? Call them off. Let us handle it from here."

I looked around, trying to figure out who he was talking to. It was Ken, standing in the eye of the zombie storm.

"Erm, what are you doing, old turnip?" I inquired. "Why are you addressing Ken?"

"But he's not really Ken, are you? And this isn't his address."

Ken smiled, his teeth bright. Then the strangest thing happened. He reached behind him and pulled out a white top hat. Then he shrugged on a long, flowing coat.

"That's more like it," said Quayle. "Now, are you going to release your hold on them, or are you and I going to fall out?" My friend's chin was jutting out so far people could have walked along it and fed the seagulls. "I asked you a question... Baron Saturday!"

The man in front of us nodded slowly, and to my astonishment, all the zombies around us collapsed on the floor.

"Thank you."

"Today, I let you have your way." Ken... The Baron's voice

had changed now; it was much more velvety and tinged with a foreign accent. "But our paths will cross again one day, Dalton Quayle!" Then he vanished, completely and utterly, before our very eyes.

I held up a finger, jaw scraping the ground. "What just happened?"

"At the end, Pemberton, as always. I'll explain it then. But right now, I think we had better summon Inspector Le Strange and his boys." He surveyed the remains of the zombies around us, sniffing the foul air. "After all, someone will have to clear up this mess, and I can't think of anyone more suited." Quayle's relationship with Le Strange is, as you can probably tell, not on the friendliest of footings—but that's another story.

"It would certainly have been less taxing on the golf course," I said to him.

"True," Quayle replied, rubbing his capacious lower facial area. "What time is it, by the way, Pemberton?"

I consulted my fob watch. "Well, would you look at that—it's just past teatime."

"The teatime of the evil resident living dead? Has sort of a ring to it, don't you think?"

Again, I shook my head, and this time Quayle couldn't help chortling just a little.

✕ ✕ ✕ ✕ ✕

As we watched Le Strange directing his men to carry off the bodies, handkerchief over his nose, Quayle started to reveal what had really taken place here today.

"I began to grow suspicious when Vest looked so puzzled about the zombies upstairs. And after he'd mentioned the N'kabonaklulu jungle... Well, I feel I need say no more, really."

"I really feel you should," I urged, still scratching my head.

He sighed. "Oh, very well. You see, Vest had absolutely no idea about the dead who'd risen outside. His experimentations had been confined to his basement, using bodies he'd procured from the graveyard." The police had now taken that particular bonkers doctor away to Mayhem Asylum for treatment, along with his assistant, who had tried to wheedle out of it by explaining that he'd only become involved because he'd broken up with his lady friend and was in a dark place emotionally.

"But his shenanigans in the N'kabonaklulu had not gone unnoticed in some quarters. Just as Vest wanted to corner the market in mad scientifery, so too there are those who want sole dominion over the raising of the dead."

"And that's where this Baron Friday comes into it?"

"Saturday, but you were only one day out," Quayle said, grinning. "Yes, as you've probably worked out, he doesn't come from these climes at all."

"I knew he was a Zulu the first time I met him."

Quayle shook his head. "Haitian."

"Bless you."

"No, I meant he's... Oh, never mind. The important thing is, he's an expert in Voodoo."

"Who, how?"

"Voodoo. Tribal mysticism, including the raising of the non-alive. I've heard his name spoken in certain circles but never, ever thought to meet the chap."

"So, he was here to scupper Vest's plans, then?" I ventured.

"Exactly right, Pemberton. The zombies were meant for him—fight fire with fire and all that. We just got stuck in the middle of it all. And, of course, when we did, he needed a disguise to mingle amongst us and make sure Vest got his just comeuppances."

I let out a gasp of realization. "That's why he went upstairs first, slipping away in the confusion, to summon his troops to swarm on the place."

Quayle nodded. "They were all under his control."

"So, where does Alicia fit into all this?" She'd returned to the scene after wrestling control of Savinero from Reginald Hudsucker—who, after returning to his normal dead state, had fallen off the horse into a ditch.

"Well, you were there when she told us. Once she'd regained her memory, she remembered that she had actually been investigating the suspicious influx of strange chemicals and energy conductors to this place—working as she does for our very own Secret Service."

"Ah yes, which explains her combat maneuvers. But why was she on horseback?"

"She was undercover. Who would suspect an innocent lady simply out for a ride in the country?"

"Not me. I was certainly taken for a ride by it. Right then, I think that pretty much wraps it all up, then, doesn't it?"

"Almost," Quayle said, nodding towards the dejected Mrs. Hudsucker, who was sitting on the steps of the funeral home. She'd followed Savinero for the first half a mile, rolling pin drawn, but had given up the chase after that. "We still have the small matter of replacing the corpses in their proper plots. I'm sure Mrs. Hudsucker will feel better when her late husband is once again where he belongs?"

"He already is," Mrs. H said sharply, "the good for nothing... Ditch is too good for 'im."

I smiled inwardly. At last she'd seen the blighter for his true self, which meant there might just be the tiniest of hopes she may one day look for love again. Possibly in my direction...

"But—" began Quayle, and was halted by her holding up her hand.

"I've made my mind up. It's no more than he deserves. I'm going to sell the plot and pay you back what I owe you, Mr. Quayle."

Quayle looked worried, possibly because he thought he might lose her services without that hold over her. "Ah, yes, but don't forget the interest," he added. "In any event, we can talk about that later. I suggest for now that we make our way back home before dark."

"Absolutely," I said. I hated these places in the daylight, so had no great desire to hang around when it was pitch black. As we walked over toward the cab Le Strange's men had righted for us, and which one of them had offered to drive us home in, I asked

Quayle, "Do you think it was right what he said?"

"Mmm?"

"Baron Sunday."

"Friday, Saturday, Sunday... Why don't you just call him Baron Long Weekend and be done with it?"

I looked down. "Sorry, old chum."

"Anyway, what did you mean?"

"I was referring to what he said about our paths crossing again."

Quayle looked wistfully off into the distance. "Oh, I think so. I think... I think he was *dead* right about that."

Then he smiled and placed an affectionate arm around my shoulder as we completed the short walk to the cab that would take us away from this place of the once-living dead.

Pay the Piper

He turned intuitively.

Another one lumbered out from behind a dwelling to The Piper's left. He stopped and watched the figure, tracing its path. At this distance, it looked tragic, like the town drunkard who remains under the influence long after the taverns have closed. Bottle clutched to his chest, faint mutterings of a song escaping from his lips—or perhaps the laments of a once-happy man.

But as The Piper covered the ground between them, certain truths came to light. Instead of a bottle, the man was holding something that was pink and red and glistening in the early morning sunshine. The remains of his last meal. And in place of a song or words of regret, the sound of burbling wind was emanating from his mouth; half-formed belches released with each step the fellow took.

The Piper stopped now, a few feet from this new suspect. It looked up at him, no longer an individual in any true sense of the word; one eye glazed over and thick with cataracts, the other hanging down to rest on its cheek, suspended on strips of meaty string—the blood in its empty socket long-since dried up. It took another bite of the forearm clenched in gray, gangrenous hands, one finger bent so far back that it must surely be broken, the nails crusted and black as if this thing had been digging for coal.

It chewed the meat in an unconscious way. This was merely a habit, something it felt it must do. There was no reason for it to eat anything at all; its digestive system was no longer in any fit state to process food and it was hardly likely to keel over and die from lack of sustenance. You could only die once. That was accepted, a fact of life. One of the rules of creation.

One of them.

As it worked the muscle and bone around inside its mouth, grinding the portion down until it felt able to swallow, it stumbled forward. The rags it wore flapped behind in the mild breeze, but here and there pieces of its skin were exposed and The Piper looked upon the foul grubs and insects that had made their nests in its rotting body. Bits of earth still fell from its breeches when it "walked," gathering around its bare feet, waiting to be trampled back into the land once more.

The Piper often wondered what went through their minds if, indeed, such uncanny vagrants even had minds. Were their souls somewhere else, on another level exploring magnificent territories beyond his comprehension, detached from these ungainly vessels they once inhabited in life? Or was there still some small fragment of humanity lurking inside each one, trapped in there and screaming for deliverance? Trying to prevent themselves from committing such unholy acts because if they didn't, they would never reach the Great Hereafter and sit with The Lord and His angels and—

The Piper shook his head. He knew full well what this repellent wretch was thinking about. It looked at The Piper—as best it could, given the circumstances—and saw another succulent dinner already prepared. It did not, by any stretch of the imagination, see a person standing there. Just food, and plenty of it; enough to last a good few hours, starting with that nice, juicy brain inside his skull. This was always the first to go for some reason. He'd noticed this.

He'd noticed many things in his time.

But The Piper had no intentions of being devoured that day.

He showed not a flicker of fear as he reached for the instrument tucked into his belt, a long, wooden tube with holes down the middle and a flattened-out mouthpiece. The work of a true craftsman. His own work, in fact. The dead thing had now dropped its snack and was "speeding" toward the main course. Those shaking hands stretched out, flashes of bone poking through at the knuckles, worms hanging down off the wrists like living, squirming bracelets.

There was now only a gap of inches separating them and a putrid aroma filled this modest cavity. It was just about to grab The Piper's arm—and a second later force him to his knees—when the first note was played. The carcass stood paralyzed as the gentle sound carried past its ears, or what was left of them. A second note followed, then a third and a fourth, until a melodic tune took shape. A combination of vibration and breath jetted out of the pipe's end like a sort of magic current. Someone had even told him once that they'd seen shapes and symbols flowing from the whistle— musical notes of differing size and color. The Piper didn't actually believe this himself (in all honesty, he put the man's visions down to either terror or one sip too many of some intoxicating brew or another), but such stories could do nothing other than bolster his soaring reputation.

The Piper's long, bejeweled fingers gamboled over the holes as he blew. Slowly, the thing that had once been a living being backed away. Its arms fell to its side, bewildered by its own actions. And, aye, a slight smile appeared on its face. Its cracked lips parted, pulled back over brown-black teeth. This was more like it.

Without further ado, The Piper turned his back on his captive audience and started walking again. It would follow him; they always did. Even now, above the noise of his pipe, he heard the shuffling behind, the empty croaking. It wasn't something that could be fought or questioned. When he played, they obeyed.

All his life he'd known he had a purpose, a destiny. That he was somehow different. But for most of his childhood, he'd been wilful and directionless, finally cast out by his adoptive family because they couldn't cope (his true origins still remained a mystery;

abandoned in a basket in the village square). Training as a 'prentice carpenter had seemed like the answer for him, a discipline and direction he lacked at that time.

Old Jed had been his mentor when no one else would take him in. He'd taught him how to respect and manage the wood, to fashion it into any object he wished, from tables to chairs and even playthings for the young. He'd enjoyed his studies, but still longed for something more. Something special to happen. An objective, and maybe even riches beyond his wildest imaginings.

He used to watch the noblemen, traders, and traveling merchants who would oft-times pass through the settlement, wishing he could be just like them. To explore the provinces, and further afield than that, must truly be an amazing thing, he thought. They told stories of distant lands where a man was sure to make his fortune, and a different maiden would warm his bed each night. Jed had laughed and called him a dreamer. In a sense, he was just that. He would never live the fantasy life he'd mapped out for himself, never in a million years. Or so he had thought. That was before...

This was now.

The Piper led his new recruit through the streets of the town. At windows he saw the frightened inhabitants pointing, talking of him.

"There goes The Piper," they would say. "Listen to his music."

Children idolized him. They dreamed their own dreams of one day becoming just like the man in the splendid tunic and single-feathered hat. But he was providing an essential service for the adults as well, without which they would not dare set foot outside in the light—never mind the darkness hours—for fear of running into one of the ground-dwellers.

(This was the name they had acquired over the years. It made them sound more...human than they were. Not something that couldn't be understood or reasoned with. The Piper had never approved of the label himself, which likened them to some exotic new subterranean race who, jealous of the life above, had suddenly decided to come up and say hello. Why couldn't people just face the truth? These were—or had been—brothers, sisters, parents, cousins, friends... Folk they had buried but who refused to stay that way.)

The Piper remembered how his own community had been the first time, how they had reacted to this unheard-of occurrence. The disbelief and ignorance.

One story, in particular, had remained with him: that of a young girl he'd known and admired (from a distance, alas). However, on this Sunday aft, her family and betrothed had been consigning her to the grave, mere seconds away from placing her in the freshly dug orifice. And all the mourners were especially alarmed to hear the woman knocking inside her casket, desiring to be set free.

Now, in spite of the fact that all the people there present were conversant with how she had met her end—attacked and beaten on the way home from market—they convinced themselves that by some divine miracle she was still alive. Her beau ran to the wooden box (a box, incidentally, The Piper had helped to make, sobbing as he worked), urging those round about to prise open its lid. The banging became louder and more frenzied. She wanted to be with her loved ones again, and he—being a devoted, caring swain—wished the same. All those lonely days since she went away, all the tears he'd shed, enough to fill a small lake, were forgotten. It had simply been a nightmare that had now relinquished its hold.

But the true nightmare was yet to come.

As the cover was wrenched off, the man had fallen gratefully into his beloved's extended—if disjointed—arms, hugging her tightly, kissing her cheeks, her lips, her forehead, every available patch of skin.

Bystanders looked on, puzzled, as the girl went to do the same. *Had she simply been rendered unconscious by the ordeal,* they asked one another. *Had the local healer been hasty when he declared the lass to be dead?* Quite obviously she was not deceased, the way she was embracing her love like that. Oh mercy, another few minutes and she would have been six feet under. A dead 'un alive.

How apt that last description had proved, for the *dead 'un alive* was opening her mouth, staring vapidly up at the sky and faces above. But instead of kissing her paramour, her teeth had gnawed their way through the side of his face.

His scream had been muffled—so those who'd escaped had said—blocked off by the girl's shoulder. The first inclination they had that something was wrong was when he started to kick his feet against the side of the coffin. Then one observer noticed all that blood inside. A horrible display to be sure.

And there were more to come, as barely recognizable hands broke through the sacred soil of the churchyard. Remnants of locals once fondly remembered were climbing out of their graves and attacking the guests at this rather premature funeral. Soon, the place was filled with the unsteady hordes, some almost skeletal, they'd been horizontal for so long. All hungry for those who still enjoyed the benefits of breathing.

Most fled from the ground-dwellers as fast as their legs could carry them. But some did not make it. The elderly, the infirm, those frozen with fright, all were overwhelmed by sheer numbers.

The strong young men of the village, those who had not yet been drafted into service but bragged about their fighting prowess to all who would listen (aye, and laughed at The Piper because of his scarecrow-like frame), came out to oppose the withered masses before they progressed too far into the settlement—where people hid in their houses and prayed for salvation. The bang of gunpowder and swish of swords could be heard all around. But in the end, it did no good.

An arm here, a leg there. The outcome was never in any doubt. How could they possibly kill that which had already expired? The very utmost all these warriors could manage was to slow them down before they too joined the ground-dwellers in death, some as rations, others as converts to their tacit cause.

And this is how it went on. In village after village, town after town, they sprang up, one following the next. With no explanation, no reason. The more superstitious said it was a curse on the land, witchcraft and sorcery afoot. The rational thinkers banded together and stated that it was some strange malady, one that placed its victims in a deathly state, then reanimated them after a certain amount of time had passed (but why then, critics argued, was the time period different in each case? Some ground-dwellers had been interred many, many years ago, while others, like the woman at the funeral, had barely started to turn cold). No one could offer any real solutions. No one understood what was happening. But perhaps no one was meant to.

There was a shrill cry from up ahead and The Piper ceased his playing. The ground-dweller halted also. When he saw who was calling out for help, he began running across the town center, leaving the corpse where it was. It wouldn't attempt to move now; it would simply wait there patiently for his return—the stony grin breaking upon its face.

The Piper could see what the trouble was. Someone had disregarded his express instructions and dared to step out. A lad of no more than fifteen was being dragged across the dirt by his hair. The ground-dweller was female this time, a woman who had probably been sturdy in life but was now like a deflated pig's bladder; the pleats of flesh dripped from her, dry cuts all over her face and arms where she'd swum her way through wood and packed turf in her hurry to reach daylight. It never ceased to amaze him how they could do that, how strong they could be if they set their sights on something. Why, before now he'd even seen them turn over carts and punch through solid rock to get to their victims.

The boy was yelping as the ground raked his backside. The dead woman was hauling him off to a place only she could see, a place where young, tender striplings were for dining on only.

The Piper positioned himself in front of her, avoiding her free arm as she swung it at him. Great clumps of hair had fallen out, he observed, and that same glassy expression possessed her, the one they all wore. Until, that is, he started to play again, concentrating intently on what he was doing. Then it was quite a different tale.

She let go of the boy and cackled peaceably to herself, almost as though she'd been expecting this to happen.

As he led her off to join her own kind, he heard the bleating youngster shout out after his mother. A mother who had died a good year or so ago, by the look of her. And The Piper understood now why he'd broken cover, if only to see his late ma again one final time. The Piper had never known his own mother, abandoned as he'd been, but he could appreciate what drove the youth. Except this was no longer the loving parent the boy had known, as he'd found out to his cost. The Piper felt a trace of emotion and anguish for the deluded boy. Told that his mother was gone, only to witness her walking as large as life—as death?—along the street. Then the empathy disappeared. The Piper picked up the other ground-dweller, and they were on their way again. Stumbling behind him, they resembled touched lunatics. But never did he look back once. For if he had, he might have seen the boy again, the boy who was so familiar. A mirror image of himself at that age. Before...

Before his name had been known far and wide? Just a carpenter's 'prentice with a big mouth and even bigger aspirations. That would all change soon enough, though. As soon as he discovered his secret, his latent ability. Something no one else in the world could lay claim to.

Aye, he had been a face in the crowd who hid when the ground-dwellers stormed their village that first time, fresh from the funeral. Covering his eyes as the mayhem outside his workshop gathered strength. The dead like a festering wave sweeping into the alleys, trying to break into houses. Old Jed had seen the things take those young 'uns, had seen how easily they'd swallowed them up...in some cases, quite literally. But still he insisted on going out to face them, armed only with his few craftsman's tools. He ignored the teenage Piper's pleas, his half-mumbled explanations.

"I won't just sit here and watch 'em take the village, son!"

Those were his last words, unless you count the pitiful screams as he vanished beneath a swell of decaying forms, his bones picked clean in a matter of minutes.

If only there was something I could do, The Piper had thought. But he couldn't control them. This was beyond the wisdom of his years. It was only when they burst into the workshop itself, splintering doors and smashing tables, that he discovered there *was* something he could do. There was plenty he could do (if only he'd realized it sooner). Instinctively, as the first of them drew near, its chin hanging off on a piece of gristle, the cheekbones dirty-white where they split skin as crumbly as dried parchment, he became aware that he *could* control them, could master this new power rushing through his veins.

He just needed to channel it somehow.

But he was also scared, overcome by the forces unleashed upon his home. So terrified, he scrabbled around on a nearby bench for a weapon in case he should falter. And his fingers, those long, artistic fingers, had closed around the pipe—a child's trinket he had been making all that week. As yet, it remained untreated, the wood still naked and cream. Hardly resembling the shiny brown object he now carried about with him everywhere.

But something told him to play.

To his surprise, the devils curtailed their advancement into the workshop. More than that, they all fell back—about eight in all, including the girl from the funeral—smirking and bobbing their heads to his tune. A tune he played confidently, though he'd never picked up a whistle in his entire life before now, other than to plane and chisel one.

The ground-dwellers parted and allowed him safe passage outside, where he discovered his music had the same soothing effect. Of course, he knew it wasn't the flute or the music alone that was doing this, but rather his own persuasive knack. The pipe merely allowed him to direct the energy from within. He couldn't explain it. It was just so. However, the villagers didn't know this. They believed it was The Piper's harmonious notes that kept the savages at bay. So, as he strode out to the edge of the village, the ground-dwellers fighting to keep up, he became a legend—his old family being the very first to offer praise. How did he do it? No one knew, including The Piper himself! No one cared. He had saved them all and was amply rewarded for doing so.

Thus began his travels. The fulfillment of his dreams. Dressed in an outfit more suitable for his purposes, the pointed hat with a feather stuck in it a finishing touch (the people expected no less of their heroes), he visited "infected" towns and hamlets, ridding them of the ground-dwellers in exchange for a few nights' board and lodging. That and a modest payment. Well, modest compared to losing their lives, he argued. And most folk agreed. They were happy enough to oblige. Nobody could offer the same service as him, at least nobody *he* had ever come across, leaving the field wide open for him to set out his stall.

He'd earned prodigious sums of money during his time abroad, had met so many people—some good, some bad—and his myth had grown in proportion to his remarkable feats. One day, he'd decided, he would retire and live like a king when the scourge was over. But for now, there was still work to be done.

The Piper led his two prizes through the streets. He resisted the urge to dance to his own rhythm, although he had been known to do so on occasion in other locales, where the inhabitants cheered him on from the windows. There was no such outward encouragement from these people.

He made another sweep of the town to pick up any stragglers he may have missed on the first few rounds. The Piper found two more to add to his collection, then took them to the boundary, where he had deposited his earlier hostages. He looked out over the assembly of around forty ground-dwellers, each one in various stages of decomposition. They gaped back at him, as if waiting for The Piper to decide their fate.

He had an idea they already knew. They had been on their little excursion, enjoyed the freedom while it lasted, but would be glad to return to the only homes they recognized now. The Piper played his tune louder, steering them back. It must have been an eccentric sight, the carrion procession marching on like that. Though no less astonishing than the sight of them coming over the hill in the first place. The Piper arriving some time later to save the day once more. Payment had then been swiftly negotiated with the town's spokesman, a sly-looking man by the name of Halberry. Could he be trusted? The Piper hoped so.

Now the graveyard wasn't far away, and it didn't take long for the corpses to find their respective plots. The Piper directed the operation, urging them to settle back into holes they'd made themselves. One by one they pulled the sod back over, like a sleeper pulling blankets up over their head. Bedding down, asleep once more.

The Piper took the whistle from his mouth, another job finished. As he walked back down the town's path, he meditated silently. Would these folks pay as they had promised? Sometimes, when they saw the ground-dwellers were gone, people foolishly believed they didn't need his services anymore. Why should they compensate The Piper now that the crisis was over? He prayed they wouldn't take that attitude. They seemed like fairly nice people (an image of the boy flashed through his mind). He would hate to see what happened in the last town happen here again. Today.

But if for some reason they did decide to renege on the deal, he would just have to persuade them. It seemed to be what he was best at, persuasion.

Of the living and the dead.

No, if they refused to pay The Piper, it would not bode well for the population of this town. He might be forced to undo all his crucial work, a waste of everyone's time and effort. However, The Piper would have no choice but to make another example of them, calling the dead to rise just as he'd seduced them back to their mounds.

After all, had he not raised them up in the first place? Raised them *all* up in his time. In village after village, town after town...

And if this were true, if he really was The Piper, what on God's green Earth was there to stop him from doing so again?

Nine Tenths

He'd been watching the place for a few weeks.

In his line of work, patience and persistence paid off. You couldn't afford mistakes because they got you caught. So he'd camped out, watching. Always watching.

As far as Ren could discern, the new owner—a middle-aged man going both gray and bald at the same time—lived alone in that big place. He was usually out in the evening (some kind of shift worker, perhaps?), but when he was gone, he'd be gone for hours. Ren would watch him leave in that sporty Mazda number, during which time he'd phone the house randomly to see if anyone picked up. No one ever did, and there was no sign of any wife or family at all.

No sign of anyone.

Ren also made recces, gaining access to the wall at the back through the wooded area beyond. What would have been a selling point when buying the place—a nice, quiet, isolated spot—was a major bonus in his specialist field. The wall was fairly standard size, offering no obstacle to him: he'd been climbing like a monkey since he was small. He'd been doing this almost as long, graduating in the ranks from petty thief to professional burglar. One gig these days could last him a good few months because he chose them so carefully and always scoped out his targets.

The house itself was alarmed, which he could spot from the outside. It would be easy enough to cut the lines to that, though. What he was also able to do on those research missions was take a look through the windows and see whether it was actually worth breaking in. It was amazing how many properties looked like they'd be Aladdin's caves but turned out to contain nothing of value at all.

This one was different. No sooner had he pressed his face up against the glass than he spotted the works of art on the wall; the LCD TV and home cinema system, not to mention Blu-rays; the music system, racks of CDs; the various statues and ornaments scattered about the place that would make a mint when he sold them on (so much stuff that he considered bringing someone else in, but decided ultimately that he could handle it). This was a person who enjoyed the finer things in life.

It was also while he was looking through his third or fourth window that he spotted the locked door just off the hallway that led into the spacious kitchen. In Ren's experience, locks always meant that there was something of worth on the other side—and he hadn't come across a lock yet that wouldn't yield to him. It would probably be where this guy kept his serious money. There might even be a safe on the other side. Again, Ren had the tools and the skill to handle any kind of job.

So he'd waited for the man to leave once more that night, tested the phone for the final time, and when there had been no answer, he'd made his move. Did he feel any kind of sympathy for the people he stole from, any guilt at what he did? After this long? Hardly. Besides, Ren had always subscribed to the philosophy that possession was nine-tenths of the law. Once he had all he wanted loaded up into his van—parked down the side of the house, out of view—it would *belong* to him. And if he chose to sell it on, well, that was his affair. He'd lose no sleep over it.

In his black clothes and mask, he blended into the shadows—not that there was anyone around to see him. Ren brought along the tools necessary to disable the alarm, which took only a few minutes. Next, he pulled out his glass cutters and armature to gain entrance through the back door. Long gone were the days of him trying to use a screwdriver to jimmy doors on his estate. Now he had much more finesse.

He'd popped the locks and bolts on the door in a matter of seconds, gaining access quickly and stealthily. *Start with the larger stuff,* he told himself—he'd brought along a trolley to pile it on. But there was just something nagging at him about that locked door. Beyond it, there might be cash—or better—that would render all that hefting redundant. *Have a look inside there first. Go on.*

Ren couldn't resist. It was like a magnet was drawing him to the door. The lock was again a fairly standard one, but probably hadn't come with the house. He checked the seals for another alarm, just in case, but there was nothing. The lock sprang open and he pushed on the door, flicking his small torch-light into the blackness. A set of steps led downward, into some kind of cellar. A wave of cold air greeted him.

Ren frowned. Was it worth going down there when he could just load up on the ground level? Hell, he hadn't even checked the upstairs yet—who knew what kind of finds there were? To his surprise, Ren found his foot on the first step. He'd come this far; he had to know what was so priceless that it needed to be kept down here.

His beam flashed over a room; metallic cupboards lined the walls. *Could be storage,* he thought to himself, *the kind they use in banks.* In all his time, he'd never pulled off a bank job, so maybe he was in over his head. *Don't be silly; you still know how to crack those kinds of locks,* he reminded himself.

But there were metallic shapes in the middle of the room as well, plus what looked like floor-to-ceiling storage cabinets. Ren moved further down into the basement, one ear still cocked for any noises upstairs. These days, if you were caught by the owner of the place and they attacked you, *they'd* be the ones going to jail. But he'd rather avoid that kind of messiness if he could.

He couldn't see properly using just the flashlight, but found a light switch on the wall nearby. Ren hesitated before throwing it, but decided that the light wouldn't extend upstairs. Now he could see the room as a whole, the cupboards and the table not far away—the edges of which he'd only just brushed with the torch.

Ren wasted no time in trying to open the cupboard doors. They were steel, and remarkably cold, but he managed to fling open the one nearest. It was full of glass vials, each containing liquid. He picked up the closest and read the label on the side. Ren had no idea what it was for, but he did know one thing: drugs were drugs, no matter which way you cut it. He'd been right; there was a fortune waiting just in this cupboard alone.

Moving to another, he opened it and found containers. White, plastic, that opened at the top. They ranged in size from the very large to the really small, each with a temperature gauge. Ren frowned again. He should just fill his backpack from the first cupboard and leave, but he wanted to see if there were any more of the vials in the cupboards.

He made for another one on his right, tugged at it. The metal finally came loose, and Ren stared at the contents of this cupboard now. He staggered backward, hitting the edge of the table. He felt nauseous but tried not to throw up inside his mask. Breathing long and slow, he opened yet another cupboard. This one was even worse.

Ren swallowed, a sour taste in his mouth. He turned and looked at the larger cabinets. Against his better judgment, he reached out his hand. Before he could stop himself, Ren had opened that door, too. He caught only a glimpse of what was inside before he felt the blow on the back of his neck.

But that glimpse was more than enough.

⚔ ⚔ ⚔ ⚔ ⚔

When he woke, Ren still felt sick, but it was a different kind of nausea.

He tried to move, then realized that not only was he doped up, he was also strapped down. *Are you happy now?* he said to himself. *You got your drugs, all right.*

A face appeared above him, the gray-bald man whose home

this was. Just behind him was another figure, much larger, the one who must have struck him from behind. They were both dressed in aprons, wearing rubber gloves.

"Ah," said the owner, "back with us?"

Ren attempted to say something but found that his tongue and lips were completely numb.

"You've kept us waiting, almost as long as you did deciding to rob us in the first place." He smiled; it was a terrifying sight. "That's correct, we've been watching you for some time." Ren tore his eyes away, then wished he hadn't. The cupboards were still open, the contents clearly visible.

"What? Oh yes. You're probably wondering what I do, what pays so well? I sell them on, you see. In just the same way *you* sell things on, I'd imagine. It's a specialist field."

Could he be comparing what they did? It made Ren's stomach churn to think about it. He never…he'd never do anything like that!

"About ninety percent of each 'unit.' The rest…" His eyes flicked over to the larger cabinet. Ren looked, too, seeing the poor thing inside again. "It's just a hobby of mine, really. Isn't it, Maynard?" he said to the larger man, who nodded.

Ren was able to take in the full length of it now, the oddness of the body with its parts stitched upon parts—the bits that were left over from this man's organ-stealing operation. There were both male and female bits spliced together: it had three eyes, each covered in cataracts and not viable for selling on; two mouths, one almost where it should be, the other on its cheek; but just two holes where its nose should be. Ren gasped as it moved, the warmer air obviously wakening it. Those three eyes opened and looked at him, blind but pleading, as it moaned and strained against its own bonds.

What kind of madman was this?

"We're not so different, you and I. Finders keepers, isn't that what you people say?" *Not quite*, thought Ren. "You were on my property, and now…" He held up his scalpel. "You *are* my property."

Ninety percent (nine tenths) sold on. The rest—

Ren tried to struggle again but realized it was useless. As the scalpel came down, he had to concede that the man had a point. It was his rule as well, wasn't it? His law?

The law of possession.

But that thought didn't comfort him much as the blade sank into his flesh, cutting deep—some of which he felt, some he didn't.

Nor did it help in the slightest when, at last, the man reached for his power tools. Nonetheless, they were his final thoughts.

Nine tenths, Ren turned over and over in his mind as he lost consciousness.

Nine tenths...

The Corpse Identity

Who was she?

She had no idea. Did she have a family? People who cared about her, who…loved her? Nothing. What was her story? Who knows? How did she get here? Again, not a clue. All she knew was what had happened after she'd woken up, scaring the men who'd been around her. Who'd carried her from the riverbank where she'd washed up apparently.

Who'd carried her body.

Because that's what they'd thought initially. That she was a floater, a corpse. A…Jane Doe. She might not have a real name, but that's what Aleksander eventually ended up calling her because he couldn't just keep saying "Hey, girl," whenever he wanted to get her attention. Because that's what they called all the dead people in the morgue: either John or Jane Doe.

"But I'm not— I woke up," she'd protested.

Aleksander chuckled. "Yes. Yes, you did. Lord in Heaven knows how! But you did."

She had definitely *been* dead. They'd checked her pulse, Aleksander and his other hunter friends, right there on the banks of the Vistula River where they'd found her. She'd been gray, completely devoid of color—"Not that you have much even now!" Aleksander was fond of joking—and definitely not breathing.

He'd checked her himself: checked at the neck, the wrist, listened to her chest through the jumpsuit she'd been wearing. Leisurewear, he'd assumed; fashionable in the cities these days, or so he'd been told. Aleksander tended to steer clear of the population centers.

"And then there was that," he'd said, pointing at her head, the first time they'd discussed all this on one of their walks through the forest—a place that was, even now, holding on to the snow that had lain all winter.

Jane reached up and touched the wound that he'd stitched, those taxidermy skills having come in quite handy: his cabin out there in the wilderness filled with stuffed and mounted creatures, the heads of some adorning his wooden walls. He'd fixed her up, just like any other dead thing back in his makeshift workshop, where they'd dumped her on the table. It had just seemed like the right thing to do.

But then she'd snapped awake, reached up, and grabbed Aleksander—the other men standing back and letting out expletives in Polish, words she understood but didn't know how. Was she Polish, too? She didn't believe so. They'd crossed themselves; one had even raised his rifle until she'd relieved him of it. Demanded to know where she was, who they were, and what had happened to her.

For the longest time, nobody answered; they just stood and stared with mouths gaping open. Then Aleksander had said to her, "Let me go, girl. We mean you no harm, I promise you."

Still frowning, confused, wracking her brain for information that evaded her, she'd opened her fingers and done as he requested. Then she'd asked them another question: "Who...who am I?"

A good question; they all were. But these men couldn't possibly know the answers any more than she did. Aleksander had come up with a working theory, though, mainly to calm down the other men, his friends. He suggested that she'd fallen in the icy cold waters, that the temperature had slowed her heart, making it appear that she was dead. It had kept her in a kind of suspended animation. But when they'd got her into the warm...

"She was shot in the *head!*" one exclaimed, a scruffy-looking man with a scar over his left eye, not believing a word of it.

"Must have just glanced off, a flesh wound," Aleksander informed him, his wavering voice telling her that he didn't believe it either. He had seen those wounds, stitched them closed.

A man with wide shoulders had urged Aleksander to fetch the authorities, to report this. Her unlikely ally urged them just as fervently to give him a bit of time. "We don't know why she was shot in the first place. There might be people looking for her. Bad people."

She didn't know much, but she knew she trusted this man. There was kindness in him, his voice, his ways. And so Jane collapsed back onto the bench again, unconscious.

Aleksander had told her later on, once the other men had gone—some of them actually running away, but only after promising they'd give him his time—that she'd slipped into a fever. That she'd shaken, twitched in her sleep, so much so that he'd had to place her in a bath of cold water to bring that temperature down again. It was one of the reasons why he'd doused the fire in the cabin itself; the only thing she'd seemed to respond to.

"You don't remember anything?" he'd asked her when she woke again. "Not a thing?"

And there had been flashes, especially while she was asleep, but nothing she could hold on to. Every time she tried to grab a memory, it would slip through her fingers like water from that river. "Falling. I remember falling. Blackness." Jane shook her head, then took in Aleksander's features: his hair and beard shot through with silver.

She'd asked him who he was then, why he lived out here all alone. That was much easier to answer: he *hadn't* lived here alone until quite recently. "My wife... She passed a couple of years ago," he informed her, and she thought he might cry if he dwelled on it for long. "She got sick." It was his turn to shake his head. "There was no curing it. She is buried out in the back, with... I'd give anything if she could—" He laughed then, a hollow laugh. "If she could come back from the grave, as you seemingly did."

"I-I didn't come back from... I mean, I wasn't... I couldn't have been..." Jane thought about the faces of those men, the shock and terror, the way they were crossing themselves.

"Just superstitious," Aleksander told her. "Simple men who don't know a miracle when they see one. Remember Lazarus?"

Jane did, but she had no idea how or why she remembered the name. A tale from Sunday School, from when she was little? Was she particularly religious? Another thing she didn't have an inkling about.

She'd stood in front of the mirror the first night, gazing at the face that was staring back at her. The old hunter was right; she barely had any color to her cheeks. Jane pulled down the skin under one of her eyes, those brown-verging-on-black eyes, seeing the lack of blood there. She wasn't attractive in the conventional sense of the word, or at least she didn't think so—a Plain Jane, then?—but there was something about her, the high cheekbones, thin lips, short hair. Someone had loved her, once. She knew that. Felt it somehow.

Just like someone cared about her now. The man who'd saved her. And she had to wait a short while before she found out why, when he came to join her sitting outside on the porch (she spent more time outdoors than in). "Would you like something to eat? I have just made a stew."

Jane shook her head, she'd barely eaten since she'd arrived and knew that he was worried about her.

"You must eat; it will give you strength."

"I'm not hungry, but thank you." To stop him asking about food more than anything, she'd changed the subject. Asked him about what he'd begun saying before, about his wife out back. Why there were two graves.

Aleksander's eyes had brushed the floor as he'd sat down and told her about the daughter who had only lasted a week after being born. "I always wondered what she might have turned out like," said the hunter, looking older than ever at that moment. "Maybe she would have taken after me. Maybe she'd have been a little like you, eh?"

Jane had remained silent, neither nodding nor shaking her head. "You don't get lonely out here?" she asked him next, following his gaze now out into the woods. "All on your own?"

He looked over at her. "But I am not on my own." For a second, she thought he meant his hunter friends, who appeared to have abandoned him; then she thought he meant her, that he had company now, though for how long was anyone's guess. But he meant neither, as he clarified: "They are still with me, my Hanna, my Zofia. The dead are not really gone."

She had nodded, and they'd sat in silence as the darkness fell.

It was only on their walk the next day that Jane realized the other hunters had not abandoned Aleksander at all; they had just been scared to return alone. Scared of her. So scared, that they'd come back in greater numbers. Decided to handle things their way.

They'd both stiffened at the same time, her and Aleksander. "You sense it, too?" he'd asked, adjusting the cap he always wore outside.

"Multiple targets," Jane had replied, not really knowing how she knew that. "Moving toward us through the woods. Twelve o'clock, three o'clock—"

Then the shooting started. Bullets pinging off trees, splintering bark. She'd shoved Aleksander down, but it was too late—he was already hit. "Go!" he told her. "Move! Save yourself."

"You know there is something wrong with her!" shouted a voice, which Jane easily traced. "Something unnatural. She should not be alive Aleksander. That girl has the Devil inside her."

"Do not let your feelings for your dead daughter cloud your judgment, my friend," said another. More bullets. More wood flying everywhere. *Some* friend.

Jane moved; she'd gone, but not to save herself. She moved fast and low, reaching the first man doing the shouting: the one with wide shoulders who'd wanted to alert the authorities. She leaped at him, kicking the rifle from his grasp, and then kicking him into a nearby tree trunk. The sound of cracking bones was like music to her ears.

Next, she found the second speaker, rolling and taking out his legs from beneath him. It was the man with the scar, the one who was so sure she was dead. She blinked once, twice, then elbowed him in the chest.

Jane dispatched the rest of the hunters with as little effort as it had taken to bring down the first two. Ten in total, two of which she'd lured into a crossfire and had shot themselves. By the time she'd finished and returned to a fallen Aleksander, he was breathing his last breaths. "You... You *are* like me. You are a hunter," he told her, and now the tears flowed. Not just his, but hers: for this man she hadn't known all that long but had grown so attached to. Felt some kind of kinship with. Who she would have been proud to call her father.

Such a waste, killed by his so-called comrades for trying to help her. She would bury him at the back of the cabin, with his Zofia, with his Hanna; Jane didn't even know which was his wife and which his daughter. But she'd bury him with them because that's what you did with the dead. With those you cared about anyway, with those that were never really gone. With others you—

Aleksander had been right about one thing: there had been bad people—bad men—who'd come for her. And it wasn't until she rose from his side that Jane realized. After all this time of refusing meals, of not wanting to eat cooked stew or beans or anything else on offer back at the cabin that the old hunter had kindly made for her.

Only now realized just how hungry she was. Realized what it was she wanted to eat.

Even as she was approaching the first of the men she'd incapacitated rather than killed, she realized that, yes, they might well have had a point.

She *was* wrong, unnatural. As she bit into them, leaving their heads for last—knowing that sweet deliciousness inside would taste like cherry pie to her—she agreed that she shouldn't be alive.

Understood that she, Jane Doe, was, in fact, actually still dead.

A shady room, filled with shadier figures.

Not just how they looked in the dim light that masked their features, but what they thought. Their very natures. Men and women with no consciences, just agendas and missions.

They sat around a horseshoe table, facing front as the screen ahead of them finished playing the recorded footage, leaving the hovering rectangle a chilly blue.

"And that's all there is?" asked a deep voice near the front of the table. A man who was known only as Mr. Nine.

"Yes, all we have until just after the bodyguard shot her," answered someone else, male, but the voice was thin and wheezy. Mr. Seven. "After that, it just went...well, dead."

"And the diplomat?" a female voice now. Ms. Four.

"Arrived safely at his destination," answered Seven. "And there was no sign of our resource on the train."

There was a bang that made them all start, a fist striking the table. "I told you this was a bad idea, that sending her was—"

"Mr. Three!" barked the woman. "What's done is done. We all agreed that she was the best candidate for the job, a test of her—"

"The test failed!" snapped Three.

"Only because of a lucky bullet to the head," Seven pointed out. "No one could have foreseen that it would—"

"So she was pushed, or fell, from the train?" This was Mr. Nine again.

"One would assume," replied Seven. "The footage seems to indicate a fall, then—"

"And the tracker?" asked Three abruptly.

Seven shook his head but spoke up when he realized they probably couldn't see him in the darkness. "Offline, same as the camera."

"I see."

"Chances are the resource is also offline. Permanently."

"You and I both know there's no such thing as permanent, Mr. Seven." There was silence after Three had spoken.

"We're keeping an eye on the area for unusual activity and can have agents in the vicinity within the—"

"If she's still operational, you won't find her. I shouldn't have to remind you of that. We spent a hell of a lot of money making sure of it!"

"So what's our next move?" asked Ms. Four.

"We'll just have to wait," Three suggested.

"Wait for what?" the woman asked.

"For her to resurface again," Three replied somberly.

Heading towards the surface, breaking through.

Breaking free. After the fall. After—

The train? There had been a train (not the first time, there hadn't), she was sure of it. The sounds of a train, the rattling of lots of parts moving together, working in unison. Like the organization she was a part of, that was how it had been explained to her... Hadn't it?

Then those sounds replaced by a single one, a kind of a *pffttt* noise rather than the bang you'd expect. Something hitting her, hitting Jane in the head. Being pushed, or falling backward. Falling a long way.

Hitting the surface. A hard surface. And suddenly being underneath it, darkness replacing light. Knowing nothing. Everything slowing down, stopping. It felt like—

Felt like dying.

Waiting, waiting, waiting. To emerge again (from the water, the river, the bath, or...). To break that surface and—

Jane snapped awake, looking left and right, ready to grab someone, attack, incapacitate. But there was no one there. She was alone in here. They hit a bump and she rocked back on the crate she was sitting upon, trying to claw back the memories of what had happened to her. What had happened even before being shot in the head. And before that...?

All that would come were the more recent memories, of being at Aleksander's. Of what had happened in the woods, what she'd done to those men. The people who'd killed him. Accidentally, because they were trying to kill *her*, she reminded herself. He had died because he'd found her, helped her. Believed in her.

Unnatural.

When those other hunters had been right all along to fear her. Had no idea what she was capable of because Jane didn't even know herself at the time. Not until she'd had to use those skills, and until she'd needed to feed. Aleksander had never tried to feel for a pulse since the riverbank, but if he had done, like she had done many times on her journey, he still wouldn't have found one. Lazarus? He'd come back, but come back all the way. He'd been alive, he'd been... human, hadn't he? Or was she remembering the story wrong? How could she even remember that at all, and not what had happened? How she'd been—

What, murdered? And come back wrong.

Unnatural.

Maybe she did have the Devil inside her. Was that it? Was *He* powering her? A dark reflection of what Jesus had done, an imitation that wasn't quite right? A "fuck you" to God?

How. Had. She. Come. Back?

She'd ransacked Aleksander's cabin and workshop, put everything she thought might be useful in a bag, and changed into a shirt, trousers with braces, boots, and a coat—not that she needed one, she didn't seem to get cold; instead, she thrived on it—and donned one of his caps, which she could pull down low to disguise her face. Looking in the mirror, she could pass for either sex, which would be handy out in the world.

Then she'd rounded up whatever cash was lying around—not much, it had to be said, because Aleksander had lived off the land—and whatever weaponry. A couple of knives—one with a serrated edge—and a revolver, complete with a box of ammunition. She'd buried his rifle with him because, again, that felt like the right thing to do—and besides, it would have been too cumbersome to carry. Too conspicuous. Jane didn't need any weapons at all, not really—she'd done okay out there against those hunters with her bare hands—but something was telling her to pack them all. So she'd tucked the revolver into the inside pocket of her coat.

Finally, she'd set fire to the place, making it look like an accident, logs from the open fireplace rolling onto the rug. Leave no traces of your presence, that was the golden rule. Time was ticking on; she should get as far away from the cabin as possible. Had no idea whether the hunters had actually kept their word or whether they'd contacted the authorities; probably not, or they'd have been swarming all over this area. But she'd already hung around longer than she would have liked.

Jane followed the direction of the river, but not on the riverbank itself because it was too exposed. Unlike Aleksander, she needed to get to a population center. Wouldn't find the answers she was looking for in the back of beyond.

The river brought her to Warsaw, with its red, green, and yellow buildings. And from there, she would have to think about transportation because she was beginning to feel a pull, a need to head in a certain direction. It crossed her mind to perhaps befriend someone, pay them to take her in a car. But she really didn't want to drag anyone else into this business—whatever the fuck this business happened to be.

Walking the streets as night fell, she came across some muggers relieving a tourist couple of their belongings in an alleyway.

"What are you looking at?" asked one of the thieves when he spotted her watching. He had a scarf pulled up around the bottom of his face to conceal his identity and was brandishing a switchblade, waving it around. In the direction of the terrified victims. In Jane's direction.

This particular business was none of hers; Jane knew that. She should just leave well enough alone, not draw attention to herself. Instead, she found herself moving forward. Quickly, stealthily.

The man's companions, one wearing what looked like a stocking over the top part of his face and another who simply hadn't bothered at all—maybe because he was so ugly—came to head her off at the pass. Jane easily ducked the first one's blow, Stocking Guy, tossing her bag aside to give herself greater maneuverability. When she came back up again, her fist connected with the man's chin and almost tore it off. He dropped to his knees, wailing, or as close to wailing as he could manage, so she twisted his head sideways to shut him up.

His companion, who was clearly as stupid as he was repugnant, continued his attack. She grabbed him by the neck and lifted him off his feet. Obviously surprised by this, the man was even more shocked when she hurled him at the wall of the alley like a child discarding an unloved toy.

That just left the guy with the scarf and knife. Abandoning the tourists, he took a few steps toward her, still swinging the blade. The lunge, when it occurred, was sloppy, and she saw it coming from a mile away, had analyzed his fighting pattern, such as it was, before she'd even engaged the others. Knew what he was going to do before he did, and with that knowledge, she had stepped aside and grabbed his arm as it flew past, snapping it sideways so that it broke at the elbow. Even before he'd had a chance to register this—and scream—she'd delivered a blow with the side of her hand across his throat, crushing his windpipe. Seconds later, he was on the ground and keeled over sideways.

"Oh, thank you! *Thank you!*" the crying woman was saying in an American accent. Jane said nothing back, merely waited for her partner to usher her away from the scene. She hadn't done it just to save the pair of them, however—although deep down she suspected that had been one of the motivations. That made her a good guy, didn't it? But did the rest of it? The other reason she'd stepped in and got involved. Jane had also been hungry. The sustenance from the woods had kept her going this far—the fight admittedly taking it out of her—but...

The top-off nourishment the muggers gave her didn't have to last that long, as it turned out, because the very next day she picked up the tantalizing scent of raw meat. A meat-packing plant, by the looks of it. Breaking in that night, she ate her fill and made use of the giant freezer to keep her core temperature low. What's more, she discovered a way of traveling off the grid—west, which was where she felt she should be heading. The direction she needed to go next. Don't ask how she knew; she just did. Something from before the... What? Accident? She'd been shot, hadn't she? Killed? How could that possibly be an accident?

She'd hidden in the back of one of the delivery lorries, which was where she'd fallen asleep and dreamed about the fall. The darkness. It was heading for the border into Germany; she'd discovered this by checking the itinerary. And—now awake—she hopped from the back before they hit the checkpoints, just in case the truck was searched.

Jane would make her way into the adjoining county her way. Heading for yet another city, heading for a building she was seeing flashes of now—as strongly as she'd seen the other images from before, and after, her death.

An itch she needed to scratch, just like trying to figure out who she was. Only this one she could get to, could reach and rake her nails over. It might even provide those other answers, she thought.

The who? The why? And the what next?

They'd been able to piece it together.

A report of men, hunters, being attacked in the woods—the local authorities had put it down to an animal attack because they'd been savaged and parts of the victims had been eaten. But the people in that shadowy room knew differently. Knew what their missing resource needed to survive.

Couple that with another report of a cabin fire nearby, and she might as well have been waving a flag or setting off a flare for them. Of course, she was long gone, so none of it did them any good. All that it told them for certain was she was still alive.

All right, still *active* then, if you wanted to be pedantic.

Then had come Warsaw, and the police reports about a mugging gone sideways. The American tourists had been vague when describing their savior, but the remains that had been found in the bins not far away had confirmed it was their girl. On the move, heading west.

None of them had been surprised when Mr. Seven had burst into the meeting and announced that they'd had word from their contact at the hotel in Berlin. One of any number of places she might have been heading for, the conditioning still working that well, at least.

"Several squads have been activated and sent in to reacquire her," Seven had announced proudly.

"And you really think it will be as easy as that?" Three countered.

Seven opened his mouth, then closed it again.

They all knew the answer to that question.

Hotel der Lotos.

The Hotel Lotus, a nondescript building that looked exactly how she'd pictured it. How she *remembered* it? Jane had visited this place before, maybe stayed here, quite possibly not that long ago—just before her accident? Or further back even? The staff at the front desk had recognized her anyway, although they seemed a little bewildered by her clothes. They welcomed her back and called her by the name "Fräulein Tod."

"Your room is just how you left it, number four forty-four."

Jane thanked them, resisted asking when that had been—because shouldn't she *know* herself when she'd been here last?—feeling a little uncomfortable that they seemed to know who she was when she didn't. But then that was all part and parcel of finding out who she *really* was because it sure as hell wasn't this Tod person. Part of finding out what she'd been doing on the train and what had happened to her. Risky, definitely, but worth it, she reasoned.

Jane had gone to the room, letting herself in and tossing her bag onto the bed. It was a pretty standard-sized room, nothing too fancy, with a little kitchen and bathroom attached. Somewhere you could stay for a while if you had a mind to. Perhaps until you were needed for something?

Inside the wardrobe, Jane found more stylish clothes—including a couple of dresses—but also some functional ones tucked away in the top. Another jumpsuit with pockets like the one she'd been wearing when the hunters had found her, which she'd changed into because it would be more comfortable; it was obviously molded to her frame. She also discovered a safe, which she apparently had the combination to, hidden in a corner of her mind. Nestled inside was money, a few IDs—including passports, which might come in handy—so she zipped all of this into her pockets. There was also a much more modern Glock pistol, complete with spare clips and a silencer, which screwed onto the end.

She was beginning to suspect that not only was she not normal, but whatever "job" she did—and she had a few ideas about that—wasn't run of the mill either.

There were also some open, empty envelopes. All that was written on the outside of these was some code made up of numbers and letters; fortunately, it was a cipher she knew how to crack, and she jotted down the word it revealed using one of the hotel's pads and pens.

That word was "Tombstone."

Jane frowned as she read this, having no idea what it meant other than the obvious. It made no sense that she was able to break this code yet didn't know what it was trying to say. Another secret beneath the secrets.

She had no more time to think about it, though, as she sensed something was happening inside the hotel itself. Jane could hear raised voices out in the corridor, people speaking German demanding to know what was happening. Being informed there was a criminal on the loose. The thud of boots on the floor, orders being shouted, telling people to remain in their rooms until the situation was contained.

Jane went to the window and looked down on the street. She saw dark vans outside the entrance, men in dark uniforms milling around wearing helmets and masks, brandishing machine guns. She slapped a mag into her gun, snatched up her bag, and poked her head out to see more of the soldiers emerging from the lifts on this floor—joining the numbers already gathered.

They were here for her; she knew that instinctively. Jane was "the situation." More hunters, just a different kind. Professionals, deadly. More deadly than street muggers, that was for damned sure! She should just go with them, surely? They might take her to the people who could provide all the answers. But something was stopping her, an instinct. A sense of self-preservation. Something was telling her to run, not to let them apprehend her. That she needed to find those answers for herself or she never really would.

And anyway, it was too late: the lead figures had already spotted her, were pointing in her direction, calling out for Jane to stay where she was. She did the opposite, racing toward the stairs at the far end of the hallway.

"Go, girl! Save yourself!"

More footfalls—bootfalls—behind her, but Jane reached the door and swung it open. Slammed it shut again and bolted it behind her. It had never been her intention to go down because that's where the vans were—but the choice was taken out of her hands when she spotted more of the uniformed men jogging up the steps, their arms and legs just visible down there through the well of the stairs.

Up, then. The only option, and where she'd been planning to head anyway. There was another building close enough to the left of the hotel that she'd noticed when she scoped out the place; Jane could make it over to that, jumping the gap, leaving the troops behind her. This didn't have to get messy.

Unfortunately, she could already hear the choppers approaching. Could hear the ropes being let down so the men could rappel onto the roof and cut off her exit that way as well.

Jane was being left with very few choices. None, actually. She didn't want to hurt anyone, but...

The first of the bullets ricocheted off the wall just behind her. A warning shot. Or had they been *trying* to hit her? Did they have orders to take her in, dead or— Dead. They'd be taking her in dead whatever happened, wouldn't they? If she didn't want to go with them—and everything inside her was screaming not to be taken now—then she had no alternative but to fight.

Unlike the others she'd faced so far since the river, she had no idea whether these men were good or bad. If she took them down, did that make *her* good or bad? Well, they were shooting at her so—

"Okay," she said under her breath. "Let's do this."

"Save yourself!"

Above her, someone suddenly wandered through a door and onto the stairs. An innocent bystander, just a guy staying there who had no idea what was going on. Jane glanced up, glanced down. "Get back!" she called to him in German, and he looked puzzled but then stood frozen to the spot. *"No!"*

But it was too late again; bullets flew in her direction. She pulled back, heard the man above her grunt and cry out as he was struck. More projectiles peppered the door she'd bolted nearby as the men there finally forced their way through.

Gritting her teeth, Jane levered herself forward again and fired her own gun—all of her bullets hitting their targets. Wounding where she could, finding their marks between Kevlar vests, taking out kneecaps. The soldiers from her floor burst on the scene at that moment, almost as one. And she had to swing around to tackle them now, pulling knives from her bag and stabbing one in the shoulder—ramming the blade all the way home and pinning him to the wall.

Jane kicked a second man in the stomach, whirled around, and threw another knife at a third. One of the men from below reached her, shooting at her gun hand and sending the pistol flying out of her grasp. She ducked and flung a small knife back at him, returning the favor as it skewered him through the back of the hand, causing him to drop his own weapon. A high kick to the face knocked him backward and into more troops coming up the stairs, sending them all toppling like pins in a bowling alley.

She climbed up onto the railing, balancing on top, then leaped and grabbed the rail above her, pulling herself up and over just before another smattering of gunfire found her. Jane scrambled to her feet and ascended the stairs, pulling Aleksander's old revolver out of the bag as she went, the only weapon she had left. She tossed the bag over, more to give the soldiers something else to shoot at than anything, then raced up to see how their uninvited guest was faring.

There he was, slumped against the wall in a puddle of blood. Coughing up the redness.

"Shit!" said Jane, taking his hand and trying to get him to put pressure on the wounds. He needed medical attention, and quickly, or he'd—

More gunfire, this time from above. The soldiers who'd landed on the hotel's roof. Without even thinking, Jane pulled away and ducked for cover, but of course, the man couldn't, and now he faced another barrage. This time he was dead for sure, and unlike her, wouldn't be getting up again anytime soon. Jane was under no illusions that she'd get the blame for his death, living up to the description of the criminal they'd been calling her. Not that she hadn't murdered before on her journey, just not this particular man. Not someone who hadn't deserved it.

She fired upward at the figures above her, winging a pair but running out of bullets before she could actually make any headway. Someone rolled a smoke canister down the stairs where Jane was crouching, but all that did was give her cover. It wasn't as if she needed to breathe.

So, she wound her way up the stairs, taking out the men one by one, seeing them clearly enough without the need for a mask like they all wore. Jane snatched up a couple of their machine guns and fired down into the stairwell to keep back the troops from below, then rushed through the emergency exit that had been left open.

More were waiting for her on the roof when she emerged with the smoke at her back. She fired over their heads and watched as they all dropped to the ground for cover. There were two helicopters overhead, but thankfully not enough space on the roof for either of them to land. Jane weighed her options.

Suddenly, she dropped the guns and made a run for it, readying to spring up and aim for the nearest chopper, its blades *thwupping* above. Her plan was to climb up into it and force the pilot to fly away from here. But as she jumped, reaching up toward the landing skids to grab one, she felt a weight dragging her back— dragging her down. Not one, but three men had hold of her, were throwing off her momentum, her aim. So much so that they all fell, hitting the edge of the hotel roof and rolling off it. Now she was plummeting with the men clinging on to her.

One fell away almost immediately, but two continued to paw at her, causing her to drop more heavily than she would normally have.

Falling, falling... Not from a train this time, but—

Jane maneuvered herself around, making sure the soldiers were beneath her. They all bounced off the side of the building, a tangled ball of arms and legs, before hitting the ground. Before everything went black again.

Blackness. Falling and—

Jane snapped herself awake, forced herself to wake up because she knew more men would be trying to find her on the ground. She had no idea whether the two beneath her were alive or dead, nor the other man who'd fallen with them—but she had to get out of there!

The choppers were circling again, no doubt reporting what had occurred.

Jane crawled away, then managed to get to her feet, stumbling sideways and rebounding off the side of the hotel again—this time at ground level.

Then she spotted it. Her means of escape. Jane staggered toward it, bending and tugging it free. More blackness.

By the time the other uniformed men had made it around to this side of the hotel, she was already gone. Leaving the manhole cover aside, leaving them to gather around the tiny hole in the ground that she'd hurled herself into.

To be carried away by the water once more.

"What a fucking absolute shambles!"

Mr. Three's voice echoed off the walls of the office. Nobody responded. "Four dead, including a civilian, six in critical condition. And we still don't know where the fuck our resource is!"

All the outlets had been covered once they realized that she was in the sewers, but there had been no sign at any of them. She'd simply disappeared. Again. They shouldn't have been all that surprised, really; it was what the resource had been trained to do (what made her a resource in the first place). What she'd been trained to *be*. A ghost: a solid, walking-around-punching-and-kicking-people ghost, but a ghost nonetheless. She would go to ground once more now, wait for things to die down a little—but where would she go after that? That was the question.

There was one thing in their favor, and that was no matter how cool the resource kept herself, no matter how much raw meat she consumed, she would be feeling the effects of the lack of treatment before long. Of course, there was no limit to the amount of damage she could cause them all in the meantime. Someone like that, out there, unsupervised...

"Fuck!" Three snapped again for absolutely no reason. "Okay, okay. I don't see that we're being left with many alternatives here, people. Do you?"

"You can't possibly be suggesting..." began Ms. Four, but she didn't finish her sentence.

"I'm *absolutely* suggesting *that*," Three answered.

"But we could end up escalating things," broke in Mr. Nine.

"What do you call Berlin? And, I hate to say I told you so, but... Well, I fucking *told* you so. All of you!" He glared at Four now. "Twice!"

She swallowed dryly, knew exactly what he was driving at. That the resource shouldn't have been sent on her original mission in the first place.

"Suggesting...?" asked Seven, who still hadn't caught up.

"He wants to activate another one." This was Five, who very rarely spoke. Very rarely felt the need to. "Don't you?"

"Yes. I want to fight fire with fire."

"And which—"

"The Salamander," Three stated plainly. "I want to send The Salamander after her."

There was silence again, but Five spoke for the second time in weeks. "Very well. But this is your call, Three. You'll accept the consequences."

Three nodded. He wanted this over and done with now, finished.

As the meeting ended and everyone left the room, he sat down and reached for the phone. Made the call to put his motion into practice.

Then he swallowed dryly himself and hoped to God in Heaven— if there even was one—that he'd done the right thing.

Blackness, blackouts.

Waking.

The falling, the rising up. Breaking the surface again. It was all a cycle these days. Jane was aware she was getting worse: the headaches, the shakes, they were just a part of it. Since Berlin, she'd stuck to the coast, following it around, sticking to the more rural areas once again. She hadn't even been aware of it, but she'd been shot several times during that encounter. It hadn't hurt, hadn't even really slowed her down. But she'd fixed the wounds any- way, breaking into an army surplus store at night, using a mirror to see where the entry points were and pincers to lever out the bullets before stitching herself up.

There had been a hell of a stench, but it wasn't just from the sewer water. It was coming from her, she realized. Her dead body.

It was rotting.

No need to worry about putting antiseptic on the wounds then, but she dressed them anyway. Cleaned herself as best she could with wet wipes, then changed clothes—dark combats and a sweater this time. Took everything she thought she'd need for camping out, like a tent, a really good hunting knife, a flashlight. No need for a campfire either, Jane preferred the cold, and it wasn't as if she'd be cooking anything she caught.

So that's how she'd moved around. Aware that every day, every hour, every moment that passed, her body was breaking down. But she didn't know what to do about that; it had presumably been happening since the train, since the river.

Maybe she should just hide out here and be done with it, wait for nature to take its course, if it ever did. Wouldn't she just end up skin and bone at some point, still aware of what was happening to her?

Answers. She still needed those answers, needed to know who she was, who she'd worked for, and why what had happened happened. Was it part of some kind of experiment, creating unkillable operatives? Super-soldiers?

Who had she been?

In the end, the itching—not a real itch, because her nerve-endings, her pain receptors didn't work anymore—got her moving. The need to scratch the itch in her mind, her brain. She thought about paying someone to smuggle her across into Sweden by boat, heading north. It would have to be under the counter; the IDs and passports would do her no good now. But instead, she found herself drifting sideways, making her way toward the Netherlands. West, always west.

It wasn't until she was on the outskirts of Amsterdam that she realized she was being tracked. Being hunted again. Whoever it was must have picked up her trail from that farm she'd raided, from the animals she'd had no choice but to kill and eat—raw, naturally—because she was starving. Not that there was anything natural about this. As with Aleksander's "friends" back at the start of her little adventure, she'd tried her best to make it look like wild creatures had done it, covering her tracks. But if you knew what you were looking for...

All this time, trying to steer clear of the CCTV cameras that were the bane of modern life, and it had been this slip-up that had flagged her. Her pursuer had picked up her stink, literally, and followed her to the nearest population center; Jane figured she'd stand more chance of losing herself there. Except the people avoided her on the streets, pulling faces and nudging each other. It had been a mistake, this tactic, but too late to rectify.

Ducking into the underground, she'd spotted her shadow, an average-sized but lithe man, moving easily in and out of the crowds. Snaking his way through them. Jane had hopped on a train, only for him to do the same. There would be no shaking him; she realized that.

Jane felt herself flagging, felt the blackness rising. No, she had to stay awake! Had to keep moving.

So she'd jumped off again, letting the sea of people carry her this time, up and out onto the streets, going with the flow. To the nearest car parked by the side of the road. Jane had no time for niceties; she'd smashed the window and hot-wired the thing without batting an eyelid: a small, blue Toyota, adequate for her needs. It got her mobile, or more mobile than the person coming after her, at any rate.

Only he did the same, shadowing her in more ways than one. Stealing his own car, a large silver Seat, to continue the chase. Jane gritted her teeth as she watched him in the rear-view mirror, getting closer and closer, ramming her when he was close enough and nearly sending her spinning off the road. She skidded, braking and turning up a side-street, narrowly avoiding a collision with another vehicle at the other end.

Her shadow caught up with her on the other side, having driven around the building. Speeding up in an effort to ram her again, sideways on, and it was only then that she saw what he looked like up close: his buzzcut, his eyes. Those brown, almost black eyes. Just like hers. Not simply a hunter like her then, but *wrong* like her. She'd known it even as he'd followed her back there in the station, felt it. Another unstoppable thing like Jane, maybe even stronger than her—especially given what had been happening to her corpse in the time since the river. Yet still, she didn't sense that he meant her any harm, not if he could help it.

Jane yanked on the steering wheel, then let it slip through her hands as the Seat clipped the back of her Toyota. "Damn it!" she spat, stamping on the accelerator.

She pushed the speed to its limit, trying to get away. But the Seat easily matched her, ramming her once again, trying to steer her in a certain direction. Steering her onto the wrong side of the road. Jane pulled on the steering wheel again, and the Seat kept going...

Slap bang into the path of an oncoming truck.

The behemoth practically tore the silver vehicle in two. Then, when that had ground to a halt in a flurry of sparks, it was clear the crash had done the same to its driver. The owner of the truck got out, almost throwing up on the spot as she watched that half-a-man drag himself away from the Seat, intestines slipping and slopping out behind him.

"Oh, Jesus! I didn't see... He was—"

Jane was out of her car and telling the woman it wasn't her fault, to go and fetch someone—mainly so she was out of the way. Already there were other drivers getting out of their vehicles, some just wanting a look at what had happened, others wanting to help. She had to be quick.

Walking over to where her pursuer was, she knelt beside him—yet still out of reach in case he tried something. "Who are you? Who sent you?"

The man looked up at her with those black eyes, and she almost felt sorry for him. "S-Salamander," the man hissed.

"Salamander sent you? I don't—"

The man shook his head; Christ, he was a mess! That wasn't what he was trying to say: *He* was the Salamander. A codename. "Who am I then?"

All he did was laugh; it was the most surreal sight.

"What is Tombstone?" Jane demanded next.

The man touched his chest, then pointed at her. There was sorrow in those eyes, an apology for what he had done, perhaps? People were gathering, phones out. Jane needed to get out of there right now. He sighed, this pathetic creature in front of her who refused to die. Like her. Who couldn't be killed in the conventional sense. And it was almost as if he understood what he was at that point. "Look..." he managed. "Look at what they've done to us."

"Who? *Who* has done this?" Jane bent her head closer to his ear. But then she saw the river of petrol pooling. Saw the sparks nearby, this time from the electrics. Realized that their time together was shorter than she thought. "Keep back!" she rose sharply and began shouting, waving her hands. The last thing she needed was more innocent deaths on her conscience. "Get the fuck back! All of you!" Some of the people listened; others just stopped where they were.

Then one spark created a flame, the flame turning into an explosion—and they had no choice but to back off. Run off, some of them. As fire consumed the so-called Salamander. As plumes of smoke rose, concealing Jane's escape.

And she blended in with the blackness of it, letting it take her: a different kind of blackness now. Walking with determination, a newfound hope. Because of what this hunter had told her. A location he'd whispered. An address.

An address where she could find Tombstone.

When the shady figures gathered that day, the talk was of one thing and one thing only.

Mr. Three had been discovered in his office, head back against his leather chair, brains splattered all over it. The gun he'd been chomping on had fallen from his grasp when his arm went limp, dangling by his side. His failure to bring the resource in after ordering the activation of the Salamander would not be tolerated, and he knew that. It had been his call, his responsibility. His price to pay.

Or had it?

In this line of work, you had to wonder whether it had been his choice at all. Failure often meant that whether you wanted to go or not, you were often given a... "push." Fired, in the very real sense of the word.

Of course, they were all involved in this operation—Ms. Four was the one who'd suggested sending the original resource on her mission, which had wound up being "sub optimum"—so they couldn't help wondering who might be next. Perhaps all of them; everybody was expendable here. No one was irreplaceable.

As if to prove that point, Mr. Three walked into the meeting about halfway through, apologizing for his lateness. Not the same Mr. Three, obviously; he hadn't been part of the program, so wasn't likely to rise from the dead (even if he had been, those brains were so much mulch). No, this was another Mr. Three, slightly more even-tempered with a less gruff voice. It was difficult to tell if he looked like the other Mr. Three, as it was so dark in there.

"So, moving forward: options?" he'd asked, seeking their opinions.

No one answered at first, probably because the other Mr. Three had never asked for suggestions—and if he did, he would have dismissed them out of hand. Or maybe it was just because they were fresh out of ideas. Where could you go from there, the debacle that was Amsterdam? The clean-up was still going on from that one.

No, it was difficult to know what to do now except wait. Certainly, sending out yet another resource wasn't on the table, not after the best of them—hunting her, the rogue—had failed. Back to square one again; watch and wait for the resource to crop up again. Or waste away. That was another thing that might happen without access to the treatment.

It was difficult to know what to say because there really was nothing to say. Dead in the water: the recovery mission, all of it. Maybe even Tombstone itself.

All just dead in the water.

⚕⚕⚕⚕⚕

Dead, that's how she felt.

As Jane crawled out of the river, soaked through. Coming full circle, some might say, back to how this had all begun. Not the same river, but a river nonetheless. It was where she'd waited for night to fall, for the cover of darkness. Waiting in the stretch of water Jane had used to get close to the place, the address she'd been given. Waiting in the cold, in the wet.

But that just about summed up this country, didn't it? Wet and cold, yet somehow, strangely, she felt at home here. In England, just outside London, to be precise.

This time she had used the cash from Berlin to buy passage across the water in the hull of a ship transporting petroleum derivatives. Couldn't have been meat again, could it? No such luck.

By the time she was let out at the other end, Jane was starving. She practically fell out!

She was aware of the fact that things were breaking down; her body was breaking down. The fall from the train, the consequences of that finally catching up with her. She'd survived on roadkill as she made her way up toward London, taking the back routes, the occasional kindly motorist offering her a lift. Though not for long, as the smell put them off.

"It's... It's not catching," she promised one white-haired woman who'd stopped. "I'm just..." Jane shook her head. What, dying? Too late for all that, way too late. "Not well," was all she could come up with. That was one way of putting it.

At last, she got close enough to put the first part of her plan into effect. From a map she'd stolen, Jane knew her best bet was to use the river that ran alongside her final destination, letting herself drift down it until she was far enough along. She'd drifted in more ways than one, unconscious for some of the journey, allowing herself to just be taken. Blackness, oblivion. Was it calling to her?

Not yet. Not yet. She'd had to snap herself awake again, though it was getting harder and harder all the time. Jane felt herself slipping away in pieces, bit by bit. She couldn't let that happen, though, not until she'd found her answers. Some of them, at least.

Answers she hoped would be in there. The building beyond those gates, off the beaten track. The next part of her plan had been to climb the walls, jump the gate, but now that she was here, it seemed like an impossible task. Jane just felt so, so weak. How on earth she intended to take out potential guards that might be lurking was anyone's guess. Luckily, there didn't seem to be any—on the perimeter, at any rate—and not long after she arrived, she found the perfect way to get inside.

A car pulled up and stood idling at those gates as the driver got out to key in a code, in much the same way she'd done back at the Lotus to gain access to the safe. While he was doing that, Jane tried the back of the vehicle and found it open, then slipped inside and ducked down. Seconds later, the man got back in, and she heard the sound of the gates opening so he could drive forward.

If he could smell her, he didn't show it. Probably wouldn't, given what he was used to transporting in that car, given he was used to ferrying what she was back and forth all day. It wasn't long before they pulled up again, having traveled along the drive and parked outside the building. Jane waited for the click and the slamming of the driver's side door, waiting again a few moments for him to be clear.

Then she got out of the back of the hearse.

Almost dropped out of the thing, catching herself at the last moment. All of her stealth had abandoned her along with her strength, but again, there were no guards on duty in here. Jane cast a glance sideways, seeing the graveyard there adjoining the building. The funeral home: Tombstone Funeral Home.

The building itself looked like something out of an old black-and-white horror movie; she kept expecting thunder to roll and a bolt of lightning to flash across the sky. But, of course, it didn't; this was the real world, not a movie. Even if it felt like one at times.

Facing front again and holding on to the hearse as she rounded it, Jane noticed that the main door had been left open a crack. Why worry about security, she guessed, when you were sitting behind those walls and that gate. Although she had found out the cemetery was open to the public during office hours, as was the business itself—but it was all just another front, she guessed. More hiding in plain sight.

It was what went on here after office hours that concerned her, the experimentation on people, so the last thing they needed was a plot over there in the ground.

Jane stumbled forward, just about making it to the door unaided. Using it to hold herself up, she pushed it further open, then crept as quietly as she could into the home itself. The foyer was similarly old-fashioned, all dark woods and red velvet. Off to her left was an open-plan room with seats; she squinted and thought she saw a coffin resting on a table at the far end. Before she could investigate further, there was a noise off to her right, and she saw the driver disappearing inside a room there.

Slowly, she followed, because she couldn't really do anything else. The room she found when she eventually got there looked to be a preparation area. Another table positioned in the middle, metal this time, with various medical instruments strewn around. Jars of various liquids filled the shelves—embalming fluids, she assumed. Or something more? Something connected to the experimentation?

No. That would be better hidden than this, surely? Jane's suspicions were confirmed when she heard another noise further ahead, down another corridor. The driver, tapping yet another code into a panel on the wooden wall. A concealed door rolled open, and the man walked quickly through—walked *down,* judging by the sounds of the echoing.

Though it took everything out of her, Jane stumbled toward that door to catch it before it shut again, just making it in time. She heaved it back open again and saw that, yes indeed, there were stairs leading down into the darkness and a faint light beyond that.

A wave of nausea washed over her, a feeling like she was going to pass out.

Not yet! Damn you, not yet! I have to see, I have to know...

Jane straightened herself and began her descent. Once or twice she almost tripped on the steps, nearly pitched forward headlong, but she hung on to the banister for dear— She hung on to it tightly, with everything she had.

It seemed to take forever, but at last she made it to the underground level. Just in time to see the light that had been coming from there go out. Still squinting, she shambled along into the blackness, a state she was more than familiar with by now. She needed to see what was down here, felt that it might explain everything to her about what had been going on. Her fingers found yet another doorway, an opening anyway, and she went inside. Into more darkness.

Before she could even search around for a light, it came on: motion activated, which meant that the driver must have exited the room and it went off on a timer. And, yes, there was yet another opening ahead of her that he must have gone through... But what concerned her more than that was what was in this room.

On the walls were similar instruments to upstairs, similar to the ones in Aleksander's own workshop, in fact: the tools of a mortician, a taxidermist. Here and there were canisters mounted with tubes running from them. And taking up the majority of floorspace, rows of tables, each containing a coffin like the one in the open-plan room above. Some had their lids off, exposing the corpses inside, and some were still nailed on. Indeed, on one, Jane could still see the dirt from when it had been dug up. She frowned again, trying to work out what this meant. Its connection to her, to her predicament.

Only she was distracted by what was on the table in the middle. Like the preparation table she'd already seen, this was definitely meant as a place to work on dead bodies, except this one wasn't empty. There were human remains lying there on top.

Jane inched closer, hanging on to the coffin tables at times to keep her upright. But finally, she made it, was close enough to get a better look at whatever this was. A blackened, crispy husk of a thing, barely human at all in shape, really.

It moved, moaned, and she started.

Didn't mean anything. Very often the dead expelled gases and shifted, groaned. Hadn't she read that somewhere, seen it on TV or in a film? Except this one sounded like it was trying to talk! Not only that, Jane recognized the voice.

It should have been a clue enough that what was left of this body was in two pieces. A set of legs and a top half—a top half she'd last seen crawling from the wreckage of a silver Seat.

"The Salamander," came a voice from the back of the room, and Jane jumped again. Since when was she this nervous? "I believe you two have met?" She peered into the gloom. Was it the driver? No, apparently not. The man—lean, with a suit on, bald except for wisps of hair on either side of his head and a bit of a comb-over—stepped forward but didn't step fully into the light. It was as if he wasn't used to it, almost afraid of it. He was carrying what looked like a metal briefcase. When he gazed at her, his left eyebrow arched and his right eye closed to almost a slit. "And so the prodigal daughter returns," he said after a pause.

"W-Who are you?"

Now he smiled, and it was a chilling sight. "I am known as Mr. Two."

"Mr...." She touched her chest.

"Oh, don't worry, you're not Six. 'I am not a number' and all that. We don't have a Six currently, but I do so love that show." Jane was frowning again; she had no idea what this newcomer was going on about. "You are not a prisoner. You never were. You are paying off a debt. The debt of extra time we handed to you."

"Who am I then?"

"You, my dear, are the Phoenix."

"The—"

"The mythological creature, rising from the ashes. Rebirth. It's all about rebirth, you see. What a pity the poor Salamander doesn't have that particular talent." The tall man nodded to the remains of the hunter from Amsterdam. "We had to clean up the mess you made, the mess one of my colleagues elsewhere made as well. Couldn't just leave him there—too much evidence on the scene—but he'll never really be functional again. Never be of service again. We can fix a lot, but we can't repair that kind of damage. So all we can really do is wait until he...lets go. Drifts away, I suppose."

"I thought... I mean, we can't die, right? You made it so we couldn't. That's why I came back when I was shot, when I fell from the train. Fell into the river back in Poland."

Mr. Two laughed. "Came back? My dear Phoenix—"

"Jane," she interrupted. "Call me Jane." If she was going to be known by an alias, then at least let it be one somebody she gave a shit about had given her.

Two cocked his head. "Jane, is it? Very well... Then, my dear Jane, you didn't 'come back' after the train, after the river."

"But I did; I came back. I was dead. I *am* dead," she argued.

Another laugh. "Haven't you figured it out by now? You were dead long before we sent you on that mission, Phoen... Jane."

"What?"

"I mean, look around you. Where do you think people like you come from? Thanks to this place, we have access to all the resources we need, including a fresh supply of bodies. We bury them, dig them up again, then bring them back." And to illustrate his point, he waved a hand vaguely toward the coffins, open and closed. "You know, people used to believe that if you didn't put lids on, the souls of the dead would escape." He shook his head, and it was unclear whether he himself believed that or not. "We brought *you* back almost a year and a half ago."

Jane had no idea what she'd been thinking this was, that they'd given them something to make sure that even if they were killed in the field, they returned. Super-soldiers, super spies, but not... "Who...who was I before?"

"To answer your first question, though, about Salamander," said Two, changing the subject. "Everyone, every*thing* dies eventually. Especially without access to this." He held up the case for her to see, opening it. The container fell into two halves, both filled with what looked like epi-pens. Whatever was inside those was glowing a strange green color. Jane didn't know what it was, but suddenly her whole being was craving it. "I mean, just look at yourself. You're falling to pieces! It's what, weeks since your last dose? Oh, you're wondering what it is? The formula for the serum was developed back in the eighties by a scientist who went mad because of his creation. They often do, you know. It took us a while to realize what he'd done. To enhance it, refine it. Find a purpose for it. That, combined with the programming and training at Tombstone... Well, you can imagine how useful it could be."

"I-Is that why I can't remember anything? You did that, wiped my memory?"

"None of the subjects really remember who they were before, my dear. Just snatches occasionally, and even then, we try to weed the memories out with conditioning, with therapy. It's not good for them, you see. Not good to remember their lives. Better that they stay on mission. Stay on target."

"Better for you?" growled Jane.

"Better for all concerned. But look at what we give them, what we gave you. Would you prefer nothingness? This way, you're serving your country. Serving the common good. We gave you strength, skills, knowledge. We gave you purpose. Turned you into—"

"Weapons! That's what you're turning us into here. Weapons, which you use for your own selfish purposes," Jane spat.

"Potato, potahto." Two nodded at her, and she frowned again, wondering why. But then realized he wasn't actually nodding at her. There was a presence behind her, two... No, three figures there when she turned, one of them the driver she'd followed inside Tombstone on her left. He grabbed her by the wrist as one of the others clamped a hand onto her shoulder. Even in her weakened condition, it appeared they were afraid of her and what she might do. "The Jackal, the Crow, the Scorpion... You've met them before, too; you just can't recall it. Might sense it, I suppose, like you sensed Salamander, or knew where to go in Berlin." Two tapped his head. "That lucky shot. We lost the feed from your..." Now he tapped his eye. "And the tracker, everything. If only you hadn't been distracted. That was another mistake by my colleagues elsewhere, to send you to complete that particular task."

Jane opened and closed her mouth, then said, "I knew the target, didn't I? It was... I think it was someone I cared about. Who was it?"

Two batted away the question with his free hand, then sort of answered it. "No one you need concern yourself about now. A diplomat."

"Who?" she demanded again. "Who were they? Who am *I*?"

"Soon, you won't care, my dear. Soon, none of that will matter anymore and we can get back to where we were before." Another smile. "You were always meant to return here, would have gravitated towards this location even if Salamander hadn't given you a prod... Oh, that was part of his mission, to direct you home. He wasn't just doing it out of the goodness of his heart!"

"No," Jane said quietly, remembering the look in Salamander's eyes after the crash. "No, I think he wanted me to come back here and stop you. Put an end to all this." And at these words, the burned shape that had once been the Salamander twitched and moaned.

Two laughed harder than he'd done since she came down here. "How do you propose to do that, exactly?"

Another opening and closing of her mouth. Jane didn't have the first clue how she was going to do that.

"Multiple targets."

"Go, girl! Move! Save yourself!"

"Look at yourself! You're falling to—"

Pieces. She was falling to pieces... Jane wrenched her arm away, the one that was being held at the wrist by the driver (the Scorpion?), heard the tearing sound as her left hand was ripped off and fell to the floor. At the same time, she stepped away from the Crow (wasn't it?). The guy who was holding her by the shoulder. Anyway, she felt that part of her body give as well, the flesh there ripping under her jumper. Suddenly she was free, throwing herself forward, heading for Mr. Two at the other end of the room.

He took a step back, shouting, "What are you doing? Stop her!" Two, as thin as he was, could probably have stopped her himself—but she guessed he wasn't used to fighting. Had spent far too long behind a desk or in conference rooms. So much so that when she barreled into him, she knocked him flat on his back.

The open case fell out of his grasp. Jane rolled off him, rolled toward it. Reached out and grabbed the nearest epi-pen inside and snapped it from its housings. Rammed it into her right leg and depressed the end before anyone could stop her.

"My... My dear, please—" mumbled the prone Mr. Two.

"I'm not your fucking dear!" screamed Jane, who could already feel the serum coursing through her. Feel it working to reverse what had been happening to her since Poland. Feel it maker her stronger. Which was good because three of her own contemporaries were now bearing down on her, following Two's orders.

Jackal, the one who'd been standing by while she was grabbed, reached her first. Pulled her up and threw her against the nearest table, knocking a coffin to the ground. Its inhabitant dropped out face-first. For a second, Jane expected him to get up as well, but, of course, they hadn't had the treatment, the programming yet.

They were just prospective Tombstone agents.

Though she didn't really want to hurt any of her opponents, felt that same kinship she'd experienced when the Salamander had been chasing her, it didn't mean she wouldn't defend herself. Jane brought up her right foot, the serum having reached that now, and kicked Jackal full in the face.

It would take more than this to drop three of them, however, and before she had a chance to think about it, Jane brought up the second epi-pen she'd snatched just before being grabbed and stabbed herself in the other thigh. If one injection could do what it had done for them, what would two do? Overdose her? Jane was hoping not, even though she was on the verge of blacking out again.

"Go, girl! Move!"

"Multiple targets!"

Both Crow and Scorpion were on her now, trying to grapple her to the ground. Jackal was rising, pulling a pistol out of his jacket. Jane gritted her teeth, willed herself to stay awake, to feel the double doses of serum inside her. Feel the strength it was giving her, the energy, the way it was fixing her.

She rose, shrugging off the two men like they were nothing. With one hand, she grabbed Jackal's gun arm before he could shoot at her—and the bullet went wild. Tugging on it again, he fired a second shot at the floor, which ricocheted. With her stump, she whacked him in the face a second time, sending him reeling back.

Scorpion came at her from the side, and she managed to avoid his blow easily, headbutting him away. With Crow, she rolled and took out his legs just in time to see where one of the stray bullets had landed. Chipping the side of a canister on the wall, releasing the contents—whatever they were—which promptly jetted out.

The entire room was pandemonium, but Jane did spot Mr. Two escaping back into that room at the far end, out of harm's way. Or so he thought, because another shot was fired, and the gas ignited. It was like the very air was on fire now, slipping and sliding over everything.

Jane bumped into one of her attackers, Crow she thought, and screamed at him to get out. But he grabbed her again, still following the last set of orders he'd been given by his superior. Jane brought both of her arms up, freeing herself. Knew that she had to escape, no matter what the others were doing.

But before she did, she ducked and crawled. Searching for two items. She found the first quickly enough because it was bigger than the second. It took a few minutes more to find the other, which she tucked under her arm, during which time one of the men tripped over her and fell headlong into a coffin that was now on fire.

Grunting, Jane rose. There was nothing more she could do here, and if she stayed, she'd end up like the Salamander. So she ran, out through the main doorway and up the stairs—praying there was a release catch on the secret door.

About halfway up, a hand grabbed her by the ankle, pulling her back. One of the agents, she couldn't tell which now because they were aflame, was still trying to prevent her from leaving. Still trying to "stop her," as Two had barked. Jane twisted and hit him with one of the objects she'd scooped up. There was a satisfying clang, and the figure dropped, rolling over and over down the steps.

Jane got up, headed upward, and didn't even bother searching for a release—simply rammed the door open, knowing it would give because of how strong she was now. Up, rising out of the inferno below. Surfacing, sprinting down the corridor she'd had trouble navigating on her way inside, passing the preparation room, making for the still-open door at the front of the building.

Making it outside, then running so far down the path until she felt she was safe.

The building above didn't take long to catch fire, too, and soon she could see flames licking the windows. Heard another explosion from below, then one above; she hoped there had been no one else inside. No innocents (was there even such a thing as that at Tombstone?). There were so many flammable materials in that place, it would have been a miracle if it hadn't gone up like a bonfire. Jane shied away from the heat, the warmth, just like Mr. Two had done with the light. Embracing the cold night air instead, knowing it was helping the regeneration of her dead body.

It was then and only then that she looked down at the two objects she'd brought with her, one she was carrying and the other still tucked under her arm. The case, folded shut and full of more of the serum—though what she'd taken tonight should last her a good while—and her hand, which she'd re-attach when she got the chance. It would be good as new, thanks to the miracle green drug in her system.

She looked over at the graveyard. There was no time right now to explore, but she'd once been in there. Buried in there. People Jane cared about and who cared about her, who loved her, had mourned at the plot. A father, she wondered, like Aleksander? A family?

Maybe even the diplomat they'd sent her to kill?

Jane had clues to follow; she'd get to the bottom of all this if it... There was more to Tombstone than just this facility, she felt sure.

"My colleagues elsewhere..."

And she'd find them, as well. The other numbers. Wondered absently as she made for the gate—feeling confident she could bound it in one now—if Mr. Two had gotten out of the conflagration behind her. If he had, she'd find him as well. Find whoever was above him, Mr. One: the person really in charge. Make sure this never happened again anywhere. Would make sure the others like her out there, because she knew there would be others like the Salamander, Jackal, Crow, and Scorpion—who all had families themselves that knew nothing of how their loved ones had been used—she'd make sure they found their own peace. And if she ran out of serum in the meantime... Well, she'd find more of that. Or get the stuff analyzed, get more made for herself. Find *all* the answers she was looking for.

"Go, girl!"

Jane knew how she'd got here, knew more than she wanted

to about that. And although she didn't know yet who she really was, she had an identity—identities, plural. She was Ms. Tod. She was the Phoenix, rising (out of flames rather than water this time). She was Jane Doe.

And her story was only just beginning.

Planet of the Dead

Chapter One

It was the discovery of her life. Ironically.

Not the planet itself, which had cropped up during a routine survey of this system. Star scanners, actually, those very "exciting" people who specialize in creating maps of space: cartographers, or a variation of. She'd once been stuck next to one at a dinner party and had almost dropped off listening to him drone on. But, God bless 'em, because without those guys, she wouldn't have had her find. Imagine if it had been scavs who'd come across this place; they'd have stripped it bare—relics from ancient alien civilizations being even more valuable on the black market than those from their own...whatever was left after the last war.

That particular scouting craft had been owned by The Corporation, a conglomerate of all the major businesses that had survived the last 70 years and who had joined forces to basically run the Earth. Unofficially, of course. There were still figureheads—Kings and Queens, Presidents and Prime Ministers, same as always—but everyone knew who really pulled the strings, and who'd probably been pulling them for a lot longer than just the last century. The Corporation was also all over space travel like a rash because it knew how valuable the resources were out there to the people back home.

And, so, it staked its claim on this specific locality: a creamy-red ball a fraction of the size of Earth in the middle of deepest, blackest space, with an atmosphere that was lethal, unfit even for "plough and scatter"—modern slang for terraforming. When teams had been sent down to take a look, they'd reported that a civilization had once lived there but was long gone. Where, nobody really knew. Scans had picked up no signs of bodies, so maybe they had just upped sticks and moved on one day—though they saw very little sign of the kind of technology that would be needed for space travel. Certainly, no "Elastic Drives" like the ones fitted to most ships that journeyed out this far, so-called because, in layman's terms, they stretched the space between two points, and when it snapped back, the vessel was flung to its location. It was faster than normal space travel, but you could still be talking about a year or more for greater distances. There were risks, naturally—it took a lot of calculating to plot the route, some of it the computer making last-minute decisions to avoid obstacles. And obviously, mistakes *were* made from time to time, the same as with anything. You couldn't foresee all the variables; even a chunk of meteor suddenly wandering across its path could damage a ship, if the flight comps weren't fast enough to course correct in time.

The G-forces on the body in order to accomplish such a thing were incredible, as well; therefore, people making the trip had to be cocooned inside a thick, viscous substance that had a very long and complex name but people tended to just call "jelly." Light-hearted techies had been known to joke that the whole pro-cedure was just a trifle, but to those who underwent it—which included the jelly being pumped in as a gas before solidifying and a breathing tube being shoved down your throat while you were placed in suspended animation—the whole palaver was anything but funny.

She didn't find it funny, either. Especially when all your functions were lowered for this kind of hibernation, and the jelly-filled containers looked more like coffins than anything else...

So, anyway, the inhabitants of the planet probably hadn't left. Cremation, then, maybe for those who'd passed away? Would have left one body behind, however, the last of them. Yet the planet was still called what it was called, perhaps because it had absolutely no natural resources they could exploit: Thana. An in-joke, a shortening of Thanatos, who was the Greek personification of Death. Essentially, a dead planet. Or a planet of the dead.

Because of the legal restrictions on buying and selling anything that was found there—the only thing stopping The Corporation from flogging off artifacts, just like the scavs would have done—it was soon deemed pretty much useless.

Only it wasn't to people like her. Enter Dr. Helena Kirby, who'd gotten wind of this planet through the grapevine. With degrees in History and Classics, doctorates in both Archeology and Xeno-Archeology, she was perfectly placed to uncover the hidden secrets of this world—that's what her pitch had been to those running the show anyway. Perhaps something of worth had been overlooked, which would then, in turn, belong to them? At the very least, the information they could gain by studying the civilization would be invaluable to academics around the world. "Exactly *how* valuable?" the suited representative from The Corporation had asked her, wanting the doctor to put some kind of price tag on it. Helena had leaned forward on the table dividing them. "*In*-valuable," she'd repeated.

Perhaps it had been her "persuasive" manner that had sealed the deal—or maybe it had just been pure greed, as she'd also offered them three-quarters of any potential virtu-book and docu-sales to the webworks. Whatever the case, Helena soon found herself in the position of putting a team together for the trip. Just a handful of people she knew, those who she'd worked for and with in the past. This included anthropologist Dr. Anna Blackwell, a scarily intelligent woman who also happened to have the figure and good looks of a model, blonde hair and blue eyes to match.

Something Jay Musgrove, a history and archeology lecturer at the University of Haddenberg could definitely appreciate—one of the finest in his field, he was also unfortunately a bit of a throwback to the previous century where males were concerned. For Musgrove, it was almost as if the equality acts of the 2060s had never even happened. Helena also added her research assistant, a young Asian post-grad by the name of Kelso, to the list—who coincidentally had a flair for linguistics. His sense of wonder at the sites they'd visited together never ceased to amaze Helena, and she figured this would be a massive opportunity for him. Finally, she'd had to include Professor Douglas Grable—a former boss and associate, and probably the one person who knew her best in the whole world. He should, too; they'd been engaged for a while back in the day.

Douglas had taught her so much during their time together, touring the wonders of the ancient world; he had been a mentor to Helena in a lot of ways. But he'd also taught her a more valuable lesson—*invaluable*, if you like—when he'd cheated on her... several times, with several different women (just one of his "addictions"). Taught her that she preferred the company of the dead to the living, that where matters of the heart were concerned, you could trust them so much more. That they would never, ever hurt you like the living could.

"You'll be okay," he once said. "You're a survivor, Hel."

He was right, but she'd *had* to be. He'd *forced* her to be.

Oh, they'd got past it eventually and moved on with their lives—had stayed in touch, and even became friends again after a fashion when she could see Doug had cleaned up his act—but it was still there, floating between them, unmentioned. Nevertheless, she could think of no one else who was more qualified to be part of her team—and this trip was business all the way.

Add to that the crew of their ship, not a bad lot as far as Corporation people went, although from what she could gather, they were independent contractors hired by that organization: Captain Nathanial Wayne, whose beanie was apparently glued to his head and who smoked what looked like *actual* cigarettes, rather than the synth-versions that had replaced e-cigs in the late 2020s as the substitute of choice; bearded pilot Rod "Handles" Hannigan, who was also on navigation duties; Med-technician Dr. Susan Rains; Security Officer Meghan "Meg" Thomas, who boasted more muscles than any man Helena had ever seen; Rafferty, the Engineer, a second-gen clone who was covered in grime and oil from head to toe, the only clean bit being where his goggles had protected his eyes; and Science Officer Phil Burch, who was so thin a draft from a hand fan could probably blow him over. Her team had been introduced to the crew of the *Artemis*—which looked from the outside, from their shuttle, for all the world like a concrete slab with engines—when they boarded the vessel itself. Sorry, *herself*, as Wayne would no doubt have corrected her.

Drinks in the rec-room the evening before setting off was their preferred method of getting to know one another—although anti-social Rafferty had left after about five minutes. Helena knew exactly how he felt; it was her idea of Hell. "Are you sure you should be drinking so much on the eve of our mission?" she'd asked both Wayne and Hannigan, who'd looked blankly at her, then at each other. Their reply, which hadn't exactly instilled confidence in her, had been to knock back more of the whiskey, then head off to play holo-pool at the nearby table, grabbing tabs and extending hard-light versions of old-fashioned wooden cues.

Helena had caught Susan Rains on the way to the toilet, her chocolate-colored ringlets loose and cascading over the shoulders of her flight-suit, and she'd asked her the same thing. "Aww, let them have their fun for now. They'll be total pros tomorrow; I guarantee it." When Helena pulled a face at this, Susan added, "Look, after you've flown as many times as we have, you'll need a stiff drink before you set off. Trust me." And that, ladies and gentlemen, was the ship's physician. About as far away from a McCoy or a Franklin as you could get.

But then, this whole operation was about as far away from those classic sci-fi shows that Helena remembered from her childhood—illegal downloads, what was left of the entertainment industry from the 20th century.

"A stiff drink or…something else," Rains added, nodding toward the bar, where both Musgrove—hair slicked back, which made him look sweaty rather than trendy, especially with his fleshy face—and Kelso were vying for the attention of Anna Blackwell. They'd be lucky! As would Rains, it seemed, when Meg Thomas came along and linked arms with her, planting a kiss on her cheek.

Helena was shaking her head and turning back toward the direction of the captain and pilot when she bumped into Douglas. She hadn't had much to say to him at the briefing, nor on the way up here, but now it seemed they couldn't really avoid speaking to one-another. "Helena," he began. "I… Well, I just wanted to say thank you, really. For asking me to be a part of this."

She nodded. "You're the best person for the job, Doug. Simple as that."

"The chance to explore an entirely new society, its culture, religion…" There was that faraway twinkle in his eye, the one that used to melt her heart; now it simply gave her heart*burn*.

"Technically, it's not a *new* society. Far from it," Helena corrected, brushing back a lock of her raven hair over one ear.

He laughed. "You know what I mean. So…looking forward to the big New Year's bash when we get back home?" He was talking about the turn-of-the-century parties that were already being planned on Earth. To be honest, she'd been intent on just staying in with a couple of bottles of wine and reading a good book; if you listened to all the doom-and-gloom merchants, it was going to be the end of the world anyway. Y2K all over again apparently, the end of civilization as they knew it. Helena shrugged; she understood all too well what he was trying to get at, though. Was she looking forward to the celebrations…with anyone in particular? "Listen, can I get you something to—"

Helena held up a hand to stop him in his tracks. "I'm good, thanks. Going to have an early night, I think."

Douglas nodded. "You know, Artemis is the Goddess of the Hunt," he said then.

"Yes, *of course* I knew that," she answered back a bit too quickly. "I'm not stupid, Doug." It was perhaps a little uncalled for, but part of her was flashing back to when he used to point things out on digs—and she was no longer his "student," if she ever really had been. She was the one in charge now. Luckily, he didn't seem to take it personally, was in a more philosophical frame of mind than spoiling for a fight.

"I wonder what we shall find when we get to the end of *this* hunt? Seeking, always seeking."

"Well, on that note…" Helena began to walk away from him but dared a look back over her shoulder as she did so. Only to see that Doug was also making his way toward Anna to join her fan club. "Men," she said, sighing, then continued on to her quarters.

She barely slept that night and began to think maybe she'd been too hasty about that drink after all. Too excited and nervous to even keep her eyes closed for more than a few moments at a time. Perhaps a couple of belts would have put her under; perhaps that was why people like Wayne and Hannigan did it as well. And before Helena knew it, the alarm was going off. Time to put themselves to sleep and be hurled into the depths of space.

Seeking, always seeking…

The next thing Helena remembered was a feeling of suffocation, of being smothered. Of *dying,* in fact. But it was just a consequence of being released from the "jelly," from the coffins, the trace memory of being inside it. Helena was freezing, shaking, and was glad when a blanket had been placed around her. "Easy," Rains told the woman as she opened her blurry eyes. "Give it a moment or two." Helena tried to speak but couldn't; she started rubbing her sore throat. "A side-effect of the oxy-tube. That'll wear off too soon enough. Welcome back to the land of the living!"

Helena had been told that the experience was a lot like being born again, but in actuality, Rains hadn't been far off. It was more like rising from the dead. One by one, they'd all gone through it, starting with the *Artemis* crew, and it had been several hours before they'd felt like themselves again. By that time, they were on a trajectory to land on Thana.

"This is your captain speaking. We are about to land at Planet of the Dead airport," Wayne had quipped over the internal comms.

"The current weather is shitty, and local time is fuck knows. Please strap yourselves in, and thank you for flying *Artemis* airlines."

"Funny guy," said Anna, who was sitting next to Helena in one of the side-lounges, but she wasn't sure whether the woman was being sarcastic or not.

However, they hadn't so much landed as flopped down on the planet like an old man in a bathtub—after riding through some of the worst atmospherics, Hannigan said later, that he'd ever encountered. "You're lucky I got us down in one piece," the pilot commented, switching off the swearing that was coming through the mic from Rafferty down in the engine room. "I could barely see the hand in front of my face!" Down they were, though, except their rough landing had caused a few side-effects itself.

No sooner were they on the surface and the *Artemis* had stopped rattling, than it began to shake again. "What the...?" asked Musgrove as they started to gather in the cockpit.

"We must have triggered a seismic shift when we landed... and I use the term loosely," Science Officer Phil Burch explained, glancing pointedly at Hannigan. When Musgrove looked slightly puzzled, Burch added, "An earthquake."

"Yes, I'm not an idiot," Musgrove snapped.

They rode it out, a large tremor followed by several aftershocks—Helena commenting that she hoped it hadn't damaged any of the structures they were here to examine. "How is it going to damage a bunch of ruins?" asked Meg Thomas.

Helena had let out a long breath, reminding herself that not everyone was here for the same thing. To security personnel like that woman, this was just another freelancing gig. Money in the bank. And time to them, as it was to The Corporation, equaled money.

So, they'd wasted no more of it by immediately heading off to the first of the sites, a small settlement north of where they'd touched down. They'd all donned their enviro-suits, and Hannigan had driven Helena, Doug, Musgrove, Anna, and Kelso there in the hover-bus. Naturally, Helena had studied the recordings made by people who'd mapped this planet back when they'd first encountered it, but none of that had prepared her for the beauty—yes, beauty!—of the environment and structures they saw that day. No styrofoam rocks, no balsa wood sets here. Small buildings, it had to be said, possibly some kind of farming community, but they were constructed out of a natural substance that seemed to be everywhere here and resembled ivory. Indeed, it looked exactly like a village made from bone. Furniture, too, the remains of chairs, tables—even some cutlery.

To the trained eye, this place told the story of a deeply religious, meditative people; Doug, Anna, and Helena all agreed that the simple but decorative building at the heart of this particular community was a place of worship.

"What do you think happened to this civilization?" said Anna, asking the obvious question through the proximity comms they were using.

"That," replied Helena and Doug, almost as one, "is what we're here to try and find out."

Kelso, too, when he wasn't marveling at all this, was put to work trying to decipher the language these people had used. "There are definite comparisons to be drawn between it and Tamil, but with some hieroglyphics in the mix, too, and a smattering of ancient Babylonian," he concluded after examining what there were of signs and, in some instances, remnants of bone-like tablets that appeared to have been used for writing on. The people who'd done the initial surveys of Thana hadn't given a shit about any of that.

"How long before you can get a rough alphabet worked out?" Helena had enquired.

"Depends on what we find in the other localities, which may have used an altogether different language. But I wouldn't think more than a couple of weeks, if we're lucky." He'd beamed then and thanked her again for bringing him along on this one. "I can't tell you how grateful I am!"

"My pleasure," Helena had replied. "Now it's time to earn your keep." She'd patted him on the shoulder through the enviro-suit, and he'd nodded eagerly.

Over the course of the last few days, they'd taken in three or four of these tiny settlements—one of them in the shadow of a range of mountains that looked like they had vague faces carved into them—working their way toward what was probably the largest city on Thana. It had been Helena's turn to marvel this time because the architecture, albeit in a state of decay, was magnificent.

The building that seemed to be the hub of this city, another place of worship, had a spire that twisted round and around—cracked at certain points but still awe-inspiring. She caught herself as she walked through the gates toward the structure, her mouth dropping wide open. And when Kelso simply said, "Wow!" she couldn't have agreed with him more.

On that particular expedition were Helena and her assistant, Musgrove and Doug, plus Meg Thomas—pistol holster strapped to her leg—and Susan Rains tagging along behind. They'd only been in the building for something like ten–twenty minutes when they felt it. The tremble of another 'quake. Not a big one, more like a delayed aftershock—although it had taken its sweet time after the initial one from the landing (they'd experienced a handful since their arrival, but quite early on). Nevertheless, it was enough to cause a section of the bone ceiling to fall in. If Doug hadn't pulled Meghan out of the way, she could have been seriously injured. As it was, a fist-sized chunk of the ceiling caught her on the upper arm, causing Dr. Rains to dash across and start fussing over her once the trembles had subsided.

"Thank Christ it didn't penetrate the enviro-suit! I'm going to get Meg back to the bus, though," Rains told Helena, looking up and around nervously. "I wouldn't hang about much longer here either, if I were you."

On their way out, the security woman had nodded her thanks to Doug, who'd acknowledged this with a tip of the head. "I think you might have an admirer there," Helena said, joining him.

"Oh, I really don't think I'm her type," Doug replied with a smirk.

It was as Helena turned, gathering her people to do exactly what the doctor ordered and get them the hell out of there, that she spotted it. There was a crack now in the base of the altar down at the far end. She moved forward, and Doug caught her arm. "Are you crazy? What if we get more activity?"

But she wasn't listening to him; she was lost—drawn toward the hole that had been created. She'd switched on her helm-torch as she moved, was pointing it at the darkness of the fissure. And no, she hadn't been mistaken at all; there was a set of steps! Hidden under the altar, for whatever reason.

In Helena's experience, the hidden always meant secrets. Secrets to be uncovered.

Seeking...

Doug was calling to her again; in fact, he was following Helena now—perhaps in an effort to drag her back. He stopped when he saw what had caught her eye. They were soon joined by Kelso and Musgrove.

"What's... What's down there?" asked Kelso tentatively.

"I don't know," answered Helena, looking back over her shoulder and almost blinding him with the torch. "Want to find out?"

What had been down there turned out to be the discovery of her life. Of all their lives.

What had been down there were the catacombs beneath Thana.

Beneath the Planet of the Dead.

Chapter Two

They didn't spend that long underground the first time. Another tremor could happen at any moment—they'd really fucked up the planet with that landing—so they didn't want to linger too long before heading back to the transport (where Rains was no doubt finishing patching up her lover).

It was enough to get a sense of what was down there, the snaking corridors in both directions, a system of tunnels that none of the scans had ever picked up, possibly because of the nature of the bone-like substance used for the flooring in the church and the creation of this place.

"Gives me the fucking creeps," Musgrove had commented, looking all around him at the low ceilings, the walls, as they opted to explore the closest shaft. "Isn't this bothering you at all?"

Helena shrugged. "No different from the caves I used to explore near where I grew up," she explained. No different from some of the places she'd explored in her career, either.

They hadn't gone very far when they spotted it: a solid barrier, another entrance of some kind with what looked like a release mechanism to one side. Above the door was more writing in that alien language Kelso had been attempting to get his head around. Helena gestured for her assistant to come forward and pointed toward the message. "Yep, I'm on it; just give me a second..." He scanned the text with his wrist monitor and punched a few of the virtual buttons. "Those are...prayers, I think," Kelso said, his turn to point at the archway. "Not unusual given the apparent nature of the indigenous population. But this bit here is looking like...'Behold' something or other. Definitely 'Wanderers,' that's what that symbol means." He gestured toward one marking in particular. "And, yes, I'm fairly sure that means 'treasure'." Kelso looked up then, realizing what he'd said *as* he said it; looked at each of his colleagues in turn. "Obviously, I haven't finished my work on their alphabet yet," he added. "So—"

"Treasure?" Musgrove mused. If he could have got to his chin through the plexi-glass of the enviro-suit's helmet, he would have been rubbing it. "Then what are we waiting for?" He reached for the release mechanism. Helena reached out as well, grabbed his wrist, and shook her head.

"We need to do more research first," she told him. "Plus, we've already been gone too long. Rains might come back to see what the hold-up is."

"She's got a point," Doug said then. "They're working for The Corporation. If they realize there's something down here that's actually worth anything..."

"We won't get a chance to study it properly," Helena completed for him. "We need to ascertain what exactly we're dealing with first before we bring them into it. That's what we're here for, after all."

She'd made a strong case, and Musgrove reluctantly nodded.

So, not long after that, they'd retraced their steps up the corridor, up the stairs, and returned to the bus—though not before Doug had leaned in and whispered to Helena, "Looks like the huntress really has found something this time."

Seeking, always seeking...

Meg Thomas's wounds had been minor, easily treatable, but Rains nevertheless took her to the med-wing when they got back on board the *Artemis*—once they'd gone through decontamination— just to give her the once-over. That warranted a "I'll *bet* she's giving her the once-over," from Musgrove. The man might have been vital to their team, but he really was a pig.

Once Anna, who'd been examining her own findings back on the ship, had been filled in about what they'd found, they'd taken their evening meal with the rest of the crew—minus Rafferty, who always ate on his own—in the mess hall. As the re-hydro'd food had been passed around, the conversation was muted, on their side at least—especially when Phil Burch asked if any of their findings so far had been significant. *By significant, does he mean lucrative?* Helena wondered. She couldn't really blame people who worked for The Corporation to be enquiring about it; she'd sold the whole trip on that, when all was said and done. But then again, had she actually expected to find something of monetary value beyond the black market price that would be paid for "ordinary" alien artifacts? Helena certainly hadn't been expecting to hit paydirt, to find "treasure," whatever form that took. The Corporation might ruin what could be a significant xeno-archeological find by wading into somewhere looking to make a quick buck.

So the question put her on edge right from the start. "Er, depends how you define significant. We're finding out an awful lot about this civilization that we didn't know. Its culture and religion." She went on to talk about statues that they'd discovered, works of art carved out of the bone-like material that seemed so common on this world, and the fact that their kind of worship apparently involved meditation and was rooted very much in the cerebral.

"We've found extensive evidence to suggest crystals were used in their 'churches'," Anna chipped in—ever the anthropologist. "They were a contemplative sort of people. Peaceful, it would appear. We haven't found a single weapon yet."

"If only we could say the same about our species," Doug commented, taking a drink of his protein shake.

"What about a monetary system?" This was Science Officer Phil again. "Coins, bullion?"

The research team exchanged glances, but it was Musgrove who answered this one. "Surely if there'd been anything like that, it would have cropped up on previous surveys?"

Phil tipped his head, conceding the point.

"Some sort of barter system then, perhaps?" Anna suggested.

"Maybe..." offered Doug. "That would seem the most logical conclusion. Certainly, a people as spiritual as these apparently were wouldn't hold much truck with material wealth."

And with that, the conversation moved on—various separate chats opening up within the group. Helena, who was sitting near the captain, told him about her plans to return to the city and continue their exploration.

"Are you sure that's a good idea, after what happened there today?" he asked her.

"I-I think it's worth the risk."

"One of my crew ended up in the med-wing, Doctor."

"Yes, yes I know, but—"

"In fact, and don't take this the wrong way, are you sure *any* of this is worth the risk?"

Helena paused before answering. "It was our landing that set off these tremors in the first place."

"Have you ever thought that's just nature's way of saying we shouldn't be here?" he asked her, taking out an old-fashioned silver zippo lighter and igniting another one of those cigarettes that looked far too real for her liking. Where in Christ's name was he even getting those from?

"Look, Captain, we've come all this way. You're getting paid."

"Not enough, trust me." A typical Corporation man—or maybe

just a typical hired-hand attitude in general? When it came right down to it, the bottom line was always money. Had been historically for a very long time. Too long, if you asked Helena.

"Captain, are you going to okay another trip to the city or not?" She hated that she even had to ask permission, but it wasn't on her ticket. Helena could never have raised the funds on her own; back on Earth, stuff like this wasn't exactly top priority. Even the resources needed to explore their own world had dried up, let alone civilizations nobody had heard of, that no one gave a flying crap about.

He sighed. "I'll tell you what, I'll take you myself—personally. All right? I wouldn't want another member of my crew putting themselves in harm's way again."

"Fair enough," Helena said, although she wasn't particularly happy that it was Wayne coming with them this time. Since the initial "getting to know you" evening, she'd come to realize he wasn't as slipshod as he pretended to be, only used the humor to mask what she suspected was quite a keen mind. The captain was nobody's fool, and the chances of them being left alone to check out more of that underground network were slim. If nothing else, he might suspect *something* was going on.

Helena thought about coming clean, even up to the moment when they disembarked the bus to return to the "church," as Anna had called it. But instead, stuck with the strategy they'd come up with after the meal. That Anna had even suggested.

"Let me take care of the captain," she told Helena. "I can distract him while you guys gather your samples or whatever."

So that's what they'd done, leaving Anna to chat with Wayne out in the open while they headed inside, Musgrove and Doug taking the lead—Helena and Kelso bringing up the rear, mainly because she wanted to make sure the captain wasn't about to change direction and follow them inside.

"Are you sure about this?" her assistant asked, a riff on what Wayne himself had asked at the meal—only this time Kelso meant deceiving that same man.

Helena wanted to nod, but the more she thought about it,

the less she was actually sure about anything. In the end, it didn't really matter because events took it out of her hands.

"Dr. Kirby... Hold up there!" It was Wayne, who'd managed to detach himself from Anna and was jogging toward them. All Anna could do was shrug, one of Helena's usual responses.

"Shit," said Helena under her breath, quietly enough it wasn't picked up through the prox-comm, then, "Yes?" turning to face Wayne, heading him off at the pass before he could get to the entrance of the church. He still had that beanie on, even under the enviro-suit helmet. Helena had to look twice to check he wasn't smoking inside there as well.

"Could I have a word?"

"Sure."

"Privately," said Wayne, glancing in Kelso's direction.

She nodded for her assistant to go and join the others, out of prox-comm range, while the captain took her to one side. "What is it?"

"*What is it?* Do you think I was born yesterday, Doctor?"

Helena shook her head. "No, of course not."

"All right, so let's cut the bullshit, shall we? What are you hiding?"

"Hiding?" asked Helena with a bit too much of a hitch in her voice. She wasn't the only one who was good at uncovering secrets, it seemed.

"Come on. I suspected as much last night, but the bit with Marylyn Monroe back there fluttering her eyelashes at me was the final straw."

"I can assure you, Dr. Blackwell is—"

"Trying to divert my attention...in the nicest possible way, I have to admit. So come on, time to spill."

Helena sighed, and if she could reach her face, she would have rubbed her forehead rather than her chin. "Okay, look, we found—"

She didn't have time to get any more words out before another tremor hit. At least it felt like a tremor, but it was coming from a more localized spot. Underneath the church. They both turned and peered inside. A fountain of what looked like cloudy wind jetted from the opening at the altar.

"What the fuck?" was all Wayne managed before they were knocked over by it. Kelso had already been batted aside as he made his way toward that part of the building. Then, as quickly as the wind had whipped up, it vanished again.

The captain managed to scramble back to his feet first, then helped Helena to hers. "What the fuck was that?" he asked, finally able to finish his sentence. But Helena couldn't answer, didn't have a clue.

Instead, she whispered Kelso's name, going over to the young man to check on him, Wayne not far behind. Her assistant was sitting up, dazed, but otherwise looked okay. He held up a thumb to indicate that he was all right. Anna had joined them by this time, and they were all looking towards the hole at the altar.

"What is that? Was that there before?" Wayne demanded, then glanced around. "And where are Dr. Musgrove and Professor Grable?"

Helena hesitated, then pointed at the gap in the altar. The captain walked over and, spotting the steps there, he leaned in tentatively, slowly.

Then something grabbed him by the front, tugging at his enviro-suit. Helena sucked in a breath, shocked, before recognizing the person reaching out of the darkness as Doug.

"Mus-Musgrove," was all he could muster before collapsing onto the top step.

Wayne gestured for the others to help move him, freeing Doug from the hole. Then they turned the Professor onto his back and checked his vitals on the suit's monitoring system. "He's all right," said Wayne. "Stay with him," he ordered Anna, then added politely, "please."

She nodded, crouching down beside the man.

"You two, come with me," he said. Wayne flicked on his helm-torch and headed down the steps, even though he had no way of knowing what waited for him; Helena and Kelso followed. The captain lit the way, looking left and right when he got to the bottom, sucking in a breath himself when he first saw the cata-combs. "Jesus Christ!" he gasped, turning to Helena. "So this is what you were trying to keep from me. From us." And by that, he meant the rest of the crew, only enforcing the divide that was widening by the second.

"Only because—"

Wayne held up a hand to silence Helena. "Save it for later," he told her. "Which way?"

She guessed that the men had headed back toward the door again and pointed. Sure enough, when they rounded that corner, they saw the prone body. Saw the hairline crack in the clear face-plate of his helmet. "God..." said Helena bending over him.

"We need to get him back to the bus," said Wayne, stating the obvious. "He hasn't got long. Kelso, grab an arm and help me!"

The young man did as he was told, and they pulled Musgrove to his feet, then began dragging him along the corridor toward the steps that would take them back up into the church again.

Helena rose, was about to follow when she saw that the door was now open. "Musgrove, you bloody idiot!" He'd opened the sealed chamber—that's where the wind had come from. Opened it and paid the price. No treasure was worth that, not if you weren't around to enjoy it.

She should have trailed the men back, but Helena found her-self being drawn to the doorway that was now gaping wide. Drawn through it, flashing her own helm-torch around.

What she saw in there almost made her take a step backward.

There was treasure, all right—just not the kind Musgrove had probably been expecting. Nor the kind The Corporation might be interested in either, really.

I wonder what we shall find when we get to the end of this hunt...

But it explained a lot. Explained everything, actually, about what had happened to the people of this world. Where they'd van-ished to.

Because Helena saw row upon row of horizontal, hollowed-out spaces in the walls. Each one was rectangular, and the more she focused, the more she could see what was inside every single one. People, lying flat—naked, humanoid people, with hands resting on their stomachs. The holes were their versions of coffins. There were bodies, at long last.

The bodies of Thana's dead.

Chapter Three

Helena hadn't kept the new discovery from Wayne—quite apart from anything else, it was too big to hide. There were too many of the hollowed-out holes, too many corpses. And there was no way any of her team would be coming back here on their own ever again.

But it did mean she had to be ready to defend her position, to try and buy some time before Wayne alerted The Corporation about what they'd found and this whole thing turned into a circus.

So, once they were back on the *Artemis*, Helena had shown him the hastily filmed vid-footage she'd taken just after the captain and Kelso had carried Musgrove back to the bus; that moron was now in the med-wing, stable but unconscious. Her thinking had been that Wayne would watch it and see what she saw, something that needed to be preserved and studied carefully. That could be the key to unlocking what actually happened here. But as he'd taken in those remains, his brow had creased, hand snaking under his beanie to scratch his head.

"Did you know these were down there? Did your friend Musgrove?" he demanded.

She knew why he was asking, but Helena had shaken her head. "He must have pressed the release mechanism for the door, maybe by accident." More lies, more secrets—and she didn't say anything about Kelso's translation. About the treasure.

"Well, we're going to have to let the bosses know right away before—"

Helena held up a hand to cut him off. "Look, just wait a second."

"Wait for what?"

"We need time to properly study all this. Document it, categorize. It's a delicate business."

"Oh, it's definitely a business; you got that right, Doctor. And I'm not about to jeopardize my crew's earnings on this one by ignoring protocol." Definitely not the laid-back man she'd thought he was when she first met him, not where being paid was concerned, anyway. "Phil's going to have to take samples first, send everything back for analysis. Then we—"

"Samples?"

"Who knows what those eggheads at home might be able to get from this kind of material." He tapped the screen as one of the bodies hoved into view, brown and wrinkled, skin like tanned leather; Helena's helm-cam moved up to the face then, long and skeletal, with protruding cheekbones and a massive cranium, a tiny nose that was little more than a couple of slits, eyes sunken but shut. Definitely alien. Turned out they were the treasure after all and did have a price tag on them as far as The Corporation was concerned—just like everything else. "You know the score. We may even have to ship a couple back."

"Captain, we need to start an examination of the site *immediately*. We don't know how long we've got before those bodies start to break down."

Wayne lit up a cigarette with his zippo, cupping his hand over the end regardless of the fact there was no wind. He blew a stream of smoke out the side of his mouth. "You were the one who just said we needed to wait, Doctor. Besides, those things look in pretty good shape to me. They've kept all right for this long."

Helena wafted the smoke away from her. "I meant wait and not contaminate the find, your people going in and causing God knows what kinds of damage! And I'm only guessing, going from what happened when Musgrove opened the door, but I think that room might have been hermetically sealed. The reason those bodies are still in such good condition is because they haven't been exposed to the elements. Who knows how long we've got now before they—"

"All the more reason to crack on and get those samples," he told her. "Keep the people who're paying our way out here happy." A reminder, as if she needed it, of how she'd been able to drum up the cash to get to Thana in the first place. She wasn't in charge at all. They were.

Helena shook her head in despair. "Just give us a day, a few hours at least." Wayne looked at her, then sucked on his cigarette. "*Please.*"

The captain sighed, letting out more of the trapped smoke. "Okay, okay. I guess a couple of hours won't hurt."

She'd beamed. "Thank you. Thanks so much!"

"But listen, Phil's going with you just in case things do start to go wrong with them. I insist on that. Oh, and Rafferty's going to have to jury rig something to stabilize the church and the tunnels. Too many people have been hurt already for my liking on this mission."

Helena nodded, not really listening to the rest after the green light—already speeding off to get her people together.

"Don't make me regret this," Wayne called out after her.

But she was the one who ended up regretting things in the end, the way Wayne's crew got under their feet a preview of what would happen once The Corporation heard about the burial chamber. Rafferty went in first, the filthy-looking man having crouched in the corner of the bus all the way there like some sort of animal, not saying a thing to anyone. He returned an hour or so later, thumbing back toward the building, his mission completed. He'd set up an energy net in the church itself to stop any more bits of it from falling onto people, and what looked like buffers modeled on the tech the hover bus used as kind of struts or props down in the catacombs themselves: columns of yellow energy that would stop various sections of the tunnels from caving in should there be another tremor. He'd also sorted out free-standing lights down there so they didn't have to rely on torches anymore.

After that, Helena had hoped they'd be left alone to get on with things—but no such luck. Not only was Phil Burch there, hovering over them like a vulture after carrion, waiting for his crack at the corpses, but also newly-recovered security woman Meg Thomas, doing an impression of an altogether different bird and watching them like a hawk. In fairness, Burch was probably just keen to examine these specimens on a scientific level, might not even be thinking about what The Corporation could get out of them. Thomas, however, was definitely there to protect the investment.

Helena's team had done their best to work around it, unloading the tools they might need—including laser-shovels and sonic brushes—filming everything with their helm-cams as they went. Kelso made notes on the carvings in here once he'd stopped gaping, more than likely the names of the dead, but also possibly their status within this society; something Anna was also helping them work out. "None of them are set apart from any of the others," she'd noted. "No leaders, kings, or heads of state. Unless we haven't come across those yet... *Hey!*" Anna said loudly, then looked over her shoulder, suddenly aware she might have activated her proximity-comm and drawn the attention of the captain's people. She hadn't, and she now switched off her cam before speaking again to Helena—who'd also killed her vid-feed. "It's just occurred to me... What if there are more of these sites scattered all over? Maybe even underneath the other places of worship we found?"

It was a distinct possibility, Helena thought. After all, this area couldn't possibly contain every single person who'd died on Thana, could it? The planet was tiny compared to theirs, but even so.

"If that's the case, we might have a few more bites at the cherry," Doug said, joining them. The professor had been shaken up by what had happened here before, but informed Helena that no way were they coming back without him. He was concentrating on more of those crystals they'd found in here, on the floor, in the "graves" with the bodies. "Other tombs that have yet to be discovered and opened."

"Well, let's not put that particular idea in our friends' heads just y—"

"What's with the meeting over here?" asked Meg, wandering

across, the prox-comm kicking in so they could hear her.

Helena shrugged. "Oh, you know, boring, old archeology stuff."

The security woman brought her wrist up, looked at the clock display, and tapped it. "If I were you guys, I'd get a move on. Captain said to get you back to the ship by eight." With her other hand, she tapped the butt of the pistol in the holster hanging at her side. What was she planning to do, shoot them if they didn't finish up in time?

"But we've barely got started here," argued Doug. Meg said nothing in reply—simply folded her arms.

"Come on," Helena said, pulling him away, "she's right. Let's do what we can in the time we have left."

"*Definitely* not her type," muttered Doug when he was far enough away. "Ungrateful as well."

"This is ridiculous," Anna piped up. "It would take weeks in here to do what we need to do."

She was right, of course, but what choice did they have? For all Helena knew, the captain might even have caved and contacted The Corporation already. What really didn't sit right with her, however, was the fact that her group was to be taken back to the *Artemis* by Hannigan while Burch and Thomas stayed behind. That certainly hadn't been part of the deal with the captain, not that it had been much of a bargain in the first place.

But again, their hands were tied. She just had to hope that Anna and Doug were right. That there might be more of these sites on Thana that The Corporation couldn't mess up before they had a chance to do a proper examination.

More of the dead on this planet that was named after them.

Chapter Four

Science Officer Philip Burch had to admit he'd been relieved when the archeological team cleared out.

Wasn't that he didn't like them as such—some of them seemed

like genuinely nice people. He'd had a good old chat with that guy Grable, for example, the evening before they'd set off for this planet. Found out they had a love of cricket in common, which had been an ice-breaker. The kid, too, Kelso; harmless enough, with an endearing puppy dog-like enthusiasm he'd once had himself starting out. And their "leader," Dr. Kirby—she certainly stood her ground when it came to her beliefs. Not as obviously attractive as the blonde woman, Blackwell, but a striking lady nevertheless. Someone he could see himself with at some point, if his vocation didn't continually keep getting in the way. But God, imagine what two people together would be like who were obsessed with what they did, especially when they were coming at things from two completely different angles.

That's what he struggled with, if he was being honest. While they were always looking to the past, uncovering how people—and alien races—might have lived, *he* was constantly looking toward the future. About what these kinds of discoveries might mean for their own race going forward. Who cared about what sort of society these people had lived in? That was gone, long gone. What mattered now was, could they be of benefit to human beings? He'd never subscribed to the whole "if you don't learn from history, you're doomed to make the same mistakes" theory. People still made the same mistakes whatever the past was supposed to teach them.

No, what mattered was any one thing in this race's physiology might be the key to unlocking the cure for something like Barrington's disease, that cruel illness which attacked both the body and the mind. Could be all kinds of breakthroughs just waiting to happen, could prevent needless deaths, help the blind to see or the deaf to hear without the need for complex implants. That's what concerned him, what was important to him. Vaccines might be developed to prevent the spread of wide-scale viruses, or techniques to extend life even more. That way, he might not have had to say goodbye to both his parents before he'd even turned forty. Yes, they'd had him late in life and had both died of "natural causes," but they might both still be here if something like that had been on hand to help.

Of course, the flip side of all this was the fact that weapons could be derived from what they'd found on this planet. Biological weapons, like the ones that had been used in the latter stages of the last war. But that had been the bane of scientists throughout the ages, their research constantly being stolen and used for more sinister purposes than it was intended; sold off to the highest bidder. It shouldn't stop you from trying, from doing what you felt was right yourself, should it? Doing your job, essentially; doing what you were trained to do. To Philip—he hated Phil, though people kept insisting on calling him that; in particular, their captain—the positives far outweighed the negatives. Kirby had her beliefs, he had his, and he stood by them in much the same way she did.

Which was why, once her team had gone and he was given the opportunity to examine these bodies himself, he quickly began to take his samples. For one thing, the doctor had been right when she told the captain they'd start to decay now that the chamber they were in was open. Philip could see it happening, the skin turning from brown to gray in places, wrinkling even more than when they'd first arrived there. He made his judgment call, got out the tools of his particular trade—laser-scalpel to slice into skin and muscle, tweezers to place what he'd detached into containers that would be temperature-regulated. Everything would be examined in greater detail back on the *Artemis*, reports generated and sent off, giving the scientists that would follow him a head start on what they were dealing with. With a bit of luck, they might even let him stay on and be a part of that group. It could be his chance to finally be noticed, a way off the ship, and a full-time job that didn't involve bumming around the universe with his fellow no-hopers.

Stop that, he told himself. *It isn't about recognition, getting ahead. Remember why you're doing this!*

He'd nodded to himself and got on with the task at hand, which was removing a nail from a dead alien's finger. Everything "bagged and tagged," as his old tutor used to say, though he'd had a background working for the police. Same principle, though; this was evidence of a different kind. Evidence that the future could be a much better one.

"Everything going okay?" asked a voice from behind Philip, which made him start. He was nervous at the best of times, but being down here surrounded by what was left of this race... The science officer looked over at Meghan Thomas. She cut a more imposing figure than most men and then some, but he'd always got on well with her—and so welcomed the woman's company while he was working. Felt a lot safer with her present than not.

Philip nodded. "Y-Yes, fine, thanks. Getting everything we need, I think."

"Good, good." The dead didn't seem to bother Meg at all, and if they did, she certainly hadn't shown it. He wondered then, and not for the first time, if she'd ever killed anyone herself. Could probably have done it with her bare hands. Might even have enjoyed it. "Do you mind if I ask you something?" she said next.

He shook his head now. "Not at all."

"What do you make of this place?" she asked.

"*This* place, you mean?" asked Philip, waving a hand around to show he meant the chamber they were standing in.

"No, this planet. This whole mission, in fact."

Philip didn't really know how to answer that. "It... Well, it is what it is. Hopefully, something good will come of it all." He gestured then to the samples in the container.

"Hhmm," Meg said. "I've had a bad feeling about it since the get-go. Nurse-maiding a bunch of Indiana Jones wannabes that—"

"Indian who?" he asked.

She flapped a hand. "Just some old movies me and my brothers used to watch on pirated downloads. He was a history guy, always getting into fixes."

"Ah," said Philip, not having the faintest idea what she was talking about. As for the bad feeling, he doubted whether having a chunk of masonry fall on you would help put your mind at ease on that score. Meg was lucky it hadn't been worse. Still, having Dr. Rains with her must have taken the edge off. It was just Philip's luck that the only two women on board his ship were in a relationship with each other.

"You know, getting into shit with cursed objects and whatever," the security officer continued.

"You think this place is *cursed*?" asked Philip. He hadn't realized Meg was so superstitious.

"I never said that," she backtracked. "Just, well, just that I've had a bad feeling."

"I can't say I—" he began but never got the chance to finish. The floor beneath them started to tremble, and the surrounding walls shook.

Meg looked up. "Another fucking 'quake!"

Philip's eyes flashed over at the energy columns Rafferty had planted in the doorway, working hard as bits of dust and stone chips fell. The top of the door seemed to bow, but the props were holding. For now. "We'd better check the others," Meg said, grabbing Philip by the hand and pulling him toward the exit; he barely had time to snatch up his samples container. He knew why she needed him with her, to fix anything that might be wrong with the supports; it wasn't really in her wheelhouse to do that.

As the rumbles continued, they went around and checked the other energy columns to make sure they were holding. One or two were flickering but seemed to be doing their job. Philip was bending to examine a final, more extreme case that was fizzing, attending to the mechanism at its base, when Meg said, "Hold on! You hear that?"

Philip cocked an ear but couldn't hear a thing through his external audio; he'd been too focused on the beam in front of him to have heard anything before. "I-I don't..."

Meg wandered away, and when he called out to her, she said, "Stay here; I'll be back in a sec."

He began to protest, but it was already too late—Meg had turned a corner and was gone. Philip should have gone after her, caught her up, but he was in the middle of making sure the prop didn't suddenly pack up on them. By the time he was done and trotted off down the tunnel after Meg, there was no sign of her. He called out her name but got nothing in return—totally out of range.

This was not good. Not good at all.

Meghan Thomas knew full well what people thought of her.

It wasn't really surprising; the image of the tough—butch even—security chief who didn't take any crap and let nothing at all faze her was one she'd cultivated herself for a long time. Had started building it up when she was little, surrounded by four brothers who all liked to tease her. She'd had to toughen up to survive in that family, become a tomboy just to get by. It was something that had just carried on into her adult life as well.

Shouldn't necessarily follow that she'd be into girls, though— but in her case, it just happened that she was. Had realized as early as those gym classes with Mrs. Verger, had silently joined in with the boys at her mixed school ogling the woman who had a body that might make you want to turn gay even if you weren't. Meg often thought about the teacher, even to this day, fantasized about her even though she'd probably be pushing sixty now. In her head, that image of her climbing up the ropes to demonstrate what she wanted them to do was a fixed point in time. A perfect, frozen moment.

Meg had never been what you'd call academically minded, one of the reasons—she guessed—why she resented people like the ones they were babysitting. While those she knew like that had gone off into fancy, high-paying careers, she'd ended up working in a series of dead-end jobs until she landed the bouncer position at a club on the East side of the town where she'd grown up. She hadn't really needed to know much about self-defense for that one but had attended classes anyway—and found she had an aptitude for it. It wasn't about hurting people, wasn't that at all; if Meg could defuse a situation without using violence, she would. Even as a last resort, she prided herself on the fact she could send troublemakers on their way with a minimum of bother. It was one of the reasons she hadn't gravitated toward the military, like her father had suggested, where she would definitely have been called upon to use more than just an arm-lock to deal with her opponents. Contrary to popular belief, she didn't actually like guns. Although rarely seen without her sidearm, she'd only had cause to draw it on a handful of occasions, and only then to threaten, to fire off a warning shot to calm things down.

While she was working in the club, she applied for the post of security at a large warehouse. Meg had worked her way up from junior to head of her section in the space of five years. That particular warehouse had been owned by The Corporation—she never did find out what was in all those boxes—and someone somewhere had recognized her talents. It wasn't long before she was being contracted out, being sent all over to manage teams of security personnel. She was getting paid a decent amount of money for it as well, didn't feel quite so inadequate compared to the boffins who were on top salaries.

Then, a few years ago, they'd asked her if she'd like to do some work "off world." Not something she'd ever really considered up to that point. Meg had never been one of those kids who dreamed about being an astronaut. But it was another step up in the pay department, and the training would be minimal. It wasn't like she'd be expected to fly the spaceships or anything; good job, too. So, she'd become attached to the *Artemis*—had gone through the motions of being interviewed, then accepted on staff, as if she was a freelancer, when, in fact, she was a Corporation girl through and through. Owed them a lot because they were the ones who'd really given her a direction in life. There would be no people working under her, but then that kept things simple. It would just be her, and she'd be in charge of all the security aspects of the ship and the missions. More of a position of trust than ever before, actually.

So she'd flown around the galaxy with these people, had even developed a respect for the likes of Phil Burch with his science degrees. A respect for Susan Rains as well, the ship's doctor. More than respect, as it turned out. She wasn't quite sure what it was they had together yet, as it was still relatively new—a year was new, right?—but it was more than simply sex, that was for sure.

Oh, it had started out like that, some innocent flirting and then hooking up one night when both of them were slammed on some kind of rum substitute they'd picked up on Station Zero-Nine—90 proof the guy had said, made it himself.

Meg suspected that it might even be love, or something approaching it, though she was loath to put herself in that position after what had happened with her last few partners. She'd rushed in, got hurt; acted in haste, and repented at leisure and all that. Meg was determined to take it slow with Rains, even gave the impression sometimes that they were still casual. That they weren't exclusive. Seriously, why did that woman even still give her the time of day?

The way she'd looked after her when that chunk of church roof had struck her had been above and beyond the call. Though Meg supposed she owed that Grable guy, too, for pushing her out of the way. Not bad for one of the tweed jacket brigade, and she felt bad about the way she'd dug her heels in back there about sticking to the time limit. But those had been the captain's orders—he'd already given them more leeway than she might have done, and especially after Kirby had hidden the entrance to this place from him initially. They'd had their turn, and now it was Phil Burch's, The Corporation's turn.

Except in the process of taking his samples, they'd experienced another one of those tremors. Bloody Handles and his shitty landings... The way they'd dropped down on this planet was still having an effect even now. His fault she'd been injured. His fault this last one had shaken the catacombs. Meg had been waiting for the other foot to fall this entire time. She might give the impression of someone who took everything in their stride, when in reality, she was probably more of a bag of nerves than Phil—quaking in his boots just because she'd spoken to him back in that tomb. She was just better at hiding it—mostly. Had told him about her bad feelings, though. Admitted that much, at least.

"You think this place is cursed*?"*

That had made her stop and think. Maybe she did. Maybe it was. They always were in those old movies with that guy something or other Ford and his hat. Also, in those old films, you never, ever went off to explore noises on your own. That was a big no-no. But off she'd gone, hearing something vague down one of those corridors through externals. Movement, echoes reaching them? Her sense of loyalty to the company that had given her a fresh start overriding those feelings of dread.

Leaving Phil to finish securing the columns, she'd gone to check it out—and now Meg wished she'd left things well enough alone. The light only extended so far down here, especially now she'd made several turns, so she'd switched to her helm-torch—and immediately saw something, shadows shifting ahead of her.

"All right, who's—" she began, using the helm-mic before realizing it was *her* shadow on the wall of the tunnel. Imagination playing tricks on her. These old catacombs... She was willing to bet they made noises all day long. Just things settling again after the tremor. It was only to be expected. And just where the fuck was she anyway? Meg realized suddenly she didn't know. She'd been following the sounds without thinking about how she might find her way back to the church's crypt. There were none of Rafferty's energy columns here, either, should there be another "seismic shift." Nothing to stop more rock from falling on her now.

But then there was another, more distinctive noise that drew her attention. The echo made it sound like it was coming from everywhere at once, all around her. Made it sound like ghosts, if she'd believed in such a thing. The spirits of the dead that they'd disturbed. The Ark opened up, and things that shouldn't exist let loose... She shook her head—complete and utter bullshit!

Meg drew her pistol. She might not have liked firearms, but there was something comforting—especially in that particular moment—about having one in her hand. "Phil?" she called out through the prox-comm, thinking maybe it was the science officer and he'd ignored her instruction to remain where he was. *Hoped* it was him—except she didn't want to shoot the poor sod accidentally.

The strange noise filtered through her externals once more, and she spun around, her torch creating more shadows as she looked left and right. Only...only one wasn't hers. This one was real. She saw it, heard it move. A scuffling sound accompanying the action, something fast.

"Hey... Hey, you fucker!" she shouted in a tone that usually stopped people dead in their tracks. They didn't know her bark was worse than her bite. "Stand still!"

More movement, off to the side of her. The left-hand side, or was it the right? She couldn't tell, especially hearing it second-hand like this. Dizzy from trying to pinpoint the source of the movement, Meg struggled to keep her balance.

The attack, when it came, was swift, and she pressed the trigger on her pistol, letting loose a concentrated plasma beam. She shot wide, however, missing whatever this was completely, hitting the wall instead, dislodging bits of it.

Meg attempted to use those self-defense techniques she'd learned so long ago, treating this as if it was another rowdy thrill-seeker from a club she had to subdue. Realizing at the last moment, when it was absolutely too late, that it would take more than those moves to pacify whatever was grabbing at her.

Then came the pain, so severe she let out a scream. Agony that seemed to be coming from different parts of her body at once, something sharp tearing through her enviro-suit. Tearing into her skin.

Everything went black—and Meg thought: *This is it, I'm dead. The real curse of the Planet of the Dead!* But it was her helm-torch that had actually died.

More sharpness, more pain, and this time it was in different places as the "something" that was plaguing her skirted around. She fell to the floor, clutching for it; she couldn't tell what it was made from through her gloves. One second solid, the next nothing at all. This shadow made flesh, this...ghost.

Meg was aware of the blood she was losing from several wounds now, could feel it escaping, pooling around her. It was so stupid, as well-built as she was, as strong as she was, all that energy was swiftly deserting her like water from a leaky bucket. She wished Rains was there. Wished that *anyone* was with her.

But Rains would know what to do, would be able to patch her up.

Then there was no point thinking about such things because everything went black for a second time, darkness upon darkness. But it wasn't the torch, wasn't the absence of any kind of light source.

It was because Meg was finally losing consciousness.

Chapter Five

Helena had barely had time to get back, grab something to eat, and get into another argument with Captain Wayne in the rec-room when the emergency call came through.

She'd started off trying to reason with the man once again, pleading for more time on the off-chance he might give it to them; Doug and Anna's words back at the church were haunting her. "Look," he'd said in reply, another cigarette—much smaller, sucked down to the filter—sticking out of the side of his mouth. "I gave you those hours you wanted. What more do you want?"

"Where would you like me to start?" she'd said, exasperated. "For one thing, I wasn't expecting your science officer to stay on there alone to do God knows what."

"He's not alone; Meg Thomas is with him."

"Now, don't get me started on her! We felt like we were being scrutinized the whole time we were working!"

Wayne couldn't help a chuckle. "That's just how Meg is."

"A cast-iron bitch?" said Helena, the words out before she could help it. She hadn't meant to say them, and they were borne out of tiredness and frustration, but once they were in the wild...

"Hey, you don't get to speak that way about my crew!" Wayne retorted, jabbing a finger in her direction. He stubbed out the tiny cigarette and immediately lit another with his zippo.

"If it hadn't been for Doug...Professor Grable, she'd be under a pile of rubble right now," Helena reminded him.

"And I'm sure she's thankful," he said, blowing out smoke.

"They're good people, Doctor Kirby. Every single one of them."

"Corporation people," Helena replied.

"We were *hired* by the fucking Corporation! We're on a bloody retainer for them. They're the ones who've made it possible for you to come on this little jaunt, Doctor!"

"Jaunt? *Jaunt?*" Helena said through gritted teeth. He made it sound like some sort of holiday. A trip to the Lunar Biosphere for a break! This was nothing more than a joke to Wayne and his people, what they did no more than a side-effect of making money. But then, what else had she expected?

Wayne held up his hands, a gesture of placation. "I didn't mean it like that. Christ... I don't know what you want me to do, Doctor! It was my job to get you here, and things were going pretty well I thought, until you started hiding shit. Then you come to me with...with this, with a fuck-ton of dead aliens, and expect me not to report it to the people I have a binding legal contract with. Expect me to put you and your people first? We're not just some glorified taxi service, you know. Our jobs matter as well!"

"*Glorified?*" Helena snorted.

"You two should just go and find a room already," commented Rains, who happened to be passing by the rec-room and had heard all the shouting. Both of them stopped their "conversation" and stared at her. "I mean, you sound like an old married couple anyway. Might as well have the fun bit, too."

"Susan..." Wayne had begun, stepping toward her, but the woman was already on her way to wherever she'd been going.

When the captain turned back to Helena, she could feel her cheeks reddening. Couldn't help it. "Don't flatter yourself," she said, a knee-jerk reaction to cover the embarrassment.

He removed the cigarette, put it out on the edge of a table, and placed what was left of it behind his ear. Then he let out a slow breath. "Doctor, can we just start again? My people are good people, I'm sure yours are as well. So am I, as it happens— though if you talk to any of my exes, you might get a different side of the story." Wayne attempted a smile. "I understand why you hid the find from me. I understand where you're coming from, wanting to examine the site, believe it or not. But you've got to meet me halfway. I thought you already had."

It was Helena's turn to sigh. "It's not your fault. I know that. You're just doing what you think is right, doing what you have to do."

"Yep," said Wayne. "Doesn't make it any easier to swallow, though, does it?"

"No. No, it doesn't."

"But we *are* in this together, whether you like it or not. And I'll do my best not to let this turn into some kind of sideshow; I know how important it is to you, anyone can see that." He wandered over to the bar area. "Here, let me get you a drink. I think we have some of the good stuff back here somewhere."

Helena looked at him sideways. "So, you're trying to get me drunk now?"

Wayne's expression was priceless, like a rabbit caught in the headlights. "No, I... That wasn't what... I just thought perhaps we could both use a belt."

"Relax," she said, putting him out of his misery. "I was just teasing."

Wayne laughed, dragged out a couple of glasses and a bottle of brown liquid, then poured two generous measures. He walked back and handed one to her, gestured for her to sit down at the table before joining her. He held up his glass. "Here's to... Well, here's to...to something."

She clinked his tumbler, took a sip, and immediately began coughing. "The *good* stuff?" wheezed Helena.

"It's a sliding scale," he informed her. "It'll put hair on your chest, though."

"My hair's fine where it is, thanks." Helena jabbed her glass toward him, toward the top of his head. "There's something I've been meaning to ask you. Don't you ever take that bloody hat off?"

Wayne grinned. "Only on certain special occasions."

There was a cough then, and Helena almost spilled her drink. Doug was standing in the doorway to the rec-room now. How long he'd been loitering before alerting them to his presence was any-one's guess. "Not interrupting anything, am I?"

"No...*no*," they both said in unison, shaking their heads.

He paused, then seemed to suddenly remember why he was there. "Hannigan sent me to try and find you," he said by way of an explanation. "Apparently, your comm is off."

"Oh, wonder why I did that," replied Wayne.

"Well, anyway, you're needed on the bridge. Some sort of emergency." Wayne frowned, looked across at Helena, who was doing the same.

"What now?" asked the captain.

"Phil... Phil, slow down. I can't make any sense of what you're saying to me."

That was what greeted them as they stepped onto the bridge, Hannigan attempting to calm down a clearly distraught Phil Burch—audio only, and even that was crackly.

"Lost... Screaming!" was what came back, though whether the gaps were due to the man's mental state or the poorness of the signal was unclear.

Helena and Doug watched as the captain leaned over Hanni-gan's station, depressing a button. "Phil? Phil, can you hear me? It's Wayne. What's happened? Who's lost? You?"

There was silence for a minute or two, and he looked back over his shoulder at the archeologists, a worried expression on his face.

"...have to come quickly!" the long-range comm spat back sud-denly, making them jump. "Meg... don't know where..." Then that word again: "*Screaming!*" They'd made that out plain enough.

"Listen, Phil, what's happened? Has there been some sort of accident?" Silence again. "Where are you now? Still in the cata-combs?" It would explain why the signal was so atrocious.

"...fucking joking!... church..."

So, he was above ground. Whatever had happened, whatever

caused the screaming, had forced him back out into the building above the tunnels.

"We're on our way," the captain said, flicking the switch off. "Handles, get a hold of Susan and tell her to meet me at the bus." He made to step past his audience, but Helena barred his way.

"We're coming, too," she told him; it wasn't a request. When he looked like he was going to say no, Helena reminded him, "We're in this together, remember?"

"All right, all right—I haven't got time to argue. You'd better get ready as well, then. Let's go and see what all this is about."

Chapter Six

They'd seen what it was about, all right.

The bus carrying Helena, Doug, Rains, Kelso—who they'd bumped into on the way to the loading dock—and driven by Wayne hadn't even come to a standstill outside the church when the figure of Phil Burch rushed to meet them. You couldn't really mistake him for anyone else with that lanky frame, even in his enviro-suit. He was clutching something to him, what looked like a samples container.

Suited up themselves now, they'd opened the door to the bus and Susan Rains had virtually caught him in her arms as he stumbled towards her. "Phil, what the hell's happened? Where's Meg?"

"I-I don't know," the science officer replied, breath coming in gasps.

"What do you mean you don't know where she is?" asked the captain, appearing behind her, Helena and the rest stepping out after him.

"Is she okay?" this was Rains again, a hitch in her voice.

Phil shook his head inside the helmet, though whether that meant no or he just didn't know wasn't clear.

Rains grabbed hold of him by the shoulders. "Phil, take it easy. Tell us what happened."

He slowed his breathing, nodded, then told them about the tremor, about how Meg had gone off somewhere while he was attempting to stabilize one of Rafferty's energy columns. "Said she heard something, I assumed through her externals, but I didn't... Next thing I knew, she was gone."

"What do you mean, gone?" asked Wayne.

"I mean, she was *gone!*" said Phil, regaining some of his composure. "She'd vanished. I tried to look for her, but... And then I heard the screaming through my own speakers, not prox-comms, so it must have been loud! Such terrible..." His eyes were wide as he remembered. "She said she had a bad feeling, but I didn't listen. Didn't..." His words trailed off.

Helena caught the concerned look between Rains and Wayne. They had to get down there and find out what had happened for themselves. Phil was no use, didn't know anything; he was clutching that container to his chest like it was his firstborn or a comfort blanket. Wayne told him to wait in the bus, that they were going to search the catacombs for Meg, and he just stared blankly at the captain.

"Come on," he told the group after Rains retrieved her medi-kit from the bus, and they headed in the direction Phil Burch had just come from. Into the church, then through the gap at the altar, down the steps.

Rains suggested they split up to cover more ground, but Wayne pointed out that was a good way to lose more of the team. He put his hand on the physician's shoulder and said, "Don't worry, we'll find her."

Seeking, always seeking, thought Helena.

Phil had given them a starting point, however, told them which direction Meg had gone off in, so they began there. Wayne placed markers on the walls so they wouldn't get *themselves* lost, and as they made their way through the snaking corridors, they called out the security chief's name over and over using their helm-mics. There was no reply, neither on externals nor prox-comms. When they eventually turned a corner and found her, it came as something of a shock. Not just the sudden discovery of the body on the floor, but also the state it was in. Helena had to admit she wasn't sure at first that it even *was* a person, a human being. It looked... Mangled was the only word to describe what had happened to it. Limbs bent out of shape, helmet cracked, enviro-suit ripped in several places. And *so* much blood. Kelso turned a shade of green, leaned against the wall.

"Slow down your breathing," Helena told him. "You really don't want to be sick inside there."

Rains, who'd been at the back, was the last to see it. Wayne tried to stop her from going any further, but she pushed past him. "Oh... Oh God," she whispered.

"Is it...?" asked Doug. "Is it her? Thomas?"

Rains went to the body, got down on her hands and knees beside it, fighting back the tears. "I think we can take that as a yes," Wayne said.

If that really was Meghan Thomas, if those really were her remains, Helena felt bad now about the things she'd said back on the ship. The woman had only been doing her job. She looked over and saw Doug's face, knew he was thinking the same thing about what he'd said: that he wished he'd let her get crushed by the rubble. And glancing across now at the parts of the wall that had broken off and fallen, thinking perhaps that wish had come true.

"Susan," said Wayne, moving forward and putting a hand on her shoulder again. "Susan, I think maybe we should be looking at getting Meg back to the bus," he suggested in a kind voice.

"S-Shouldn't we leave her where she is," said Kelso, who'd recovered a little but was still facing away from the scene. "You know, for evidence or whatever. An investigation?"

"Evidence?" Doug said. "You think someone *did* that?" When Kelso refused to answer, the professor continued: "This isn't a murder mystery, lad. It was an accident."

"*Shut up!*" snapped Susan Rains suddenly. "Shut up! Shut up! Shut up! All of you!"

There was silence that lasted for a good minute or more. Probably the reason they all jumped at what happened next.

The body moved. Twitched. Let out a breath, a moan.

"Jesus!" spluttered Wayne. "She's still alive!"

Rains was over her lover in seconds, checking the woman's vitals. "What...what kind of a doctor am I? To just... I just thought..."

Thank Christ it didn't penetrate the enviro-suit...

"Susan?" asked the captain.

"I'm getting a pulse," she told him, not able to disguise the pure joy in her voice. "Weak, but it's there. We need to get her back to the bus," the woman said, parroting what the captain had himself said when he thought they were dealing with a corpse.

From the medi-pack, she produced a hypo, which she pumped into the bloodied figure through one of the tears in the suit.

"The pain she must be in," gasped Helena.

"Here, give me a hand with this," said Rains, digging something else out and unfurling it. Some sort of sheeting that immediately went rigid. It had handholds at each end and was the length of an average person. A portable stretcher, which Wayne then helped Rains load the security officer onto. She moaned as they did so, whispering something.

At the same time, Kelso had spotted an object on the ground near where he was. Helena saw him bend and pick it up. Meg Thomas's sidearm, the one she was never seen without. He handed the weapon over to Wayne, still keeping his own eyes averted.

The captain looked at the pistol for a second, then tucked it into his belt. He got down, ready to help Rains lift the stretcher. "Wait, hold on a second," the doctor said to him. "I think Meg's trying to speak. What? What is it, sweetheart?"

Helena almost started crying herself at that. When all was said and done, these two people were partners. She couldn't even imagine what Susan Rains was feeling right now. The woman stood back, frowning, as Doug went to the other end of the stretcher to help Wayne heft up the patient.

Helena asked the obvious question: "What did she say?"

Rains gaped at her. "Just one thing, over and over. Sounded like, 'ghost.'"

"Come on," said the captain, facing front, arms back, and

hands in the gaps provided. "We need to get her back as soon as possible."

They all began retracing their steps, following the markers to the way out, Susan Rains running parallel to the stretcher, holding Meg Thomas's hand as best she could.

But Helena kept turning that word over and over in her mind. It was impossible, made no sense at all. Was Meg trying to identify her attacker? Was she trying to say that what did this to her had been the unthinkable?

That it really had been a ghost?

Chapter Seven

They'd loaded Meg onto the bus, accompanied by Phil Burch's cries when he saw her, his gibberings that she had been right and he hadn't listened to her.

"Something bad. Bad feeling. A curse. She said it!"

"Is he going to be all right?" asked Doug.

"I think so," Wayne replied. "He's just in shock."

"Aren't we all," Kelso chipped in.

The captain elected to remain behind, but only because Helena said she and her team were staying put.

"We...we are?" This was Kelso again.

"Well, *I* am," she told him. "I need to check that the site is still intact. That there was no damage." She exchanged a glance with the captain, and added, "From the tremor."

"But what about, you know...?"

The ghost, Kelso meant—although they didn't even really know that's what she'd said. Could have been anything in her condition.

"I'd advise against this; we should stick together. But I don't have time for another debate," said Wayne. "And I know you're not going to change your mind, so..." He drew the pistol from his belt, and for a moment, she thought he was going to threaten them, load them onto the bus at gunpoint. Instead, he turned the gun around and handed it to Helena. Then he disappeared inside the vehicle for a minute or two and emerged with a larger version of the gun she was holding, a rifle designed to the same specs. "So I'm going to have to stick around."

He asked Rains if she was okay to drive back, and her answer was, "Try and stop me!" She just wanted to get her lover to the *Artemis* and get her some treatment. If—and it was a big if as far as Helena was concerned because she didn't even understand how anyone could survive those fissures in the enviro-suit, let alone the injuries—if Meg survived, then they might get a few answers. But it was more likely that they'd find them down there, back in the catacombs.

"If either of you wants to go with the bus, then speak now or forever hold your peace," she told Doug and Kelso. The professor said he'd stay with her, and—probably because he didn't want to look like a wimp in front of them all—Kelso chose to remain, as well. "Okay then," Helena said, nodding to Wayne, who shut the door to the bus and banged its side. Moments later it rose and was away, speeding Meg Thomas toward the ship. It would be sent back for them as soon as the patient was settled; they'd been left with a bag of spare oxy-pods in case any of them should run out.

"Poor woman," said Doug as they walked, obviously still feeling the guilt. "Such a terrible accident."

"But was it?" asked the captain.

"You don't think so?"

"You saw the debris, the rubble, same as I did. That stuff was nowhere near her."

"Then what—"

"All I know is Meg had drawn her gun, and it had been discharged. I'm willing to bet it was what caused that section of wall to crumble rather than the tremors." Doug said nothing in response, so Wayne turned his attention to Helena. "Doctor, is it possible some sort of defense mechanism might have been triggered when the door to the chamber was opened?"

"How do you mean, like a booby trap?"

He shook his head. "Something that could have been released, that might have done that to Meg? Something to do with that strange wind?"

She thought about it for a moment, remembered that Meg wasn't the only person to have been injured so far; Musgrove was still out of it in the med-wing, though he'd probably earned that. "I-I just don't know. Anything's possible, I suppose. This *is* an alien planet."

"Or maybe some sort of animal living down there," Wayne offered. "After all, the original scans of this place didn't pick up the dead bodies, so maybe they missed something alive as well?"

"Something indigenous to this planet, you mean?" Helena shrugged. "Also possible; those tunnels look like they go on for miles." And more plausible than—

"Or perhaps it's just a vengeful spirit, like the woman said." They all turned and looked at Kelso. "Hey, my culture's full of them. They call them onryō, or yūrei: a ghost that can do harm to the living."

Whatever it was certainly did harm to Thomas, thought Helena.

"So, you're asking us to believe that this...ghost, or *ghosts* plural, wanted vengeance for us disturbing the burial site?" Doug asked, a mocking tone to his voice. "That they're the spirits of the people in the crypt?"

"A lot of ancient civilizations believed that the soul departed from the body when it died," Helena pointed out, playing devil's advocate. "And these *were* a spiritual people."

"There are no such things as ghosts," said Wayne with the kind of certainty usually reserved for death and taxes. "If whatever did that to Meg shows its ugly face, though..." He patted the side of his rifle.

Maybe his reasons for staying with them weren't as simple as safeguarding The Corporation's investment at all, or even safeguarding them, Helena pondered.

I'm sure she's thankful. They're good people, Doctor Kirby— every single one of them.

Good people who deserved what? Justice? Revenge?

"I feel better already knowing that you're here to protect us, Captain," Doug said.

The sarcasm wasn't lost on Wayne. "You were the ones who wanted to stick around, Professor," was his answer to that.

"Boys, boys," said Helena. "Enough." She had never liked pissing contests, especially when she might be partly responsible for some of that testosterone flying around. Besides, they'd reached the entrance to the underworld again, returning to the place of the dead even though they'd already rescued Eurydice. Helena held out her hand: "After you, James T."

Wayne looked confused, and she told him not to worry about it. There was a reason for leading the way—the captain had the largest weapon (and no doubt he would have made some light-hearted comment about that under different circumstances...circumstances like those back in the rec-room). If there really was something to be worried about running around in those cata-combs...

The captain ventured down into the half-light, and one by one, they followed, not knowing what awaited them below this time.

⨯ ⨯⨯⨯⨯ ⨯

They were at the entrance but were being denied access.

The bus had made good time back to the *Artemis*, Susan with her foot down on the pedal, driving like a mad person—probably pushing the engine more than it (and Rafferty, no doubt) would have preferred.

Every few seconds she would peer into the back of the vehicle to check on Meg, who was now hooked up to a bank of monitors that would tell Susan if there was any change in her condition. Phil Burch, for his part, seemed calmer than he had been back at the church. He was sitting with the patient and apologizing over and over. For not getting to her quickly enough? For not lis-tening? Susan didn't have the faintest idea. If she knew Meg— and she did, intimately—then she would have insisted on going off to check out the noise alone anyway. She would've wanted to keep Phil out of harm's way, but she also wouldn't want to have to think about another person's safety if she came up against something. A pity she hadn't thought about her own more.

That wasn't fair, and Susan chastised herself for it. Meg was the security officer; it was her job to look into anything suspicious. She knew the risks. Susan knew them as well, but it didn't mean she liked them. She spent countless hours worrying about something happening to Meg on a mission, like when she was on protection duties and they'd been delivering those replacement turbines to The Corporation colony on Beta 3. There was every chance of them being attacked by opportunistic scavs on the planet itself, but once again Susan had to remain on the ship, driving herself crazy until she knew her lover was okay again.

What the scavengers would have done to the security officer was nothing compared to what had actually happened here today. On a planet they'd been told was uninhabited. What was it that professor had said: an accident? Believed that the section of wall had caused those injuries. Rubbish! Even without a thorough examination, Susan could tell they weren't the result of any kind of trauma from falling rocks or stones—like they were when she'd treated Meg after the church incident. She didn't yet know what *could* have caused such a thing—that would come later, as the young assistant Kelso had said, an investigation. All she was bothered about at the moment was getting Meg to the med-wing and getting her stabilized.

What was stopping her was Hannigan.

He'd been alerted to the situation but wouldn't let them inside the *Artemis* without going through the hour-long decontamination process. Time Meg Thomas didn't have.

"This isn't like Musgrove. Her enviro-suit's been severely compromised," he said to Susan.

"Tell me something I don't know! Handles, look—I need to get her serious treatment *right now* or she's going to die. Do you understand?"

"I do, but regs is regs, Doc."

"You weren't saying that when I helped you smuggle that

Martian ale on board, were you?"

Hannigan groaned. "That's one thing; this is another. Bringing Meg on board could expose us to God knows what." Better that she die than him, in other words. "You, of all people, should know that. Or would if you were thinking clearly." Meaning it wasn't just the enviro-suit that had been compromised.

"For fuck's sake, Handles!"

The doors to the cargo bay remained closed. She might as well have been Kanute screaming at the sea. Then, suddenly, a chink in the armor. A glimmer of light as the huge rectangles of gray metal began to part, Moses now and the Red Sea—although Susan had absolutely no clue why.

"T-Thank you," she started to say to Handles, but the swearing that came back over the comm told her it hadn't been him. Puzzled, she turned again and saw that Phil Burch was at the console. He'd only gone and hot-wired the doors to the *Artemis* somehow! Phil raised a hand, nodded, and she repeated her thanks to the actual person responsible.

"I owe her," was all he'd say by way of explanation. "You can go in now."

Susan didn't need telling twice. She put the hover-bus into gear and pressed down on the pedal to take her up into the mouth and then, like Jonah, into the belly of the beast.

Chapter Eight

A cursory exploration revealed that nothing seemed out of place, nothing damaged as such.

They had a brief look around the tunnels, but as Helena had pointed out, those could go on for miles—and with no stabilization if there were any more tremors, the group as a whole was reluctant to go off mapping them today. She kept their theory about the catacombs to herself for now, that they could be interconnected, linked to other burial chambers underneath other places of worship in different cities or towns. That was a con-versation for another time.

Doug especially had appeared visibly relieved when they re-traced their steps back to the chamber that was already open. "If there is some kind of alien guard dog down here, or any ani-mal at all as far as that goes, I'm not sure I want to run into it," he admitted as they trailed back.

The captain—rifle raised as he turned corners, swinging it around them nose first—still looked like he wouldn't mind a crack at it. But again, there was time for that. Time to get the story from Meg—if she survived. Find out what really happened down there.

For now, it was a case of checking on the inhabitants of the catacombs, the chamber. Phil Burch hadn't really had much to say on the subject, hadn't been fit to talk about anything. Helena was dismayed to find out that the corpses were in a state of de-cay—you could see it simply by looking at them, although Doug also made the comment that their skin was "drier than kindling now." And it was obvious that the scientist had been taking sam-ples, not just because he'd been clutching his box to his chest when they came across him. His heavy-handed approach made Helena and her colleagues want to cry out in frustration. If the ghosts of these people had come back, you couldn't really blame them for being pissed off.

"This is what I was trying to say to you," Helena told Wayne, jabbing a finger in his direction; he was lucky it wasn't the pistol. "No respect, no care taken. Like excavating dinosaur bones with a bulldozer."

All the captain could do was hold a hand up, taking her point. But there was still nothing he could do about it, she knew. The damned Corporation!

The group had been in there for a little while before any of them noticed, and it was Kelso who pointed it out. "Over here," he'd said to Helena, fetching her, pulling her by the arm.

"What?"

He hadn't needed to explain, though, the closer she drew. It was obvious, explained itself. Doug joined them, and then the captain.

"What are we looking—" the professor began before stopping, seeing it as well. However they'd missed it when they first entered, Helena had no idea. The eye glossing over things, seeing what they expected to see.

And, whatever it meant, it didn't bode well.

Not well at all.

✕ ✕ ✕ ✕ ✕

Rod Hannigan was fuming.

As he stomped through the corridors of the *Artemis*, heading toward the science labs, he just grew madder and madder. What in the name of fuck did Phil Burch think he was playing at? Oh, Hannigan knew who'd overridden the locking mechanism on the cargo bay doors, allowing the hover-bus entry. Susan Rains, no matter how worked up she'd been, didn't have the necessary skills to do something like that. Actually, only two people from the ship did: Rafferty, who was currently doing his best to pretend he didn't exist down in engineering—and didn't give a shit about what was happening outside; and Phil Burch.

But why? What possible reason could he have for breaking protocol like that? He was usually the last person who'd do something along those lines. As Rains had rightly pointed out, Handles himself wasn't above bending a few rules to get what he wanted. Alcohol wasn't the only thing he'd brought on board without permission in the past. But this was serious. This was life or death—and not just for Meg Thomas. Of course, he cared about his shipmate, but there was more at stake than Rains's live-in lover here. And yes, if he was being honest, it wasn't just about sticking to procedure—although Hannigan was trying to play it more by the book these days, The Corporation dangling a full-time position in charge of his own vessel; Lord alone knew nobody had any real respect for him on this crate (take that landing for example, under difficult circumstances... Did he even get a thank you? No such thing, only abuse!). But anyway, it wasn't just about the rules; it was also about his own skin. Rod "Handles" Hannigan (so-called not because he could handle any situation, not even because he handled this ship like a dream—but because he'd been much bigger once, because his fat had spilled over at the sides) liked his own skin, always had, always would—even if it was a little loose in places. Christ alone knew what kind of shit might be kicking about on that planet out there, especially down in those fucking caves! And Meg had been exposed to it, some kind of accident causing her suit to be penetrated. How on Earth she was still alive was anyone's guess. But she probably shouldn't be.

Definitely wouldn't be if Burch hadn't stepped in. Couldn't be that the man fancied her, could it? He knew she was spoken for, that Rains had first dibs on that. Then what? It was why he was heading for the science labs, to find out, to get to the bottom of it—and maybe put the fear of God into Burch at the same time. People were always shouting at Handles, so perhaps it was his turn for a change. Time to be seen as more than just Wayne's second; when the man wasn't here, the *Artemis* was Hannigan's responsibility. The ship and the people on it. He was in charge, and he'd *make* Burch listen, have a proper go at him for acting the way he had.

By the time he got to the labs, he was ready for a rumble and no mistake. Had decided to start with their science officer, as Rains would be busy attending to Meg Thomas. And there was Phil, the long streak of piss, sitting on a stool, hunched over his microscopes, adjusting them. The screens above were throwing back an image of what he was looking at. Hannigan was no scientist himself, but they appeared to be cells. Some of the samples he'd brought back with him from the site? Yes, there was his container—open and on the table. Getting on with his business (The Corporation's business, Hannigan had to remind himself) as if nothing had happened. As if he hadn't just flagrantly disregarded orders—*his* command—and committed an offense that was actually punishable by imprisonment.

Just made Hannigan even angrier. He went over and grabbed Burch by the shoulder, yanking him back and swinging him around, the stool's seat squeaking as he did so. "Now you listen to me," growled Hannigan. And Phil *would* listen to him this time, not ignore him and just do whatever the hell he wanted to! "I know what you fucking well did! You've put us all in danger by letting Meg Thomas on board, by—"

"You're right," said the man before him, eyes wide and staring. "I-I've done something terrible. I just... Handles, I only wanted to help." He grabbed hold of Hannigan's wrists, then took his hands. "I had no idea... It was the curse you see, in the film."

Acting Captain Hannigan looked at him blankly. "The what? What the fuck are you talking about?"

"You're right! You have no idea, do you? I-I've put all of us in such terrible danger!" He looked like he'd just remembered something then. "Captain Wayne. Captain Wayne and the others, they're... We have to... No, wait. Meg! We need to get to the med-wing. Get there right now. Doctor Rains..."

"Phil. Phil slow down," said Hannigan, in a replay of what he'd said over the comms when the science officer had first gotten in touch with them. Seemed like weeks ago now but was only a couple of hours, tops. There was no anger now in his voice, only concern. Only fear. "What are you on about?"

"It must have been... Yes, it must have been... Can only have been—"

"Phil, I—"

"The curse," repeated the science officer. "Oh, Handles, something terrible is about to happen. We need to get to the med-wing. *Right now!*"

⊁⊱⊰⊁⊱⊰⊁

Susan Rains was grateful for what Phil Burch had done.

Right now, Meg Thomas was on an examination table with tubes running in and out of her, but at least she was alive. If it had been down to Handles—and she was ready the next time she saw him, would have a proper go at him!—Meg would have almost certainly died. The captain wouldn't have let regs stand in the way of saving one of his crew. Hell, it had been him who'd shipped them off back to the *Artemis*; he wouldn't have done that if he thought they couldn't get inside once they arrived. Fucking Handles, playing the big shot while her darling—

Never mind; it didn't matter. All that mattered was they'd got her here in time. Rains could start the long and painstaking process of putting this woman back together, of healing her. But good Lord, what a mess she was in! No way these injuries had been caused by those rocks, no way at all. Something else had done this.

She recalled then what the professor had been saying back in the catacombs, about a murder mystery. Not a murder anyway, thank goodness (and she still didn't know how or why that was even possible given the toxic air of this planet; although Meg's heart-rate was still terribly low), but definitely a mystery.

The ghost Meg had spoken of, what could it possibly be? To do all this to her girlfriend, as fit as she'd been. And—with the help of the medi-bot—relieving her of her clothes, getting the woman into a paper gown, she'd seen the extensive nature of those wounds. The bruising, the scratches, and the bites. Yes, incredibly, there were teeth marks on Meg's flesh. On her upper arm, her neck, her side. What kind of bloody ghost bit people?

She glanced over to the other end of the med-wing, where Jay Musgrove's prone body was spread out on another surface, on a different bed, still unconscious. Still in a coma from opening that door to the burial chamber. She'd found no such injuries about his person, and although the plexi-glass on his helmet had been cracked, they'd managed to get him back to the bus in time. So not quite the same sorry story. Yet, did his "accident" have something to do with Meg's? Were they in some way connected?

"Don't you worry, sweetheart," Susan said, patting the top of Meg's hands that she'd placed on each other, looking at her closed eyes, one of which was practically swollen shut. "We'll find out what happened and get you fixed up again, good as new. Computer, run the usual screens and do a full blood workup. Let's see what we're dealing with. I don't want any nasty surprises."

No sooner had she said this than the beeping she'd more or less tuned out, the sound that was indicating a faint heart-rate, began to suddenly slow even more. Susan ran around the table.

"Meg? No...*no!*" They hadn't come this far just for Meg to die on her now. She prepped a hypo that would deliver a massive dose of adrenalin, then delivered it into the security officer's system; the equivalent of when they used to pump it in the heart with a needle over a century ago. Her pulse was still fading. "No..." Susan repeated before hearing the oh-so-familiar sound of flatlining.

She moved Meg's hands, ripped open the gown at the front, grabbed a pair of electro-squares from the crash cart, and placed one on each side of her chest. "Computer, give me two hundred joules, *right now!*" The machine obeyed, and Meg's body rocked as the voltage shocked her.

Silence. No beeping.

"*Again!*" shouted Susan, and the whole process was repeated. They did this a number of times, her and the computer. But each time, there was nothing but silence. Tears welled in her eyes, but the doctor wasn't about to give up. She removed the electro-squares and got on top of Meg's body, straddling her in a grotesque parody of a favorite position they liked to make love in. This time, however, instead of caressing Meg's breasts, Susan folded her hands and began to pump between them, hoping against hope that she could restart the battered woman's heart muscle. Succeed where all her hi-tech equipment had failed, pour all of her feelings into the procedure and *will* it to work.

Mouth-to-mouth next, and again there was a sourness to it—the action robot-like, where once it had been all darting tongues and lingering kisses. Once more, she was willing it to revive Meg, bring her back from the brink she'd already tipped over. Even give the woman some of her own life in every breath, get lungs working that had stopped; all the time her ear cocked for that beeping to resume.

It didn't.

She carried on like this for a good ten minutes or more, then stood back from the body—realization finally setting in that it was doing no good. That she couldn't bring Meg back, no matter how hard she tried, no matter how much she wanted it. She slumped down, her back against the table, and wished more than anything that Meg would come back, that she could hold her—and be held by her. That she could talk to her again.

The tears came freely now as she sobbed into her hands. Susan had no idea how long she sat there just crying, maybe as long as she'd taken attempting to revive Meg. Maybe even longer.

But the next thing she knew, she could hear footfalls; someone was in the room with her. She lowered her hands to see Phil Burch and Rod Hannigan had entered the med-wing.

"S-She's gone," was all Susan could manage. "I've lost her."

But there was something else about the men in front of her, both pale and out of breath from running. Now they were shouting and screaming over each other, needing to convey something to her but failing miserably. So instead, probably seeing the confusion on her face, they began pointing, jabbing fingers at something behind her.

"What?" she asked, but then followed the direction they were frantically indicating, motivated by the fear on their faces. And she saw what they were gaping at, saw what they must have come here to warn her about.

Susan Rains saw, but she hardly dared believe.

"It's empty," said Wayne, the last one to see it, stating the obvious, stating what they'd all seen. "Was it empty before?"

They were staring at the space in front of them, one of the hollowed-out enclaves that contained the bodies of the dead—or at least should have. This one was, as the captain had pointed out, completely empty.

"I...no, I don't think... They were all full," said Helena, then questioning herself, "weren't they?"

"Definitely," confirmed Kelso. "All of them. All occupied."

"Which means..." began Wayne but couldn't bring himself to finish.

"One of the bodies is missing," finished Doug.

Helena rounded on Wayne then. "Is this your man Burch's doing? Has he taken one back to the ship with him?"

The captain looked stunned. "How? When? You were here when we arrived and met him, for fuck's sake!"

"We were in the tunnels looking for your security woman for a while," Doug reminded him, standing beside Helena, almost shoulder to shoulder. She was well aware that he'd take any kind of opportunity to stir it with Wayne, not that the captain wasn't giving them reason.

"Fucking hell! You saw the state of him when we got here. Besides, Phil Burch is about five stone soaking wet!" argued Wayne in defense of his crewman.

"They wouldn't exactly be heavy," Doug replied, taking up the argument, and gesturing to another one of the corpses.

"Even so," said Wayne. "Now Meg, she could have slung one over her shoulder easily. But she's—" He shook his head.

"There is another explanation," Kelso finally waded in.

"Oh what, your bloody vengeance ghost took it? Reclaiming what was his?" snapped Wayne.

It was the young man's turn to shake his head. "That wasn't what I was going to say."

"Go on," Helena prompted.

"All right," said Kelso. "But you really aren't going to like it."

※ ※ ※ ※ ※

Philip gaped at the scene in front of him. Looked to the side, saw that Hannigan was doing the same.

There was no time to ask, no time to find out whether... Rains there, on the floor, back pressed against the table said it all, though. Told them what had probably happened to Meg.

What was happening right now, in front of their very eyes, told Philip that he was absolutely right. Proved what he'd been telling Hannigan on their way there, once he'd managed to get him out through the door of the lab.

"I don't understand," said the pilot.

"The samples I took from the bodies back there. The tissue... It's not dead."

"What?"

"I mean, it *is* dead...but it's still alive, the cells still replicating."

"How can... Phil, you can't have it both ways. Something can't be... I mean the dead...dead alien, it can't be living *and*—"

"I don't know how to explain it; I've never seen anything like this before. Perhaps it's something to do with the composition of this species; perhaps it's something else. All I know is that the tissue, the corpses back there underground... They're living—"

"Dead?" offered Hannigan with a fair amount of skepticism in his voice. "You're kidding me."

"Do I look like I'm joking?" asked Philip, who wasn't one for humor at the best of times.

"It's not going to... I mean, those samples back there you've got, they're safe, right? That's what I'm asking."

"Don't worry; *they* can't harm you. But if you happened to come into contact with any at a cellular level..."

Again, Hannigan frowned, not really getting there. So, as they proceeded apace to the med-wing, Philip spelled it out for him in no uncertain terms.

"Holy shit!" gasped Hannigan. "And *you* bypassed the decon process."

Philip said nothing. It was his screw-up, certainly. But he'd only been trying to help, trying to get Meg the proper care she needed. If he'd been thinking straight, he'd have pieced it all together himself. If he hadn't been living on his nerves, shaken by the sight of his colleague. How could she have possibly survived? Sure, you heard tales of people still alive after enviro-suit failures and the like in hostile surroundings, but that was usually only for a short period. The time it had taken them to get that man Musgrove back to the bus after the accident, and look at the state he was in. Still comatose.

But Meg, she'd been down there too long. It didn't make sense... Until you knew about the samples. About what they were and what could be transferred. Until you realized what must surely have done that to her. Not an accident at all, but an assault. Attacked by—

It had broken the skin, sent her system into turmoil, into confusion. Even more confusion than Hannigan had experienced trying to get his head around all this. Alive one minute, dead the next. Alive, dead. Dead, alive.

Then both: living and dead at the same time.

Of course, it had only been a hypothesis. Just an unproven theory until they reached the med-wing. Until they saw Dr. Rains on the floor there, crying her eyes out, telling them her partner was dead. Philip absently wondered what lengths the woman had gone to in order to prevent that. Had she given her mouth-to-mouth? Had the contamination been passed on?

It didn't matter right at that moment, as both he and Hannigan began shouting at her to get away. That she was in terrible danger.

Because behind her, on the table, the woman who had once been Meg Thomas was sitting up, gown ripped down the front and exposing her discolored chest, scratch marks across both breasts.

Sitting up, regardless of her injuries. In spite of wounds that should have killed her back there in the catacombs, the one eye not swollen shut glassy and unseeing. Philip was aware of all the color draining from his face, glanced sideways to see the same was true of Hannigan. But it was nothing compared to the strange grayness of the person in front of them. Their former security chief, alive, then dead. Dead, then alive.

And now both at the same time.

Chapter Nine

Susan Rains's first thought was: *My wish has come true; she's come back to me!*

After all that effort, all that work, Meg had done it herself. She'd returned from wherever she'd been, unwilling to be parted from her. Thought it even more so when the woman got off the table, wrenching out all the tubes attached to her flesh, and raised both arms. Susan stood up herself at the same time so they were both at roughly the same height. She went in to accept the embrace, ignoring the shouts of "No!" from behind her, ignoring even the fact that the monitors hadn't started up again. There was still no beeping to indicate Meg's heart was working properly.

None of that mattered. All that mattered was she'd come back. That they could be together again, once she'd patched her up, that was; Jesus, she was such a mess! But the injuries simply couldn't have been that bad if she was on her feet now, holding out her arms. Susan stepped forward so that she was touching Meg, so that she could put her own arms round the woman, the same as she clearly wanted to do with her. Heads coming together as well, Meg's mouth open for a kiss.

Only…only the angle was wrong, surely? Meg wasn't aiming for her face at all; she was tilting her own head as if to lay it down on Susan's shoulder. That was okay; she could comfort her, rub her back and tell her everything was going to be all right. Which it was, or would have been, had Meg not suddenly sunk her teeth into the exposed flesh between the neck and shoulder. That was called the Trapezius muscle; she'd learned the name in medical school, remembered it because it sounded like those acts in the circus, the people who swung many feet above the ground. And it was part of that Trapezius Meg was biting into now, biting and tearing away, yanking back so that the strips of skin and muscle tore off at the roots. Biting, like some kind of rubbish bride of Dracula.

Susan opened her mouth in turn, but this time it was to scream. She'd wondered about the amount of pain Meg had been in, what it felt like, and had been granted a small taste—not funny!—of this. The answer was: *incredible!* She gazed at the person who'd done the deed, chewing away on the gristle like it was a delicious hydro-burger. Susan stopped screaming for a second, the sight so surreal it took her mind off the agony she was enduring briefly. She wanted to ask why, ask what had gotten into Meg that she would do this? But before she could, the woman was coming in for seconds. Susan couldn't shift either because her lover was holding her fast in that embrace she'd so craved just seconds before. Had walked into willingly, never thinking that this would... *Why would I?* she thought to herself, coming back to that question again: Why?

Not that Meg was in a position to answer her anyway, even if Susan could get the question out. The moans and groans that were emanating from the woman she adored were guttural, feral.

Hungry.

Just before the security officer could take another chunk out of her, Susan felt herself falling. She wasn't dropping to her knees or anything, wasn't able to because of the bear hug Meg was giving her. No, she was falling sideways. Falling *with* Meg.

Then she saw the reason. Hannigan was standing over them with one of the metal chairs from the med-wing, having just whacked Meg with it. The momentum had carried them both over, and when they hit the floor, Susan found that she was suddenly released, was rolling over onto her back so that she had no choice but to watch the farce taking place beside her. Hannigan attempting to pin Meg to the ground with the chair, to keep her there.

The "patient" was growling now, actually *growling*! Like a wild dog or something. Susan was aware of hands grabbing her again, and flinched, only to realize they belonged to Phil Burch and he was trying to get her away, trying to help her up. At the same time, Meg was clutching at the chair legs, and as strong as she'd been before, she never would have been able to bend them inward like that. Whatever had caused her to behave like this—caused her to come back from the dead!—had obviously given her un-natural strength.

Phil was practically dragging Susan through the door, but she didn't want to go, was reaching out even now for Meg. "No...*no! I can't leave her like this. I've got to—"

"It's too late, Susan. We have to get out of here," said the man. "Besides, your neck!"

It reminded her of the pain, the blood pumping out, and she put a hand up to try and stem it.

Hannigan bought them just enough time to clear the doorway before abandoning the chair and following them. Only just making it as Meg scrambled to her feet and hurled herself after him. Hannigan slapped the button to shut the door, and there was a thud on the other side of the metal.

Cautiously, the man moved sideways to the oval window of the med-wing and looked inside, presumably to check whether Meg had knocked herself out. He peered in, then took a hasty step back as the woman materialized, beating at the toughed glass.

"Don't worry," Phil said, still holding on to Susan in case she made a move to get back inside; a wise precaution. "It should hold."

On the next punch, the window splintered, cracked.

"Fuck!" shouted Hannigan. "Come on!" Susan had no choice but to go with them, as both men were ushering her away from the scene.

Away from the woman who'd come back from the grave to be with her.

And had also tried to devour her.

⚕⚕⚕⚕⚕

"So you're saying, what, that it just got up and walked off by itself?" Doug's voice was no less sarcastic than when Kelso had put forth the vengeful ghost theory.

"I'm just saying that it would fit with what happened," Kelso suggested.

"So would the notion that Burch took the body," Doug insisted. Then he regarded Kelso, realized what else he was trying to say. "What? You think this…the missing corpse did that to their security woman?"

Us and them again, thought Helena. *Their* security woman— and the rift was getting wider all the time. There was no trust left, not that there'd been a vast amount before.

Kelso cocked his head. "We're dealing with an alien civilization here. Who knows what happens to them when they die? Who knows if they're really dead at all," said the young man.

"Don't be ridiculous," snapped Doug, but he did turn to look at the other bodies in the wall cavities.

"Actually, Kelso's right," said Helena, backing up her assistant. "We don't know quite what we're dealing with here. They looked dead, granted, but—"

"Oh, come on, Helena! It doesn't matter what planet you come from. When you're dead, you're *dead*!" Doug argued. "They were showing distinct signs of decay. We've spent our lives examining sites like these, bodies like these."

"Not *exactly* like these," she corrected, throwing him an angry glance. "Nobody has."

Doug waved his hand dismissively.

"There are lots of legends from our planet about spirits leaving the body, about the soul and the body being separate," she re-iterated. "Just look at the idea of astral projection."

"Yes, but that body doesn't then get up and go walkabout— let alone attack people!"

"Unless someone, or something else jumps in," Helena mused.

Seeking, always seeking... This time the truth.

"Have you never heard of Haiti, Professor?" asked Kelso.

"Of course I have! But that's entirely different. Some might even posit that the people brought back to life weren't even dead in the first place. Just poisoned so they *thought* their souls were separated from their bodies. Superstitious nonsense!"

"Most of what we study is based on that 'superstitious non-sense,' as you call it," Helena stated.

"Studying ancient civilizations is not the same as having their belief systems," Doug came back with. "Besides—"

"Whoa, whoa, whoa," Wayne stepped into the middle of them, holding up a hand. "Let's calm this down a minute." He waited for them to stop arguing, then said, "We don't know anything about these people, you're right—but that's exactly what Phil was trying to find out. Discover a bit more about their make-up. Now, whether you agree with that, or think he was doing it just for The Corporation and for profit, he might have got some answers if Meg Thomas hadn't had her...accident."

"You think that's all it was?" Helena said. "An accident? That's why you were asking about the possibility of something doing that to her, was it? That why you brought the rifle?" She nodded at the weapon in his other hand.

"I don't know what to think anymore," Wayne admitted.

"You said maybe it was something to do with..." She trailed off. "The wind. The strange wind that was released." Helena looked lost in thought now.

"What about it?" asked Kelso, breaking into those thoughts.

"Well, what if—and bear with me on this—what if whatever was released when the door was open was, I don't know, keeping them in check?" Helena said.

"I don't follow you," said Wayne.

"I do," Doug broke in. "She's saying that maybe these bodies were in some sort of stasis, for want of a better word."

Helena nodded. "It's no more far-fetched than what we do when we travel using the Elastic Drive. The gas that's pumped in which solidifies, and then turns to gas again when exposed to air."

"It's *so* much more far-fetched! Our bodies aren't rotting, Helena!"

"Perhaps theirs weren't until we opened that door," she pointed out. "We did that. Or rather Jay did it."

Doug's eyes brushed the floor and he sighed.

"Or perhaps it was something more natural? Something naturally occurring," Kelso offered.

"You mean it did something *to* them," said Helena. "We only assumed these were graves because of our own culture."

"Two questions, if that's the case," Doug said as if he was addressing a class. "One: where's our missing friend right now? And two: how come the rest of them haven't woken up?"

There was silence for a moment or so, then Kelso had a go at addressing the second query: "Maybe it works differently for each person, like recovery times after anesthetic when you're in the hospital?"

"Or the rest are just too far gone," Wayne added, "hopefully."

There was a rumble then, vibrations in the cave. They all pitched sideways, Helena falling into Doug; Wayne and Kelso doing the opposite, separating and tumbling back to hit different walls. The 'quake was only a minor one, lasted just a few moments. And when it was over, Helena stepped back from the man who was holding her upright. Through the plexi-glass in the helmets, they met each other's gaze. Helena glanced away first, flushed. There was a noise off to their right. Both looked at the same time.

Because at least one of Doug's questions was in the process of being answered. Because one of the corpses in the alcoves had reached out and was attempting to grab Kelso by the arm.

Because the rest of the "dead" were now waking up.

⚔⚔⚔⚔⚔

Though she didn't know it, Dr. Anna Blackwell was about to answer Professor Douglas Grable's other question.

She'd been in the "office" allocated for her work, had been there while all the excitement had been going on back at the church, in the catacombs, and then when the bus returned to the *Artemis*. Helena had filled her in before she left, calling on the vid-screen; said Meg Thomas had gone missing or something, and Science Officer Phil Burch was in a bit of a flap. "We're just going to check it out; you carry on working," Helena had told her.

Her work, always her work.

Anna had left the screen on, configuring it to show the loading bay so she could keep an eye out for when the bus returned. And she'd gladly done as she was told, got on with her study of this alien race they were still trying to fathom out. She was making quite a bit of headway, as well. From the evidence gathered so far, she'd already determined that this had been a society with no hierarchical structure, which was mind-blowing, especially given Earth's history. It was hard to imagine a world with no levels of leaders and followers, who just got along with each other. Who worked together for the betterment of their race. They could certainly have taught humans a thing or two, she thought to herself as she narrated her findings and watched them appear as words on the monitor in front of her.

And she wondered whether that equality extended to males and females, whether they'd actually managed to crack that divide here. Anna hoped so. Oh, they'd made efforts over the course of the last few decades to do that on her own planet, but there were still those like Jay who thought they were back in the twentieth century. No, scratch that, the nineteenth, or even eighteenth century! Who thought laws were there to be bent or even broken, guidelines at best. Anna shouldn't, for example, have encountered the kind of resistance in and to her career that she'd had. She was clever, scarily so—but just because she looked like she did, men thought it was an open invitation to try and bed her. Things hadn't really changed since the stone age in that respect.

Offers of jobs that would advance her up the ladder, but only if certain favors were granted. She'd declined, naturally, and had even reported some of those involved, only to find herself going down a snake instead. Back to square one. Wouldn't stop her taking her own stand, though.

But not even her own parents had taken her seriously or backed her up when she told them what her chosen profession was. Certainly not her older brother, who'd delighted in teasing her from the moment she was born.

But then there was the work to comfort her, always the work.

Thank God, then, for women like Helena Kirby, who she'd met at a conference and had bonded with over cocktails—moaning about the quality of the lectures, given by some of the dullest academics who'd ever existed. She'd said she would bear Anna in mind if anything cropped up, and as far as the anthropologist was concerned, that had been that. People didn't really mean what they said when they were at those sorts of things, and especially when they were tipsy. But, to her surprise, Helena had gotten in touch less than three weeks later about a dig out in the former Egypt. She'd gone away and checked out Anna, liking what she found. That had been the start of it all, and Anna had been on her team—give or take—for several years now. So, when this opportunity had popped up, Helena had come to her and asked, "How do you feel about a little trip? Further than we normally go, but I think it'll be worth it."

A little trip? She hadn't been kidding! The furthest Anna had been before that had been Mars Colony, although she had done a pass of Jupiter on a holiday excursion once. But out here... She'd never imagined... And, *of course,* the answer had been yes; there hadn't even been a moment's hesitation. The opportunity to study an alien civilization first-hand, to be the one who wrote the papers (they were still called that, even though paper was in rare supply these days, just like the trees it came from), who was part of the team that wrote the virtu-books, made the holo-docs about this subject... Well, it was just too good to pass up. It might even give her the recognition she needed. Dammit, deserved! She'd worked hard enough for it, more so than other people in her profession, male or female.

But enjoyed the work, embraced it.

Now, she hadn't been averse in the past to using how she looked for a good cause—and Anna recalled the way she'd tried to distract Captain Wayne as a favor to Helena. If men were stupid enough, so easily manipulated... But he hadn't been, to his credit. Knew there was something going on. At the end of the day, though, it was all about the work. That came first, before anything. Before sex, before relationships, before... Friendship? No, maybe not that—not where people like Helena were concerned. They went hand-in-hand, then. One and the same. Working together toward the same goals.

Work, always the work.

So that's what she'd been concentrating on when those images flashed up on the vid-screen of someone being brought back to the ship. Carried off the bus on a stretcher by Burch and their medic Dr. Rains. It had to be Meg Thomas. They'd found her, and she was in a much worse state than the science officer by the look of things. Of the rest of her team, of Wayne, there was no sign. She'd thought about calling through on the comms then to find out what was going on, perhaps even contacting the pilot, Hannigan. But they looked like they had their hands full down there. Rains especially appeared stressed, unsurprising really given the nature of her connection to the security chief. Plus, she didn't really know any of them that well; something which she couldn't really say bothered her too much. Apart from Jay Musgrove, who was spark out in the med-wing, she was all that was left of the archeological team on board. Maybe she'd have a wander down there later and see what was happening; she could at least see how Jay was doing—not that she could really stand the creep. An excuse, then, to see what was going on with the rest of them.

Work, stick to the work. Her one true companion throughout her life. Her one true *friend.*

And she'd got lost in it again for a while, probably longer than she'd expected or wanted to, without coming up for air. It had been movement on that screen again, however, which was still focused on the hover-bus and the cargo bay, that had caught her eye. Something in the periphery of her vision, actually.

She'd thought it was one of them, Rains or Burch, returning—perhaps to go and retrieve the lost members of the crew and her team. But it hadn't been either of them. Someone else was making their way around the side of the bus. Anna couldn't tell whether they'd come from inside or not; probably not because she hadn't noticed the doors opening again or anything. Which meant they'd been on the *outside* of the vehicle somewhere—but that wasn't possible. Clinging onto the bus, on its side or roof, at those speeds over open ground, it would take more strength than—

She blinked as she realized exactly who—*what*—this person was. From its gait, the fact it was almost bones, from the huge forehead and cranium, it could only be one of the things they had been examining down in those catacombs, down in the crypt. But it was moving, alive! No, she wouldn't exactly call whatever condition it was in alive, not yet. How could…

Anna blinked again, wondering if she'd somehow nodded off while doing her research. It was true she hadn't really slept that well since she'd stepped foot on the *Artemis,* unless you counted the long sleep she'd had while they were traveling here in the first place. But she wasn't prone to just dozing off over her work. Hadn't even done that when she'd been a student, as most typically did.

Another blink and the image was still there—indeed, she'd drawn closer to it for a better look. Definitely one of the "dead" they'd been studying. Definitely walking around down there in the cargo bay.

Definitely meant trouble.

She'd pushed away from the monitor, flipped the switch for the comm, and tried to raise Hannigan, who she assumed had been left in charge if the captain was off ship. Nothing. No response at all.

Anna tried every comm now, including the med-wing. Didn't give a shit if they were still in the middle of an emergency; there was another one developing right now. Nothing again. The only answer she got was a pick-up down in engineering. That weird guy Rafferty she'd only seen a couple of times, but he'd hung up before she could get more out than, "Hello, can you—"

Static spat back at her, and she snapped, "Well, fuck you as well!"

What to do now? She checked the monitor again. The alien had gone. Disappeared, maybe even got out of the cargo bay? Anna thought about leaving, then thought about staying—weighing up which would be the safer option. She'd be trapped in here if that thing found her, but out there, would she stand more of a chance of bumping into it? Not that it had shown any signs of being malicious—hadn't actually done anything at all. It was just a sense that she got, the same way she could work out things about a civilization from just looking at objects or buildings. Something in the way it moved, it carried itself. Like when you see an insect and knew that, intrinsically, it was just...wrong. That it would bite or sting you.

They'd been examining that alien's final resting place, for Heaven's sake! Except it hadn't been, had it? Not it's *final* resting place...

But maybe it *had* just been resting, Anna thought to herself.

Maybe the others were as well. Which made her think about her teammates for a moment, and what they might be going through down in the catacombs. It also made her think about that security woman they'd brought in and what might have happened to her.

Stay or go? What would be best? Anna couldn't decide.

Go, probably. Yes, *go!* At least she might be able to find some kind of weapon out there to defend herself. The most she had in here was knowledge and theories. Couldn't batter someone to death with conjecture.

If that thing could be battered to death. If it could even be killed? And she felt guilty about thinking that, about killing anything. Those kinds of thoughts didn't come naturally to her like they did some people. But the alien had certainly put them in her head.

She was up and had made it to the door of that makeshift office, was reaching out to open it when there came a banging from the other side. Anna stepped backward, hand to her mouth.

It was here; it had found her.

The banging came again, harder now. Holy crap, it was going to break its way in!

...would take more strength than—

Anna searched around again, looking for something she might have missed that she could use to defend herself. There was nothing, really. Nothing that would be effective against—

Bang-bang-bang!

She backed into the corner of the room, sliding down into a crouching position. Convinced she was going to die here, alone, except for her best friend in the world. Her one true companion, who had comforted her.

The work, always the work.

Chapter Ten

They'd manhandled Dr. Susan Rains through most of the corridors of the ship—that's what it felt like, at any rate.

Especially to Philip Burch. He wasn't the fittest person on the *Artemis* crew by a mile, nor the strongest, and even with Hannigan helping, it still felt like they were carrying a dead weight. No, not dead. Not yet. Dear Lord, not yet!

Because if she was...

So, first things first—they had to find somewhere they could patch her up. Rains was bleeding profusely, her hand dropping from the wound at her neck now like she didn't have the energy to hold it there. Hannigan tried to help her, pulling her hand up and placing it on the bite—those dark ringlets of hers matted with redness—then attempting to stem the blood-flow himself when that didn't work. But they needed somewhere to take her, access to medical equipment. Not the obvious choice, the med-wing, for equally obvious reasons.

"The rec-room," Hannigan had suggested, nodding ahead to the part of the ship in question. Philip had agreed without hesitation, if only because it meant they weren't lugging Rains anymore; he was tired. Philip understood the logic of it; if nothing else, he was a logical person—although the events of the last few hours had challenged his notion of that quite a bit. Put some distance between them and whatever Meg Thomas had become. It was a good idea, all things considered.

But it also meant that Rains was in a seriously bad way when they got her to their destination, when they—mainly Hannigan—lifted her onto the holo-pool table, laying her back as the blood continued to pump out.

"Medi-kit... Medi-kit?" said Hannigan, partly to himself—trying to remember where it was kept—and in part asking Philip.

"Behind the bar there," the science officer said, pointing.

Hannigan raced off, leaping over the surface, and started rooting around for the kit. He returned moments later, opening the case and reading the instructions to himself—attempting to figure out which instrument did what.

"*Hurry!*" shouted Philip.

"I'm...I'm hurrying."

"Just a bandage, anything!"

"Look, it's been a while since I did the course," Hannigan said absently. "Chem... chem-healer. Cortical—"

"Give it to me!" grumbled Philip, snatching the medi-kit from Hannigan. The pilot didn't protest, but instead stared at Rains, who was coughing up blood.

"Fuck," Hannigan said, stepping back. It was the first time they'd been able to stand back and just look at the damage that had been done. And Philip knew what the man was thinking, that it could have been him bleeding out like that. One lucky swipe or bite and Meg would have had Hannigan as well.

"Where are you going, Handles? Hold her down for me," Philip told him, taking out what he hoped was the stero-foam filler syringe, which would slow down the blood-loss and form a protective barrier over the wound. The only problem was Rains had begun bucking on the table, finding reserves from somewhere. It was the most active they'd seen her since she'd wanted to go back into the med-wing and be with her partner.

Hannigan took a step toward Philip again, then stopped. The science officer frowned, avoiding one of Rains's flailing arms in the process. He was about to ask what Handles was playing at when he saw the problem clearly enough himself. Hannigan's legs were moving, even his feet were moving, but they were not propelling him forward. Because they were not connecting with the floor. He was being lifted off the ground by something behind him, and it was only when Handles was thrown several feet sideways to collide with a table and some chairs that Philip heard the moaning of the "person" responsible.

How she'd caught up with them quite so quickly was anyone's guess, but standing there was the former security chief and Rains's lover, Meg Thomas. Only she no longer resembled that woman, not really. Yes, there was still the damage from the attack, but even Philip could see it was more than that. She'd...*changed.* Her head was more dome-shaped than it had been before, her limbs more skeletal in nature. She was becoming more like the thing—or things—that must have attacked her. Those aliens back there from the tomb. Passing this infection on, altering her at a molecular level. Both living and dead at the same time, as much alien DNA as human.

Philip dropped the stero-foam syringe, took a tentative step away from the pool table. The creature that had once been Meg Thomas threw back its head and groaned. Suddenly, it sprang forward, and for a second or two, Philip was frozen to the spot. Then he ducked and rolled—right under the table, coming out the other side. When he rose again, he spotted one of the hard-light cue tabs stuck to the side of the table and peeled it off. As he rose again, Philip saw "Meg" rounding the obstacle to chase after him. He pointed the square at her and depressed the button. The cue shot out, extending from both sides of the small square—the thin end ramming straight into his attacker's shoulder.

It was enough to pitch Meg off balance, the force of the cue elongating enough to make her stagger back and right. Philip grabbed his chance to run, but he, too, found that he couldn't. Something had a hold of him, as well.

In all the confusion, he hadn't noticed that Rains's convulsions had stopped. Now she was sitting bolt upright on the pool table in much the same way Meg had done on the examination bench back in the med-wing. That wasn't the only similarity, either, because the doctor's eyes were just as glassy in death; the bite at her neck the only thing animating her.

She'd reached out and grabbed Philip by the sleeve of his jumpsuit, preventing him from going anywhere. It wouldn't be long before she'd roll around and grab hold of him completely.

Philip wrenched his arm away from her, tugging and tugging. Conscious also that this woman's partner was upright once more, the cue sticking out of her like a giant needle in an oversized pincushion. The "weapon" apparently had little or no effect on the thing, hadn't slowed it down in the slightest—and it was intent on picking up where it had left off. Or mopping up after Rains had finished, perhaps? Philip made a concerted effort, pulled back with what little weight he had, and felt the material of his suit giving way; heard the ripping moments later.

Then suddenly he was falling backward, just in time for the two monsters to reach each other. Philip watched, fully expecting Meg to start trying to devour Rains again, as she had back in the wed-wing. Instead, the deformed hybrid seemed to recognize a kindred spirit and broke off the lunge. Sensing, or even smelling, that the virus had been passed on. Or perhaps there was a simpler explanation: Rains's flesh was no longer appetizing enough now that it was necrotic. Was no longer of use as food. Which left—

Almost as one, they turned and regarded Philip—a much tastier morsel.

Philip scrambled to his feet, now with two of the things to worry about, to somehow evade. He skirted around one of the bar tables, pushing it toward the living dead things in pursuit—Susan having jumped down from the pool table to join her ex. Now partners in another way, possibly even more connected than they ever were before.

He threw a couple of chairs at them, continuing to make his way along the walls of the bar—the open doorway in sight. They both lunged at him, leaping forward with a speed he wouldn't have believed possible had he not seen it before, but even after all that, it still took him by surprise. They would have had him as well, were it not for the intervention of various projectiles being thrown at them.

One hit "Meg" on the side of the head—a tankard of some kind Philip had seen Wayne drink from a few times. It connected and shattered completely, causing the glass to explode in the air. Philip instinctively raised his arm to protect himself. More objects were thrown at the pair, drawing their attention. Anything and everything Handles—who had recovered enough from being thrown to make it to the bar—could lay his hands on.

"Move! Get out of here!" shouted Hannigan. "I'll follow!"

A couple of bottles collided with the pair, spraying them with alcohol but hardly slowing them down at all.

Handles broke another bottle on the counter and, as the larger of the two corpses drew close, he rammed this into its face, causing it to jerk back. When "Rains" joined her partner, he did the same with one more, this time bringing the smashed glass up under her chin, making even more of a mess there than the bite had done.

Philip was already at the door and turned back, expecting Hannigan to only be moments behind him. But as he'd begun his bid for freedom, Handles had been swooped on by the two "women," who had renewed their efforts, going after him more vigorously than they had Philip. It was almost as if both of them held a grudge against the pilot for something, and not simply the glass attack.

They grabbed him and lifted, Rains under the arms and Thomas by the legs. Hannigan reached a hand out to Philip, pleading with him for help—the help he'd just given the man so he could escape. A distraction, even calling out to them, something, anything, that would draw their attention away from their task. Philip stepped back inside, then halted. What could he do? His mind was racing.

"Phil...*please!*" Handles called out.

Still, Philip hesitated. And his course of action had been determined even before Handles's dead shipmates started biting into him, meaning there was no hope for the man. Philip always knew he was going to run away from the mess he'd created. Just like he'd done when his parents had been dying, not able to cope with the stress of it all. Just like he had when he'd heard those screams back in the catacombs, getting to safety outside the church.

Screams similar to the ones that were following him now as he turned and started to move out of the rec-room and away from the trio. He looked back over his shoulder only once, perhaps to make sure that neither of the dead creatures were following him, but saw instead Handles being ripped in two, top and bottom halves coming away as his attackers pulled in opposite directions. Blood exploded from both ends, organs and intestines falling out of his torso section. Philip tried to look away again but couldn't. Even when he faced front and began to run in earnest, he could still see the sight of Handles being torn apart.

And all he could hear were screams that had rapidly turned into gurgles.

This can't be happening. It's impossible.

Eddie Kelso was gaping at the scene in front of him. He tended to do that, had done it since he was a kid, taking in things around him. Certainly had on this trip—something Helena found quite funny, though she told him it was endearing. But this was on another level. It was one thing to talk about legends from his own culture, from others as well; it was quite something else to witness people—all right, aliens—you thought were deceased climb out of their "graves." Not dead, not really. Quite lively, actually, as the one who'd tried—and failed—to grab hold of him testified; as the one nearest to Professor Grable was ably demonstrating.

It had clambered out in seconds and seized the man, throwing him sideways and sending him skidding across the floor, sending up dust motes too. Kelso thought for a moment Grable was dead himself, but he was merely winded and, once recovered, managed to prop himself up on an elbow. Two more aliens were behind him, though, and Kelso cried out in warning—then realized he had his own problems to deal with, as the one who'd attacked Grable leaped in his direction. He just about had time to duck sideways, avoiding the thing, but when he righted himself again, two arms wrapped themselves around him from behind.

At that moment, he would have given anything to have been wrong. For Grable, the unbeliever, to have been right. Because it would mean he wasn't about to end up like Security Officer Meg Thomas, savaged in that tunnel by what must have been one of these guys' companions who'd woken up ahead of the rest of them.

There was a loud crackling sound, then a bright flash that almost blinded Kelso, and he was free again. He looked over to find Captain Wayne hefting the plasma rifle he'd brought with him, the end of it still smoking.

Kelso waved to say thanks, before realizing that the dead alien Wayne had hit wasn't staying down for long. The captain gave it another blast, but again it seemed to shrug this off.

Grable was crawling across to the tools that had been left in the tomb, pursuers in tow. When he reached them, Kelso saw him dig something out and then bring it around in an arc as he rolled over. The las-shovel struck the nearest corpse, wedging in its fore-arm. Grable tugged on it, pulling it out again, and the arm came away with it, flying off into the distance. The dead thing didn't even seem to notice; it just kept coming at the professor, more of its kind behind it.

Kelso looked across to see the captain adjusting the settings on the side of his rifle. Urging the young man to get out of the way, he fired again, and this time he blasted a hole in the body of the creature who'd been hugging Kelso. You could see right through to the other side—and Eddie again stared, opened-mouthed at the sight.

"No time for that!" Wayne shouted down the prox-comm. "Get with it. These fuckers are everywhere!" When Kelso just gawked at him, the captain clarified with a simple, "*Fight!*"

Unlike Wayne, who, Kelso wagered, had probably been in more fights than a champion boxer (probably not against the dead, but apparently that didn't seem to matter), this was actually his first one. He kept away from trouble if he could help it, was never keen to rock the boat; it was one of the reasons he'd put up with all that bullying at school when his dad and his uncle had told him to stand up for himself. Now, though, he didn't really have much of a choice.

Helena, his boss, his mentor—the person he looked up to more than anyone else—was having just as much difficulty motivating herself. Hesitating, like he'd been doing moments before. Maybe she was having trouble believing her own eyes, too? But then he heard her say: "We...we can't..."

This can't be happening...

"We have to...have to preserve the—"

"*Helena!*" Wayne barked at *her* now. "These new friends of yours are going to kill us!"

She looked around then, at Wayne and Kelso, at Grable struggling with his own attackers. He knew exactly what she was thinking, weighing up whether they could still preserve the tomb, the catacombs, maybe seal them off somehow? This was their fault, after all.

But also thinking that they needed to stay alive in order to do that, and as Wayne so colorfully put it, these "friends" wanted to slaughter them. Maybe even eat them. She drew Meg Thomas's pistol and began to fire. That must have already been set to maximum because the plasma discharge from it blew away the side of one dead alien. However, as they were soon to discover, not even wounds like that were deterring them.

The one Wayne had shot in the chest, for example, was still coming on strong. Still after Kelso. "The head!" called out Grable. "Go for the head—or sever the brainstem!" He was in the process of hacking at the neck of one of his attackers with the las-shovel. Hacking, until that went flying off in the same direction as the arm from before.

Kelso hadn't pegged Grable as a fan of old horror movies from the last century—the ones you had to go on underground webworks to find now (his flatmate in college had gone through a period of watching them while Kelso had been trying to study; trying very hard not to look as the really gory bits came on). Grable had heard of Haiti, though, he'd said, was familiar with the lore. Or perhaps he'd just worked out, like so many of them did in those old flicks, that you had to cut the head off the snake to make the rest of it dormant. Puncture the brain.

Looking about him, Kelso saw one of those crystals Grable and Anna Blackwell had been studying; long and to a point. Was thinking of it now not so much as a cultural artifact as a means of defense. The alien with the hole in its chest was advancing, so Kelso shifted to the side and grabbed the crystal. Then, gulping loudly, he jammed it into the side of the corpse's head. Unlike the laser and plasma weapons, using this didn't instantly cauterize the wound, and as dry as this being's skin was, a pulpy discharge still ran from the fissure Kelso had created. He fought down the urge to vomit. But the corpse did drop onto its knees, then fall over sideways.

Helena, following suit, aimed the pistol at an alien's head and depressed the trigger. The energy discharge punched a cavity right through its cranium, and it fell over backward.

More and more of the dead were waking as they fought, climbing out of their alcoves. Ten, twenty, maybe even thirty or more—and that was only the tip of the iceberg. There had to be a hundred plus in here, Kelso figured.

"We've got to try for the entrance!" Wayne hollered over the comms. "Before they hem us in. Make for the steps back at the church, then block that off."

It was a solid plan, the only one that made sense. So they started to inch backward, toward the door, Wayne blasting the aliens that were bothering Grable, then helping him up. Helena provided covering fire as they retreated, Kelso joining her to stand side by side.

It wasn't until they were almost at the doorway that the dead began to surge forward en masse. And, yes, Kelso spotted the ones they thought they'd dispatched, rising again in spite of the craters in their heads. The one Grable had decapitated was just a body now, but it still joined the rest.

"I-I don't understand," gasped the professor.

"Understand later," Wayne snapped.

The four of them half-stumbled, half-fell out through the entrance—but they weren't alone. A wave of the alien dead was there in seconds, spilling out, too, and by the time Kelso and his friends were ready to head off toward the steps and the church, several bodies were already standing in their path.

"Shit!" said Wayne, backing away from them and urging the others to do the same.

"What now?" asked Kelso, hardly able to keep the panic from his voice.

"We'll have to head down there," Helena said, thumbing back toward the tunnels where Meg had been found as she shot the security chief's gun, winging one of the living cadavers. None of them were in a particular rush to go further into the catacombs, but it looked like they had little option. "Maybe we'll be able to find another way out?"

"They'll just follow us there, too," argued Grable, saying out loud what they were all thinking.

"Get back," shouted Wayne, signaling for them to move behind him and then firing off a couple more shots of his rifle. They did as they were told, leaving him to hold off the dead. "I have an idea," he told his companions.

More and more figures were filling the tunnels, emerging from the tomb until Kelso could no longer see the walls or floor. Just heads and limbs, biting and grasping. Wanting to reach them. One snatched at Wayne, and he stepped sideways to avoid the lunge, only to fall into another body. Then one of the others grabbed his rifle and pulled it out of his grasp.

Kelso watched, holding his breath. He thought that was only something people said they did in times of crisis, didn't realize that you did it automatically...probably not a bad thing, the amount of oxygen they were going through. Wayne tore himself free, staggered backward, then he kicked out. Kicked the closest alien right into one of the energy props Rafferty had set up to stabilize this area.

The prop fizzed and buzzed, the alien glued to it, writhing about as it was fried. Then the power blinked out, the prop failing. Wayne shoved another one of the dead into a second prop and sprinted for Kelso and the others, waving them back. "Run!" he urged. "Just fucking run!"

So they did, the other prop cutting out as they went, the roof of the catacombs coming down behind them, nearly burying Wayne under the rubble. The whole tunnel started to shake, not because of another earthquake this time, but because what had been holding up the ceiling after the last one was now gone. Wayne fell forward, dust at his heel, covering him. Helena and Kelso helped pull him further away from the avalanche of bone-rock.

Then they turned, almost as one, to look back at the makeshift wall that had been created. A blockade they'd intended for the mouth of the church entrance but which had now effectively cut off their escape route. It had also separated them from the dead, which had been Wayne's primary intention, Kelso guessed.

"Congratulations," Grable said eventually, once the dust had—quite literally—settled. "You've trapped us down here!" There was no gratitude whatsoever for the fact Wayne had helped him escape from the tomb.

"I don't know if you noticed, Doug," said Helena, "but we were already trapped."

"I stopped them from coming after us, didn't I?" Wayne said, facing Grable. They stared at each other for a moment or two through the plexi-glass of their helmets, and it was the professor who turned away first.

Kelso stepped closer to the pile of rubble, listened through externals that filtered the noise outside through to him. There was the sound of the dead on the other side, grunting and groaning, furious that their prey had escaped—if they could even experience emotions. But there was also something else he could distinguish, the sound of rubble being moved. The sound of all those bodies working together, digging to try and get through to them.

Can't be happening…impossible.

Except it was.

"Maybe not for long," he said, gesturing for them to come and hear it as well.

"Excellent," spat Grable. "That's just excellent! Better hope there is a way out down there, Helena, because we need to find it quickly."

"Okay," she said, "so what are we waiting for?" Switching on her helm-light because the remaining artificial lights on this side of the barrier only reached a few meters down into the blackness, Helena began marching off in the opposite direction.

"And you'd better hope the one that attacked Meg isn't waiting for us," Grable added, causing her to stop for a second. Then Helena continued on.

"You know something, Professor," Wayne said as he pushed past Grable, igniting his own helm-light. "You're really kind of a dick."

Kelso couldn't help laughing at that but soon stopped when Grable shot him a withering stare. Then the professor headed off himself, leaving Kelso next to the pile of rocks. He listened for a few seconds more, then when he heard more of the digging, he ran off to join the others—just as they turned the first corner and disappeared.

Chapter Eleven

The noise again, this time more urgent than ever. Trying to get through.

Blocking her ears had done no good; she could still hear it through the balled fists she'd made. But now, as she took her hands down, Anna Blackwell could hear something else as well.

It was a voice.

"Anna? Anna, are you in there? Let me in!"

Her brow furrowed. She hadn't been expecting that dead thing from the catacombs, from the tomb, to be calling her by name. To be asking her to let it in.

"Come on love, stop pissing around," said the voice, and suddenly she recognized it.

Anna got up from her sitting position in the corner of the room, drifted toward the voice, and the door. "Musgrove?" she ventured. "Jay, is that you?"

"Is it... Who the bloody hell were you expecting, Father Christmas?"

Definitely Jay Musgrove.

Anna reached for the door release, but still she hesitated— as if thinking perhaps she was being fooled. That the dead thing was somehow able to imitate her colleague? That it was able to hypnotically suggest Musgrove was on the other side of the barrier just so she'd let it in. But why would it suggest that pig of a man? Under normal circumstances, and if she wasn't already half out of her mind with worry, he would be the last person she'd let into her proximity. As it was, she opened the door.

"About fucking time!" Musgrove complained. He looked sweatier than usual, lips plumper and slimier than ever. "What the fuck's going on around here?" he asked as he stepped into the room.

She just stared at him blankly.

"Anna?" When she still didn't reply, he looked around, looked behind him, closed the door again, then went over to the monitor and started trying to key into the other cams on the ship. His clearance—like Anna's—would only allow him to see the major communal areas, like the docking bay.

Shaking her head, she joined him. "You...when did you wake up?"

It was his turn to look at her but not say anything.

"You were in a coma," she told him. "In the med-wing."

"The med-wing is covered in blood," he replied.

Anna put a hand to her mouth. "The creature," she whispered.

"The *what*?" Musgrove's face was a mixture of confusion and anger.

"From the catacombs, from the tomb."

"The tomb," he said as if trying to remember. Anna hit him on the arm. "Ow, what was that for?"

"This is all your fault," she shouted. "You opened the fucking door!"

"The treasure," Musgrove said to himself. "Kelso's treasure."

"There *was* no treasure; don't you get it? Just dead bodies. Well, we thought they were dead. But one of them attacked Meg Thomas...I think. One of them found their way back here to the ship."

"*How long* have I been out?" he asked, and she couldn't tell whether he was being serious or trying to be funny. Before she could answer, he changed the subject. "Where's Helena? Where's the rest of the crew?"

"She stayed behind after they found Thomas, with Kelso and Professor Grable. Captain Wayne's with them."

"And Rains? Hannigan? Burch?"

"They all returned, must have taken Thomas to the med-wing. But then I saw... Musgrove, there was one of them down in the cargo bay. It hitched a ride with the bus."

"Shit," was his only reply. He continued scrolling through the monitors.

"What happened down there?" she asked him.

"I-I don't know. It was all over by the time I... Nobody was around. There was just the blood. Place was a real fucking mess, window smashed... The works." He paused for a second. "There was a trail of it leading off up the corridor."

"Did you follow it?"

"Of course I bloody well didn't. I'm not insane!"

"You let that thing out, Musgrove. You're responsible for all this!"

"I-I didn't." He shook his head. "I don't remember doing that. I—"

"It left you alone," Anna said in response, with more than a hint of accusation in her voice.

He opened his mouth to answer, closed it again. Then said, "Maybe it was because I was immobile? Not moving around?"

"So you didn't follow the blood?"

Musgrove shook his head. "No. I tried the comms but couldn't get through to anyone. I knew you'd camped out in here and it was in the opposite direction, so I made for this place. And I—"

He suddenly stopped speaking, and when Anna followed his gaze to the monitor, she realized why. It had settled on the rec-room, which was in a similar state to the med-wing as he'd described it. Blood everywhere, tables and chairs knocked over. That must have been where the trail ended, and someone—or several some-ones—had also met their end.

"Christ," Musgrove said under his breath.

"Christ is right." Anna rubbed her temple. "Do you know how many of those things are down in that tomb?"

"Of course I don't," snapped Musgrove. "I didn't sodding well see it!"

"*I* did," said Anna ominously. "If just one of those things did all this, then our friends are in some serious trouble."

He held up his hands, nodding to the monitor. "I think we're in just as much, don't you?"

"We need to warn them, Jay!"

"We need to get to an armory or something," was his answer. Typical Musgrove, always thinking about himself. "Look, I tried outside comms as well. Nothing. Couldn't get through to anyone. And we'll be no good to them dead," he added, clearly countering what she'd be thinking.

"This is all your fault," she repeated, not knowing what else to say.

"No," he insisted. "No, it isn't! I didn't—"

"You don't know what *the fuck* you did," she said and hit him again. But this was getting them nowhere, and she knew it. Musgrove's suggestion was a good one; they did need to arm themselves in order to survive—and maybe mount a search and rescue for the team. "Okay, okay," said Anna, breathing in and out to calm herself. "Armory."

Musgrove nodded.

"Any ideas where it is?"

"Not the first inkling."

"Would a ship like this even *have* an armory? I mean, the odd gun for defense. Thomas always had a pistol with—"

"That's it!" said Musgrove, clicking his fingers. "Meg's quarters! We know where they are, on the same level as ours. There are bound to be some guns in there."

So, they had a location. Somewhere to aim for. But as they got ready to leave again, various questions were still nagging at Anna. If, as Musgrove maintained—and she still didn't know if she believed him, or even if his memory of events was intact—he didn't open that door to the tomb, who did? How were Helena and the others? Were they even still alive?

More importantly, if it hadn't been the dead alien responsible for all that knocking on the door to this room, and they hadn't been able to find it on the cams, then where in Heaven's name was it?

It was the one place in the entire ship that had no cams. He'd made sure of that.

Rafferty liked his privacy, and down here with the engines—in the ship's hull—was his sanctuary. The one place he was certain of not being bothered...much. Where he could control which comm messages he answered and which ones he didn't—like the one from that blonde woman earlier on. If it were something work-related, he'd always take it, like when the captain requested he go and rig up the energy nets and props in that alien church, then in the tunnel system below it. In the tomb. He'd always answer a call like that, even if it meant exposure to other people. His crew wasn't *so* bad—all right, bad enough—but these new strangers? Forget about it. He would always answer a call that intrigued him because the work was interesting, tested his abilities. He liked that.

And, of course, he wasn't averse to contacting others when their actions threatened a part of the ship—like when that moron Handles executed his landing on this planet like someone dropping an anvil from a cliff. Rafferty had felt like executing *him*, the mess he'd made down here. Still, it gave him something to work on. Tinker with. He did like to tinker. Liked to be alone and liked to tinker.

Alone... Now that wasn't strictly true. He didn't like the company of other *people*, but he did like to create his own company. His little friends, his "helpers," who he could control. He knew where he was with them; they weren't cruel like most of the human race. If Rafferty could go the rest of his life without contact with humans, that would suit him just fine. That compulsory evening in the rec-room when they'd held the "getting to know you" session had been like torture for him, and he'd only managed a few minutes.

He knew that if they saw him—actually saw him, away from the dark lighting of the engine rooms, without all the muck and grime all over him—they'd only make fun. Shun him for the monster he resembled. Rafferty was a second-gen clone, but something had definitely gone wrong somewhere in the mix. Yes, he could remember things from the original donor's life, and even the first gen who'd gone before him, which was the point, both engineers and very good ones at that. Not as good as him, and that was to be expected when you were building upon two sets of people's experiences; it was what had made him so sought after in his field. But it was a bit like copying a copy. Or trying to boost a signal that was getting fainter the further you traveled.

Rafferty's molecules were breaking down, scales and boils appearing more and more on his skin. His flesh was essentially rotting. He had maybe five, six more years tops. Though perhaps that was a blessing. God knows how the clone that came after him would fare. Not that Rafferty believed in God. No, he believed that after this came darkness. Nothing. And he was happy enough to embrace that.

When you were gone, you were fuckin' gone.

Or were you? Little did Rafferty know, something was about to happen down there in the belly of the *Artemis* that would test that theory. He knew when someone was in there, trespassing on his territory, intruding in his space. He could just *sense* it, that something was off. The crew had more brains than to venture into the engines, but that new lot... They didn't know, couldn't care less. Maybe it was the blonde woman coming down because she didn't get any answer from him on the comms? It was possible. Ill advised, but definitely possible.

Rafferty had been fixing yet another one of the coolant leaks that had appeared in the aftermath of the landing when he first realized someone was on his patch. He immediately took his finger off the trigger of the las-torch, lifting the protective mask he was wearing, eyes searching the gloom. Then he saw it, the shape there at the other end of a corridor that had piping flanking the sides.

"What do you want?" he croaked, using vocal cords that had also seen better days. He didn't even ask who the person was. "It had better be good!"

No answer. But the shape was still moving, heading toward him.

"You deaf?" Rafferty said.

Apparently, they were, because he still didn't get an answer.

"Look, just fuck off. I'm busy."

The figure kept on coming. Rafferty was swiftly losing patience with whoever this was.

"Don't make me tell you tw—" The sentence dried up in his already parched throat. Because the shape...the figure had moved into the half-light between sections, revealing at least part of it-self.

It was rotting, just like he was. One of the dead from the tomb he'd stabilized so that the archeology team could do their thing, and so The Corporation could get their samples. Rafferty blinked, not really understanding why it should be here; he hadn't kept tabs on what was going on above his decks, didn't really give a flying shit, so this development was new to him. Had they brought one back here to study, perhaps? And, in doing so, somehow reani-mated it? Wasn't the weirdest thing he'd ever come across. More to the point, what was he but an echo of a dead man himself—and one that was dying, too? They were dealing with an alien species after all, one they'd never encountered before.

But that still didn't explain why it was down here in the en-gines, unless it was looking for the place that most resembled its home? Those catacombs, the tomb? That was *this thing's* home. Down here, though, well... It was Rafferty's—and he didn't take too kindly to visitors, alive *or* dead.

"Okay," he said, stepping forward. The alien matched his move-ments, lurching, and at the same time reaching out with both hands. Each finger had claw-like nails attached, and when it opened its mouth, Rafferty could see sharp, ragged teeth. If it were possible, this creature was less friendly even than him.

But it'd picked on the wrong person today. Rafferty pulled down his mask again, cranked up the torch. When the creature—a real-life, honest-to-goodness monster—was close enough, he ad-justed the side and let the thing have it, full spread. It seared the front of the corpse, blackening it instantly, but it pushed against the beam like someone fighting a water cannon to get to the person wielding it.

Then suddenly, the torch was knocked from Rafferty's grasp. The beam cut out as soon as his finger wasn't on the trigger anymore, a safety feature, and one he was glad of now because it would have blown the entire engine deck apart if it had hit the wrong pipe.

The alien barreled into him with the force of a pile driver. Rafferty was shunted backward several yards, landing awkwardly on the floor, mask falling from his face. He sat up and coughed, noticing darkness in the phlegm when he spat. That wasn't good.

What was worse was the dead alien was still approaching, smoking where the las-wounds were now dying off. If he'd hit it with a proper flame, then... But it would have led to the same problem again—*boom!* He wasn't so much concerned about the crew or the archeologists as he was about his beloved engines. Do what you like to him, he didn't care. But touch those and you'd wish you hadn't been born, let alone died.

Rafferty got to his feet, holding his fists up in a boxing stance—something his original had been very good at, he recalled. "Come on then, ya bastard; let's see what you've got!"

Before the alien could hit him again, though, something grabbed it from behind. Grabbed it by the leg, preventing it from advancing any further, for the moment. Rafferty looked beyond the creature to see one of the 'bots he'd created—one of his "friends," the one he called Rex because it resembled a mechanical dog to some extent—holding the alien fast. More soon followed, including the chimp-like creature he'd named Bonzo, which clambered onto the thing's head and scrambled around it. Rafferty had always loved animals, and he got that from his previous incarnations as well, back when there had actually been more animals on Earth.

The corpse kicked out at Rex, trying to shake him off, and grabbed Bonzo, tearing the 'bot from its face and taking skin with it, before wrenching it in two. If the alien felt any pain at all, it didn't show it—though Rafferty supposed the first clue should have been the torch. If being blasted by that had no impact, then his fake monkey's attentions would be nothing but a mild annoyance.

Pip, the 'bot he'd fashioned to look like a bird—generic, as he couldn't settle on any particular type—came out of nowhere and flew at the alien now, talons also raking its dead flesh. Gunge oozed out of the deepest wounds, but the creature fought on, snatching at the bird and finally grabbing it and dashing it against the nearest pipe. Then it reached around and took hold of Rex, crushing the 'bot with both its hands so that it looked like it was in a decompression chamber. The strength that must have taken!

Rafferty's fists had dropped as soon as his 'bots had come to his defense, but he raised them again now as it continued with its mission of heading toward him. Rafferty got two, maybe three punches in, all of which glanced off and had no effect whatsoever. Then he was grabbed by the neck and lifted off the ground.

"J-Just...just fuckin' get on with it," Rafferty managed.

The alien cocked its head, stared at him, and for the briefest of moments, the engineer wondered if it was seeing beneath the surface, beneath all that grime and muck, to realize that they were brothers of a kind.

Then it opened its maw wider than Rafferty had ever seen anyone or anything do (except perhaps a snake on one of those old documentaries) and bit into him.

It wasn't long after that he was given his answer about death, about whether there really was only blackness afterward. Nothingness.

About whether if you were gone, you were actually fuckin' gone.

Chapter Twelve

They'd sat down to rest eventually, and to conserve what oxygen they had left.

Nothing but corridor after corridor. They had no idea where they were going or whether it even led anywhere at all.

Seeking, always seeking...

"Why make them, though, if they don't go somewhere?" was

Helena's argument.

"They could be a natural phenomena," Doug replied.

"You heard what Anna said. She was speculating whether they connected that chamber, those catacombs, with more from other towns or cities. I'm willing to bet she was right."

"Betting with our lives," said Doug.

Helena shook her head in despair. What choice did they bloody well have? Why was Doug being like this?

"So we could be looking at running into more of those things, just from another location?" Wayne had said.

"Not unless someone's opened another door we don't know about," she replied.

"So, assuming that's not the case, all we're looking at is running out of oxygen or those guys back there breaking through and trying to kill us again." Wayne let out a slow breath.

"Pretty much," said Helena.

"Just don't expect the cavalry to arrive." When she looked puzzled, he explained. "I promised you I wouldn't call in The Corporation yet, and I didn't. I'm beginning to wish I had, though."

"No outside help, then?" said Doug.

"Correct," Wayne informed him.

"But the ship... The bus. They've got to come back for us at some point," the professor concluded.

"Oh no," said Helena suddenly.

"What?" asked the captain.

"The bus... Meg." She looked from Wayne to Doug, then back again, but they didn't get what she was driving at, so she laid it out. "What if whatever's reanimating those corpses back there is communicable? What if that's what kept her alive down here?"

"Bollocks." Wayne looked like he needed a smoke, badly. And what he'd called a belt earlier. "But quarantine protocols would have been in place; they wouldn't have been let on board the *Artemis*."

Doug shifted about where he sat. "You're quite sure about that, are you?"

Wayne's silence spoke volumes. He knew as well as the rest

of them what lengths Rains might have gone to in order to get Thomas the treatment *she thought* was necessary.

"At the very least," Helena continued, "we have to assume that Rains and Burch might have been—"

Wayne held up a hand. They'd all seen the state of Meg Thomas, and she was someone who'd been left alive...sort of. "We've no way of letting them know either," he said. Signal through to the outside world was bad enough back there near the tomb, but the further they went into the cave system, the less likely it seemed their chances would get any better.

"What a fucking mess," said Wayne at last.

"And it's all my fault."

They turned, almost as one, when they heard Kelso's voice. He'd been sitting there quietly, Helena assumed just getting his head around the whole thing. That marveling at stuff could be a real drawback sometimes, and as for bloodshed...

But no, it seemed he'd been tapping things into his wrist computer—which he now held up, as if to show them he had actually been doing something. They couldn't see it from where they were, so he explained. "It's all my fault. If I hadn't said there was treasure in that room."

"Kelso, you can't blame yourself for what that idiot Musgrove chose to do," Helena assured him.

The young Asian man shook his head inside the helmet. "It isn't just that. I got it wrong. I got it so, so wrong. 'Behold, wanderers—treasure.' That's what I thought it said."

"What's all this about?" asked Wayne, who hadn't been there when they'd initially discovered the message above the door. "You guys thought there was treasure in there? That's why you opened it? And here I was thinking *we* were supposed to be the money-obsessed twats."

Helena shushed him and motioned for her assistant to go on. "It's actually a warning. It's a mistake anyone could have made... Look, see how that bit curls round at the end and—"

"Cut to the chase, kid," said Wayne, and for once Helena agreed with him.

"What it actually said was: 'Beware wanderers.' And I think the last bit, the word I thought was treasure... Well, I think it really says: 'Threat.' Or something along those lines. Terrible danger anyway. Like I said, it was a warning not to open the door."

"Can't imagine why, can you?" Wayne said, sarcasm dripping from the words.

"Threat?" Doug said. "It said *threat*?" He stood now, went over to Kelso. "You stupid, bloody idiot! I can't believe... Look what you did! Look what you bloody well did!"

Helena was up, too, tugging on Doug's arm to pull him away. He looked like he was going to just punch Kelso right there on the floor, punch his helmet until the plexi-glass broke. "It wasn't his fault. He made an honest mistake."

"A *mistake*!" Doug shrugged her off, grabbing Kelso by the front and practically hauling him to his feet. "You little shithead. You—"

Then Wayne was there, pulling Doug off Kelso. "That's enough!" he told him. "Calm the fuck down!"

Doug wrestled out of the captain's grip, turned his back on them. Helena wouldn't let him, though, and went round to stand in front of him. "Listen to me; it wasn't his fault. Kelso didn't force Musgrove open that door; *he* made that decision. It was his choice—and he paid the price for it."

"We all did," Wayne said from behind them.

Doug, taking deep breaths, looked down at the ground. Then up and to the side. Helena had seen that face before, knew what it meant. And the last time she'd seen it, she'd been terribly hurt. "Doug, what aren't you telling us? What aren't you telling *me*?" He looked at her then, eyes like a puppy dog waiting to be told off— and she knew. She knew who'd really opened that door. "Oh no, Doug... Why?"

"What's she talking about?" asked Wayne of no one in particular. "Why what?"

"I-I've got debts, Helena," Doug said in a low voice, but it didn't matter because the proximity-comms picked it up anyway. Wasn't like he was talking to someone in a corner at a crowded party.

"I'm… I owe the wrong people a lot of money."

The gambling again. Just one of Doug's vices that she'd known about. But one she thought he'd kicked a long time ago.

"So when you offered me this job, I jumped at it. The chance to put some distance between me and them."

"And make a bit of cash from alien artefacts on the black market at the same time," Helena added, hardly able to hide her disgust. Not really wanting to.

More bites at the cherry, he'd said, regarding those other potential tombs. Now she knew what he'd meant.

"No…no, that wasn't it at all. I—"

"You've put all of us at risk just because you thought you could pay some gangsters off with whatever was in that room? What the hell's wrong with you? What happened to that man I used to… used to look up to?" she asked him.

Doug's eyes were watering. "I'm sorry. I'm so sorry, Hel. They were going to—"

"To what? Kill you?" This was Wayne, the penny finally dropping, and he took hold of Doug now by the front of his envirosuit. "I just might save them the trouble!"

Helena tried to get between them but failed. Then it looked like Wayne was pulling Doug in closer, before throwing him down. Except she was moving as well, losing her footing. Kelso too was shifting sideways.

Another tremor.

The section of passageway they were in began to shake, dust and bone-rock falling from the ceiling. Wayne pointed ahead of them. "Move!" But Helena wasn't quite sure what good that would do. Without Rafferty's energy struts down here, they had no protection whatsoever.

Still they tried, moving forward, out of the way, attempting to dodge one rock after another, like they were in some kind of arcane computer game. One hit Wayne on the shoulder, pitching him to the right. Helena and Kelso stopped and went to help him up. They managed to pull him out of the way just as another two pieces of ceiling fell. Clouds of dust flew up everywhere, reducing visibility to practically zero—even with their helm-torches.

Then the tremors stopped, and the last bit of falling debris rained down. They waited there, just to make sure. But then the noise of rumbling was replaced by something else.

"Do you hear that?" asked Helena.

Kelso listened through his externals. "What is it?"

"Where's Doug?" This was Wayne, whose priorities were apparently somewhat different to theirs. The rage was still in his tone, the need for some sort of vengeance. But it was true; somehow they'd become separated from Doug when the rubble started falling.

The noise was getting louder, though, and at the last second, Helena realized what it was. The sound of lots and lots of feet. Heading their way. "Oh no," she said again, drawing her pistol at the same time.

Then the alien horde was suddenly in the tunnel with them, clambering over the bits of rock like they'd done back at the make-shift wall Wayne had created. One leaped straight for him, bringing the captain down and straddling him. Helena turned her pistol in that direction, but before she could fire, she was knocked into Kelso, who also toppled over.

Righting herself, Helena blasted the monster closest to her at point-blank range, causing it to fall back into its brethren. Then she remembered what she'd been doing and drew a bead on the one still plaguing Wayne. They were too close together, and her aim wasn't the most accurate at the best of times. As if realizing that, Wayne managed to get an arm underneath the thing's chin and push it upward, creating a gap between them. Helena took the shot, vaporizing half the creature's middle and allowing the captain to scramble backward on his elbows.

Heads were appearing through the dust, as if teleporting into the cavern. Helena shot at half a dozen, trying to hold them back, but it seemed like an impossible task.

Wayne was on his feet again, drawing up beside Kelso and helping him. "Th-There's too many of them," said the lad, shaken. "They'll kill us all!"

Pushing him to the rear, the captain joined Helena now, who was still firing. "What was it your professor said back there? Skin dryer than kindling? Let's test that theory, shall we?"

He raised his zippo, which he'd brought with him—for what reason, Helena had no idea, it wasn't like he *could* smoke inside the suit; maybe it had sentimental value?—and he lit it. Helena stopped firing for a second, long enough for him to run forward and set light to the nearest alien. The skin did indeed catch fire quickly, spreading up and across that creature's torso. It stumbled into another, setting that one on fire as well, causing a domino effect that would buy them precious moments to fall back.

Now, instead of a wall of dust behind them, there was a wall of flames. It wouldn't last long, Helena knew that, but it was better than being torn apart or eaten alive right there and then.

They stumbled on, the dust clearing a little. She risked a look over her shoulder and saw that even though they were on fire, those things were still coming. She had a feeling that they'd come even if they were just cinders. They'd hunt them. Facing front, she then saw where Doug was. He'd run off down the corridor, his shadow stretching along the wall.

"*Doug!*" she screamed, not knowing if the prox-comm would reach him—or whether he'd respond if it did. He turned, though, and looked back.

Just as the creatures caught up with them again. Helena fired back a couple of times, then her gun just died. Out of charge.

"Doug..." she repeated, sadness and pleading in her voice.

Then she heard his reply, even from this distance. "I'm sorry," he said again. And he was gone.

With tears in her eyes, Helena turned just as Wayne and Kelso had done. Facing the flood of cadavers, those on fire and those not. Facing their destiny together.

Facing, what had to be, their certain death.

Chapter Thirteen

"You want to hurry it up in there?"

The voice came from the doorway, where Anna Blackwell was keeping watch. She might be incredibly easy on the eye, thought Jay Musgrove, but she was a complete and utter pain! He was beginning to wonder why he'd gone off to find her at all when he woke up in the med-wing. Yet, she'd been the first person he thought of when he couldn't get through to anyone on the comms.

Go and find Anna.

And why wouldn't he? He'd hardly been able to stop thinking about her since they'd met, since that night in the rec-room when he thought he'd been getting somewhere with her. This one was going to take a while, he knew that, but it would be worth it in the end. Good Christ, would it be worth it! *I mean, just look at her!* he thought again, even as he was searching Meg Thomas's quarters, glancing over at the woman in the doorway. The things he'd like to do to her. That they could do together!

"Come on, Jay. Hurry up!"

But man... Okay, okay, these were somewhat trying circumstances—he'd give her that. The blood. The dead alien on the rampage. All the more reason to try and take their mind of things, though, wasn't it? He'd figured himself as some sort of hero, rushing to her rescue, ready to protect her—that kind of crap. Yes, he was fully aware that things weren't like the old days, like when his granddad met his nan—or even his mother met his father. There were rules and regs now; you could get into serious trouble for some of the shit he was thinking, for some of the things he said to women—and he very nearly had on occasion. Had been called all sorts in his time, "throwback," "selfish," "sexist shithead"; the works. Yet he was still firmly convinced that they liked it, for the man to take charge or whatever.

"*Jay!*"

"I'm lookin', I'm lookin'!"

She scowled at him. Didn't fool Jay. She wanted him, he just knew it. All they had to do was survive this. That's why he was looking for a weapon in the first place, he reminded himself. Survival, yes, but also—

Although there was the small problem that Anna thought he was responsible for it all in the first place. That he'd opened the doorway down in those catacombs. It had all been so muddled to start with, his memory of those events. He'd be lying if it hadn't crossed his mind to do it, open that door and see what the treasure could be, that Kelso had said was on the other side. But he hadn't, Jay was sure of it. He would have remembered doing something like that.

All he could recall was going down those steps with Grable and— *Grable!* It had to have been him who'd done it! Let all that weird steam out that had flattened him, knocked him out until he'd come to all that time later. Except when he'd tried to convince Anna of that on their way to Meg's quarters, she'd been having none of it.

"Why would Douglas have done something like that?" she retorted. Douglas, not Professor Grable anymore. And Jay's lip curled when he thought back to that night in the rec-room, the way that man had been trying to muscle in on his action with Anna. The way most of the men had tried by the end of the evening, when it came right down to it. Why not? Look at her. Just *look at her!* Jay licked his lips...

No, he had to try and concentrate on the task in hand. There was time for all that later—he hoped.

"What are you staring at?" snapped Anna. "Get looking!"

He'd show her, he'd win her over. Get in her good books again, no matter what it took.

"Jay... Jay hurry. I think I can hear... Shit, I can hear footsteps!"

Fuck! thought Jay. *What now?* He couldn't believe he'd been envisioning a scenario where he'd have to be "the man" to stand up and protect her. Especially when he couldn't find a bloody thing in Meg's quarters apart from some quite nice lesbian porn, which had held things up a little, he had to admit.

Maybe he should just run away? No, run off and take her *with* him. Grab Anna by the hand so they could hole up somewhere cozy and wait this out. Too late. She was coming in. Closing the door and locking it behind her.

"It's in the corridor," she said, biting her lip.

"What?"

"You heard me!"

"But...but you've just trapped us in here now," Jay gasped.

She flashed him a look that in part said she hadn't known what else to do, and also that she didn't need reminding of it. Anna looked terrified, was practically shaking. He should just shut up about it. What was done was done. She clearly *needed* him.

Jay rose, took a step toward her, then hesitated. From what she'd said, that dead alien was strong. *Really* strong. It was why she'd thought he was the creature trying to get through the door earlier on. Did he want to get too close? If it did tear down this door, maybe Anna would be able to buy him some time to get away?

Then again, maybe this was his chance to get closer *to her*? If he was going out, perhaps he should just go out with a smile on his face? A few minutes, that was all he'd need if Anna was up for it?

No, what *are you thinking?*

Maybe just a hug then? They probably both needed it. Needed to feel safe. He approached her, arms wide, about to put them around her—when Anna shoved him away.

"What in God's name are you doing?" she snarled.

"Com...comforting you," he told her.

"I don't need bloody comforting," she assured Jay. "I need that thing to be wiped off the face of the Earth...the ship!"

He nodded. Yet, when the first of the bangs at the door came, Jay leaped backward. Couldn't help himself. The self-preservation gene; always outweighed the need to get laid.

Anna backed off as well, but in the opposite direction—into the other corner of the room. He wondered whether he should go and join her, but then thought twice when the sharp, urgent banging came again.

She started looking around, searching for something to fight it with.

"I looked, there's nothing here," Jay promised her. Didn't she trust him or something?

Anna ignored him and carried on rifling through stuff as the banging intensified. Getting frustrated when she realized Jay was right, that there was nothing useful inside this room. Nothing but laundry and personal effects.

Bang! Bang!

Any minute now it would break through. Any minute now it would—

"Please… I saw you come in here. Please, open up!"

They turned and looked at each other. The voice that had drifted through the door wasn't alien, and definitely didn't belong to a dead alien on the rampage. It sounded as scared as they were.

"*Please!*" it said again, and Jay recognized it as belonging to that prick—the science officer who'd explained what a damned earthquake was to him. Arsehole!

Burch, that was his name. The long streak of—

Anna was rising, going to the door. Recreating the scene of when she answered it to him. Jay sprang to his feet and headed her off, beating her to it. "I'll handle this," he told her. Taking charge, being the man.

She hit him on the arm again as it slid open. Playful, jokey; he knew that was all it was. S'alright, he told himself. Still in with a chance.

And there he was, thin as a rail, all the color drained from his face. "Oh, thank God! Thank *you!*" Jay looked down and saw all the blood covering him. Burch followed his gaze. "It isn't mine," he assured them.

"What happened?" asked Anna.

Burch shook his head. "We don't have time for explanations. We need to get off the ship, right now!"

"Off the ship? But where would we go?" asked Anna.

"Somewhere, *anywhere* safe!" he spluttered.

"Look, we just need to kill that thing," said Jay, then realized what he'd said, the fact that it was already dead. "I mean destroy it. Do you know where the armory is? Weapons?"

"What thing?" The science officer looked bewildered.

"It came back with you on the bus," said Anna.

"You mean Meg?"

"We're going around in circles here," Jay said, sighing. "Do you or do you not know where we can get our hands on some bloody big guns?"

"Weapons won't stop them."

"*Them?*" Anna bit her lip again. "You mean there's more than one of those dead aliens running around out there?"

"Dead aliens..."

The ship lurched, a tremor shifting it and sending vibrations up Jay's leg. "Are those things still happening?"

"Unfortunately," Anna replied. "But I think right now that's the least of our problems."

"Agreed," said Jay, then turned again to Burch. "Guns?"

"I'll take you to them," he said, nodding.

"Lead the way." Jay held out his hand for the man to go on ahead. Then he took Anna's arm to escort her out. She pulled it sharply away.

You can't fight it forever, he said to himself as he padded after her. She was crazy about him, he could tell. *It's only a matter of time...*

⚰⚰⚰⚰⚰

It was just a matter of time.

Douglas Grable knew that. Time before his oxygen ran out, time before those dead things caught up with him—though Helena and co. would keep them occupied for a bit—time before, if none of that killed him, his past caught up with him instead.

That was the reason he'd done what he'd done, the cause of all this. If he didn't pay what he owed to Harold Metcalf and his boys, there wasn't a planet in the universe that would be far enough away; they'd reach him anywhere. Loan-sharking was in Metcalf's blood, along with the rest of it; his family had been in the business of organized crime for well over a century, dating back to his grandfather: the bastard son of notorious gangland boss, Nicholas Metcalf.

Douglas had said sorry to Helena back there, and he'd meant it. Sorry for letting those things out, sorry for letting her down after she'd given him this opportunity. Sorry for leaving them behind. Well, her anyway. Douglas didn't give a toss what happened to her idiot assistant and that wanker of a captain.

Sorry for screwing up her life all those years ago. For not being the man she'd thought he was, that she deserved. He'd cared about her, of course he had. Still did, sort of. Not enough to go back there and help her, especially after she'd made it pretty clear whose side she was on. How she felt about the aforementioned flyboy of the galaxy. He'd seen that look before, the way she gazed at the guy. She used to look at him that way, before he'd blown it.

Douglas shook his head. None of that mattered now; she'd made her bed and she could lie in it. He just needed to get away, get back to the ship—somehow. If he didn't run out of air first; there was that. If the dead creatures from the tomb didn't catch up.

There was still a way of salvaging something out of all this mess. Get back to the *Artemis*, get away from this planet, sell his story. That would make enough to pay off Metcalf three times over and still have enough left to set himself up for life. He was trying very hard not to think about what Helena had said, about whatever this was being communicable. That Meg Thomas might have carried it back to the ship and he'd be no safer there than he was down in these caverns.

He was good at not thinking about things. The consequences of things. He'd made a career out of doing that, and he'd been more successful at it than he had all that academic stuff. Just one more bet, what harm could it do? Just one more lay, one more drink?

No, he'd get back to the ship and all would be right with the world. Might even get to know Anna Blackwell a little better. Let that moron Musgrove take the fall for unleashing those monsters, fly away from here and—

It was as he was thinking this that he saw it. The chink of light in an otherwise pitch-black tunnel. It wasn't coming from his helm-torch because the closer he drew to it, Douglas actually turned that off and was able to see just fine. Because the light wasn't coming from down here at all; it was coming from up above. A way out!

Wasn't exactly as he'd imagined, as Helena or Anna had said—the tunnel connecting with another town or city. But the gaping hole above him, letting in sunlight from above, would do just fine, thank you very much. Especially as the ground that had caved in and created it formed a sort of stairway up to the surface. Must have happened during the last quake, he reasoned. That wasn't important either; it was here, and it was exactly what he'd been searching for: a way out.

Seeking, always seeking... Just like he'd said to Helena.

They'd walked quite a way through these tunnels, so maybe the ship was closer now? At the very least, being above ground would make getting through to them easier. Douglas thought about going back then, to see if anyone had survived. To see if Helena had, if he was being honest.

But instead, he began to climb up the rubble toward the brightness. It would take him a little while, but he'd get there. Then he was on the home stretch. He could put off thinking about everything else.

And he was so focused on the task at hand, in getting up through that hole, he didn't hear the echoes. Making so much noise climbing, he didn't hear the footfalls coming from the opposite direction, from further up the tunnel where he'd been heading.

If he had, he would have known that Helena and Anna's theory was correct. That the catacombs all connected to each other. But nobody had needed to open the door in the tomb belonging to the next church along, because the quake had cracked it wide, split it down the middle.

Allowing more of Thana's dead to escape.

Chapter Fourteen

Two things happened in the catacombs, but the second thing didn't happen quickly enough.

Definitely didn't happen in time to save Kelso, after the surge of dead bodies filled the tunnels. Helena and Wayne kicked and punched the first few at the front, working together, but the mob easily swamped the young assistant, biting off his hand for starters. Then pretty soon it was like he was drowning in the things. Helena saw his other arm and hand appear once or twice, even tried to reach out for it.

Then it was gone.

"Eddie!" she cried out, but there was nothing either of the survivors could do now.

Almost didn't happen in time to save Wayne either, pinned up against the wall of the corridor—although this was probably what stopped him from being hit when the shooting started. Helena, for her part, ducked as soon as she realized what was happening; instinctively getting down and throwing herself to one side when the blasts began.

Beams of different colors filled that tunnel, making it look like the dead were being attacked by rainbows. But where these struck them, it ripped them apart—the firepower incredible, putting their own efforts with the rifle and pistol to shame. It didn't take long to clear a path this way, figures appearing behind the wall of dead that had been attacking them.

Wayne and Helena exchanged puzzled glances; he even shrugged. But she saw now that his suit had been ripped there at the shoulder, where the rock had hit him before. If he didn't sort that soon, he'd be in serious trouble. Luckily, one of the first people who appeared was wearing a black enviro-suit with a red cross on the chest. He had ginger hair, Helena saw through the plexi-glass of his helmet, and was looking round, trying to ascertain if anyone needed treatment at all. When the medic spotted

Wayne, he ran over and started to patch up his suit with filler. He then started rummaging around in the bag he was carrying for spare oxy-pods to give the pair of them.

"Hold on, hold on," said the captain. "Who *are* you? What are you doing here? How did you *get* here?"

More of the people dressed in black—no, not black, but dark green, she realized—appeared then behind the medic, although their suits seemed to be more like armor than anything. Scaly, green armor for ease of movement. And they were carrying some heavy-duty rifles, a couple of them so big they almost didn't fit in their hands.

The one at the front of this group, the one clearly in charge, stepped forward, having heard Wayne's questions through the prox-comms. "In order," said the man, who had a crew-cut so short he might as well have been bald. "I'm Sergeant Hannibal Rowland, Medusa Squad. We're here to save your butts."

"The cavalry," she found herself saying.

Rowland took her in, looking her up and down. "If you like. As for how we got here... Well, if you don't mind, I'd rather we walked and talked."

✕✕✕✕✕

Captain Wayne might have kept his promise not to let The Corporation know, but Security Chief Meghan Thomas had done no such thing. Hadn't even made the promise in the first place. So, as soon as she heard about what was down in those catacombs, she'd pushed the panic button.

"Loyal to a fault," Rowland said and glared accusingly at Wayne when he said this. "Corporation girl to the end. Good job, as well."

Wayne, in turn, looked over at Helena. She felt bad now, knew that the favor she'd asked of the man would get him into bother; she'd talk to his bosses, hopefully get them to see it wasn't his fault. But, for now, Wayne had to settle for changing the subject. "Even using an Elastic Drive, it would have taken you—"

"We set off not long after you did," Rowland interrupted. "Kept at a discreet distance. It's Corporation policy on missions like this one, just in case there's any…unpleasantness."

Missions where there might be a profit for The Corporation, thought Helena, but said nothing. Given the circumstances, it would seem more than a bit ungrateful.

"Now, I know what you're thinking Miss Kirby—"

"*Dr.* Kirby," she corrected.

"All right, Doctor, then… You're thinking we were sent to keep an eye on you. But let me assure you that if we hadn't been alerted to this—if we hadn't picked up on the fact something was going on down here—you never would have known we were even around."

"Comforting," said Helena.

"Should be," he told her, missing or ignoring her point. "As it was, we thought we'd bring a shuttle down to the surface and check out your little discovery. Imagine our surprise when we saw all those fellas flooding out of the church back there. Pretty spry for a bunch of dead guys, ain't they?" Rowland gave a small laugh at that, and not for the first time, Helena thought that he was taking all this quite well. In his not inconsiderable stride. Then again, grunts like these—Corporation grunts at that—who knows what kinds of things they'd encountered in their time. "Pretty deadly, too," the sergeant added. "But nothing we couldn't take care of. They don't call us the Medusa Squad for nothing. We show up and it turns our enemies to stone."

"Yeah, I got the subtle reference." Rowland chuckled again at her remark. "I'm going to assume that there's not much left of the tomb then?"

"You still want to study this place, Doctor? Even after everything that's happened?"

Helena didn't reply, just carried on walking forward. Heading in the direction Douglas had gone. She still couldn't believe they were bothering to look for him, but it had been because of what Rowland said really. "We read four life-signs down here, back when we could get a reading, that is. Actual life-signs, as opposed to just movement. What happened to—"

"Dead," Helena had answered, holding back the tears, trying not to think about what Kelso had gone through during the skirmish. She was going to leave it at that and felt sure Wayne would have done so in a heartbeat, but she couldn't just abandon Doug as he had done them. "Well, one of them. My assistant. The other..."

"Ran off," Wayne finished for her. "It's his fault all this is happening in the first place. Fucking Professor Douglas Grable."

"Right," said Rowland, then turned to Helena. "Your call, Miss... Dr. Kirby. But, personally, I hate to leave a man behind, no matter how much of a yella-belly he is."

Helena had shrugged herself then. If they didn't at least try, she probably wouldn't be able to live with herself. Though Doug seemed to have no problem doing the same. Wayne just shook his head but joined them when they set off.

So, on they pushed ahead. He couldn't have gotten that far, they reasoned—and yet, it felt to Helena like they'd been walking for miles with no sign of Doug anywhere. It was as they turned one particular corner that they spotted the shaft of light: a hole in the ceiling of the tunnel, with a convenient "ladder" of rubble to climb up.

"I bet our missing professor made use of that," Rowland said, jabbing a finger in its direction.

"Maybe we should follow him?" offered Wayne, but the sergeant was all for heading back to the shuttle now and picking him up that way. In any event, it was taken out of their hands. They heard the echoing sound first, filling up the catacombs. Then the dead bodies themselves doing the same, rushing toward them. Nobody had been expecting it, and like the other attacks, it all happened so quickly.

Another wave of aliens rushed toward the group, with no end to them in sight.

Chapter Fifteen

The attack had taken them all by surprise.

Rounding a corner and suddenly being confronted with two of the dead aliens, only there was something different about them. They'd been following Burch, and when he saw them, he hung back—almost knocked his companions over in his retreat.

When he said the names, then it clicked: "Susan, Meg..."

Anna gawped at the figures, pretty much unrecognizable now as the people they'd been. Had the alien got to them, changed them? Certainly would have explained the blood back at the med-wing. Burch hadn't really said a great deal since they encountered him back at Meg Thomas's quarters—and Jay's constant prattling to her, pestering her, had prevented Anna from questioning the man further—but now what he'd said there made a sort of sense:

"What thing?"

"It came back with you on the bus."

"You mean Meg?"

Had she been changing since the catacombs, passed this on to Rains? Which meant they weren't just dealing with the one who'd hitch-hiked, but now three? And where was the pilot, Hannigan?

Didn't matter. All that mattered was they hadn't reached the armory and were facing two...monsters. It was the only word for them. Rains and Thomas were monsters, simple as that. Burch was still pulling back, Musgrove joining him.

"What...what *are* they?" he was whimpering.

When it came right down to it, and even with all of Jay's bluster, they were just like scared little boys. Someone had to do something—the time for backing off into corners and pretending this wasn't happening was over. Time to make another stand, no matter how it worked out.

Then the smell hit her. "What's that, alcohol?" Looking around, she saw Burch nod. No explanation as to why they were doused in it, these two creatures who had once been human, who looked like they needed a drink even more than her trio did but would probably prefer to just eat them instead. It was something she could use, though, something they could fight them with.

"Here," she said to Musgrove and Burch, "help me with this." She was pointing at a panel off to one side, then digging her fingers into the grooves to loosen it.

"What...?" asked Jay again.

"There isn't time, just *help me!*" Anna screamed at him. She risked a glance ahead to see the pair advancing, working out that their prey was only minutes, seconds away.

The two men were practically useless, and in the end, it was probably Anna's sheer force of will that pulled off that panel. Revealing wires and coils behind it. The real workings of the ship, the guts of it hidden behind that façade. And the lights were still on, the electricity still flowing, which meant...

"Stand back!" she said to the two men. Burch didn't need telling twice, but Musgrove looked like he wanted to help now that he'd figured out her plan. Take control now that she'd done the hard work. Bloody men! "*Back!*" she warned him, then ripped out the insulated wires she was holding, exposing the live bits at the end.

Rains and Thomas were only inches away, so she thrust the wires at them, into the nearest body: Thomas, who jerked as the voltage ran through her, instantly catching fire where the booze had soaked in.

Then Rains, in turn. The pair almost embracing as they must have done hundreds of times, now as one again. A single flaming alien hybrid.

Anna was backing off, dragging both men by the arms and pulling them around yet another corner for cover. She peered back round to see what was happening, the flames engulfing not only the couple but that section of the corridor. They were on the floor now, writhing about. But they still refused to just lie down and accept they were dead. That they had, to all intents and purposes, died a while ago.

Now they were crawling toward them, spreading the fire as they went. An alarm started up, and CO_2 sprays were doing their best to try and combat this, but already it was in the walls, had gotten back into the very electrical system she'd used to fight the things.

"Fuck!" said Anna. "Come on, move!" They had to get out of there. Maybe even off the ship altogether because there was at least one more dead alien around that was as tough as those two. Get to some suits, get to the bus? She wasn't thinking any further ahead.

Survival, that was all. Just survival.

It was all they could do to survive by the end.

The Medusa Squad had stepped up and opened fire on that first batch of the dead, cutting them down as they must have done the others from the tomb under the first church. But it seemed to Helena that there was a never-ending supply of replacements this time, and that no matter how many they hit with those rainbow beams of theirs, more would appear to take their place.

They'd started the retreat, naturally, as soon as the first lot of corpses had shown their faces. But it was a slow process, not helped by another quake rocking the catacombs only moments after the throng descended on them. The falling rock alone took out four or five of Rowland's troopers, despite their armor. Nothing they could do for those who were buried under it, not when the dead were clambering over them and there was debris on top.

Helena had snatched up an abandoned rifle at that point, preferring to rely on herself for protection rather than any of the soldiers. She hadn't missed the tip of the head Rowland gave her, either as approval or simply in admiration. One of the dead leaped at her, and she swung the weapon, depressing the trigger and hoping it was no more complicated than the pistol she'd been using earlier. It wasn't, but it was a lot more powerful—the beam cutting her adversary in half, yet at the same time, the kick throwing her backward.

Once she'd steadied herself, Helena glanced around to see how the captain was faring, if he'd managed to grab a weapon himself. He hadn't because he'd been thrown against the wall. She heard the crack of his helmet before seeing the massive breach it caused. Much bigger than Musgrove's had been. He fell to the ground, not moving, limbs out at awkward angles, almost certainly broken.

"Wayne," she breathed. Helena wasn't going to lose another person on this mission, from either her team or the crew: one and the same now in her head. So, she continued to fire, holding the dead at bay until she could reach the man. She had no idea how she was going to help him.

Another rumble pitched her sideways, and she found herself fighting alongside a member of the Medusa Squad. Far from turning anything to stone, the terrified look on this young female—maybe even a rookie?—soldier's face should have made anyone feel sorry for her. But she was up against things that apparently had no feelings at all because they rushed her and started biting and clawing into the girl, tearing through that armor like it was paper. Seconds later, she was a bloody mess that Helena had to get away from as fast as she could. The rookie at least bought her some time to finally get over to Wayne.

Ahead of her, she saw Rowland aim his weapon at a section of roof; he was not willing to wait until it caved in of its own accord, targeting it instead. Shooting and jumping backward as it fell in on several of the dead, blocking all but a small bit of the tunnel at the top and slowing down the advance of the horde. Forcing them to funnel into a smaller space to reach the living.

"We need to fall back, regroup!" Rowland ordered, his tone much less assured than it had been when they'd first met.

"Wayne," Helena repeated, this time jabbing the end of her rifle toward him to show that she wanted to help.

Rowland shook his head. "Look at him. He's dead." Helena went over anyway to make sure, bending and shaking him. "He's gone, Dr. Kirby." The sergeant might hate to leave anyone behind, but he also knew a lost cause when he saw it; the troops he'd lost back there, and Wayne here.

She reluctantly nodded, got up, and was about to go with Rowland when she heard the cracking. This wasn't like Wayne's helmet; instead, it was the cracking of bones that she'd figured were definitely broken. Helena turned back to see Wayne moving. Twitching at first, perhaps in the spasms of death? But no...he was rising up, arms straightening and helping himself up the wall, his back to her. More cracks as his legs straightened.

"Wayne?" This third calling out of his name was the charm, it seemed, because he turned, facing her. But that face! His whole head was altered. When it had happened, Helena had no idea. That first attack? The last one? That wound from the falling rock, which perhaps hadn't been caused that way at all. If only the medic had taken a proper look and not just patched it up... Would it even have done any good?

None of that was important now; none of it was as important as being proved right about the contamination (Christ alone knew what was happening back on the ship); about the fact that Wayne's head was elongating, his beanie no longer fitting, eyes sunken and strange. None of it was as important as surviving, when all Wayne clearly wanted to do was kill her.

Now the tears did come, and she didn't even understand why. She'd only known this guy a short time, and yes, there had been a connection—maybe even more of a connection than she'd experienced with that silly bastard, Doug Grable—but why was she weeping and why now? Because he represented the last of them down here? Because he was a missed opportunity? Because he might have been her Kirk, her Sheridan? That in another time and another place, they might have...

No, it's because you've got to do it yourself, she thought. *Because it's down to you. It's all down to you now.*

So as Wayne made to spring forward, Helena finally raised her rifle, sniffing back those tears.

Then she pressed the trigger and said a silent goodbye.

Chapter Sixteen

It wasn't just the next town along that the quakes were affecting.

In all the towns, all the cities, and former population centers on Thana, the violent shaking was dislodging the borders around those underground doors, creating gaps that let out streams of the strange wind that had knocked Douglas Grable and Eddie Kelso on their backs and put Jay Musgrove in a coma. Or the doors were obliterated again, cracking under the strain.

Opening up the tombs that spanned the length and breadth of this planet. Waking the dead, *releasing* the dead, so they could claim the world that was rightly theirs once more.

✶ ✶ ✶ ✶ ✶

A slog was the only way to describe it, their journey back through those corridors again to reach the original crypt.

The dead would break through in twos or threes, clambering through the gap left when Rowland brought down that section of the tunnel. Easy enough to handle in small batches, but it slowed their own progress down considerably.

Then, at some point, the aliens must have cleared the blockage in the same way they did with the one that saved Helena, Wayne, Grable and Kelso, cutting off their escape route, but also preventing their deaths at the same time. Now, there was only Helena left of that quartet, standing with the soldiers who'd come to rescue them.

Standing and fighting with them as the bodies rampaged up those enclosed spaces once more. She counted only something like a dozen of Medusa Squad left with her, a few having bought it since they set off back toward the church. Shared their disappointment when they finally reached what should have been the entrance, leading back up to the surface, only to find that had caved in as well.

"What now?" asked Helena, pumping out several more blasts from her rifle. She'd found that if she nestled it in the crook of her arm, it steadied the thing enough that it didn't kick so much.

"Well," said Rowland, "I've been reluctant to use any of these down here, but..." He detached something from his belt that was metallic, disc-shaped, and had a button on the top. Helena knew a grenade when she saw one, no matter what its shape was.

It was then that they heard it. Masked at first by the noise of the dead following them up the tunnel they'd just retreated along, this was a similar sound—only it was coming from somewhere else.. From the corridor on their other side, leading away from the tomb and church in the opposite direction.

More of the aliens, from yet another location—they'd be trapped by them soon, attacked on two sides instead of just one.

"Use it, *use it!*" shouted Helena, and Rowland nodded.

He depressed the button, tossed it at the landslide covering the crack they'd all used to get down here, then shouted, "Fire in the hole!" Rowland, Helena, and the rest of the troops all hit the deck as the grenade flashed green, then red, then blue, orange, and yellow. If the beams from the rifles were individual rainbow colors, then this thing was all of them combined. It blew seconds later, and Helena gave a grunt of satisfaction as some of the flying chunks of bone rock hit the approaching dead from either side. She'd gone from wanting to study these things, to feeling sorry for them, then wanting to wipe every last fucking one of them off the face of Thana.

Looking up when the dust settled, she saw the blast had punched another hole in the church, more ragged and haphazard than the natural one that had been created under the altar, but it looked like the most beautiful thing she'd ever seen.

"Everyone okay?" called out the ginger medic, who'd not been able to do much to save any of the lost members of his party up to now. His question was met with a series of mumbles and murmurs and several thumbs in the air.

"Right, then let's shift it, people!" said Rowland, waving his men before him between letting off shots left and right into the tunnels, trying to stem the stream of the dead. "Now you, Dr. Kirby," he said, clapping her shoulder as she went past. An honorary member of the squadron, Rowland's respect for her was clear. The last to clamber up, making sure his men were safe first, Rowland was halfway to the top when he stopped. Something was pulling him backward.

"Go, go!" he barked at Helena and the others, waiting up top in the church. But she stepped forward, jammed her gun into the gaping space, and pumped off several rounds. A couple of soldiers on either side pulled Rowland free, but it was clear his leg was injured, that the dead had grabbed hold of it. There were marks on the armor at his thigh, but she couldn't get a clear look between the scales, couldn't determine whether the suit had been punctured. And there wasn't really time; they had to get back to the shuttle. Rowland was helped by the troops closest to him, given covering fire by the rest.

That cover multiplied when they got outside the church and Helena saw someone in a dome on top of an equally reptilian shuttle, operating a much larger cannon from his mount. The man was blasting the dead indiscriminately as they emerged from the building, sending them up into the air and giving the beleaguered squadron time to reach the landing craft.

A flap-door opened at the back and the soldiers practically tumbled in, one after the other, helped by more inside, the sound of heavy breathing filling the prox-comms. "Get her up!" Rowland called out through gritted teeth, and the pilot did as he was told.

Helena went to the first available window and looked out through it, watching as the gunner's fire struck clump after clump of the alien dead filling the church and the streets outside it. Soon, that city was overrun and she was glad to be above it, not down there on the ground, or even under it.

Now they needed to see what was happening back at the *Artemis*, and if there was anybody else left who'd survived.

They'd survived so far, that was the main thing.

Okay, so they hadn't made it to the cargo bay, to a bus, but they had managed to grab three enviro-suits before being cut off by one of the aliens (it looked scorched on the front, on his chest, like someone had really done it some damage) barring their way, having returned there. With Rains and Thomas at their backs, not to mention the fire that continued to ravage the *Artemis*, and that thing in front of them, they'd opted for going upward.

Managing to lose it by climbing up into a service hatch and then closing that behind them, Philip and the two members of the archeology team he'd picked up along the way got into their suits and came up with a plan of action.

"Maybe we can access the cargo bay from the outside, get to the bus?" Musgrove had suggested, then asked Philip if it was possible.

"Perhaps." After all, he'd been the one who'd bypassed the doors in the first place to give Meghan Thomas the run of the ship. The one who'd caused the deaths of both Dr. Rains and Handles. He shook his head, had to stop thinking like that. He hadn't known at the time what would happen. But he'd had the bus's computers back then, had been able to hack into the *Artemis*'s control network and order the doors to open. From the outside it would be much more difficult, but not impossible.

"That's good enough for me," Anna Blackwell had said. This woman who'd shown remarkable strength and courage back there when facing the two changed crewmembers. So much more than he'd displayed in this entire debacle. "Let's go!"

So, they'd followed his lead once more, up and up, through more service hatches to reach the top floors of the ship, and then, finally, to the hatch that would open up onto the surface of it. Quakes continued to rock them as they climbed, and when they finally got outside—standing on the top of the craft—they saw the consequences of all that activity.

"My Lord," whispered Philip. Handles, whether he'd intended to or not, had really done a number on this planet. There were cracks in the surface, running away from and toward the ship.

Holes in places, big craters that revealed a network of tunnels running below, confirming, Blackwell said, a theory she'd had about the tombs all being interconnected. Bodies were climbing out of those spaces, however, climbing up above ground, like they really were rising from their graves. More of the alien dead, gathering and making their way toward the ship.

He felt a tapping on his shoulder and turned to see Musgrove pointing at the hatch they'd just climbed through. They had more immediate concerns, if that were at all possible; the smoke billowing through that hole told them that the fire had spread again, had climbed as if chasing them.

Yes, they'd survived, but for how much longer? Philip Burch had to ask himself now.

Chapter Seventeen

It was as they were banking away from the city, on their way to the *Artemis*, that the pilot shouted it out.

Someone was running—or what passed for running in an enviro-suit—across the bleached earth of the planet. A human figure, or as Rowland said, "Looks like your yella-belly professor, Dr. Kirby."

Regardless of the fact his oxy-pods must be practically out, he was propelling himself forward—going where, they didn't have the faintest. He was certainly nowhere near the ship, and he wouldn't get to it without help. Then they all saw why he was running.

A mass of the dead aliens had followed him up through the opening in the ground and were in pursuit. He'd gotten a fair way since climbing up, but they were as fast as they were strong, those things. Even as Helena watched, they narrowed the gap between Doug and themselves in a matter of minutes.

"So..." said Rowland, as if waiting for her to give the command.

She stared at him. Was it really her decision? Back in the

catacombs, she'd felt like leaving him behind just like he'd left them. But now, here, and seeing what was about to happen to Doug... No one deserved that, not even him. Helena shrugged, then nodded, and Rowland told the pilot to drop down for a pick-up.

They were almost there as well, as near as dammit—so close that Helena could see Doug's sweating face through the plexiglass of his helmet, and she felt like he could see her, too. Then the dead put on a spurt, racing to catch him, bringing Doug down and swarming over him. He managed to get an arm up, a hand, then all she could see was a geyser of blood exploding where he'd been, flashes of his body as they ripped it to pieces and greedily ate. It was practically a repeat of what had happened to Kelso.

"Pull up, pull up," Rowland called back to the pilot. "It's over."

As they gained altitude again, Helena found herself saying, "Sorry," to Doug, just as he had to her when he ran off.

Whether or not she actually meant it was another matter, and something she didn't even know herself.

✂ ✂ ✂ ✂ ✂

It was the same story everywhere as they drew nearer to the ship.

More and more quakes were wracking the planet, splitting it open like an Easter egg. And where there were cavities, where chasms appeared, the dead were not far behind. Joining together, covering the bits of the world that weren't devastated by the seismic activity.

"It's increasing exponentially," said one of the soldiers monitoring a screen inside the shuttle—possibly the closest person the Medusas had to a Phil Burch.

"Meaning?" asked Rowland.

"Meaning this planet is fucked," replied the soldier.

It wasn't the only thing, Helena thought as they arrived at the *Artemis*. The parts of the ship that weren't on fire were sinking into the ground, into deep trenches that were opening up, tipping the whole slab of a thing on its side.

But... Yes! "*There!*" Helena almost wailed, spotting the three suited figures clinging to the edge of the ship.

"I see them," said the pilot, but still awaited instructions from Rowland before doing anything.

"Well, let's get on with it then," was the only reply the sergeant had to give.

The back of the shuttle flopped open once more, but the pilot was having trouble getting close enough for the survivors to climb on board. An explosion didn't help matters, rocking both vehicles and causing one of the suited figures to almost lose its grip. But there were other problems, as Helena could now see. On the side of the ship were two...no, *three* more figures. Two looked like they were on fire, the third like it had come off worse in a fire*fight*. They'd emerged from what looked like a hole blown in the ship and were heading toward the humans.

"We have to hurry!" she said, calling back into the shuttle.

"I-I can't get any nearer," the pilot warned.

Helena looked around, desperate for something to help get down to them. For some way of hauling them in. "Here," said a voice from behind her. "Let me."

Rowland was standing there, his suit attached to a tether that he was uncoiling behind him. Before she could say anything, he'd jumped from the back of the shuttle, the length of cable trailing behind. It looked like something he'd done a million times; he probably had.

He landed with a bump not that far away from the first couple of figures. There appeared to be some debate as to who was going with Rowland first, and Helena, well aware that they couldn't hear through prox-comms, said under her breath, "For Heaven's sake, just pick!" Then one of the suited figures pushed the other one forward, and Rowland grabbed on. The cable started to retract.

Helena jumped when several blasts went off at the side of her, but then she saw soldiers were targeting the dead. They were clambering up the other side of the *Artemis*, some reaching the top and attempting to leap from there into or onto the shuttle.

Then the rescued survivor was at the mouth of the shuttle,

and Helena was helping them inside. It was Anna Blackwell, who fell into her arms. "It's...oh, it's so good to see you!" said the woman.

"You, too," replied Helena as they parted. "Who else is—"

"Jay, and Science Officer Burch."

"*Jay?*" Helena exclaimed. The last time she'd seen him, he'd been flat on his back in the med-wing.

Anna nodded. "He wanted me to go first. Insisted in the end."

"I see," said Helena, watching as Rowland went down again for the others. There was no debate this time, however, because the suited figure at the rear was suddenly toppling, being dragged backward. Not by any of the creatures on fire, or the other alien, but by what appeared to be half a corpse. The top half clawed at the suited figure, grappling with him. Helena couldn't be sure, but she thought it looked a little like the *Artemis*'s pilot, Hannigan.

The pair rolled off the edge and started to slide down the tilted ship, leaving only one clear choice for Rowland to zero in on. He picked up the last survivor just as another blast from inside rocked the ship below them. Rowland and his charge swung to and fro, like a toy being dangled in front of a kitten.

"Retract," said Helena. "Come on, Rowland, retract!"

The cable started to pull them upward, and Rowland managed to lift the figure for Helena, Anna, and one of the troops to pull on board. It was Musgrove she saw behind the plexi-glass. Then the cable slid forward, and for a moment, Helena thought Rowland was going back down again. Instead, he swung sideways and smashed into the side of the shuttle. He dropped a little further, hanging there, clearly unconscious.

"Help me!" Helena said to anyone and everyone around her, grabbing the cable with her hands and trying to haul him back inside. One of the dead made it onto the door flap, fingers catching the edge.

"Watch out!" Anna screamed, but it already had hold of a soldier who'd been firing on the dead—momentarily distracted by his commanding officer's plight. The alien scrambled up the man and bit through his suit at the neck, teeth ripping away green armor to get to the flesh inside, like a starving person trying to open tinned goods. Seconds later, there was blood spraying everywhere, coating the shuttle's door flap.

More soldiers were there immediately but hesitated because they thought they might shoot their comrade, even though he was surely dead by now. There was a thump, and another corpse was at the open back of the shuttle, making for Anna. This time it was one of the figures on fire, gunning for her like it was seeking some sort of revenge. And at this range, didn't it look a lot like a distorted Dr. Rains? thought Helena.

It was unclear whether Musgrove was intending to head this one off, or if he just slipped on the bloody floor—but the effect was the same, and he slid sideways into the flaming figure, knocking it backward toward the drop. Anna was rushing across, maybe to thank Musgrove or just to help him find his feet, when suddenly he was pitching backward as well, the fiery corpse having caught part of his suit. Anna didn't reach him in time, and he fell, taking his attacker with him.

Helena was aware of hands helping her now, other members of Medusa Squad tugging on the cable to get their Sergeant back on board; which they eventually did, dragging his prone body into the shuttle. The others had decided their friend was a lost cause, it seemed, because they were firing at him *and* the alien. Firing until they both went the same way as Musgrove, over the edge.

Looking below them, Helena saw what must have been hundreds of the aliens clambering over the *Artemis*, forming chains and steps to try and reach their shuttle. Working together to get to the food, like ants on a hill.

They needed to get out of there, now! "Pilot, shut the back door! Get us up and away!" ordered Helena. She wasn't in any position of authority at all, but he did as she asked. The flap started to lift, the door closing. Anna was still staring at the space where Musgrove had been.

"He...he saved me. I-I can't believe he saved me."

Whether it had been intentional or not, his last action had been to put himself between Anna and the creature coming after her. "Come on," said Helena, placing an arm around her shoulder and leading her away from the door. Leading her into the shuttle proper.

From the window, as she passed, Helena looked down at the planet below. At a planet that was tearing itself apart, at the beings on the surface looking up at them accusingly for causing this. For waking them from their slumber.

Rowland sat up with a start, groaning. It was only now that Helena remembered his leg, the injured leg they hadn't even looked at since the church. He sat up and rocked from side to side, jerking. Helena and Anna stepped around him, backing off.

The sergeant tugged at his helmet, pulling it from his head and tossing it across the shuttle. His face was turned away from them, and he was still shaking. Changing?

Medusas gathered around with rifles half raised. They didn't know about the contamination thing, hadn't seen Wayne change. But Rowland was freaking them out all the same.

Then he held up a hand, waving it. Turning to them. He shook his head from side to side, and Helena searched his features for signs he was turning. Half-human, half-alien. Dead.

But he was normal, absolutely normal. "What the fuck happened?" he asked, rubbing his forehead. "Did we win?"

Helena and the others let out the breaths they were holding. "We survived," she told him, detaching her own helmet now that the pressure in the shuttle was equalizing. "We survived."

✕ ✕ ✕ ✕ ✕

Philip Burch watched as the shuttle flew off into the atmosphere.

He'd managed to detach himself from Handles, the thing that had been Handles anyway, the top half that had survived the attack in the rec-room and managed to follow them out here. Follow him?

And now Meghan Thomas was crawling along the side of the ship, making her way toward him as well. They were all here together, the monsters he'd created. It was only fitting, he supposed.

Not that they had long, he could see as he looked around him. Watched as the planet began rumbling and quaking into oblivion. He'd die here with them, taking its secrets with him. No cures for anything. But no weapons either, so that was something, he guessed. If these things were ever to find their way off this world, then...

He could feel the ship sinking beneath him, sinking into the troughs. Into the planet, to be buried where the dead had been before they all arrived here. Wouldn't be buried for long, though; wouldn't be a planet for long. Even someone without his science background could see that.

However, as he looked up again at the shuttle, he saw something else. Something that at first made him frown, then tremble. Then laugh maniacally.

He might not have survived, but something definitely would. Something already had.

It was then that Meghan caught up, pulling him to her. Setting him on fire and biting through his enviro-suit at the same time.

And Philip Burch was still laughing as the blackness took him, as he sank lower and lower into that oblivion.

Chapter Eighteen

It was confirmed by the medic as the shuttle broke atmosphere, heading back to the Medusa Squad's ship—what else but *The Gorgon*?—that Rowland was fine, nothing more than a mild concussion. The attack hadn't penetrated his armor back at the church; there was not a scratch on him. "What, you thought...?"

Helena, free from her enviro-suit like the rest of them—and feeling more human by the second—told him about her theory, which Anna Blackwell backed up. "Dr. Rains and Meghan Thomas were definitely changed by those things," the blonde-haired woman reported, and Rowland looked very sad about the latter.

"Shame," he said.

"Same thing happened with Captain Wayne," said Helena, gratefully accepting a hot cup of synth-coffee. Now it was her turn to look sad. "So...?" she said, turning his usual question on him.

"So?"

"What are you going to do about that place? The planet?" she asked him.

"What would *you* do?" he asked her.

Helena shrugged.

"I'm all for nuking it personally," he said. "No disrespect to your ancient civilization, Doctor."

"*Doctors*," Anna reminded him.

He gave a small salute, then ran his hand over his cropped scalp. "And let me just say, you...*Doctors* are some pretty tough customers." They both looked at each other, knew exactly what he was getting at. "But I honestly don't think it'll be necessary. I'm told it's going to live up to its name before too much longer. You know, the Dead Planet."

"Yeah, I got the subtle reference," said Helena with a slight grin. "You don't want to take one back for The Corporation's Weapons Division or something? Isn't that what you guys always do?"

"Fuck no," said Rowland, returning her grin. "You saw those sons of bitches. Why would I want to take one back?"

"And, of course, it isn't as if you didn't download all the information from the *Artemis'* databanks as soon as you were in orbit anyway," said Anna.

"I can neither confirm nor deny that," replied the Sergeant.

The pilot interrupted then, telling them they were locked in for a landing in *The Gorgon*'s docking bay. "All right," said Rowland, "we're pulling into our station. If you'll take your seats and strap yourselves—"

They shifted sideways as the shuttle lurched. It was like being back on the planet, another quake rocking them back and forth.

"What the...?" Rowland began.

"Something's wrong," said the pilot up front.

"No shit!" came the response.

"It's affecting our guidance system. Hold on; I'm going to have to bring her in manually. Too late to pull out!"

Helena and Anna tried to make it to one of the seats, but the shuttle lurched again, sending them flying backward. The soldiers behind flew forward instead, one ramming the wall of the shuttle with such force Helena heard the breaking of the bones in his neck.

There was one more shunt, and they came to a standstill. Helena rose shakily, peering out through the window at the front. Saw metal instead of space. They were inside the docking bay at least, which meant that automatic depressurization should have occurred.

"You two okay?" Rowland asked, looking back at her, then at Anna. Both nodded.

"What happened?"

Rowland didn't answer; he was too busy checking on his men. The medic and a couple of others were dead. So was the pilot at the front, a piece of metal having rammed through the side of his head from the shuttle wall.

Before anyone could say a thing, the flap door at the back was opening. "Who did that?" Rowland was shouting. "Close the—"

It was one of the injured Medusas next to the door, it appeared—but no sooner had he stepped out than something grabbed him from above, pulling him onto the roof. Moments later, blood rained down.

"Jesus!" said Rowland, snatching up a rifle. "You men, with me."

"You're not leaving us inside," snapped Helena, picking up a gun of her own and passing one to Anna.

But the remaining troopers were already outside the vehicle, training their weapons left and right. Emergency lighting kicked in, coating everything black and red. One soldier let off a shot that lit up the space in front, and the others followed his aim. Then a noise on the opposite side, and they did the same. No one seemed to know what they were trying to kill.

Helena and Anna made their way outside, eyes searching around, too. The shuttle had crashed into the wall, right up against the door that led to the rest of the ship. The outer hatch had indeed sealed them inside, re-pressurizing and giving them oxygen—so they wouldn't die from that.

Just from whatever was out there trying to pick them off. Something scuttled across the far wall, and Rowland spun, trailing it with the end of his rifle. Anna backed off, placing one foot behind the other. Didn't see it until it was too late.

The figure rose up behind her, and Helena turned to see what had once been Jay Musgrove, helmet smashed, but head bulbous and stretched. His suit was ripped where the dead alien had had hold of it, blood congealed there. It must have wounded him, but he'd held on to the shuttle, the foreign DNA saving him, protecting him as they flew up to *The Gorgon*.

It spun the woman around, and she screamed.

"Anna, move! I can't get a clear—" But it was lifting her, its strength incredible. Crushing her to it like he was trying to kiss her, then sinking sharpened teeth into her face. However, Anna still had the rifle in her hands and pressed the trigger as this happened. The beam blasted upwards, frying off both their faces, sending them toppling in opposite directions.

Helena felt sick. She wanted to run, but there was nowhere to run *to*. Another scream made her snap out of it. One of the soldiers was also being lifted, but this time because he had a hand rammed through his chest. Something behind *him* now. If it hadn't been Musgrove out there—only Musgrove—then...

Helena saw it. The alien with the burnt front, looked like someone had tried to kill it once already and failed. She'd lost track of it while they were trying to save the others from the *Artemis*, and it must have jumped for the shuttle, hung on as well. Christ, its strength!

Which it ably demonstrated, tearing the soldier in two, though not before he coughed up enough blood (which appeared alternately black then red in this light) to paint the entire bay.

More beams targeted the thing, but it dodged this way and that, avoiding them easily. She didn't know how she knew, but Helena just did: this was the first one to wake. The one who'd done that to Meghan Thomas, who must have hitched a lift back to the *Artemis*, just like it did on this shuttle. It was somehow stronger, faster than the rest.

It was a survivor.

The dead alien took out two more of the soldiers. There weren't many left, a couple plus Rowland. Then there weren't any. The sergeant was batted across the bay like he was nothing, a ragdoll. Another toy, like the kitten's plaything.

Helena stared at the creature. It stared at her. She was aware of movement behind her, to the sides. Those not shredded by its onslaught, plus Anna, Musgrove, all getting to their feet again. Dead but not—

She looked around. Seeking, always seeking... For something, anything. And then she saw it. The vent, up there and to her right. She could reach it if she used the top of the shuttle.

Helena fired at the original monster, then let it come, ducking and sliding under it as it leaped for her. It hit Anna and Musgrove instead, buying her some time, allowing her to start climbing. She was almost at the top when it grabbed her by the foot. Helena looked around, tried to bring the rifle to bear with one hand, but it fell from her grasp.

Then something struck the alien instead. It was Rowland, charging it, forcing it to let go, taking Helena's trainer with it. She scrambled to the top of the shuttle, which gave her a bird's eye view of what was going on. The dead rising again, Rowland in the thick of it.

"Go!" he called after her, then showed her what he had in his hand: a disc-like thing with a button on the top. "Survive!"

Helena threw herself at the grill just as the grenade went off. The colored patterns of light blew anything within spitting distance to pieces, and it unfortunately blew a hole in the outer hull of the ship.

She clawed at the grill as her legs were swept out from under her. Felt an incredible force tugging at her. Helena wrenched the grill off, pulled herself inside the cramped space, fighting for breath that wouldn't come. She scrambled further in, not minding the tightness of the tunnels one bit. It was just like the caves when she was small, like the catacombs.

Helena got to the end of the tunnel she was in and fell down into another. Would continue onwards until she found her way out of them, looking back when space allowed, certain that something was following her through them.

Not able to relax, never taking it for granted that she'd survived until she reached the other side and there were hands there to help her. Techs and more soldiers, those left behind on *The Gorgon.*

Never thinking, even as she was taken to their med-wing, even as she recovered, as Thana finally tore itself to pieces and she was prepped for the long voyage home again—encased in the jelly, in her "coffin" while the Elastic Drive did its thing...

Never once certain that she was even still alive.

Chapter Nineteen

Not alive and not alone, either.

As she "slept"—as she rested—Helena dreamed, or at least she thought they were dreams. She knew now what happened on Thana, and why. Secrets finally revealed to her. Knew that the spiritual race, the one who'd prayed and sought enlightenment, had indeed worked out how to separate their consciousness from their earthly bodies. Astral projection, humans called it, only they'd gone much further than that. Figured out how to detach themselves so completely they could wander the stars.

However, it came at a price. The body, what they considered the shell, what they left behind, became violent, cannibalistic; its strength tripled, even quadrupled in some cases when they'd experimented. If the mind was the spiritual, the "good" part of themselves, then surely this crude, base matter was the ugly, "bad" side of them. It only highlighted the need to end this reliance on the physical. And so it was decided that they should separate forever, but they couldn't simply leave those monsters behind. What if travelers should land and be attacked? the Elders said.

Eventually, they struck upon the solution of the tombs, filled with ancient gases that would keep the bodies inert. Sealed from the inside, the Thanians (actually a race that couldn't even be pronounced by humans) would then use the crystals to meditate and leave their mortal coils behind, their spirits now free to travel. Even if, by some stroke of misfortune, the barriers should be breached, then the dead would be doomed to roam the catacombs for all time—and at least they would all be together. Warnings would be put in place above each of the doors to make sure anyone who did find the tombs by accident would leave well enough alone. Only a race as arrogant as theirs might assume that every species would be able to read their language.

Of course, this process was made all the more urgent by the fact that they knew the planet was dying. The quakes that had plagued the crew and passengers of the *Artemis* weren't caused by their landing at all, but were instead the final death throes of a world that had been steadily decaying for centuries. Just a case of the wrong place at the wrong time.

The Thanians didn't care. They would be off on their journey of discovery by then. Seeking, always seeking. Other planets, other dimensions. Their other halves would be destroyed at the same time as the creamy-red ball—a fraction of the size of Earth in the middle of deepest, blackest space—that had been their home for over a millennia. Destroyed before any harm could be done.

Or so they thought.

They hadn't bargained on The Corporation, hadn't bargained on Helena Kirby's thirst for knowledge about civilizations that had brought her and her team to Thana. In her own—and in their own—way, seeking as well. Doing the same thing as those "spirits," those wanderers. Setting free that first troupe of the dead, one waking long before the others. But they would have woken anyway, as they eventually did, at the very end—when Thana shook itself apart.

What those ancient people didn't know and didn't bother to find out, though, was that their other selves—those bodies they assumed were shells—had an order of their own. Yes, they were violent, yes, cannibalistic. But that in itself served a purpose; nothing ever going to waste. A collective consciousness of a kind, experiencing everything the others experienced.

Just as Helena was experiencing it now. She saw it all from the other side, felt the loss as those souls were ripped from them. Bringing an end to their long symbiosis, housings that were chosen for them long ago, to endure. To be survivors...

Like her.

She saw what they had been trying to do for Meghan Thomas, Susan Rains, even Captain Wayne—and no longer hated them for it. How could she, when they had returned those people to her, if only in memory? She no longer wished to fight them. But then, maybe that was because in her coffin, encased in jelly, Dr. Helena Kirby was becoming just like them.

The scratch on the sole of her foot had been tiny, had happened as the dead alien had pulled off her shoe. Nobody on board *The Gorgon* had noticed. Nobody had checked. But it had been enough to pass on the DNA, the contagion as she had once called it, though it was nothing of the kind. Helena had always felt more comfortable in the company of the dead than the living; they couldn't hurt you as badly—and these beings never would. Surrounded by them, her tribe now, she felt safer than she ever had before. Safer even than being cocooned in the jelly, from which she would eventually wake. Be pulled free from at the other end, to rise again. To be born again...in death.

That would be a week or so before New Year's Eve, New Year's Day. And boy... Did she have plans now! By that time, she aimed to have taken over this ship and the space station it was heading toward, passing on the knowledge and the strength—turning everyone she came into contact with. Turning them into survivors. By that landmark, by the year 2100, Earth would start to be theirs.

And, given time, it would be dominated by the dead. A new home for them. A new world, a new planet. One that wasn't perishing this time, that didn't have an expiration date on it.

Silently, she gave thanks that she'd come across Thana in the first place, that The Corporation had stumbled upon that glorious find with all of its...its treasure. Those catacombs, those tombs. Her family.

The discovery of her life, ironically. No, not of her life. Of her *death.*

Thana...the dead planet.

Planet of the Dead.

The Face of Death

"Now comes the mystery."
Henry Ward Beecher – Last Words

It was like a corridor leading to another world. Gone were the multitude of windows from the upper floors, the white walls seemingly absorbing the sun's rays and bouncing them back into the rooms, giving everything that bleached, sterile look.

Down here it was much darker. But it was more than just the design of the place, this level being appropriately underground where the sun couldn't shine. No, it was almost as if the building itself knew the purpose of this section and had created a suitable atmosphere. One that repelled most people, kept out inquisitive wanderers, and ensured that any person volunteering to work here knew exactly what they were letting themselves in for.

Jonathan Prichard stepped out of the lift and the door clanked across behind him. His exit was blocked off now. No easy means of escape. It didn't bother Jonathan in the slightest. He'd walked down this hallway many times before. He recognized every faulty panel of strip lighting, knew where every "NO SMOKING" sign was, could point to every crack in those bleak, gray walls. This was where he spent most of his free time. No pubs or parties for him.

It was the only way to find out what he needed to know. What he'd been searching for all these years.

As he put one foot in front of the other, the sounds echoed all around. He tightened his grip on the bag he was carrying, but his hands refused to sweat. Jonathan's walking took him to a set of double doors at the far end. Swinging past these, he found it lighter, though only just.

The smell struck him instantly, just as it always did: a funny, antiseptic aroma mixed with traces of meat. He should have been used to it by now, but it always took him by surprise. Same with the lack of heat. Jonathan felt gooseflesh prickling his arms, dancing along his shoulders and down his back.

A bulky figure stepped out of nowhere. Jonathan jumped.

He hated it when Colin did that.

"Got you!" said the man, grinning wildly, his eyes twinkling like stars.

Jonathan forced a grin. He had to play along, keep him sweet. He needed Colin too much to risk offending him, no matter how strange his sense of humor might be. "Yeah, you sure did. Frightened me to death."

Colin clapped him on the arm and started to snigger. "Frightened you to death. Good one, that." His laughter was punctuated by repugnant snorts.

Jonathan nodded, not realizing he'd said anything quite so hilarious. "Listen, Colin, what have you got for me?"

"Got for you?"

"You left me a message." Jonathan took off his glasses and started rubbing them with a tissue.

"Oh, right, sorry. You're in luck, my friend. Four just came in a couple of hours ago. A family: mother, father, two kids— one of each."

Jonathan's eyebrows stooped, a serious look on his face. "What happened?"

"Dunno really. Police brought 'em in from the Conway Estate. A neighbor found 'em all in their flat." He leaned in closer to Jonathan and whispered, "Throats are slit, every one of them."

"Oh God."

"Don't reckon there'll be much of an investigation, though, from what they were saying." Colin's voice was still hushed, but the echoes made it seem far louder. "A lot of trouble with drugs on that estate, see? Hard to know who's involved and who's not. They've even been known to steal stuff from upstairs in the past."

Jonathan replaced his glasses then peered into the room just beyond Colin. "When are the autopsies?"

"Scheduled for tomorrow, first thing."

"And there's nothing going on now? You're sure?"

"Positive. Wouldn't have phoned you otherwise. I know the drill."

Jonathan reached into the inside pocket of his coat and pulled out a leather wallet. Colin's eyes sparkled again when he saw the notes nestled within.

"Here, is that okay? Same as before," said Jonathan, handing him a couple of bills.

"Ah, well, with there being four this time, I thought..."

Jonathan stared at him for a moment, considering this new deal. Then he thumbed out more money. It would wipe him out, but so what?

"Cheers. Hey, you mind if I ask you something?"

"You can ask..."

Colin missed the joke entirely and carried on. "Don't you see enough of these things in the week? I mean, you use them to train on, right? Medical students."

Not again. Jonathan smiled weakly. "I'm a houseman, Colin. But no, I don't see enough of them during the week. Not nearly enough. Call this homework, if you like."

"And you won't, you know, damage them or nothing? Nobody'll be able to tell you was down here? Only it's my job on the line—"

It was Jonathan's turn to pat Colin on the arm now. "No one said anything all the other times, did they? I'll be careful."

Colin visibly relaxed. He knew he could trust the young doctor. Anyway, he wasn't doing anything wrong. Just wanted to bone up on his anatomy, that was all. Colin chortled to himself. "Okay, I'm going off for an hour or so. 'til then, you've got the place to yourself. If the phone goes, let the machine get it. I'll tell 'em I was in the loo or something."

"Thanks. I'll see you in a bit."

Colin began walking off and had one hand on the double doors when he turned sharply. "Oh, nearly forgot. They're in the drawers closest to the entrance. First on your right."

Jonathan repeated his thanks, a little too impatiently, then waited for the attendant to leave.

Once he was alone, he made his way briskly into the morgue.

✕ ✕ ✕ ✕ ✕

The room was a large rectangle with several "beds" spaced out evenly in the center. They looked uncomfortably hard, but then the people who made use of them were not likely to complain. Each space had a long light hanging over the top, sort of like the ones in pool halls, but these were switched off for the time being in favor of wall lamps. Trolleys with instruments on them were lined up along the left-hand-side wall, and at the back was a bench that ran the width of the room. Various pieces of equipment had a home here, including one very expensive-looking microscope.

On his right were the rows of drawers that always reminded him of filing cabinets, only they were much larger and the contents slightly more unnerving than your average bundle of tax records. But Jonathan felt no such fear. He was used to all this by now.

Inside each cold compartment lay a reminder of man's greatest mystery: what happens when life slips away and emptiness takes over?

It was a question that had plagued humanity since time began, but it had become a virtual obsession for Jonathan Prichard.

Slowly, he went over to the first set of drawers and placed his bag on the ground. Taking the smooth handle of the middle drawer, he pulled on the frigid metal. The front slid away from the wall and a flat, steel slab followed suit, rolling on squeaking castors. Resting on top was a white shape, a five-foot lump covered by a sheet. If the linen had been any longer, it would have looked as if the body was levitating at waist height. Jonathan gripped the sheet and dragged it back.

Hair, long, straight and brown, then skin, almost gray—as gray as the walls in the corridor—confronted him. The eyes were next, round and lifeless, unable to see him anymore. Only sights he wasn't privy to yet. He tugged the sheet back further to reveal a delicate nose, then two lips that would have been full and red when blood still coursed through the woman's body, but they were very nearly blue in color now.

Jonathan brought his face closer to hers, mere centimeters away so that they were almost touching. And he looked into those marbled spheres, scrutinizing. Quickly, he took a pair of surgical gloves out of his pocket and slipped them on. It was a familiar, practiced action, relegated to the subconscious part of his mind while he concentrated on other things. The doctor brought one hand up to the corpse's left eye. With great care, he placed his index finger above and his thumb below, then opened the eye wider until the shadows inside the socket were visible. His face was reflected in the pupil, that captivated expression he always wore by this stage.

"What did you see?" he asked her. "What did it look like? Please, I need to know."

Disappointment soon replaced fascination. He moved his head back and closed his eyes. It took him a moment or so to regain his composure, then he crouched down and retrieved a black object from the top of his bag.

Jonathan raised the digital camera and prepared to take a picture. But before his finger found the button, he realized he must pull the sheet down still further. Down over the chin, past the cords of the neck to bare the wound that had killed her: a slash from one side of the throat to the other, severing the jugular veins and carotid arteries precisely. The dark rip in the skin was curved with straight edges. In a macabre way, it seemed to be smirking at Jonathan. An extra hidden mouth that was so happy to be finally exposed.

He took his photograph. There was a slight whirring as the close-up autofocus adjusted itself, then a flash lit up the room momentarily. As the frozen image appeared on the screen, he examined it, looking for something—anything—his cursory exploration had missed.

There was nothing.

Jonathan repeated this ritual with all of the victims. The father, his square-jawed face the very definition of surprise. And the two young children, so innocent and vulnerable, their own upturned countenances like those of pale angels.

He took photos of each and stared at the results. But as he did so, unwanted memories came back to disturb him. It wasn't his fault. This work reminded him too much of his father, and the reason why he was doing all this. Why he had set himself such a task. The comparison with these people was inevitable, he supposed. Except, of course, his father had died of natural causes.

Jonathan's mind spun a web of distant recollections. It ferried him back to that time in the hospital. He had just turned twelve, on the brink of manhood, when his father became ill. It was particularly upsetting because he was all Jonathan had in the world, the only family he'd ever known. Since his wife had died in childbirth, struggling to deliver their long-awaited son, Jonathan's father had been sole provider. But he never blamed his boy. Instead, he loved Jonathan more than any child on Earth, playing with him, clothing him. Overcompensating for the fact that there was only one parent, not two. And Jonathan had paid him back with all the affection he could muster. In those twelve short years, his father had given the impression that he would always be there for him no matter what. Always.

However, fate had other plans. And so did his father's heart muscle.

The attack came on suddenly while he was at work, they'd told Jonathan. But he'd known as soon as those men turned up at his school that something was very wrong indeed.

Nothing could have prepared him for the sight of his dad, though. He just looked so helpless, lying in bed with those tangled wires attached to his chest. A complete contrast to the strong, fit man Jonathan had known all his life. It was like someone had come and taken his real father away, leaving a hollow husk behind to mark his place 'til he returned. In those final few hours by his bedside, Jonathan came to understand what death really was, and how unfair it could be.

A second attack occurred while he waited. His father jerked up from the bed as if he were on strings, his eyes bulging twice their normal size. He looked at Jonathan even as he fought for his last breath, and his son just caught a flash of something amazing, yet wholly terrifying, in those eyes.

"I-I see it," his father stammered, so quietly it might have been Jonathan's ears playing tricks. "The face..."

Then it was over.

There was nothing left of his dad in that body, and although the doctors and nurses battled to save him again, Jonathan knew it was already too late. For that man had seen what no other being alive had seen: the face, the very face of Death itself. And Jonathan would never forget the look in his eyes as he'd done so.

Funny how something that can happen in the space of a day can so affect one's life. Jonathan decided right there and then to go into medicine. Not to help people, as others might, but to study death further. To be around those who were dying or close to the end. Just as his father had been in the hospital on that day.

The fact that Jonathan went into a children's home didn't deter him. It just made his resolve stronger, drove him on to get decent grades and earn his place at a university on a scholarship. He would not be denied the chance to investigate this topic in greater detail. Jonathan found all he needed at medical school in books, by examining cadavers and visiting terminally ill patients who thanked him for his kindness—little realizing that it was he who should be thanking them.

But it was during his first few weeks at St. Hollister's that he struck gold, when he bumped into Colin down here for the first time. Colin, who had been so helpful in allowing him access to the recently deceased, so—

Jonathan's ears pricked up when he heard the double doors go. No one must find him here. It was bad enough that his fellow students once called him a ghoul because of his interests. He didn't want that reputation to follow him here.

He stood rooted to the spot, expecting at any moment to see the pathologist, Dr. Castle, walk into the room, hunting for a lost set of reports or maybe eager to take a look at the new arrivals— despite the fact it was after six p.m. on a Sunday.

Nothing happened. Jonathan waited, but nothing happened.

Dammit, if this is another of Colin's practical jokes... But there was only one way to find out.

Leaving his camera next to the body of the young girl, he walked silently toward the entrance of the morgue. Jonathan peered around the corner and through the glass panes in the doors. As far as he could tell, no one was in the corridor, though it was still hard to make out anything with those faulty lights.

"Colin? Colin, is that you?"

A solitary muffled groan came in reply, but from behind, not in front. It emanated from the cold meat he'd been examining. This was not an unusual occurrence. The dead would often make noises long after their souls had departed. Jonathan knew this, he was a doctor after all. Yet his hands still shook.

His anxiety intensified when he turned to see the bodies absent, all four of them. Those metallic slabs bare. Jonathan let out a gasp.

In the hall, the defective lights finally gave up the ghost and plunged the passage into total darkness, a thick black that spilled into the morgue itself.

This was strange, he could acknowledge that at least. A trick of the light, perhaps? Or lack of it.

No, they were definitely gone. And although he looked around, Jonathan could see no sign of them.

"Colin!" Anger and frustration crept into his tone now. "If this is down to you, I swear I'll..." But his brain was thinking too clearly for its own good. How could Colin have possibly slipped past him when there was only one way in or out? And how could he have lifted the bodies and hidden them so quickly?

Another moan, more distinct, and coming from several directions at once. It was joined by another, then another still. Jonathan twirled this way and that. Without thinking, he drifted further back into the room.

Something was moving around beyond the edge of his vision. Each time he turned, it would be gone. Then he'd sense movement from another direction, more shapes just out of reach.

The shadows at the door lengthened. They congealed into a pitch-black form on the wall, rapidly gaining substance.

It was too much to take in.

Jonathan turned suddenly one final time and came face to face with the woman from the drawer, the white sheet still draped over her shoulders. His scream broke free only as a series of coughs in the back of his throat.

The smiling cut at her neck was open fully now, and thick pulp forced its way out, spilling down the cloth to create abstract art. The woman's expression was a mixture of curiosity and disdain, her lips sneering, eyes full of something akin to hatred. Those eyes, oh, those eyes! The pupils he had inspected so thoroughly were now the very things he longed to shut out. But no matter how hard he tried, he found himself drawn to them.

She began to raise her hands. As she did so, Jonathan stepped backward. He came up against a large and immovable thing—the wall on the left, had to be. He soon realized his mistake when two muscular arms closed around him.

The husband pinned him with the strength of ten men. If Jonathan's knees hadn't buckled at that precise moment, he would have been crushed in the loveless embrace. As it was, he collapsed onto the floor and cocked his head back to see the towering attacker.

When the dead man bent to look where Jonathan had gone,

the bones in his neck and shoulders cracked like brittle twigs. Another guttural noise emerged from his mouth, deep and despairingly hollow.

Jonathan put out his hand to ease himself away. It brushed against something round and knobbly. To his dismay, he found it was the little girl sitting cross-legged next to him, her stringy blonde hair tied up. She giggled, putting a hand to her mouth.

A shuffling on his other side and Jonathan saw her brother, his chestnut hair the only contrast to bloodless skin and linen, which was arranged around him like an emperor's robes.

These were the faces of death he'd come here to view, to document. But he'd expected anything other than this.

Jonathan crawled between the girl and her mother's leg. Scrambling to his feet, he held his hand flat out to ward them off.

"Don't...don't you come near me!" He barely recognized his own voice.

The black thing near the door was approaching. It came to join the family and gathered a cloud of gloom around them. Jonathan could feel that somehow it knew what he had done.

Once again, memories were stirred by what he saw, partially repressed remembrances of bygone deeds. Because, in the past, it had not been sufficient to just observe others dying. So strong had been Jonathan's compulsion to discover what lay in store, to see what he had seen in his father's eyes that day, to look at that expression again and again, he had taken the liberty of intervening himself. Speeding up the process in some cases, or simply visiting death upon those who were fit and healthy.

At first, it had only been animals, but this achieved nothing. Jonathan soon realized that he needed human subjects. Patients in the hospital were easy targets, but too risky after a while. So he looked for the face of death elsewhere: on the streets, down back alleys, in the seedier parts of the town. Seeking it out and taking souvenirs of his exploits, before and after photographs. But each time looking into the eyes as it happened, desperate to see what he'd only glimpsed once before.

And Jonathan remembered how he'd killed that family. How

easy it had been to break in during the night and inject them. The panic as they all awoke to find themselves bound and gagged. The look of horror as he pulled the scalpel out of his bag.

Except he saw nothing in those eyes as their lives ebbed away, limbs twitching in defiance. So naturally, he had welcomed the chance to view them again when Colin called. Jonathan knew who the fatalities would be even before he pulled open the drawers. Even before he'd entered the hospital.

Then afterward, the guilt; an overwhelming sorrow that he'd denied yet more people of their right to life. And for what? Nothing! It was a burden that threatened to overwhelm him at times, pacified only by the prospect of the next time. Maybe this will be the one, he'd tell himself.

But there would be no more now.

He quaked as the inhabitants of the morgue closed in, egged on by something he couldn't quite see.

"I-I'm sorry. Please, I just needed to know. I had to see!"

The group came closer, holding hands to form a semicircle, preventing him from escaping. Jonathan backed away once more. His breathing was erratic, his chest felt peculiar. A twinge inside on the left made him cry out. A numbness spread down his arm.

The family stopped. They watched his suffering, then allowed the silhouette to sweep forward. It filled the room, engulfing everything in its path.

A spasm, then stabbing pains needled his ribs. There was no doubt about it; he understood what was happening all too well. He'd seen it so often before, seen it happen to his own father. The hereditary condition he knew he'd have to confront one day. But not yet. Heaven above, not yet!

The intensity of the heart attack took him by surprise, however. Jonathan dropped to the floor again. He could see nothing but the limbo ahead, wrapping itself around him.

Tasting him.

He made one last effort to rise, gripping the nearest piece of furniture to steady himself—the slab where the little girl had resided.

But his fingers wouldn't obey, and he succeeded only in knocking his camera off the edge. It landed heavily just opposite his face. The button jammed, and one flash followed another, absorbed by the expanding dark.

Jonathan couldn't move. His body was locked in a ball on the floor, his stomach somersaulting. His vision was fading fast. But as he expelled his last lungfuls of air, he did see something.

It was the answer to the question he'd been seeking all these years.

✳ ✳ ✳ ✳ ✳

When Colin returned to the morgue, he couldn't find Jonathan Prichard anywhere. The bodies of the four murder victims were stretched out under sheets on their respective slabs, undisturbed as if the doctor had never even touched them. Colin shouted his name over and over but received no reply. Was Jonathan getting payback? Playing a trick on him now?

It wasn't until he came fully into the room that he noticed his friend's bag on the ground, and next to one of the bottom drawers was a digital camera. He didn't scare easily, being a morgue attendant and everything, but this was all very bizarre.

Hesitating briefly, Colin picked up the camera, which was turned off. He pressed the power button, found the menu, and selected preview to find the last set of pictures to be taken.

The first were just photos of the cadavers, specifically their faces, their eyes. Then, as he kept pressing the arrows, he came to the ones that were dark and blurred. He could just about make out parts of the floor, then the walls. Then a shot that looked like the side of someone's head. An ear and a jawline. Another face, then, closer. Jonathan's face from just above the nose, framed against a dark background. Colin squinted at the picture, zooming in. He saw complete and utter terror in those eyes, but he also spotted something else reflected in the corner of Jonathan's glasses. It was an ebony shape of some kind, with a white patch at the top.

Curious, he continued to zoom in even further, as much as the machine would allow. He had to know what the reflection was. As he magnified the frame, it transformed into a figure. The figure of a man swathed in a curtain of black.

And the chalky spot became a face, one he recognized instantly.

Indeed, the young medic had discovered the answer to his question that day. Had seen what his father saw so many years ago.

For Jonathan Prichard had looked into the face, the very face of Death itself...

And he had found it to be his own.

ABOUT THE AUTHOR

Paul Kane is an award-winning (including the British Fantasy Society's Legends of FantasyCon Award), bestselling writer and editor based in Derbyshire, UK. His short story collections include *Alone (In the Dark)*, *Touching the Flame*, *FunnyBones*, *Peripheral Visions*, *Shadow Writer*, *The Adventures of Dalton Quayle*, *The Butterfly Man and Other Stories*, *The Spaces Between*, *Ghosts*, the British Fantasy Award-nominated *Monsters*, *Shadow Casting*, *Nailbiters*, *Death*, *Disexistence*, *Scary Tales*, *More Monsters*, *Lost Souls*, *The Controllers*, *The Colour of Madness*, *Traumas*, *Darkness & Shadows*, and *The Naked Eye*. His novellas include *The Lazarus Condition*, *RED*, and *Pain Cages* (a #1 Amazon bestseller). He is the author of such novels as *Of Darkness and Light*, *The Gemini Factor*, and the bestselling *Arrowhead* trilogy (*Arrowhead*, *Broken Arrow*, and *Arrowland*, gathered together in the sell-out omnibus edition *Hooded Man*), a post-apocalyptic reworking of the Robin Hood mythology. His latest novels include *Lunar* (which is set to be turned into a feature film), the short Y.A. novel *The Rainbow Man* (as P.B. Kane), the critically-acclaimed and award-winning *Sherlock Holmes and the Servants of Hell* from Solaris, the sequels to *RED*—*Blood RED* and *Deep RED*—*Before* from Grey Matter Press, *Arcana* from WordFire Press, plus *Her Last Secret*, *Her Husband's Grave*, and *The Family Lie* from HQ/HarperCollins (as P.L. Kane)

He has also written for comics, most notably for the *Dead Roots* zombie anthology alongside writers such as James Moran (*Torchwood*, *Cockneys vs. Zombies*) and Jason Arnopp (*Doctor Who*, *Friday the 13th*, *The Last Days of Jack Sparks*) and as part of the team turning *Clive Barker's Books of Blood* into motion comics for Seraphim/MadeFire. His stand-alone comic *The Disease*, published by Hellbound Media, was also a 2016 Ghastly Award-nominated title in the "One Shot" category. Paul is co-editor of the anthologies: *Hellbound Hearts* (Simon & Schuster)—stories based around the mythology that spawned *Hellraiser*; *The Mammoth Book of Body Horror* (Constable & Robinson/Running Press), featuring the likes of Stephen King and James Herbert; *A Carnivàle of Horror* (PS), featuring Ray Bradbury and Joe Hill; *Beyond Rue Morgue* from Titan (stories based around Poe's detective, Dupin); *Exit Wounds*—a crime anthology featuring the likes of Lee Child, Val McDermid, Dennis Lehane, and Jeffery Deaver; *Wonderland* (a finalist in the Shirley Jackson Awards); and *Cursed*, the last three also from Titan.

His non-fiction books include *The Hellraiser Films and Their Legacy*, *Voices in the Dark*, and *Shadow Writer—The Non-Fiction. Vol. 1: Reviews* and *Vol. 2: Articles and Essays*, plus his genre journalism has appeared in the likes of *SFX*, *Fangoria*, *Dreamwatch*, *Gorezone*, and *Rue Morgue*. He also co-wrote the afterword to the latest edition of Stephen King's *Night Shift* collection. He has been a Guest at Alt.Fiction five times, was a Guest at the first SFX Weekender, at Thought Bubble in 2011, Derbyshire Literary Festival and Off the Shelf in 2012, Monster Mash and Event Horizon in 2013, Edge-Lit in 2014, HorrorCon, HorrorFest and Grimm Up North in 2015, The Dublin Ghost Story Festival and Sledge-Lit in 2016, IMATS Olympia and Celluloid Screams in 2017, Black Library Live (Warhammer 40k) and The UK Ghost Story Festival in 2019. Paul delivered the keynote speech at the 2021 WordCrafter conference, and has been a panelist at FantasyCon and the World Fantasy Convention, plus a fiction judge at the Sci-Fi London Film Festival. He is a former Special Publications Editor of the British Fantasy Society, has served as co-chair for the UK arm of the Horror Writers Association, and was co-chair of ChillerCon 2022 in Scarborough.

His work has been optioned for film and television, and his zombie story "Dead Time" was turned into an episode of the Lionsgate/NBC TV series *Fear Itself*, adapted by Steve Niles (*30 Days of Night*) and directed by Darren Lynn Bousman (*SAW II-IV* and *Spiral*). He also scripted *The Opportunity*, which premiered at the Cannes Film Festival, *Wind Chimes* (directed by Brad "*Hallows Eve*" Watson and which sold to TV), *The Weeping Woman*—filmed by award-winning director Mark Steensland, starring Tony-nominated actor Stephen Geoffreys (*Fright Night*)—*Confidence*, directed by award-winning Mike Clarke (*A Hand to Play*, *Paper and Plastic*) which stars Simon Bamford (*Hellraiser*, *Nightbreed*, *Starfish*), and *The Torturer* directed by Joe Manco of Little Spark Films. Loose Canon/Hydra Films have just turned Paul's novelette *Men of the Cloth* into a feature called *Sacrifice* (aka *The Colour of Madness*), starring *Re-Animator* and *You're Next*'s Barbara Crampton. His work for audio includes the full cast drama adaptation of *The Hellbound Heart* for Bafflegab, starring Tom Meeten (*The Ghoul*), Neve McIntosh (*Doctor Who*), and Alice Lowe (*Prevenge*), and the *Robin of Sherwood* adventure *The Red Lord* for Spiteful Puppet/ITV, narrated by Ian Ogilvy (*Return of the Saint*). You can find out more at his website www.shadow-writer.co.uk, which has featured Guest Writers such as Dean Koontz, Robert Kirkman, Charlaine Harris, and Guillermo del Toro.

Other Books by Paul Kane:

Novels

Arrowhead
Broken Arrow
Arrowland
Hooded Man (Omnibus)
The Gemini Factor
Lunar
Sleeper(s)
The Rainbow Man (as P.B. Kane)
Blood RED
Sherlock Holmes and the Servants of Hell
Before
Deep RED
Arcana
The Red Lord
Her Last Secret (as P.L. Kane)
The Storm
Her Husband's Grave (as P.L. Kane)
The Family Lie (as P.L. Kane)

Novellas & Novelettes

Signs of Life
The Lazarus Condition
Dalton Quayle Rides Out
RED
Pain Cages
Creakers (chapbook)
Flaming Arrow
The Bric-a-Brac Man
The PI's Tale
Snow
The Rot

Beneath the Surface (with Simon Clark)
Blood Red Sky
Confessions (as P.L. Kane)
Corpsing (as P.L. Kane)
Coming of Age (as P.B. Kane)
Murder on the Golden Sands Express (as P.L. Kane)

Collections
Alone (In the Dark)
Touching the Flame
FunnyBones
Peripheral Visions
The Adventures of Dalton Quayle
Shadow Writer
The Butterfly Man and Other Stories
The Spaces Between
Ghosts
Monsters
The Dead Trilogy
Shadow Casting
Nailbiters
Death
The Life Cycle
Disexistence
Kane's Scary Tales Vol. 1
More Monsters
Lost Souls
The Controllers
White Shadows (as P.B. Kane)
The Colour of Madness: Official Movie Tie-In
Traumas
Darkness & Shadows
The Naked Eye
Tempting Fate
Nailbiters – Hard Bitten

Editor & Co-Editor

Shadow Writers Vol. 1 & 2
Terror Tales #1-4
Top International Horror
Albions Alptraume: Zombies
The British Fantasy Society: A Celebration
Hellbound Hearts
The Mammoth Book of Body Horror
A Carnivàle of Horror: Dark Tales from the Fairground
Beyond Rue Morgue
Dark Mirages
Exit Wounds
Wonderland
Cursed

Non-Fiction

Contemporary North American Film Directors: A Wallflower Critical Guide
(Major Contributor)
Cinema Macabre (Contributor)
The Hellraiser Films and Their Legacy
Voices in the Dark
Shadow Writer – The Non-Fiction. Vol. 1: Reviews
Shadow Writer – The Non-Fiction. Vol. 2: Articles & Essays
Leviathan – The Story of Hellraiser and Hellbound: Hellraiser II (Contributor)
Hellraisers
War is Hell: Making Hellraiser III: Hell on Earth (Contributor)
Stuart Gordon: Interviews (Conversations with Filmmakers Series)
(Contributor)

The Caribbean Sea, 1708 AD.

In Port Royal, many have heard the legend of the Black Brig, a ship of the damned bringing a fate worse than death to the isolated colonies of the Caribbean Sea. But few know the true story behind the tavern tales. As the war between the Northern Alliance and the League of the Antilles looms on the horizon, an old captain is ready to embark on a venture to cease the blight of the Black Brig once for all and have his revenge.

Set in an alternate historical setting, where a supernatural plague caused the fall of the European powers and where what was left of humanity struggles to survive in the New World, DEAD MEN TELL NO TALES – THE FULL TALE narrates the ghastly voyage pirate captain Daniel Drake Davies underwent in 1676, and the events that will force him to confront those same horrors thirty years later. For the dead do not rest peacefully in the Devil's Sea. Pirates, voodoo, and seagoing undead await you in this fantastic journey in a land that never was.